THE STRAITS OF TSUSHIMA

Marcus Baxter Thrillers
Book One

Tim Chant

SAPERE
BOOKS

THE STRAITS OF TSUSHIMA

Published by Sapere Books.

20 Windermere Drive, Leeds, England, LS17 7UZ,
United Kingdom

saperebooks.com

ISBN: 978-1-80055-331-6

Front cover picture credit to Drachinifel: Personal
Collection.

A NOTE ON NAMES, DATES, AND NOMENCLATURE

Imperial Russia utilised the Julian calendar. The Battle of Tsushima, to the men of the Russian Pacific Fleet, was fought on 14-15th May (the Julian calendar). To the rest of the world, it was on the 27th-28th May (the Gregorian calendar). As Baxter would think in those terms, I've stuck with the Gregorian calendar. Similarly, measurements such as gun calibres are in Imperial (inches) and formation designations are those that would have been familiar to our protagonist. The smallest ships in the Russian force I have seen described as both destroyers and torpedo-boats — given that those that survived were latterly reclassified as destroyers I have gone with that designation as it more closely describes the vessels (in my view).

I have seen the names of both people and vessels rendered in a number of different ways. All I can say is I have tried to be consistent in the spellings (greatly aided by the excellent team at Sapere) — this was a particular struggle with Vice-Admiral Rozhestvensky.

PROLOGUE

His world has narrowed down to simple sensations. The smell of cordite and powder, hot metal, fire and blood. The sight of a seemingly endless cloud of smoke from the fires raging uncontrolled on the deck, through which enemy ships could occasionally be glimpsed. But above all, the noise.

Surrounding, all-encompassing, so constant that all the elements of it form a single unbroken cacophony. The immediate symphonies are the crash of the gun he crouches beside, the *thunk* of the heavy breech slamming open and the distinctive rattle of the spent brass cartridge hitting the deck to join the mound surrounding them. The heavier guns — one 6-inch gun still operational on the cruiser, so many of the enemy's weapons still hammering away at the squadron — are the bass counterpoint; the rumble of the main battle an increasing drum roll. And the crew, the choir.

The shouts of the gun crew, his own hoarse voice — almost that of a stranger, bellowing in a foreign tongue. No orders to speak of, just men exhorting each other to fight harder, stand their ground. Somewhere, someone screaming in pain or rage or fear, it's hard to say. Petrov Ilyich's sobs, gradually diminishing as no help comes — soon enough they'll be sliding his body over the side. It's shattering, consuming, and something Marcus Baxter knows he'll never forget.

A hand grabs his arm. His muscles are aching from the constant exertion, moving up and down behind the line of unprotected guns helping where he can while enemy shells wail overhead and shrapnel wickers past viciously, and he appreciates the moment's pause.

Cristov Juneau's face is grimy, sweat-streaked dirt and crusted blood from a shallow head wound. He leans in close to be heard. "It seems we have made a proper Russian of you — I could hear you swearing from the bridge!"

Baxter grins back. "And I've made proper sailors of you lot!"

CHAPTER 1

Port of Leith, Scotland, October 1904

A train was rattling under Great Junction Street bridge as Marcus Baxter sauntered across, jangling his last few shillings in his hand to prevent their escape through the holes in his pockets. He hummed tunelessly; the sound lost in the shriek of the train's whistle as it announced its approach to the station.

He stopped halfway across to look down on the Water of Leith. A tramp steamer was manoeuvring up to the concrete slipway, grimy dockworkers standing by to lift off the coal required by Edinburgh's insatiable rail network. The wind coming in from the Forth blew smoke across the road, making him cough as he caught a lungful. It would have reminded him of being on the deck of a ship under way, but it wasn't the finest Cardiff coal that went into the boilers of His Majesty's warships. The locomotives that plied the network of rail that connected Leith and Edinburgh, moving goods from the port to the city, didn't warrant anything like that.

Baxter darted around a rag and bone cart onto Ferry Road, head down and hands shoved in his pockets. The wind had cooled, bringing with it the smell of rain overlaying the reek of packed people. A dray, heavily laden with beer casks, rattled past as he turned up Madeira Street and almost absently counted the doors along.

The cheap whisky he'd had earlier hadn't helped his black mood, just lay in a sour coil in his gut and reminded him of the humiliation of another berth lost because of his damned name. At least this time it had been the merchantman's owners, finally catching up with her by telegram. Her captain had seemed genuinely distressed to discharge him.

He pushed the memories away — they wouldn't do him any good.

"Good evening, Mrs Dunbar," he said as he pushed open the door to his lodging house.

"Rent's due next week, Mr Baxter." It was said with a hard-eyed stare, flour-dusted hands planted firmly on broad hips. A tone of voice and a posture that would brook no demure. "Any luck finding a new berth? The Teuchter ferry always needs more hands."

He grimaced. In truth he had spent the day wandering between the pubs of Leith, which were many and varied. He knew there was little point trying to lie to the formidable Scotswoman — she had so many children he hadn't quite managed to take a reliable headcount. Tomorrow he would try some of the freighters currently berthed in the harbour, or failing that the puffers which plied the coastal route. Protesting that he would act tomorrow, though, would be as fruitless as trying to lie to Mrs Dunbar.

Instead, he tried his most winning smile, one which had turned more than one lady's head. Mrs Dunbar merely sighed. "Pork chops for dinner, and you have visitors. I showed them up to your rooms."

He blinked, slightly nonplussed that she hadn't seen fit to mention that before. As far as he knew the local plod wasn't currently looking for him, and he couldn't imagine anyone would have tracked him down to offer him a job. He shrugged and headed up the rickety stairs to the garret she grandly referred to as his rooms. It was a roof over his head, though, and board, and he'd lived in worse conditions.

The door was standing ajar — it took a certain amount of physical force to close it properly — and light spilled out. He shouldered it open and strolled in, not acknowledging his visitors until he'd dropped his newspaper on the bed and deposited a small bottle on the rickety table.

He sat on the bed, as the sole chair was occupied. As the dandy who had the presumption to commit that sin opened his mouth to speak, Baxter held a finger up and then proceeded to work his left boot off. His big toe protruded from a hole in the sock, and with a deep sigh of real relief he finally freed it of the constriction.

The man in the chair watched the ostentatious performance with a certain amount of amused indulgence. His companion, half-seen in the dim space under the rafters, shifted from foot to foot in annoyance.

"Mr Baxter."

"You have the advantage on me, sir." Baxter wasn't quite sure why he'd called him 'sir', but there was something of a senior officer about the man.

"Arbuthnott. Naval Intelligence." A long-fingered hand pushed a card across the table, forcing Baxter to lunge forward to rescue his bottle as the surface tilted. He let the card drop.

The mention of Naval Intelligence told Baxter everything he needed to know. That Arbuthnott really should have been in uniform but was more comfortable out of it; particularly in this sort of environment. That his bulky shadow was not just there for show. His pulse quickened slightly. "Russia desk?" he asked.

Arbuthnott uncrossed his legs and he leaned forward, lacing his fingers, giving the impression of a vulpine schoolmaster. A smile creased narrow features. "I see you keep up with current affairs at sea," he said, nodding to the copy of *The Times* on the bed. "What do you make of the so-called Second Pacific Squadron?"

Baxter thought of the Russian Imperial Navy's almost-mythical formation of vessels a lot. Particularly the big, beautiful *Borodino* battleships that formed its core. Destined to restore the Russian situation in the Far East and deal with Togo's so-far unbeaten Japanese fleet, if it could manage the journey to the other side of the world.

"Broadside weight is more or less on a parity with the Japanese," he said at last. "And some of the ships are brand new."

"I suspect a 'but'."

"If weight of broadside counted for everything, Nelson wouldn't have won at Trafalgar. The new ships and crews haven't been properly worked up, and the rest of the squadron is something of a hotch-potch. And the less said of the officers the better."

Arbuthnott nodded, almost as though he was seriously listening to the analysis of a former RN sub-lieutenant, and a disgraced one to boot. But then, Baxter suspected the question was more of a test of his own capacities. "There are," Arbuthnott now said, "of course, many in the Admiralty who share that exact view. However, while we remain neutral in this affair the decision has been taken to assist our Japanese allies as much as we can. Mostly this will mean requiring strict observance of the laws of the sea when it comes to neutral harbours."

Baxter wanted to urge the fellow to get to the point. He wasn't a patient man, but he guessed the gentlemen dilettantes drawn into intelligencing liked playing these sorts of games. He contented himself with studying Arbuthnott. Slim, but not the leanness that came from hard work. Soft hands, more like an artist's than a naval officer's. High intelligent brow and a long nose, hair starting to thin. The very acme of a desk officer, who if he had ever served at sea had probably found the whole experience miserable.

"However, we are also resolved to provide the Japanese Navy with as much intelligence as possible. If Rozhestvensky's ships make it there, our allies will need all the information they can get their hands on."

"I recommend *The Times* as a good source. The make-up, nature and trials of the squadron have already been well-reported on."

"Perhaps. I imagine this speculation will reach something of a peak now that the squadron has entered the North Sea. But I am sure I don't need to tell you how things can become … blown out of proportion. Exaggerated to the point where any kernel of truth is lost."

Baxter felt his expression become stormy. Civil inhibitions, already loosened by whisky, were almost overcome by the temper that always lurked just below the surface. "Get to the point," he snapped.

The intelligence officer made an apologetic gesture, his expression bland. "I am here to offer you a job."

"You want me to observe the Russian squadron as it passes. See what … kernels of truth I can extract."

"Specifically, a single ship. Three days after the squadron finally managed to clear harbour, the Russians despatched a reinforcing vessel. So far we have been unable to ascertain any details."

"Sounds like a job for a destroyer or two, if you even want to bother with a single ship. We already know the modern Russian battleships are all in the squadron, and they're the only ships that'll count."

"Perhaps it is of little import, but we are keen to have all the relevant details. As to why a destroyer is not being sent to have a look, we feel it is best if this is done … incognito, so to speak. Our warships getting that close to the Russian ships could provoke all sorts of unwanted unpleasantness. We are given to understand that Russian intelligence networks have led their Admiralty to believe that the North Sea will be thick with Japanese torpedo boats. As you say, the standards of training and discipline on the Russian ships are not expected to be high."

Baxter snorted. The very thought of the RN shying away from getting a close look at some uppity Russians passing through their own waters. A little bit of him, that quiet bitter corner of his mind, stirred at the idea of Russian and British warships firing on each other. A war would mean the Navy would need good, experienced officers — no matter any previous blotches on their records. Previous rearmaments had saved or resuscitated more than one career.

"You'll offer me my commission back in return?" he blurted, now the idea was in his mind.

Arbuthnott laughed, a thin sound. "My dear Baxter, that would be quite impossible, as you well know." The smile left his face as Baxter threatened to rise from his reclined position. As well it should — Baxter knew the impression he made at his full height, towering above most men, certainly physically more powerful than most of his contemporaries. "However, as I said, you will be well-paid." Arbuthnott's voice had lost some of its smooth self-assurance — he had come expecting to offer payment, rich payment, to a man who had been an officer but hardly a gentleman, to do ungentlemanly work. He obviously hit upon a new idea. "Of course, if you do this well, you will be seen favourably within my own department. We always have use for capable men who know the sea."

Sly dog. In truth, though Baxter would not admit it, the money would have been enough. "I assume you don't want me to swim out there?"

"A boat has been procured. Currently berthed in … Granton, I think? She has a small crew, picked men, but they need someone with an eye for warships, and to add an aura of … verisimilitude. It is, after all, a gentleman's pleasure boat." Arbuthnott reached into the expensive-looking briefcase beside the chair, placed a plain manilla envelope and a slim file on the table. "We expect the ship to pass through adjacent waters two days from now."

"Well, I'd best make an early start then."

Arbuthnott looked momentarily discomfited — he was obviously the sort of man who liked to signal the end of an interview — but then his minder stepped forward into the light. Quite obviously a former prize fighter, he was broader than Baxter but not as tall. One ear was a cauliflowered mess and his nose had been broken at least once. The two men measured each other without speaking, then the burly old boxer gave Baxter a gap-toothed grin that acknowledged that it would be an interesting fight.

"One last thing, Mr Baxter, by way of satisfying my curiosity," Arbuthnott said from the doorway, his smart trilby already on his head. "I understand your father lives scant miles from here — I'm curious why you have chosen this … abode."

"I wouldn't let Mrs Dunbar hear you use that tone about her home," Baxter said evenly, belying the rage coming to a boil in him.

Arbuthnott's minder, recognising that violence could very well occur, swiftly bundled his lord and master out and closed the door, hard enough to latch it this time.

Baxter yanked the cork from the bottle and took a drag straight from the neck, letting the burn wash away some of the anger. The folded notes in the envelope went the rest of the way towards calming him. Or near enough.

He found a glass, poured himself a generous measure and sat, flipping the folder open. One thing that had struck him was that Arbuthnott had continuously said 'we'. Not their Lordships of the Admiralty desire. *We* desire.

He scratched his chin. This whole thing seemed … wrong. His gut told him that he should have said no. It seemed like a lot of effort to get a look at one Russian ship, and not even a guaranteed look — even with details of the assumed course he couldn't promise an interception. Chances are it was just another fleet tender or supply vessel, part of the long logistics chain Rozhestvensky would need to get his ships to the far side of the world.

And there was just something … off about Arbuthnott. Baxter knew that he could still get out, return the money, destroy the folder. Or not return the money and make damn sure he got a berth on something bound for distant shores.

His tatty clothes and the fact that he was not far off losing the roof over his head meant he had to ignore the former, and a vestigial honesty inherited from his Presbyterian father quashed the latter notion.

"It'll be fine." He drained the whisky, rose and yanked the door open. "Mrs Dunbar!" he boomed down the stairs. "I have an early start tomorrow and must trouble you for a solid breakfast. And I have your rent money!"

CHAPTER 2

A sea haar clung like a shroud to the buildings and streets as Baxter made his way down towards Granton. He went by the coastal road past Newhaven, to give himself time to clear the vague, throbbing headache that lurked behind his eyes. The cold air was certainly achieving that. His brisk walk and the thought of fresh funds in his pocket kept him warm.

It was early still, the sun still hours from rising, but the streets were coming alive around him with cries of 'gardyloo' and the rattle of wheels over cobbles. The mist would be keeping the fishing boats in Newhaven harbour for now, the fishermen chafing at the herring that would escape their nets. Baxter knew it would lift soon and the small flotilla would put out. He smelled yesterday's fish from the market, and the brine of the Forth, and that more than anything put the spring into his step.

"But ya promised!" a voice piped at his side, threatening to dampen his cheerful mood. "Ya promised me ma as well!"

Little Tommy Dunbar bounced along beside him, forgotten about until he'd got over his sulk and spoken up again. The youngest of Mrs Dunbar's extensive brood — Baxter thought he was about twelve or thereabouts — and the literal runt of the litter, it had apparently been decided that it was time he started earning his keep. And as Baxter had been until recently on the impecunious side, he'd made the rash promise to see about taking the boy to sea, help him get his sea legs before he was packed off to the Navy.

"I did promise, Tommy, that I did. But..."

"And Ma said you're the skip, an' all, so ya don't even have to worry about squaring it with the skip!"

"Seeing as that would be myself," Baxter said drily. Tommy's voice was threatening to resurrect the sore head he'd previously managed to shake off in the cold morning air. "However, this is…" He stopped himself short — part of his instructions had been not to discuss the job. A somewhat ridiculous requirement, but he was suddenly seized by a sailor's superstition about not tempting fate over a berth.

He looked down at Tommy. He knew he should send him packing back to his mother, with a hefty clout over the ear if it was required. If the job had been as innocent as he'd portrayed it, he would have no qualms about bringing the boy. He could not very well now say that the work was too dangerous.

His headache was coming back with a vengeance. In truth, he thought, there was no danger. It was unlikely they'd even see this Russian ship, even if it existed, and even if they did he certainly had no intention of standing in too close to it. And if he could keep Mrs Dunbar happy it would mean more guineas left out of his pay.

"Very well. I see your Ma has already put you into a warm coat, and you have your duffel bag."

"An' a piece, to keep me going."

"Well, if you have a piece already, I can find no fault in your preparations. Come along."

Doyle, the boat acquired by Mr Arbuthnott, was moored not far from the mouth of Granton harbour, where she wouldn't get smashed into matchwood by the first run of the ferry to Burntisland as she nosed her way out into the Forth, smoke belching from her stack.

"Looks like he acquired it from the breakers," Baxter muttered sourly as he eyed the vessel. A single-masted 25-footer, she might have been a real beauty once, not unlike some of the drabs who frequented the dockside pubs. Those days were long past, though. An attempt had been made to restore at least a veneer of her former style, but the fresh coat of paint had been slapped on over the old peeling colours and the whole effect was one of a shambles pretending to be genteel. He grinned. Much like himself.

"I think she's braw!" Tommy exclaimed, darting forward only to be restrained by the big, meaty hand of a foredeck gorilla who came up the side more swiftly, and with more grace, then a man his size had any right to.

"You'd be the skip, then?" The hand was shoved out and Baxter didn't hesitate in shaking it, which seemed to surprise the brute. "Billings. Mate."

And formerly of His Majesty's Navy. Baxter didn't need to see the tattoo on the man's forearm to know that. "Baxter. Are we ready for sea?"

"Near enough. Didn't realise we're taking on supercargo, sir."

The honorific was perfunctory, almost grudging. "Mr Dunbar is coming to sea, to see if the life suits him. A promise to his mother, you understand."

"Can't say as I do, sir," Billings grumbled. "But…" He met Baxter's warning stare and slight shake of the head. "Never mind, sir. Welcome aboard, Mr Dunbar."

There was something about the man that put Baxter into an ill temper. He had to admit, it didn't take much to do that these days, but the false cheeriness with which Billings greeted the lad raised his hackles. His next utterance hardly helped.

"There's a fresh suit in the deck cabin, sir, seeing as you have a part to play." This said with a slightly dismissive glance at the clothes Mrs Dunbar had spent some time patching for him. "Same as us."

"Very well, Mr Billings. You may take her out while I change. Tommy — Mr Dunbar that is — keep out from under foot and watch the crew like a hawk. You'll never meet finer seamen than those who have been in the Navy."

Billings just snorted at that. Baxter turned away from the small cabin's hatch, catching the mate's eye. He wanted nothing more than to give his head a rest, but his years of training kicked in and told him that he had to get a grip on this crew immediately.

He straightened up, standing a bit closer to Billings than the other man was really comfortable with, and waited until the petty officer dropped his gaze. "On second thoughts, I think I shall take her out myself. Standby to cast off bow lines, Mr Billings."

Dawn the following morning found Baxter wedged against the old teak wheel, feeling the life of the yacht through every vibration and jerk of wood polished smooth by many hands before his. She was a decent enough sea boat, something he'd be able to get a lot out of if he'd made more time to study her trim and sail plan. He patted the wheel, silently apologising for his comments earlier.

Tommy Dunbar emerged from the cabin, his face wan. He'd lost the piece from his ma, over the side during the dogwatch, and now huddled in his duffel coat against the cold wind. He was still doing better than Baxter had, the first time his father had taken him to sea. Boat and protégé, then, were causes for some degree of satisfaction. He wished he could say the same for the sailors Arbuthnott had engaged. Picked men, indeed. Billings was up in the bows with a pair of glasses keeping a watchful eye for the Russian ship that should be passing through their area soon enough. The other two were tending to the trim of the sails at his occasional direction, but otherwise huddled in the lee of the railing as the wind rose. He noticed the dark glances they threw his way on occasion.

The whole enterprise seemed more and more odd to him. One civilian ship captained by a disgraced officer in a borrowed suit, looking for a single ship that probably wasn't worth finding. He was reaching the conclusion that Arbuthnott was both hopelessly optimistic and incompetent.

He grinned suddenly, as the deck heaved, *Doyle* cutting through the crest of a particularly large wave. The rest of it didn't matter — he had a deck under his feet, at least for a few days, and a decent packet of crisp five pound notes for his time. "Good God, I've missed being afloat."

That caused one of the sailors to smirk in a fashion he really didn't like. He wondered, briefly, if they knew of his somewhat chequered history, or whether there was in fact something more going on.

"Weren't you a sailor on a steamship, Mr Baxter?"

"Indeed I was, young Master Dunbar, but in the RN every officer must learn how to handle a ship under sail." He patted the wheel as it bucked in his hands again. "It's the only way to learn the sea."

"How come you ain't in the Navy no more?" came the innocent question, the piping voice crushing his mood.

Before Baxter could respond, even if it was to tell the boy to mind his own business, Billings' shout from the bows drew his attention: "Smoke off the port bow!"

"Bradshaw, take the wheel!" Baxter swarmed forward, feet confident on the rolling deck, and took the glasses that Billings proffered.

"Two points off the port bow, sir."

Baxter swept the magnified view across the horizon, a slow scan that would take in the indicated direction. He almost overshot, unused as he was to this type of duty, but picked up a twin column of black smoke staining the sky. The ship it belonged to was already reaching up over the horizon and he fiddled with the focus to get a better look. She was still tiny and indistinct despite the glasses, but Baxter could still make out the fact that she had an auxiliary sailing rig.

"Definitely an old'un," he said, having held her in his view for a while. "Slab-sided bucket and a secondary sailing rig."

"No sign of the rest of the fleet, sir?"

Baxter closed his eyes briefly, visualising the last time he'd seen a Royal Navy squadron under full steam. "None. Half the sky would be black with coal smoke, and if Arbuthnott is right they're already south of us."

He was already working out time over distance, wind speed and the mood of the sea. Assumed speed of the Russian ship — for so she was, he was certain. A warship, he had no doubt, and the RN didn't have many hybrid steam and sail vessels still afloat. "We'll work up ahead of her and then have a proper look on the way back towards Blighty. Shouldn't surprise me if the wind veers anyway, but even if it doesn't this old girl will tack well."

"Very good, sir. I assume we'll give her a wide berth?"

Baxter thought of Arbuthnott's warning of how jumpy the Russian crews could be. "I doubt they'll see a pleasure yacht as a threat," he said with a grin. "But we'll give them the sea space that courtesy requires."

The wind hadn't veered as he'd hoped and they'd had to tack back along the way through increasingly heavy seas, *Doyle* running gamely up one side of a wave before pausing breathlessly and sliding down the reverse; only to begin the process all over again. Tommy seemed to have been infected by Baxter's own enthusiasm and was even allowed to haul on lines — never by himself of course. The three experienced seamen got on with the work without complaint but without much enthusiasm either.

Despite that, they were running down across the Russian's bows rather than crossing her stern as he'd previously intended. A smidge closer than he'd intended, as well. "Either I'm getting rusty, or she's a lot slower than I anticipated."

He was up in the bows again so he could get a proper look, Billings on the wheel and his two mates standing by the lines. "Definitely Russian!" Baxter called out over the sound of the rising wind in the rigging. Tommy was poised over the notebook with a grease pencil, taking notes. "Definitely last century, not one of the new cruisers."

"I were hopin' for a battleship, sir!" Tommy said, his voice disappointed.

"She can't be the *Monomakh* — they left all those old rust buckets behind." She was tall for a warship, high sides that would invite a hell of a pounding, with barbettes at the corners of a central armoured citadel, mounting her main battery. "Four main guns — eight, nine inch maybe. Broadside of a half dozen lighter guns." He lowered the glasses, wiped spray from his face. "Don't be too disappointed, lad. You won't see many of her like again — she's one of the old guard, the transition from sail to steam. Battleships are two-a-penny in comparison. I do believe she is the *Monomakh* — make a note of that, Mr Dunbar!"

A signal light was flashing from one wing of the ship's open bridge. Baxter patted his pockets — he could guess what the Russians were suggesting, but was in the mood to make trouble. "Tommy, run back to the cabin and fetch me the signal book," he ordered as he waved cheerfully to the Russian and then shrugged apologetically, exaggerating the movement in case they were watching him through glasses.

Billings arrived next to him. "Smith has the wheel, sir," the burly sailor said. He was standing just very slightly behind Baxter's left shoulder and seemed to be shifting uncomfortably from foot to foot.

"Something you wanted, Mr Billings?"

Billings remained hovering just in the corner of Baxter's eye. "You don't remember me, do you, Mr Baxter?"

Baxter twisted round, squinting at the man; irritated at this interruption. "Did we serve together?"

"On the old *Inflexible* when you was a middy, sir. 'Eard about what happened to you on *Naiad*. Me and the buffer was mates."

Baxter turned to face him properly, noticing the way the man's feet and shoulders were set; the way he had his hands behind his back. "Did you indeed?" he said, trying to keep his voice level. Trying to work out what was going on. Something had changed on the *Doyle*'s deck. Smith wasn't at the wheel, for one, which was lashed to hold her present course.

And Bradshaw had the little towed dinghy up at the quarterdeck rail, ready to board.

"Always thought you were hard done by, sir, so did old Harry, *Naiad*'s buffer." Billings looked deeply uncomfortable, even embarrassed. "So I wanted you to know, sir, that this is nothing pers—"

Baxter hit Billings, hard, in the guts. It was like punching a side of beef, but he had the satisfaction of knocking the sailor down. He stepped forward to follow up, but Bradshaw's shout brought him up. "You just stay where you are, Mr Baxter, or the boy gets it!"

Where Billings was a solidly-built jack tar, Bradshaw was a weasel of a man well matched to the little pistol he pressed to Tommy's temple. Baxter had no illusions that he wouldn't pull the trigger.

Billings pulled himself up, wheezing for breath. "Like I said," he gasped. "Nothing personal. Despite that. Now you just stay there, sir, like a good gentleman, and we'll make sure Tommy gets back to Edinburgh and to his ma. He looks like the sort of lad who knows how to keep his mouth shut."

Baxter could barely hear Billings over the pounding of blood in his ears. He stood rooted to the spot, not out of fear but indecision; follow Billings' insolent demands or make a play for the gun, risking Tommy getting a bullet in the skull? He glanced over his shoulder and realised the mutineers had set a collision course for the Russian cruiser, rather than heading to run across her bows with a quarter mile to spare as he'd intended.

The tableau held for a moment, Tommy pale and sweating, looking miserable; Billings and Baxter locking eyes, testing their wills and resolve.

None of them noticed the deck gun being laid on them.

"Tommy, you just stay there," Baxter called out. He knew he was about to order the boy to take a risk, but less of a risk than he would face if he stayed aboard. "Go with these men, and keep your mouth shut when you get ashore." He looked back at Billings, who at least had the good grace not to gloat. "You might want to think carefully about what you're doing, Mr

Billings. I'm not sure, but they may still hang people for piracy. They certainly do for murder." Baxter sounded calmer than he felt and knew the effect his level tone would be having on Billings.

"I wouldn't worry about that…"

The crash of a shell exploding in the water off their port beam drowned out whatever Billings was saying. The noise was stunning, the detonation close enough to send a plume of frigid water over the deck.

Baxter took a moment to recover his senses — a tiny calm corner of his mind was pleased he hadn't panicked, despite this being the first time he'd been under heavy fire. Billings, no doubt more experienced, recovered a second faster. Bradshaw, however, lost his grip on the boy in a blind panic. Tommy dashed forward, showing remarkable spirit for a boy his age, and threw himself onto Billings' back, wrapping his arms around the brutish sailor's neck just as Baxter hit him again.

The Russian ship was firing continuously now, whether attempting to hit them or warn them off, Baxter didn't care. All he could see was Billings' ugly, broken-nosed face and all he knew was the desire to smash it in. He went forward again, hands up to protect his face as he'd been taught, driving short hard jabs into the mutinous sailor. He switched from midriff to head and back again, not giving Billings pause, ignoring the pain in his knuckles. Blocked a returning round house with his left forearm and delivered a punishing counterstrike with his right fist, smashing it into Billings' mangled ear.

The man howled with pain and staggered clear, blood streaming from his face and ear, Tommy jumping off him at the last second. Baxter was prevented from following up as the yacht jerked in the water, a very near miss indeed that caused him to duck for cover and gave Billings enough time to scramble back to the stern, obviously deciding beating Baxter wasn't worth further risk. His mates were shouting to him from the wave-tossed dinghy, their voices increasingly panicked.

Baxter ignored him — his roused blood told him to follow up the attack, but the rational part of his mind told him that there was no point trying to catch the trio of mutineers now. Tommy was pressed against the side of the yacht, flinching and whimpering every time a shell hit the water nearby, dousing them with spray.

"You should have stayed with them, lad!" Baxter yelled over the explosions. His own death here didn't matter much to him, but he couldn't rightly leave the boy to his own devices. Particularly in the off chance that his father was right and there would be judgement after death. He raised his head over the gunwale and waved frantically at the Russian ship, which had paused in its furious if hopelessly inaccurate bombardment. "We surrender!" he bellowed across the intervening water, watching blue-jacketed figures dashing about on deck. He realised they were reloading and trying to correct their aim as the cruiser thundered forward, still on a collision course with the miraculously undamaged yacht.

"English vessel!" a voice yelled from the cruiser's foredeck, the English remarkably unaccented. "Change course or we will destroy you!"

"Not with that shooting you won't," Baxter muttered. Tommy was pale, shaking, but his expression was resolute. "We surrender! I have a boy aboard, for Christ's sake!"

"Adjust your course or you will be destroyed!"

Swearing under his breath, Baxter scrambled back along the pitching deck. The dinghy with the three mutineers aboard was already standing well away, scudding over the iron-grey waves with its single sail bellied out. The wind was shifting to drive the bastards back towards Britain, but he still didn't envy them the run in that toy boat. The change in direction was also driving the *Doyle* faster towards the slabby sides of the Russian warship — he couldn't even begin to imagine what Billings had thought to achieve.

"Hang on, Tommy!" Baxter shouted as, with increasingly numbed hands, he struggled to unlash the wheel so he could change their heading. Billings had done a thorough job of it, though, lines wound through the spokes and then belayed on the once-bright brass railings on either side of the narrow hull. Baxter reached for his clasp knife then remembered he'd left it in the cabin when he'd changed. He sprinted forward, almost losing his footing despite the sea boots he wore, and let go the sails, just letting them flap in the wind. It would take the way off them, anyway.

"This is your last warning!" The Russian cruiser was terrifyingly close now, looming over them. Even they couldn't miss at this range, though at least they wouldn't be able to depress the big guns to obliterate the fragile wooden hull. The deck guns, 9-pounders and Hotchkiss gatlings, were being depressed to bear and Baxter could even make out files of men with rifles lining the railing.

"I'm trying!" he bellowed back, then dived into the cabin, cracking his head on the low combing and casting around desperately for his trusty knife. He'd just snatched it up when the Russians' patience expired.

The first few rounds, even at that range, didn't manage to hit, but the explosions shook the yacht. He could hear ominous groans and creaking that suggested her hull was broken. He ran back out and madly waved his hands over his head. Tommy was crawling along the deck towards him, one hand clutched to his shoulder and leaving a trail of red that was swiftly washed away. He started towards the boy, but rifle rounds were now hammering into the yacht, clawing up splinters and ringing off the metal work. He ducked back, locking eyes with the desperate boy, and then the yacht finally took a direct hit.

Baxter's world dissolved into fire and noise, uncontrolled movement, and then the hard water hitting him and cold darkness.

Baxter went deep, stunned by the explosion that had wiped away the bow of the yacht. He let himself sink, limp in the water; but some survival instinct kept his mouth closed when the rest of him just wanted to breathe in and have it all done with.

Then the familiar, hot anger returned. He jerked his limbs into action against the aching cold that had started to seep into them. His lungs were burning as he struggled out of the heavy, waterlogged tweed jacket and then his boots. He kicked towards the very slightly brighter patch that he had to assume was the surface. He was dimly aware of fragments of his brief command settling through the water around him, and for a terrifying moment he almost got caught by a section of hull as it slid towards the seabed.

Then, abruptly, he breached. Into the light, and life. Cold air flooding his lungs until he became giddy, spray on his face and his body lifting to the familiar rhythm of the waves. A section of the mast was floating nearby and he grabbed onto it, letting it support him as he gulped down air and stared about wildly for Tommy.

A small head broke the surface not far away, the lad flailing madly. "I cannae swim!" Baxter heard just as he struck out from his improvised float.

Tommy went under again and Baxter, always a strong swimmer, dove down after him, hands grasping. He saw a pale round face, huge eyes, and just managed to snag the boy's slightly-too-long hair, dragging him back up to the surface and clinging onto him as they both breached.

The cruiser was churning water not far away, bringing images of being dragged down into those massive bronze screws. She was holding station, though, while a longboat nosed its way gingerly through the wreckage towards where he trod water.

He was shivering uncontrollably by the time it reached him. A haughty-looking officer stared down at him contemptuously. "*Est-ce que vous rendez?*" he asked in perfect French.

"Do I look like I have a bloody choice?" Baxter managed to snap back from between chattering teeth, pleased at that little bit of defiance.

He regretted it a second later when one of the bluejackets smacked him in the head with an oar, rendering further defiance impossible.

The blow didn't knock him out entirely, just dazed him. The following minutes were a blur, from which some moments stood out with stark clarity. The angry stare of the officer who had captured him counterpointing the dull disinterest of the bluejackets on the oars; a precipitously groggy clamber up the ladder to be bundled into the care of armed Russian sailors; Tommy cursing their captors in language a boy of twelve had no right knowing as he was carried away. Worst of all, watching the last pathetic pieces of his little command being swallowed by the cold grey waves.

Baxter passed out properly at that point, overcome by the blow on top of his almost-drowning and the shock of being caught in a shell blast.

CHAPTER 3

"It was an audacious plan, but one doomed to fail."

Baxter tried to pull himself up on the hard cot. His whole body ached, as though he'd been subjected to a thorough beating from head to toe, and a bandage bound his head tightly. The worst of the pain radiated from his brow, where the oar had caught him.

What was stopping him rising, though, were two somewhat large paws on his right shoulder. Opening his eyes, he found himself being surveyed calmly by something that could quite easily be described as a wolf.

"Well, I thought the weather might turn a bit dirty for a sail, but I'm not one to back down from a challenge," he found himself saying, pleased that his wits remained about him until he realised he was talking to the canine.

The Russian officer laughed at that, clapping his hands with delight. Even seated, it was clear he was not a big man, and he had an open, friendly face and intelligent eyes. Baxter was a little rusty on Russian ranks, but guessed he was probably dealing with a senior subordinate rather than the captain.

The dog looked back at his master, then set about licking Baxter's face — a slobbery assault he was in no position to fend off.

"I see Maxim likes you, so I think we shall get on. He is a fine judge of character."

"That or he is determined to drown me."

The officer said something in Russia, not too sharply, and the big hunting dog reluctantly abandoned his task and padded over to a corner of the small cabin. "My name is Juneau,

31

Cristov Sergeyivic, Second Captain. Yes, I know, a French name for a Russian officer! I have the honour of being first officer of the *Vsevolod Yaroslavich*. Might I have your name?"

"Baxter," he grunted. He noted the name of the ship, that she wasn't the *Monomakh*, but didn't want to give a clue as to what he was about by admitting he'd recognised the class at least. "Late owner and master of the *Doyle*. And might I enquire as to what the ruddy hell you think you were doing, opening fire on an unarmed yacht?"

"My dear Mr Baxter — it seems clear from the course you were steering and the fact that your crew had abandoned ship that you were attempting to ram us. We were expecting suicide attacks by Japanese vessels, but to find a British gentleman attempting the same somewhat perplexed us."

It was Baxter's turn to laugh, through the hammering in his head. It was a harsh sound even to his ears. "Why the de'il would I try ramming a cruiser with a sailing yacht? Even if I was quite mad — and I assure you I am not — I wouldn't be daft enough to think it would achieve anything."

Juneau made an expressive gesture, somewhere between acknowledging and dismissing his point. "I can only assume that there was a bomb of some description, or you were closing to fire torpedoes."

Baxter stared at him, flabbergasted. "I may not be daft, but you quite clearly are, sir! Dear God, there was a boy aboard! The very thought…"

Juneau rose, confirming Baxter's first impression of him as a small, trim man. He seemed neither angered nor intimidated by Baxter's rising choler. "We all recruit young men into your navies. I myself was thirteen when I first donned the uniform."

"I can assure you, Mr Juneau, that I am not a member of the Royal Navy, nor am I a member of any department or organisation associated with the RN!" Which was the truth, as far as it went.

"That is an interesting assertion, Mr Baxter, given that we recovered this from the wreckage of the vessel."

Juneau lifted a somewhat ragged jacket into Baxter's view. Though it sent spasms of pain through him, Baxter managed to pull himself up far enough to have a proper look at it.

"Do you deny that this is the uniform jacket of a Royal Navy sub-lieutenant?"

"I do not, nor could I. I can certainly deny it's mine."

"And yet we retrieved it from the water where your yacht went down." Juneau's voice had hardened. "The captain will wish to interview you personally — I suggest you carefully consider how you respond to his questions. He is not as … congenial as I am."

Baxter found himself at a loss for words. The pain that reverberated around his skull was making it hard to think, to come to any sort of sensible conclusion about what was going on. It was rapidly becoming clear to him that Arbuthnott was up to something far more sinister than just spying on the Russian squadron, but it was beyond him what that could be.

He pushed that all aside — it could wait until he had a clearer head. "Mr Juneau," he said, controlling his emotions and trying to modify his tone towards the contrite. "Might I know how the boy is?"

Juneau paused in the cabin's hatch. "Mr Dunbar is certainly in fine voice if not in fine form," he said. "He was injured by a wood splinter, but not seriously."

Baxter let himself sink back onto the pillows, but only briefly. He pushed himself upright, ignoring the pain, and swung his legs over the side of the bed. "I must insist that we are returned to shore. At your earliest convenience."

Juneau made an apologetic gesture. "Alas, that cannot be. The captain has decided that we cannot reveal to your masters that your attack failed and that we have taken you prisoner. You will both remain in custody until we can determine how to handle this … rather unique situation."

Baxter made to rise from the cot, but sank back groaning as the pain threatened to split his skull open. Even if he hadn't been incapable of launching an attack, he realised it would not have been a wise idea.

Juneau beckoned an enormous bluejacket into the cabin. "This is Vasily Ivanovitch. He does not speak any English, I am afraid, but will assist you in making ready to be interviewed by the captain."

The Russian captain's day cabin was perhaps the most opulent thing Baxter had seen afloat. The floor was highly polished wood, but strewn with deep rugs; the furniture was all heavy mahogany. An enormous icon of the Virgin Mary and Christ dominated one wall; the others were dotted with portraits of the young Tsar and Tsarina and what he could only assume were family members in positions of lesser import. A side table almost groaned under crystal decanters.

"Captain Alexander Petrovich Gorchakov," Juneau announced pompously, in English for the benefit of the prisoner. "May I present Mr Baxter?"

Where Juneau was cheerfully open, Captain Gorchakov had a closed face surmounted by an impressively jutting beard and a tall, spare frame. Baxter got the sense that the opulence of the cabin was as much for appearance's sake than any desire for creature comforts. It didn't make it any more practical, of course.

Gorchakov did not look up from what he was writing, and merely raised a finger to instruct silence. That casual contempt and a natural inclination to go on the offensive tipped Baxter over the edge. "What the devil do you mean, opening fire on a British gentleman's yacht?" he barked. "Threatening the lives of his crew and taking them prisoner in contravention of all rules and conventions of the sea?"

Gorchakov rose then, snapping ram-rod straight and resting his clenched fists on his desk, his prominent eyes almost popping from his skull. He snapped something in French, his voice somewhat reedy and scratchy.

"Captain Gorchakov says…" Juneau began, his voice calm with perhaps the slightest warning note in it.

"I speak French, thank you." With an effort of will, Baxter mastered himself and re-ordered his thoughts. "I apologise, Captain," he said, slipping into his slightly broken French and mustering as much contrition as he could. "As I'm sure you understand, this is a frustrating situation for me…"

"I am glad," Gorchakov spat, "that we have frustrated your sabotage!"

"Captain, as I have already explained to your first officer, I had no ill intent towards your vessel." It was becoming an effort of will for Baxter to keep his tone level. "I was merely curious about your vessel, and certainly had no intention of ramming her."

"And yet you sailed on a collision course while your crew abandoned ship."

"They fled when you opened fire!" Baxter dropped back into English and deliberately let his voice rise. It was the only outright lie he had told, and he'd often found that shouting a lie often made it more believable. "Quite understandably!"

"Nonsense!" Despite the certainty of his tone, Baxter could see a flicker of doubt in Gorchakov's eyes. Fights were messy things and it was often difficult to recall the exact order of events after the fact.

Juneau coughed gently, and said something in French to his captain, quickly and quietly so that Baxter could only make out enough to guess that Juneau was mentioning the uniform they had recovered from the water.

He managed to resist the urge to demonstrate picking this much up, and instead waited for Gorchakov's black eyes to swivel back to him.

"And how do you explain the naval officer's uniform we recovered, as you deny being a Royal Navy officer?"

Baxter had thought hard about this while he was being guided through the cramped confines of the cruiser. He had one or two suspicions, the voicing of which would not help, but there was a perfectly simple explanation which had the benefit of being the most likely. "The *Doyle* was a recent acquisition, sir, and I believe the previous owner was in fact a RN officer. I can only assume that he left an old jacket behind, which my crew had yet to dispose of." It came off pat, perhaps overly so, but for a moment Gorchakov almost seemed to believe him.

There was a sharp rap on the hatch, breaking the tense silence that had fallen. Juneau flinched and Gorchakov's head snapped round. "*Voyti!*"

A young officer entered, somewhat hesitantly, and hurried across to Juneau, a message slip clutched in one trembling hand. Juneau read the message swiftly, broke into rapid French that Baxter couldn't follow.

Gorchakov shouted something at the junior officer, who hurried from the cabin. The Russian captain snatched his white cap up off the desk and jammed it onto his head. "It seems your attempt on us was only the first wave!" he snapped at

Baxter, before turning to Juneau and waving a dismissive hand at Baxter.

Baxter didn't resist as Juneau guided him from the cabin, following the long, hurried strides of his captain. "What's going on?" he whispered to Juneau.

"The squadron has identified Japanese torpedo boats closing to the attack," Juneau said, his voice excited. "We are going into action!"

As he said that, bugles started sounding throughout the cruiser. After a longer pause than Baxter would have liked if he was one of her officers, *Vsevolod Yaroslavich* came alive with running feet and shouting as the crew dashed to its action stations. Baxter couldn't tell if the shouting was panicked or excited, but he knew enough to recognise that a lot of the bluejackets clearly had no idea what they were supposed to be doing. A ship closing up for action could resemble pandemonium to an outsider, but the chaos was very much of the organised variety with a properly worked-up crew and taut officers. As they ploughed through a milling mass of shouting sailors, it was clear to him that this was just chaos.

"Torpedo boats? Here?" Baxter shouted above the noise. "Are you people quite mad? There's no way the Japanese could deploy torpedo boats here!"

Juneau threw a glance over his shoulder. "Not without the connivance of the English, certainly," he snapped. "Here!"

They exited onto the deck, behind one of the deck guns, and then Juneau led him up a steep, narrow gangway past the armoured wheelhouse — the most important compartment on any ship — and finally onto the ship's old-fashioned open bridge platform.

Juneau gestured to Vasily Ivanovitch, who had appeared silently from somewhere, and the big Russian sailor drew

Baxter to one side, out of the way of the only slightly more organised chaos on the bridge. Gotchakov was already barking orders from his tall chair while the bridge crew scurried around. Baxter couldn't help but feel a little bit of contempt for this effort compared to the calm, ordered efficiency of the navy he'd been thrown out of.

It was night, slightly misty, and he realised from the sound of bugles echoing across the water and the searchlights springing into life that the cruiser had managed to join the 2nd Pacific Squadron. The whole sea seemed to be full of the great, dark shapes of ships that were beginning to sprout the beams of searchlights. He could make out the hulking shadows that were the four *Borodino* battleships at the heart of the fleet, and arrayed around them the myriad of older battleships, what might have been cruisers, and support vessels.

And ahead of it all, caught in a pool of day-bright light, was a collection of tiny, fragile-looking trawlers and their steam carrier vessel.

Baxter felt his stomach turn as he realised that all of the warships appeared to be bringing their batteries to bare on the defenceless fishermen.

"They're just —!" he started to yell, but his shout was drowned out by the sudden thunder of artillery.

The entire squadron seemed to open fire at once, the long muzzle flashes of the battleships' enormous twelve- and ten-inch guns lighting up the night when the smaller armaments merely prickled the darkness between the main salvoes. The sea for hundreds of yards around the trawlers was churned to white froth by the shell spouts and whirling shrapnel.

Baxter stood in open-mouthed astonishment, partly at the sheer physical shock of being so close to so many guns firing, and partly at the truly abysmal state of the Russian gunnery.

His hands gripped the wooden screen around the bridge so tightly that his knuckles hurt as he willed the Russians to continue being atrocious. The lead Russian battleship — he could only guess it was the *Suvorov* — was narrowing the range to barely a hundred yards though. It seemed unlikely that they would continue to shoot wide.

Juneau appeared at his side. "I am told there were torpedo boats hiding amongst the trawlers," he shouted over the guns. "Our bombardment is driving them off."

Baxter seized the smaller man's arm, so hard that the Russian flinched. Vasily's hand landed on his shoulder, but he didn't care, bending close to growl into Juneau's ear. "There are no torpedo boats here! You are in danger of murdering innocent trawlermen, just as you almost murdered me and Tommy!"

Juneau blanched at Baxter's intensity, his certainty. "The captain is convinced," he said, voice low enough that it was almost lost in the noise of the 'action'. "There is nothing —"

Baxter's mouth twisted into a sardonic grimace. "Just tell your gun crews to continue what they're doing."

"I don't —"

"Juneau, they couldn't hit a battleship let alone a little fishing boat!"

The lie was put to Baxter's words a moment later when a cheer went up from the crew of a 6-inch gun below the bridge wing. "*Udar!*"

Baxter snapped his attention back to the hapless targets. Something had quite obviously hit the lead trawler, which seemed to be bearing the brunt of the attack. Many gun crews would be claiming the hit, though none of them would ever be able to prove it. The cruiser was steaming close enough past the boats that he could see blood on the decks and at least one headless corpse.

Some of the fishermen were on their vessels' decks despite the danger, and it took him a moment to realise that they were holding fish over their head, trying to signal to the Russians that their business was purely peaceful.

He almost laughed then, at the tragedy of it all. He knew that, now the Russian gunners' blood was up and they were starting to get the range, a few fish would not discourage them. Juneau was no longer by his side, and to his relief he saw the officer moving along the line of the secondary battery, earnestly giving the crews instructions. It was impossible to tell in the storm of shellfire landing around the trawlers, but he got the impression that Juneau was deliberately mislaying the guns.

Gorchakov was shouting more orders, his voice urgent. The bridge deck shifted under Baxter's feet as the *Vsevolod Yaroslavich* changed heading. She was moving with the rest of the squadron, and he realised through the ringing in his ears that the battleships' big guns had fallen silent. They merely seemed to be changing target, however — searchlights stabbing out of the misty darkness were illuminating the great vessels as their ponderous turrets swung round to a new bearing. Those of the ships' secondary guns which could bear were still firing while undamaged trawlers pluckily braved the bombardment to reach the stricken lead ship. She was obviously sinking but there were men still on deck, unable to lower their own boat, and Baxter felt like cheering as the other civilian vessels disregarded their own danger to come to their colleagues' rescue.

Shells were whizzing overhead now, the main guns of this new threat. He didn't see any hits scored, the rounds disappearing into the darkness, and for an ecstatic moment he thought that a passing Royal Navy force — perhaps Beresford's Channel Fleet returning from Tynemouth — was intervening. Flame spat from the Russians' main batteries again while the searchlights were trained round.

Juneau appeared by his side again, his expression furious. "No torpedo boats indeed! But Japanese cruisers, yes!"

Baxter was staring into the darkness as this new force continued to fire, hopelessly inaccurately. "Not Japanese!" he shouted back over the cruiser's continued bombardment of empty sea.

"How can you possibly know that?"

"Japanese gunnery is better!" Baxter grinned suddenly, then bent over laughing, pounding his thigh with a clenched fist.

Vasily dragged him upright to face Juneau's wrath. "How dare you! How *dare* you! I demand to know what you find so funny!"

"You're firing at your own ships! Only Russian gunners could be *that* inaccurate."

Baxter had the pleasure of watching the colour drain from Juneau's face again. "Enkvist's cruiser squadron. But they should be fifty miles from here!"

"If their navigation is as bad as their gunnery —"

Juneau struck Baxter then, an open-handed slap delivered at his full reach. Baxter jerked his head back, surprised more than hurt, and Vasily's hand returning to his shoulder made any reply impossible. The little officer stormed off, calling out to his captain.

"Don't hurry on my account," Baxter muttered. He realised Gorchakov was watching him, his stare piercing even across the busy and crowded bridge. The captain shouted something to Vasily, who tightened his grip on Baxter's shoulder and started pulling him towards the hatchway.

Baxter let himself be dragged — while his first instinct was to fight back and try to escape, he knew they were miles from a friendly coast and, as strong a swimmer as he was, he really had nowhere to go. As a minor act of rebellion, he reached up one hand and slowly but surely prised Vasily's meaty paw from his shoulder. It took a lot of effort, despite the bluejacket obviously not exerting himself too much.

Free of the grip, he turned and grinned at the Russian. "Lead the way, my good man!"

Vasily grunted, shaking his head and shooing Baxter before him.

Obviously understands more English than he's letting on, Baxter thought as he was led from the deck and back to confinement. Learning that was only a small triumph, but still a victory of sorts.

CHAPTER 4

"Bugger this." Baxter peered at his reflection in the dim light of a bare electric bulb that swung with the steady roll of the cruiser, casting a puddle of unpleasantly yellow light that illuminated an arc of the sparse cabin.

The hours after the 'engagement' had been a mix of pure tedium, frustration and apprehension for him. Although he was locked into a small cabin deep in the armoured bowels of the ship, he could still tell when the supposed battle had come to an end. Even the light guns could be heard, the vibration of their recoil felt; when the firing petered out the relative silence, broken only by the throb of the ship's engines, had been unnerving.

Exhausted, he had slept at some point, but woke from a nightmare about being dragged into the deeps by a woman wearing expensive perfume; he could almost smell it in the cabin after he woke and for a good few minutes afterwards.

The face that peered back at him from the mirror was unsurprisingly drawn, slightly haggard, shadowed with stubble. Pulling the grubby bandage from around his head, he was pleased to see that the Russian oar hadn't left him with extensive injuries. More like heavy bruising around a slight cut. He grinned when he noticed Juneau's blow hadn't even left a mark.

"Vasily Ivanovitch!" he roared, wincing only slightly as the stitches in his hairline pulled. "Come on, man, in here!"

The door opened almost hesitantly, and the big Russian peasant stuck his head round it. He'd obviously been asleep, the deep rumble of his snore giving Baxter a clue as to who was there. "Shaving gear and hot water, if you please," Baxter boomed, miming shaving when the sailor just stared blankly at him. "And clean clothes." He plucked at the front of the shirt he'd been wearing when he'd gone into the North Sea. It was stiff and scratchy from dried-in saltwater and grime. "And please inform Mr Juneau that I would be glad to speak with him at his convenience." He couldn't quite work out how to mime that, but the mention of the officer's name seemed to get the message across.

Everything seemed to arrive at once — not just hot water, soap and a razor but also the ship's barber. Juneau and Maxim were hot on his heels, all sign of the first officer's anger during the action dissolved into what appeared to be his usual bonhomie.

Juneau perched on the cot, his enormous hunting dog lying across his feet, while Baxter submitted to the barber's attentions. The man had thick, stubby fingers but a light touch; he had a sailor's habit of moving with the roll of the vessel to keep the shave close, but not too close.

"We have anchored opposite Brighton," Juneau announced. "Taking on coal."

"Were there any casualties from the night's action?"

Juneau heaved a heartfelt sigh, perhaps slightly exaggerated. "Some injured and one or two killed. I regret to say that you were right — Enkvist's cruiser squadron was off-course and we mistook them for the enemy."

"I can state with a fair degree of confidence that you will not meet the enemy until you've reached the far side of the world. Those trawlers were certainly not your foe."

"And I regret they were caught in the crossfire." As far as Baxter could tell, Juneau's contrition was real. "The sooner we are out of these foggy waters, the better!"

"I trust Gorch … Captain Gorchakov, I should say … has reconsidered and that Tommy and I will be put ashore here?"

Juneau twisted his hands miserably. "The captain feels that it would be … impolitic to land you at this time."

Baxter knew exactly what Gorchakov would be thinking — it would be a little while before the battered fishing vessels made it to shore and reported what had befallen them. The news would spread like wildfire then, and the last thing the Russians would want would be reports being made of an unarmed yacht being destroyed as well. They'd know that the three sailors had made their escape in a dinghy, but they could be ignored, discounted. A Russian cruiser putting a British gentleman ashore would cause something of a stir.

A few things started to fit together in Baxter's mind, causing him to start and put himself in danger of a good gash from the sharp straight razor.

Causing a stir was *exactly* what Arbuthnott had been after. If he had to guess, the attack on the trawlers was an unhappy accident. His own circumstances, however, were entirely created. He'd known in his gut, right from the start, that there had been something fishy about the Naval Intelligence officer — if he was even what he claimed to be. He cursed himself now for letting his desperation for paying work override that niggling sense, and moreover that he'd put Tommy in danger as a result.

A thin, sallow, nervous-looking chap tapped on the cabin door. "Ah, Gregory. He is the officer's tailor — I have asked him to prepare attire more suitable for you."

"Thank you for that consideration, though I do not think I shall need it for long."

"I see you are a sanguine man, Mr Baxter."

"I'm more often characterised as choleric, Mr Juneau."

"When you have changed, Vasily Ivanovitch will take you to see young Mr Dunbar."

The cruiser's sickbay was slightly busier than Baxter expected, and not just with the usual seaman's complaints. Several bluejackets had been injured in the night-time blundering. The injuries were all consistent with the sort of things he'd seen amongst inexperienced RN ratings operating a ship's guns — burns from contact with hot breech blocks, sprains or breaks from standing too close to the guns as they leapt back on their springs. Tommy was at the far end, in a curtained-off bed.

"Mr Baxter, sir!" Tommy piped as Baxter lifted the curtain and stepped through. Vasily courteously remained standing outside, no doubt listening intently.

"Mr Dunbar, how're you fairing?"

"Well, my shoulder is reet sore." The boy looked desperately pale, upper body wrapped in bandages to hold his shoulder still. "The doctor said it was broken by a shell fragment."

Baxter settled onto the stool by the bed, shifting uncomfortably. "I am sorry this has happened, lad. Should never have brought you with me."

"You weren't to know these Russian blighters were going to open fire on us, sir!" Tommy said, his voice maybe a little too loud for comfort.

That's the thing — I should have known it was going to be dangerous. I should have seen the betrayal coming. Baxter wanted to explain that to Tommy, but he remained certain that Vasily spoke more English than he'd let on. Or at least understood more. "Well, life at sea is dangerous," he said eventually, wincing at how stiff and pompous he sounded.

"Was there a pagger, sir? I heard the guns firing."

"I wouldn't call it a battle, lad." Baxter dropped his voice. "If you can believe it, these Russian blighters opened fire on a fishing fleet, thinking they were Japanese torpedo boats!"

Tommy's eyes lit up and the thought of action, then the implication struck him. "Were any of them hit? Oh, they must have been destroyed!"

Baxter snorted with disdain. "These chaps were trained by the French, Tommy, which means their gunnery was shockingly poor. Sad to say one trawler was hit and I do believe some fishermen killed…" He realised that tears were welling up in Tommy's eyes and remembered that a number of his brothers had taken to the fishing boats. "But not to worry about your family, Mr Dunbar," he said, forcing himself to sound stern. "I imagine that fleet was out of Hull or one of the other northern English ports."

"Rotten thing to happen, either way, sir." The boy sounded more subdued now. "Will it lead to war, d'ya think?"

Baxter rocked back, running a hand through his hair to give himself time to ponder the question; or rather how to answer it — the thought had been in his head since the incident. "I don't know, Tommy. It might do. But those bugg … honourable gentlemen in Whitehall probably won't go to war over a few fishermen, and the Russians will be in a hurry to apologise once enough pressure has been brought to bear. No, I shouldn't wonder if this won't all blow over in a few days."

Tommy digested this information, then asked the most pressing question. "When are they going to put us ashore, sir?"

"I'm working on that, Tommy, trust me. Just have a … misunderstanding to clear up with the captain."

Bizarrely, the boy brightened slightly. "Maybe the nice lady will come back to see me, then!"

Baxter shook his head. The boy was obviously more ill than he'd realised, hallucinating a woman aboard a warship that was sailing towards battle — albeit one a long way away. Even a Russian warship.

"A woman!" Juneau declared. "Quite preposterous!"

They were standing on the cruiser's quarter gallery. In better climes, it would be a pleasant space at the back of the ship, onto which the wardroom gave. Now they wore heavy fur coats. Baxter's was, of course, borrowed, from a slightly smaller Russian. He was glad of it as the wind that whipped in from the North was icy; he could smell snow on the air.

Baxter took a slug of the fine brandy that Juneau had offered him, savouring the warming burn. There was something about his denial that seemed to quick, too heated. He shook his head, putting such notions aside. There was no point antagonising the Russian over the ramblings of an injured boy; it would be hard enough for him to muster sufficient diplomacy to negotiate his and Tommy's freedom.

He stared now across the expanse of choppy water towards the physical embodiment of that freedom. The *Vsevolod Yaroslavich* was anchored within sight of Brighton, and even though the light was failing he could see throngs of people clustered along the pier, staring out to sea to catch a glimpse of the fabled Russian squadron. He caught the occasional glint of light reflected on telescopes or field glasses, and idly wandered how many of the people there were from Arbuthnott's organisation.

Looking around, he had to admit that they had quite a view. The Russian squadron had split, the 2nd Division under Rear Admiral von Falkerzam mooring off Brighton. The admiral was flying his flag from the only modern vessel of the division, the *Oslyabya*, a monstrous grey steel citadel that towered over the low-freeboarded *Navarin* that had no business being out of coastal waters. Beyond her lay the *Sisoy Veliky*, a slightly newer vessel but one that Baxter suspected was already outclassed by the Japanese navy. Scattered around them were a handful of destroyers and cruisers of various vintages.

The ships gently rocked on their anchors, the crews enjoying a rest after the back-breaking work of coaling from the pair of German colliers that were now standing back out to sea. Baxter could not help but feel a sense of permanence and power from the sight of them, one that would be far more intense for the civilians ashore.

He scowled, knowing that it was a false impression. He could not shake the feeling that these fine ships and their crews were sailing to their doom. It was a powerful enough force, but any Royal Navy battleship squadron, or even a determined attack by cruisers and destroyers, would send this lot to the bottom if provocation was given. Given that the trigger could very well be the insane decision to bombard Brighton, the Russians' destruction would hardly be solace to the people who would be caught in the fire.

"You will coal like this, all the way round to Port Arthur?" Baxter asked, distracting himself from such morbid thoughts.

Juneau smiled. He appeared to be a man much given to smiling, and the expression came easily to him. Baxter, not for the first time, wondered how he had managed to become the first officer of an armoured cruiser, particularly at such an apparently young age. The answer, of course, was the same as it would have been in the RN — wealth, and influence. "We will coal in port where we can, of course, until we have reached … our destination."

Baxter had to grin at that. "Your own broadsheets have made no secret of the squadron's destination, Second Captain. And it is not as though I'm about to dive in and swim for Brighton to pass this intelligence along." Not that the thought hadn't crossed his mind, but he knew the water would be numbingly cold. He also could not, in good conscience, abandon Tommy.

Juneau shrugged. "I have my orders, Mr Baxter, and I am not responsible for the conduct of journalists foreign or domestic." The Russian became serious, coughing awkwardly into his hand before he continued. "I feel I must apologise for my conduct earlier."

Baxter couldn't keep the confusion from his face. "Earlier?"

"I struck you, in a most ungentlemanly manner."

Baxter grinned — in truth he had forgotten that a blow had been struck. Seeing Juneau's expression start to fall, he thrust out his hand. "My dear Juneau, there is nothing to forgive. I needled you in an unpardonable manner." He surprised himself with his own reaction, but Juneau seemed to have a way of putting people at their ease. It was easy not to be an arse around him.

Juneau smiled with relief. "Come, let us go in. Dinner should be served shortly."

The next day, Baxter stood on the same little stern gallery as the squadron steamed further south and west. The great steel behemoths had got under way in the cold light of early dawn, their smokestacks belching great black clouds into the sky in a challenge to the weak sun as it rose.

The *Yaroslavich* had got under way with little fuss or difficulty, but from his observation point it was clear that the sailors and officers of the squadron had little experience of operating in a large group or carrying out anything other than the simplest formation manoeuvres. It was perhaps unsurprising — the cream of the Imperial Russian Navy had died in the early battles in the Far East or were bottled up in Port Arthur, awaiting these reinforcements.

He hadn't moved from his vigil when the cruiser was sent to join the 1st Division, the great modern battleships that dwarfed everything else in this crowded waterway. A great dark shawl of coal smoke lay over the squadron, matching the black mood that descended on Baxter as he watched first Brighton and then the English coast dwindle into the distance. Soon enough, despite the slow pace, all he had as a reminder was the cruiser's straight white wake. Even that was soon lost in the swell and the churning screws of the other warships.

"I am sorry," Juneau said, having appeared silently at his side. He held a delicate china cup and saucer in each hand, and Baxter caught the grateful waft of coffee.

He didn't reply but took the cup. He knew what Juneau was apologising for, and it was not the blow he had struck before. "Those trawlers are slow," he said, trying not to sound bitter. "But they'll be making landfall soon."

"We will be well away from British waters by that point."

Baxter laughed. It sounded hollow even to his ears. "If the Royal Navy does decide to hunt you down, do you think that will make a difference?"

"If they do, we will fight. I should hope that our absence would offer less of a provocation, until cooler heads prevail."

Baxter resisted the urge to point out what would happen if even a fraction of the power of Beresford's fleet came down on them. Juneau was perhaps more perceptive than he appeared, though, and obviously saw the conflict on his face.

"If you are not a Royal Navy officer, Mr Baxter, it's quite clear that you were once."

Baxter shrugged, sipped the still-scalding coffee while he thought. Lying to Juneau at this point seemed churlish. "I was, for a few years."

"What happened, might I ask?" Juneau spread his hands, his expression open and inquisitive. "It is quite clear that you are not a man who would have chosen a civilian life willingly."

Baxter stirred, suddenly uncomfortable. But he had started talking about it, and for once he didn't feel the urge to close the conversation down, or box his interlocutor about the ears. "One has to be a certain sort, to be an officer in the Royal Navy. Have a certain background, the right parents. I did not quite match up to those requirements, and that didn't sit well with my brother officers. And that's more than I've said on the subject in years, and as much as I'm willing to say. I imagine it is much the same in your Navy."

Juneau laughed, perhaps slightly uncomfortably. "Why, we are a most egalitarian navy, as you will find. We may not have learnt much in the way of useful gunnery from our French friends, but we learned that much. There is even an officer on the flagship who is a *Courlander*. Imagine that! A Courlander!"

Baxter blinked, trying to remember where on earth Courland was and why Juneau should find the idea of one of its natives being a naval officer so shocking. But he could not help laughing as well. "If I might observe, Mr Juneau — you are an odd fellow."

"Oh, odd enough that I've only risen to my position purely through wealth and influence. Can you not tell?"

CHAPTER 5

"They are refusing us resupply," Juneau told Baxter, his voice glum. "The machinations of your government, I can only assume."

The 1st Division had raised the Spanish coast earlier that morning, sailing in remarkably good weather with only a gentle breeze stirring the heavy pall of smoke that they took with them. Their arrival in Vigo harbour after three weeks at sea had been uneventful — Baxter had fully expected at least one of the big battleships to hole one of their smaller consorts or smash a local vessel as they jostled into the anchorage.

Baxter shrugged. "You're a combatant fleet in a time of war, and this is a neutral port. There are rules to conduct on the high seas, as I suspect you will find out shortly."

Baxter knew he sounded surly. It was taking him longer than he'd expected to readjust to life on a naval vessel. The constant pitch and roll of the ship were not an issue for him, but even after some time ashore in a busy tenement he found the constant noise and activity of several hundred men packed into a metal shell more than somewhat unsettling.

"How so?" Juneau asked.

Baxter gestured to the mouth of the harbour. A lean, dangerous shape was steaming slowly into port, the Royal Navy's White Ensign snapping from her mastheads.

"One of your cruisers," Juneau mused. "I fail to see how one measly ship is going to enforce the rules of the sea upon us."

"It's not the ship that counts," Baxter growled, piqued despite himself at the description of the cruiser as *measly*. She was too far away from him to see which cruiser she was. He could tell she was a *Monmouth* class, modern and fast armoured cruisers designed for independent work away from interfering admirals. Exactly the sort of vessel he'd dreamed of commanding one day, before the prejudices of his brother officers caught up with him. "It's what she represents."

Juneau took a deep breath, exhaled slowly, and seemed to release a growing anger. "You are right, of course." He gave Baxter a disarming smile. "Where there is one, there will be more." It was said in a light, bantering tone and Baxter found he was unable to continue mustering his anger.

Instead he grinned back. "And there's no place in the world you can go where we won't reach you if we want to."

"I imagine there will come a day where we'll find out what happens next," Juneau said, his tone still breezy. "Now, if you will excuse me, Mr Baxter, I must attend to my duties."

"By all means, Mr Juneau. Unless you have other preferences, I shall continue to take the air."

"As long as you don't … what is the expression? … go for a goose."

Baxter looked nonplussed for a second. "A gander, Mr Juneau, a gander. And I'm sure Vasily here will ensure that no waterfowl of any kind make an appearance." The big bluejacket was an ever-present shadow in Baxter's waking hours. He seemed to have no other duty than ensuring he made no attempt to escape or launch into some madcap scheme to sabotage the cruiser.

Baxter looked back along the length of the vessel. "I doubt I could do anything that they won't manage by accident," he muttered once Juneau was out of earshot. Gorchakov seemed to run a tight ship, and Juneau despite his claim to the contrary appeared to be a capable first officer. From what he'd seen of the other officers, though, they appeared to be affable but not necessarily first rate.

He turned to survey the pleasant sweep of the broad harbour; the rows of whitewashed houses that climbed gently away from the bay. The great steel castles of the Russian ships dominated much of the harbour, a vain challenge to the peaks of the Pyrenees that gleamed in the distance. The *Yaroslavich* was moored away from the shore and the mole, and rode easily at her anchor in the sheltered space.

He'd still be able to swim it, though, even with Tommy Dunbar on his back. He had considered just going for it, running to the edge of the deck and diving overboard; there was a reasonable chance with him free that the Russians wouldn't bother keeping a Scots bairn prisoner — indeed, he had no doubt that Tommy would make himself more trouble than he was worth to keep. He couldn't guarantee that Gorchakov would be *that* reasonable, though, and he was responsible for the lad. He couldn't really leave him behind, having brought him along in the first place.

So all he'd have to do would be to shake off or overpower Vasily (not a happy prospect), get Tommy out of the sickbay, get over the side without being noticed and either swim to the cruiser or make it to shore in the hopes the Russians wouldn't risk a further international incident by landing armed sailors in a Spanish town.

He grinned. So not much at all, really.

He strolled aft and then down a companionway towards the sickbay, hands thrust into his pockets and whistling tunelessly, drawing as much attention as possible from the Russian sailors. And not a little annoyance from those on harbour watch. Vasily maintained a discreet distance, a hulking but polite shadow.

Baxter turned over possible next steps in his mind. He didn't know how long they'd be in port here, particularly as the Spanish seemed to be bowing to the demands of His Britannic Majesty's Government and would likely require a departure. His best shot was getting to the RN cruiser as well — he didn't fancy being ashore in a foreign country with no funds and only the wet clothes on his back.

Which meant that, whatever he had to do, he had to do it quickly. He wasn't sure if he could overpower Vasily, if he was honest with himself, and trying would take too much time and make too much noise.

Nothing that dash and a bit of luck wouldn't overcome, though. As he came to the companionway down to where the sickbay was tucked away in the core of the ship, he grabbed hold of the highly polished rails and lifted his feet after pushing off, sliding down the staircase. He saved valuable seconds that way and jumped the rest of the distance while Vasily was still at the top. He swung the hatch into the sickbay closed and dogged it, with a conspiratorial wink at the slack-jawed sickbay attendant.

He walked quickly to the far end, where Tommy resided in his curtained-off section. Behind him he could hear the big Russian pounding on the door and demanding to be let in. Baxter almost regretted not laying out the attendant, but the fellow seemed inoffensive and not particularly quick on the uptake.

"Tommy, my lad, we're going!" he declared, tugging the curtain to one side.

The only problem was that the bed was unoccupied, though unmade.

Baxter turned on his heel, frustration mounting. "This is what you get for going off half-cocked, old son," he muttered to himself, then switched into his broken Russian to shout at the attendant, who was struggling to open the hatch. "You! Where the boy?"

He didn't understand much of the fast babble of Russian that came back, but the one thing he did pick up was 'lady' and 'Ekaterina'. And maybe something about 'not long ago'.

"That dirty blighter Juneau lied to me," Baxter muttered as he hurried through the far door of the sickbay.

He was into unexplored territory here, a long white-painted corridor with doors on either side. As he slammed the hatch behind him and locked it, a drowsy head poked out of one of the doors. He realised, as the sailor gawped at him, that he was running between the large cabins where the bluejackets bunked. He ran down it, heart rate increasing as voices started to raise in alarm.

He stopped at the companionways at the far end of the corridor. One went up, into what he suspected was the officer's quarters on the spar deck, and one went further down into the bowels of the ship. He took the stairs up two at a time — if there was a lady on board, he couldn't imagine her dirtying her petticoats in the depths of the ship.

Baxter paused at the top, struggling to get his breathing under control. He was in officer country, that much was clear from the fact that the corridor was carpeted and had more electric bulbs strung along it. He only had seconds, but if there was one good thing about Tommy's piping voice, it had a certain carrying quality.

He followed the boy's cheerful chatter aft — right into the stern of the ship, in fact — and barged open the door without stopping to check who's cabin it was.

He stopped, poised on the balls of his feet and framed in the doorway, staring into the unwavering muzzle of an automatic pistol.

What really gave him pause, though, was that it was held by a woman.

"Well, if I have to get shot…" he began, just before Vasily hammered into him.

"I do apologise for intruding into your quarters," Baxter said thickly a few minutes later as Juneau handed him some ice folded into a starched linen napkin. He winced as he applied the icepack to his left eye.

Juneau's voice was colder than the ice. "And what did you mean by barging in here. Not to mention giving Vasily here the slip?"

Baxter was still struggling to focus — Vasily had hit him very hard indeed. Right now there appeared to be two Juneaus stood next to the single chair in the quarters. That chair was occupied by the same poised young woman who had brought him to heel. She was holding the automatic with the same confidence with which she'd aimed it, though mercifully it was no longer pointed directly at his head.

Probably not much point in lying. He could have claimed he was merely worried for the well-being of Tommy, but he liked Juneau well enough and the ship had suddenly got a lot more interesting. Instead he shrugged. "I was trying to escape but didn't want to leave Tommy behind."

Juneau's stony expression softened very slightly at Baxter's disarming truthfulness. "And you thought he would be mistreated if you escaped without him?"

"I thought he'd probably be put ashore, but I couldn't be sure. And his ma'll be missing him."

The Russian woman laughed throatily, and said something in a low, fast voice to Juneau. He replied, smiling indulgently at her, and she tucked the pistol into a clutch. "My wife assures me that the only person she was a danger to was you."

Baxter blinked. "Your wife?"

"My apologies, Mr Baxter. May I present Countess Ekaterina Andreevna Juneau, whom I am lucky enough to call my wife."

"You really weren't joking when you said you had money and power."

Juneau gave him a half-bow. "I was not, though I am sorry if I gave you the impression that I was incompetent and would therefore brook an escape attempt."

"Perish the thought. You must understand, though, Mr Juneau, that you have me in a sticky situation. You can't blame a fellow for trying."

The woman laughed again, then rose and stepped closer to inspect him. Scandalously — or it would be, to a mind more prudish that Baxter's — she was dressed in a version of a Naval officer's uniform, lacking only the embellishment of rank or other insignia; the close-fitting jacket and long skirt emphasised how slim she was. She had strong-features and pale skin, dark chestnut hair mounded on her head. The eyes she assessed him with were an emerald green, her gaze lively and intelligent. There was also something ... calculating in her inspection that warned Baxter to be on his guard around her; that she was most certainly not the sort of woman he was used to mixing with.

After a moment, she turned back to her husband and spoke again.

"My wife has decided she likes you. You have ... spirit. Maxim also likes you. This will go very well for you."

"And Vasily — how does he feel about me?"

"He hasn't made up his mind. It takes a long time for a peasant to make up his mind. He did say that you have a hard head and fears he broke a knuckle."

"Well, I can understand why you are so insistent on keeping me around if you all like me so much."

Juneau's gaze was expressionless. "The captain, however, is not overly fond of you. He wants you to know that, given the situation here, the admiral has ordered the posting of armed guards, and that you will be shot without warning if you attempt to escape again."

Baxter nodded. He almost joked about not being overly worried about Russian marksmanship, but caution for once overtook his mouth.

That evening, Baxter was permitted to dine with the Russian officers; now that the secret was out the countess also joined the men. The *Yaroslavich*'s wardroom was comfortably appointed without being as lavish as the captain's day cabin. A heavy oak dining table crossed the width of it at the stern, affording diner's magnificent views from the stern windows, while comfortable armchairs and a sideboard dominated the far end of the room. Baxter was surprised to see a number of dogs chasing each other or themselves around the compartment, though none of them were of the scale or magnificence of Juneau's great hunting dog. Maxim himself was stretched out in front of the small coal fire, watching everything and everyone through half-closed eyes.

The dinner was every bit as sumptuous as the room. As Juneau brought the assembled officers to the table, silent servants glided from the pantry bearing heavily laden salvers of food.

Baxter was acutely conscious of the fact that he was somewhere between a prisoner and a guest — while previously he hadn't cared much for social niceties, a miss-step here could cause more than the normal problems for him.

"Allow me to help you to some of this excellent cod," his neighbour to the left said, in fluent French, after they had settled and the wine had been poured. Watery but intelligent blue eyes regarded from behind small, round steel-framed glasses. The man's uniform was as impeccable as his manners and his French. "And you must accompany it with these gratin potatoes. I am Andropov, the ship's doctor."

"A pleasure," Baxter replied after a moment. He was finding his French coming back to him more quickly — most of a life spent on a merchant ship plying the waters of the globe had given him a smattering of any number of languages. None of them were little better than passing and most not even that good.

"And how is your eye, Mr Baxter?" This was said with a diffident smile. "I'm told the sailor who hit you was most impressed with how hard your skull is."

"I've heard that before." Baxter resisted the temptation to probe the bruise that was spreading across his face. "I've also had worse before — though not by much!"

"I must caution you against receiving multiple blows to the head in short sequence. I tended to you after you were brought aboard and had concerns for both your skull and the brains within it."

The dinner continued along those lines. Baxter made small-talk in his broken French or the Russians' broken English, never giving away his own slight command of their language (although he had come to the conclusion that few if any of the officers actually spoke Russian). The company was in good spirits, having made port somewhere at least vaguely friendly. Juneau at the head of the table was in fine flow; as well he should be with his wife holding court at the opposite end. The sole exception to the cheerfulness was the second officer, Yefimov Kirill Leodonovic. He was a scowling dark-haired man, approaching middle age, who said little but drank even more copiously than his comrades — one of the carafes of vodka was never far from his hand.

"The wine is not to your taste, Mr Baxter?" Juneau said, much later. They had risen from the table and stood or sat around the cabin, breaking up into amiably chatting groups. The countess had retired to her cabin and the two men were now standing at the stern windows, watching the harbour lanterns and ships' lights glitter in the darkness."The wine is excellent, Mr Juneau, but I must confess I have never been much of a wine drinker."

"And you feel you must be on good behaviour," Juneau said, with an amused gleam in his eye.

"It's been known to happen," Baxter admitted with a shrug.

"But you could not maintain this during your time in your own Navy?"

Baxter felt a scowl starting to form and smoothed his features. He wasn't entirely comfortable with Juneau's continual questioning, but as the Russian had said, he had to be on his best behaviour. "I tried, but I just reached a point that I punched one of the buggers." He couldn't help an evil grin when he said that, but it did not seem to worry Juneau.

Lieutenant Yefimov, who was sitting by the fire reading one of the consignment of newspapers that had been delivered that day, suddenly burst into a stream of angry invective. Baxter picked up enough to realise that the news about the incident with the fishing trawlers had finally caught up with them.

Juneau looked troubled as he listened to the tirade. Yefimov had the whole wardroom's attention now, reading out the headlines and snippets from the various international newspapers. He stood suddenly, clutching a copy of the *Standard* and turned slowly to glare at Baxter. "Is this wretched Baltic Fleet," he read out, in slow and deliberate English, "to be permitted to continue its operation?"

A chorus of voices joined in Yefimov's condemnation. Baxter realised, for the first time, that the officers still believed they had fought off a determined attack by Japanese torpedo boats; and that the fishing fleet had either been caught in the crossfire or had brought it upon themselves by allowing the enemy to hide amongst them.

He found himself, once again, assessing options for an escape. The obvious route would be through the windows behind him and swim for it. Young Tommy would have to fend for himself; now that he knew Juneau's wife had taken an interest in the boy he could be certain of his safety.

"Gentlemen!" Juneau snapped, in loud, clipped French. "Contain yourselves and your anger, justified or not. From what Kirill Leodonovic has read, there will be a tribunal to determine the truth of things. Let us conduct ourselves with restraint in this issue."

"But, Graf—" Yefimov began, only to be silenced by a glare from Juneau.

Baxter was sorely tempted to make a break in a less violent fashion and retire to his cabin. Juneau caught his eye and shook his head almost imperceptibly. A moment later, a slightly more muted buzz of conversation started up in the wardroom.

"I fear Lieutenant Yefimov came somewhat close to being a bugger getting punched," Juneau said quietly, his normal good cheer returning to his countenance. "And that would have been unfortunate."

Baxter grinned at the smaller man and didn't ask for whom it would have been unfortunate, choosing instead to change the tack of the conversation. "I find myself curious, Mr Juneau, about the countess."

"My wife? You mean my wife who remained in Riga and will be travelling overland to meet us in Vladivostok, once we have successfully broken the Japanese siege of Port Arthur?"

Baxter blinked. "Umm. Yes, that's the one."

Juneau's grin was positively impish. "Even that journey would not have been exciting enough for Ekaterina. She, well, instructed me to make arrangements for her to join us on the voyage."

Baxter was beginning to like the sound of this woman. "The privilege of wealth and station?"

"Indeed, Mr Baxter. But even in the Imperial Russian Navy, such behaviour is frowned upon — particularly by more old-fashioned officers." This was said with a significant glance towards Yefimov.

"Hence the open secret, and her pretence of being a brother officer."

"Indeed! You are more perceptive than you appear." Juneau's face fell as soon as he said that, realising that something may have been lost in translation. Baxter merely accepted the compliment with a slight bow.

"I assume you will put her ashore at some point before you actually face the Japanese?"

Juneau shrugged, obviously discomfited by the question. "The countess has instructed me that she will remain on board until Port Arthur. We are confident of sweeping the enemy before us, much as Tromp did to your Navy."

"You do know he was killed in action against an English fleet?" Baxter replied, very slightly emphasising the Scottish burr that underlay his accent. "If I may speak freely, Mr Juneau — I would strongly recommend that the countess is put ashore in a friendly neutral port. Like, for instance, this one. A battle at sea is no place for a civilian, whether or not you are victorious."

Juneau looked thoughtful. "Perhaps, though I fear for my life if I was to press my point."

Baxter shrugged. At the end of the day, it wasn't his business. And a little part of him, he knew, would be glad if she was aboard for longer. "Well, seeing as I have hard work ahead of me tomorrow, Mr Juneau, I think I might turn in."

CHAPTER 6

"So much for your vaunted Royal Navy!" Juneau shouted, not un-jovially, over the rising noise of the wind.

They had cleared Vigo earlier that morning, escorted out into international waters by a Spanish cruiser. Their unwilling but courteous hosts had relented to a certain extent on their refusal to allow resupply, allowing each ship to take on some four hundred short tons of coal. The crews had set to with a will, officers included, to take on double that amount from the Hamburg Amerika Line colliers which had joined them in the port.

"I wouldn't be so sure!" Baxter replied, equally affably, pointing aft.

The two of them were standing on the little quarter gallery of the old cruiser. As resentment over the way Britain was treating the Russian squadron grew, it had become something of a welcome ritual for Baxter, as Juneau didn't seem to be taking the political manoeuvrings personally.

Juneau followed his pointing arm. He squinted into the spray.

"Four of them on the port quarter," Baxter prompted. "Cruisers."

The two men watched as the British vessels — for so it became clear they were — steamed up past the Russian battleships. They were in perfect line astern, evenly spaced, and cut easily through the rolling waves of the Bay of Biscay only a few hundred yards to starboard of the behemoths they were shadowing. So close, but still too far for Baxter to make a sudden break for freedom.

"Are they trying to provoke us?" Juneau asked, sounding almost bewildered.

"It shouldn't be too hard, given what else has provoked the battleships."

"They would be smashed at this range!" Juneau protested. Then his face fell as he realised what Baxter was leaving unspoken. What he said was true — if the battleships' big guns hit the cruisers even a few times they would go down. Hitting them, though, would be the trick.

"And I shouldn't be surprised if Beresford's battleships weren't just over the horizon."

"Your vaunted battleships," Juneau said, unable to keep the bitterness from his voice. "While there may be more of them, as the admiral said only the first four will count. And our *Borodinos* are very fine ships indeed."

Baxter, for once, knew to keep his peace. The cruisers made his point for him, some little while later, as they fell astern on the port side of the Russian squadron, still in perfect order but letting themselves be overhauled until the point that they could cross over the straight wakes of the battleships and commence the process again.

"They are making sport of us," Juneau grumbled.

"Indeed they are — cruiser captains can be like that."

Juneau sighed. "Ours is not," he said, his voice so quiet that Baxter could barely make him out. The note of disappointment was unmistakable, though.

Someone on the bridge, however, was determined not to let the insult — of having literal circles sailed around them — pass. The British cruisers were lining up to make their way along the Russian line, maybe slightly closer this time, and as they picked up speed the *Yaroslavich* healed suddenly, changing course to starboard, her old boilers labouring to drive her faster. Juneau staggered at the sudden shift and Baxter — sensing it coming and with his sea legs under him — lunged to steady the Russian.

"What is Yefimov doing?" Juneau exclaimed.

"Being a cruiser captain."

Juneau's eyes widened. They both knew Gorchakov would have felt the change of course in his cabin but would not act quickly. It would fall to the first officer to rein in the officer of the watch. "Come on!"

The two of them raced back through the wardroom and up the companionways onto the deck, which was heaving under their feet as the *Yaroslavich* steamed on an intercept course with the British cruisers. A lamp was flashing from the flagship's towering bridge, accompanied by the crack of her signal gun, no doubt demanding the cruiser return to formation.

Instead she bore down on the sleeker British vessels, close enough now that Baxter could read the name of the lead vessel, *Drake*. She was coming on, seemingly oblivious to the almost quaint old Russian ship on a collision course. The Russian sailors were hooting and jeering at their British counterparts, and the water was creaming down the side of the cruiser now.

Baxter grinned at the thrill of it. He knew exactly how he would handle it, if he had the cruiser's con. Sure enough, she was picking up speed smoothly and, in a contemptuous display, passed across the *Yaroslavich*'s bows without having to alter course. It was a narrow thing, either through luck or fine judgement. Rigid silence was the order of the day aboard the British ship, in stark contrast to the hollering from the Russians, but those not on duty lined the rail to peer curiously at this ancient oddity trying to joust with them.

Yefimov was shouting again. This time Juneau was ready and clung onto the rails of the ladder up to the bridge as the helm went over to port, bringing her head round as the rest of the British flotilla passed astern. The cruisers were past, though, vastly outpacing the old Russian ship.

The flagship signalled again, this time with a pair of peremptory guns. Juneau swarmed onto the bridge, bellowing in French in a volume and a tone Baxter had never heard from the normally mild-mannered officer. He decided it would be politic to remain on the main deck as the first officer alternated tearing into his subordinate and giving orders for their return to the line.

The RN kept up its hounding of the Russian ships for three days and two nights. Baxter could feel the simmering resentment of the Russian officers and sailors as a procession of ships — sometimes only one or two, sometimes a half dozen tearing over the horizon — came to look at the lumbering behemoths. At night the cruiser crews played games with their searchlights, darting the beams across each other and then onto the Russians. He knew he should resent it, too, after the shabby way he had been treated, but the execution of the manoeuvres, the seamanship, was too perfect.

The second day of November had been particularly trying. The steering gear of the *Oryol*, one of the powerful *Borodino*-class ships, had broken down, forcing a stop while the British squadron hovered suspiciously nearby. Baxter understood that it was a perennial problem of the big battleship — indeed, the whole squadron suffered often unexplainable mechanical faults.

"Destruction to the Royal Navy!" Yefimov growled in his heavily-accented French over the celebratory lunch the following day, raising his glass high.

Baxter refused to rise to the bait, and indeed raised his own glass. A vestige of professional pride baulked at it, but he knew his and Tommy's position was precarious at best and would become more so the further away from Britain they got.

One of the junior lieutenants — Baxter still hadn't fixed all of them in his mind — nodded in assent. "They have hounded us like criminals, although we fired in self-defence. And even though the admiral, as a gesture of appeasement, left witnesses behind. Even Captain Klado was left in Riga, which will be a sad blow to the fleet."

"We will miss his acumen, certainly," the doctor agreed. "I am surprised the admiral chose to lose his counsel."

"I suspect the admiral has little time for Captain Klado," Juneau put in from the head of the table, speaking over the rim of a glass of rather fine claret. "They were at odds when the squadron was being constituted."

"Pah!" Yefimov spat. "Klado was right! The more ships we have, the more likely it is that the Japanese will spread their fire and we will overwhelm them with ours."

"The ships Klado wanted," Baxter broke in, speaking slowly and clearly, "were all old and outdated, with guns that will not throw a shell as far or as accurately as your new ships, and with engines that will not drive them as quickly. And need I remind you that Klado's strategy would have sacrificed the crews of many old ships to protect the big ships?"

Silence fell across the table, broken only by the constant noises of a ship at sea — the throb of the steam engines, somewhere deep below them; the creak of the light fittings over their heads and the clink of glasses in racks as the cruiser rolled across the long swell. All of them, Baxter knew, were reflecting on the fact that the *Yaroslavich* was an old ship and that, in Klado's mind, they were only there to draw enemy fire.

"I fear, though, that separated from the squadron, Captain Klado will make even more of a nuisance of himself," Juneau said eventually, breaking the silence. He brightened. "However, we are at sea again, which even Mr Baxter can agree is where a sailor belongs. The weather is fine, particularly for the season, and soon we will be visiting Tangier. Tomorrow is the tenth anniversary of our beloved Tsar's ascension to the throne. We have, therefore, many reasons to be cheerful!" He rose, raising his glass. "To the Tsar and his Tsarina. God's blessing on them both!"

The assembled company responded heartily, including Baxter — it would have been churlish not to.

All were full-voiced in their approval but Yefimov, Baxter noted. He had nodded along in agreement with Juneau's sentiments until the mention of the Tsar, at which point his face had closed-up entirely. It would have been impossible for him to avoid making the loyal toast, but he had been far from enthusiastic about it.

As they steamed south into warmer climes, Baxter became more and more aware of a certain resentment that existed amongst some of the junior officers and some of the more educated crewmembers.

It was never stated explicitly, but Baxter occupied a strange space apart from the crew and that occasionally made them less guarded around him. Perhaps more willing to be open, in case he was a potential ally.

Juneau was not the cause of this simmering discontent, or even the focus, but his obvious wealth and the privilege of bringing his wife aboard certainly ensured his inclusion within it. Yefimov quite clearly despised the first officer, but that was personal. Baxter couldn't help the feeling that the surly lieutenant was probably a better seaman, though with a less deft touch with his subordinates.

The others, though... The occasional pamphlet he found told him what was what. The incendiary materials weren't left lying around openly, but nor was care taken to squirrel them away. They were there to be found, and read, and this he did. He read less Russian even than he spoke, but the tracts were quite obviously written for the barely literate and he understood enough of them.

Marxism.

A word to instil fear into even the stoutest of wealthy hearts, its tendrils had even reached into Britain. Baxter had even heard that the purportedly evil genius behind it had spent time in the grime and depression of the northern cities of Britain. He was astonished this sort of thing was going on so openly aboard ship; he had no illusions that the lower decks of a British warship would have their share of sea lawyers and revolutionaries, but they would not be this blatant.

He had, however, had more of an opportunity to get to know the Russian bluejackets far better than he had during his time in the Royal Navy. It had begun with a dinner invitation in Tangiers.

"The admiral has heard of you," Juneau told him as Vasily assisted him in dressing for dinner. Somewhat clumsily. Baxter had protested that he'd been putting his clothes on by himself from a young age, but Juneau insisted. He appeared to derive endless entertainment from it. "He has asked to inspect this strange beast, an English Navy officer who claims to be no such thing."

"I ain't a bloody Royal Navy officer," Baxter growled, without any real heat. This had become something of a ritual of theirs. "I'm a merchant sailor, and there's nothing more to it."

Juneau laughed, clapped his hands with delight. "Yes. This is what a spy would say."

The performance seemed a little false, as though the Russian officer was covering for a deep nervousness. He was in his full-dress uniform, dripping with gold braid and decorations, and Baxter doubted the thought of dining with the commander of his squadron would hold much to fear for a man of his standing. He suspected it was more to do with fear of what their Britisher might get up to.

He inspected himself in the mirror. The cruiser's officers had their own tailor, Gregory, who had been commissioned to provide evening wear. He was, unfortunately, only versed in Russian uniforms and the latest gentlemen's fashion, and Baxter felt vaguely ridiculous.

He'd survived worse. Like being cashiered from the Navy. That thought gave him the spurt of anger he needed, straightening his back and shoulders in a way that would have split the seams of the close-fitting frock coat if it hadn't been cut for his solid frame.

Juneau looked him up and down critically, then nodded and straightened his pocket square. "You pass muster," he said. "Shall we?"

The Imperial Russian Navy maintained similar hours to that of Britain, and Tangier's early afternoon sun beat down on them as they emerged on deck. Sweat prickled Baxter's face and hands and he felt his colour rise, but the heat was not the only reason.

Countess Ekaterina was joining the dinner party. The further they got from Mother Russia, the less the Juneaus seemed to care about keeping up appearances. She was in a dress that befitted a lady of her station, involving a great deal of white lace, and her hair was in the latest style. Her eyes were bright with merriment and a smile curved her generous mouth.

"Mr Baxter," she greeted him. "And how are you today?" It was the first time she had spoken to him in English, slightly accented but otherwise flawless.

Beyond her, the white and tan buildings of Tangier rose, as though they had been carelessly piled, up the slopes above the crowded anchorage. The whole 2nd Pacific Squadron was assembled here, having travelled independently, and the harbour was crowded with steel behemoths. Smaller ships — cruisers and destroyers — fitted in where they could. Boats from the various ships darted about and jostled as officers and crew visited friends and colleagues, their cox'ns bellowing imprecations at the small skiffs of local traders swarming the squadron. He found his attention captivated by this odd, dangerous Russian aristocrat, though.

She started to look slightly disconcerted, and he realised he had been staring rather than speaking. "I am very well, considering my situation, thank you, Countess," he said after a brief cough to cover his embarrassment.

"You have been having quite an adventure!" she declared. "And now dinner on the flagship."

Further pleasantries were forestalled by the arrival of Captain Gorchakov. He looked ill at ease, stiff in his starched white uniform, and glared balefully at Baxter. He didn't speak to any of the other guests, instead went straight over the side, saluted on his way by a full side party.

"Good to see some things don't vary between nations," he commented, then stopped in surprise as the countess made her way to the ladder. Juneau winced as she tucked her skirts closer about her legs and went over the side, running down the ladder nimble as a boy.

"She refuses a, how do you call it? A bosun's chair," Juneau whispered to Baxter. "How she does it in that ridiculous dress is beyond me…"

Gorchakov's launch bobbed across the gentle swell in the harbour. Baxter noted that the oarsmen were all neatly turned out and rowed with precision. Most captains liked a certain precision in their boat crews, but there was something about the exact attention to detail compared to how the ship was run that told him a lot about Gorchakov.

The water the boat slid through was oily and grimy, both fresh detritus from the newly arrived ships and older deposits floating on the surface. It was the same in any port in the world, but the incredible dry heat made the crossing a dreadful experience. The countess sat neatly in the stern with a perfumed handkerchief held to her nose against the vile smell that rose from the water, undisturbed by the still air that lay like a hot blanket over the city.

Baxter forced his attention away from her as she and her husband engaged in light conversation with the captain. He turned his gaze instead to the floating steel castle they were approaching. The *Borodinos*, it was clear, were formidable ships. Nothing expressed this more than the massive 12-inch guns, the real ship killers, twin-mounted in a turret fore and aft; the rest of the artillery in turrets and barbettes on her sides merely added to the abiding sense of menace.

She sat low in the murky water, though, overburdened with supplies — coal above all. He had heard rumours that the sort of luxuries demanded by the Imperial Navy officer corps meant the ships were usually overloaded; he'd not credited them until the last few weeks aboard a Russian ship.

He looked up from the nearby vessel, taking in the dazzling white ramparts of the old city on the cliffs above, the gleam of the great mosque rising above them. Looking back to the gaggle of Russian ships, old and new, he could see a cruiser flying the White Ensign. Close, but still too far away across the foul water.

Mercifully, a few more strokes brought them into the *Suvorov*'s shadow, blocking the tantalising view of the Royal Navy cruiser.

They went aboard with the same pomp and ceremony as had seen them off from the *Yaroslavich*, though with considerably more ease as the new battleship had much lower sides. An elegantly attired officer was there to receive them. Gorchakov was stiffly formal, but Juneau greeted the man as an old friend.

"Mr Baxter, may I present the Chief of Staff to the Admiral, Constantine de Kolong. Captain, Mr Baxter, our … ah … British guest."

Constantine de Kolong gave him a formal bow, but not too formal. Baxter nodded affably and adopted a comfortable posture, hands in the pockets of his frock coat. As far as he could see, the only way through this was to maintain the pretence of a merchant sailor completely out of his depth.

Juneau gave him a hard look, quite obviously seeing what he was doing. He shrugged very slightly. *You've put me in this position, cully*, the gesture said, and the Russian officer smiled slightly as they were led below to the admiral's state rooms.

Rozhestvensky, Zinovy P., Vice-Admiral. Much had been written about the man, little of it complimentary in the British press at least. None of it could prepare him for the reality. The Russian Vice-Admiral was big — not as big as Baxter — but carried himself in a way that made him seem larger than life. Dark, intense eyes peered out above a jutting but neat beard — many Russian officers seemed to sport facial hair.

"My time is short and I have much to do," Rozhestvensky declared after formal introductions had been made, gesturing them to seats around a table already laid with a variety of dishes. He spoke English, no doubt picked up during his time in Britain in the last century learning gunnery. "Tell me, Mr Baxter, what did you hope to achieve by attacking one of my cruisers?" he continued as they took their seats. "Is killing a particular friend of the Tsar considered such a coup by your intelligence services?"

An uncomfortable silence fell over the assemblage. Constantine de Kolong, the ADC, had a long-suffering expression on his face that told Baxter this kind of outburst was not unusual.

Baxter took his time responding, using the cover of being served some indifferent, unknown fish. Rozhestvensky did not like that, and he could see the man stiffening with impatience. "Well, sir," he said at last. "As I have already told your officers here, I'm no spy and I certainly had no intention of attacking anyone close to your Royal family. I didn't even know until this moment that there was one aboard. I was merely out for a pleasure cruise when your cruiser set about me."

About half of that was true — he'd not had the slightest indication from either Arbuthnott or anyone on the *Yaroslavich* that there was a Royal favourite aboard. Perhaps one of the younger officers, the midshipmen learning their trade?

Gorchakov said something in French to Rozhestvensky, speaking low and fast enough that Baxter couldn't catch it. Rozhestvensky cut him short with a sharp chop of his hand — what would have been considered unacceptable in the RN, even from an admiral of the fleet — and the dour captain subsided, directing a murderous look in Baxter's direction.

"And the Royal Navy uniform found in the wreckage? Your crew abandoning ship, aside from the boy captured with you?"

"As to the first, sir, I can only imagine the chap I bought the yacht from had accidentally left it behind." Baxter knew he had to tread carefully here. Gorchakov was angry enough with him already, and he did not want to exacerbate that by accusing the man of fabricating evidence. He just wasn't much of a liar, particularly when put on the spot like this.

And particularly when a beautiful countess was watching him very carefully indeed. Was she his supposed target? He carefully put his cutlery down. He'd rather be facing fire or fighting off pirates in the South China sea than dealing with this. "As to the latter — what can I say? Don't hire Scotchmen to foredeck gorilla, they'll run for it at the first sign of trouble."

Constantine de Kolong laughed nervously, obviously desperate to defuse the tension in the room. Juneau and the countess joined in.

"The same could be said for your Royal Navy in general." Rozhestvensky's flat voice cut across the forced mirth.

"I understand you took a different tone when Beresford's cruisers were sailing circles around you," Baxter snapped back before he could stop himself. He knew he'd regret it, knew he shouldn't even be standing up for the organisation that cashiered and blackballed him, but dammit... He kept his expression defiant as he looked around the table. "I do think, though, that you were quite right to send Captain Klado on his way at Riga," he offered, realising he should probably do something to dig himself out of his hole. The Army dug holes and defended them, not the Navy.

Rozhestvensky continued to stare at him for a second, though there was the slightest hint of a smile on his face. Gorchakov, however, appeared almost incandescent.

"So glad you approve," Rozhestvensky said mildly. "A shame your government is being less accommodating."

Baxter, wisely, kept his mouth shut at that point, and the dinner proceeded in a sullen silence.

CHAPTER 7

Gorchakov's retribution for Baxter's speaking out of turn had been swift and merciless. Juneau had appeared entirely apologetic as he broke the news to Baxter not long after they'd returned to the cruiser.

"He is, you see, very much in agreement with Captain Klado. Which is why he lobbied so hard for his ship to be included in the squadron."

"Though I imagine having a particular friend of the Tsar aboard was a contributing factor."

Juneau dismissed that with a wave of his hand. "A very minor member of the court, in reality. But I am afraid Captain Gorchakov has declared that you are not to be excused coaling duty, along with the crew and the junior officers. Despite your status as our guest — the captain feels you must work for your keep."

Baxter had, perhaps, had a little too much of the fine wine being served at the dinner, and he was more than tired of this charade. "I think you mean prisoner," he snapped coldly. "And we know how prisoners are treated in Imperial Russia!"

Juneau's expression hardened. "Just as we have heard of the conditions in your Dartmoor!"

The two men stood glaring at each other across the small expanse of Baxter's cabin. Vasily stirred uneasily.

Baxter blew out his breath, turned to let Vasily ease the frock coat from his shoulders. "I'm not averse to physical labour, Mr Juneau," he said, keeping his tone as level as he could. He had one friend aboard, and he'd be a fool to lose him. "Being a merchant navy officer and all." He could not resist that one barb.

Juneau smiled. "Were it up to me, my dear Baxter, I would set you and young Master Dunbar at your liberty. Unfortunately, Admiral Rozhestvensky sees value in keeping you at hand."

"I had thought he had seen the error in Captain Gorchakov's judgement, and was persuaded I'm no spy."

"I believe, from what little I could hear of his conference with the captain and dear Constantine de Kolong, he is quite persuaded that there is no way even British Intelligence would recruit you." This was said with a disarming smile, taking any sting from the words. "He does, however, feel that releasing you now — after we have dragged you both to Africa no less — would perhaps not be the best timing. He would, I think, rather put you at liberty when it would best serve his purposes rather than serve to inflame tensions between our countries further."

"I'm pretty sure no one at home would give a rat's arse about Tommy and me being your 'guests'," Baxter grumbled, then shrugged. "Well, if I'm to help coal, I'd best get into some working clothes."

Coaling. The black fever. The boilers of every ship, from the big battle line units to the destroyers that darted around them, had an insatiable appetite for coal. It had to be hauled in sacks on the bent backs of sweating bluejackets and collier crews, either directly from collier to the bunkers or loaded into boats at one end and hauled up the side at the other.

But the British government, allied with Japan, had made it clear that it expected neutral countries to obey law and convention and not permit the Russian squadron to linger in harbour or conduct anything but emergency work. Which meant the fleet coaled at sea for the most part, hovering nervously just outside ports that might once have been friendly, from an intricate network of Hamburg-Amerika colliers. Each ship took on as much as she could stow, far more than was safe. Once the bunkers were filled, sacks and loose lumps were deposited wherever there was space — on the decks, between the light guns, in the crew quarters and officer's cabins.

They were a week from Tangiers, the departure from that port conducted with the sort of incompetence he had come to expect from the squadron, culminating with one of the big battleships fouling her screws in the city's underwater telegraph cable and severing it. The squadron had divided then, the oldest battleships with an escort of light cruisers and the destroyers heading for the Suez Canal. The bulk of the armada was going the long way, round Cape of Good Hope.

The load of coal they had taken on in Tangiers had been bad enough, but none of them had been ready for the slog in the broad, pleasant bay of Dakar. They were tied up alongside the collier, a stream of filthy sacks and barrows of loose coal coming over the antiquated cruiser's high sides that lowered perceptibly as she took on more and more. The bluejackets and the junior officers threw themselves into the task with uncomplaining energy and, certainly at the beginning, with gusto. Shore leave, once coaling was completed, had been promised, and a bounty of fifteen hundred roubles had been offered to the fastest ship to take on its allotted load from the cavernous holds of the colliers. Baxter often heard the hands talking excitedly about it. To them, it was a fabulous sum of money, even when split across the cruiser's crew.

"How little they understand," he muttered to himself as he took a sack, the hessian coarse in his hands, and turned, rolling it onto his back and carrying it the length of the deck to be deposited on the filthy pile growing by a fore hatch. There wasn't a part of him that wasn't coated with grime, a mix of sweat and black dust, and every muscle and joint in his body ached. The blisters on his hands would turn back into callouses soon enough, but right now they stung like hell.

He straightened, arched his back to work out some of the aches. He wasn't unaccustomed to hard physical labour — no man who worked a merchant vessel would be — but this was punishing work, particularly in the stifling heat. There was such a cloud of coal dust around the ship that the sun was a half-seen disc of orange high above, but what little relief that provided from the heat meant nothing compared to breathing the noxious fumes and particles. He took the handkerchief from around his mouth and nose so he could spit a mouthful of black saliva over the side. The French port of Dakar was an inviting spread of cool white houses and palm-lined beaches, but there would be no shore leave here. Word had gone around the fleet that the port admiral had already demanded the warlike fleet respect France's neutrality and move on. Everyone had, at least, been entertained by their admiral's supposed response that he would take on coal unless Dakar's shore batteries prevented it. It was plain to all that the peaceful, quiet port maintained no such defences.

"Water, Mr Baxter?"

He turned, embarrassed to have been caught in the act of spitting. The countess stood before him with the same slight, knowing smile that often curved her mouth. She was dressed in a version of the common sailor's uniform with a simple peasant's skirt, smudged with just enough coal dust evident that it did not appear contrived. She carried a water bucket and pail, which she offered to him. He found his mouth was too dry to speak, but wasn't sure if it was just because of the heat and dust. He took the pail of tepid water with a grateful nod and drank deeply.

It was a stroke of genius, he reflected as he looked at her — the bluejackets who could see her were all grinning, bobbing their heads in delight that this fine lady had chosen to dress herself like them. Not for the first time, he wondered what her game was. Her husband would not have put her up to this. "Thank you, madame," he mumbled as he returned the scoop. "Most kind of you to be doing this."

"This is nothing, Mr Baxter, compared to the labours being undertaken by the crew. And you, of course."

"What don't they understand, Mr B?" a voice piped from beside her. He looked down, slightly startled, into Tommy Dunbar's open and now tanned face. It had been a little while since he'd seen the lad, who'd been adopted by the countess. Tommy beamed up at him now, looking pleased as punch in a small version of a Russian sailor's uniform.

It took him a moment to remember what it was he'd said just now — he hadn't realised he was being overheard. "That the offer of a paltry reward for breaking their backs is hardly fair recompense for the labour they do," he growled, before he could stop himself.

"Why, Mr Baxter, you sound like a revolutionary." The knowing smile had disappeared from Ekaterina Juneau's face.

He forced a grin, knowing what a dangerous word that was amongst Russians — or anyone else, for that matter. The bluejackets, as far as he could tell, had about five words of English between them, but there were officers involved in the coaling.

"Just instructing Tommy in the sort of subversive thought he should avoid at all costs."

"Well recovered, Mr Baxter." She laughed with her usual full-throated gusto, then gave him a quizzical look. "You are an odd fellow."

He offered her a small bow. "I've been called worse."

He could see some of the crew looking uncomfortable, and the officers starting to look unhappy and perhaps slightly resentful, and realised the conversation was stalling further work and drawing attention to himself. He was suddenly acutely conscious of his grimy state, a sensation new to him. He bobbed his head in unconscious imitation of the sailors, trying not to look embarrassed. "Well, best get back to it, miss."

A slight change in the motion of the deck under his feet made him pause as he bent to grab a sack from the growing pile being deposited by the sailors labouring on the collier. He straightened as the cruiser lifted unexpectedly, a heavier swell from off the Atlantic carrying her into the side of the collier. The big ships had anchored further into the bay, providing some shelter from the sea, but the anchorage was so crowded that the accompanying cruisers were further out and therefore more exposed. They had fenders out between cruiser and the collier supplying her, but he could not help but think they were perhaps too flimsy.

"Boom her off, you Goddamn lubbers!" he roared at the sailors and officers who were supposed to be watching out for this sort of thing. The cruiser was riding high and fast into the side of the collier. Before anyone could act the two ships hammered together, at least one of the fenders coming free and another just collapsing under the impact. The tortured scream of metal filled the air as the two ships' hulls ground together. He saw men lose their footing, and a panicked cry came from forward, where the fender had come away.

The ships were sliding apart, the cruiser dipping and the swell carrying the collier slightly higher and shoreward. Confused shouts ran along the deck. Gorchakov was nowhere to be seen, and most of the officers seemed too confused or too worn out to respond. The crew seemed to think that the danger was past, but Juneau at least was pushing through the crowd and dodging around piles of coal to get to the bows.

Baxter could feel another, stronger swell starting to develop. He was already in motion, using his bulk to bully bluejackets out of his way or just running up and over the coal. Trained almost from childhood to work aboard a ship, his footing was sure. He seized up one of the booms the confused sailors were supposed to be using. "Boom her off!" he yelled again.

Juneau was giving much the same orders, the sailors sluggish to obey. They managed to get the spars pointed out over the side, but the weight of the ships and the momentum was such that they could not hope to prevent another contact, just lessen the blow to the hulls. He put everything he had into bracing the boom. Other hands were grabbing onto it, including Tommy's. The wood was bending, groaning under the strain.

It snapped suddenly, sending them all plunging to the deck. He didn't have time to think, just threw himself onto Tommy as splinters slashed across the deck. Someone was screaming in pain, and someone was shouting about a man overboard.

Then the hulls crunched together again, a veritably gentle bump after the grinding impact before. The colliers' crew was yelling in a range of languages, and as he looked up he saw that someone on that vessel at least had some kind of sense and was sheering away, smoke beginning to belch from her funnels as she got up speed and pulled away from the cruiser.

He pulled himself up, saw Juneau crouched behind a gun mounting. "We need to sheer off as well!" Baxter called to his friend. "To starboard!"

"Vasily! Vasily is overboard!" Juneau replied. He was moving, though, heading towards the bridge.

Baxter ran to the rail. The water below was churned into white froth, and soon the collier's screw would add to the mess. He thought he could see where Vasily had gone in. More to the point, if he surfaced in the same spot he'd probably get torn to pieces by the passing merchantman.

He kicked off the simple shoes he wore, breathing hard to fill his blood with oxygen. Then he breathed out as much as he could and went over the rail in a headfirst dive.

The water was a warm slap in the face as he hit. Probably also infested with sharks. He didn't think about that as he struck downwards, spotting Vasily trying to thrash back towards the surface. The light shining down through the clear water was cut off as the collier passed overheard and Baxter drove down desperately. The beat of so many engines nearby was a physical assault, hurting his ears and thumping his body.

He caught the enormous Russian sailor by the collar and dragged him down rather than let him try to surface. He could feel the tug of the German ship's screw, trying to pull him back towards the surface, back to be minced; his lungs were burning, aching. Vasily was struggling against him, madly trying to strike out.

Then there was light again. Baxter reversed, kicking and scooping water with his free hand, his other hand locked in a death grip on Vasily's collar. The sunlight shimmered above, seemed to be fading. His mind told him to open his mouth, breathe in. He pushed it down, fought upwards, and then breached, sucking air into himself greedily, pulling his erstwhile guard clear of the water. The great bull of a man was alive, and breathing, thrashing, an expression of mindless terror on his face. He tried desperately to grab onto his rescuer, threatening to drag them both down. Mustering all his strength, Baxter threw the best punch he could without firm footing, not hard enough to knock the Russian out but enough to stun him. He hooked a hand under the man's chin to keep his mouth out of the water and looked around.

"You're all right, Vasily. Just relax and I'll get you back to the ship."

The *Yaroslavich* was almost a silhouette against the setting sun now — Baxter was still getting used to how quickly it went down at this latitude — and he could just make out a boat pulling towards them. The cruiser was standing off, thick columns of black smoke over her funnels.

"At least we're clean," he pointed out to Vasily as he kicked water, keeping them both afloat until rescue arrived. "Though we may get eaten by sharks before the boat gets here."

Baxter's stock aboard rose after that, at least with the bluejackets. Like many sailors throughout history, it seemed few of them could swim and the mysterious British sailor had therefore taken on an almost supernatural aspect for them. Gorchakov, of course, was furious that the ship had been embarrassed in front of the entire fleet. While it was true they'd been lax even if the sudden swell had been unexpected, what Gorchakov didn't seem to grasp was that the fault lay with him as the captain. They were lucky they'd got away with mostly cosmetic damage and some repairs needed to the armoured belt.

Gorchakov, though, seemed determined to find some way to make it Baxter's fault, although Yefimov had had the watch.

Some of the older officers, who tended to congregate around the surly second officer, were increasingly frosty with Baxter. The younger men in the wardroom seemed torn, impressed by his decisiveness and the fact he'd dived into danger to rescue Vasily. He was certain, though, that his one true friend aboard was Juneau.

Tommy was a firm favourite with the crew, darting here and there, treating everything as a great jape. He was rarely far from Ekaterina as she did her rounds of the ship.

Ekaterina was not one of the people, that much was clear. She did, however, genuinely seem to care about the peasant sailors and they responded to that. She'd taken to bringing round water for the men during the sweltering work of the occasional coaling — or, more accurately, Tommy and her personal servant carried pails of water that she doled out at various points. Her wardrobe rotated between a bluejacket's uniform and a lightweight version of an officer's normal service uniform, though she was always immaculate in a gown for the frequent dinners in the wardroom.

For any of them to be within hailing distance of clean was a rare achievement indeed. Baxter felt grimy even after he'd washed and changed clothes. Dust filled the air, coating every surface. It filled his nose and lungs, and the food often had a hint of grit about it. Ekaterina made no complaint about it, though, and that was just one of the many things about her he found himself admiring more and more.

It was clear that the young officers aboard also coveted her company — although there were other women accompanying the fleet, they were more-or-less inaccessible aboard the *Orel* hospital ship, although some enterprising officers from the *Dmitri Donskoy* had been caught out by a surprise night drill, the *Suvorov*'s searchlights picking out their small boat after they escorted a nurse back to her berth. The admiral's wrathful response was seen by some as hypocritical, as it had been apparent since Dakar that the head nurse was his mistress.

Ekaterina's status, as both a noble and the wife of the first officer, of course kept her above any open declarations or anything more than an admiring glance, but Baxter felt a certain amount of tension among the younger man when neither Ekaterina or her husband were around. Almost though they were competing for the right to woo her if something befell Juneau.

CHAPTER 8

The French colony of Gabon gave some relief from both the cloying, humid heat aboard and the tension of being cooped up together. It had taken two weeks to labour the 2,000 miles from Dakar to France's equatorial colony. Two weeks of nervously watching the big battleships as they wallowed in even gentle water, sitting deep enough in the water that their lower decks were often awash. The crews had slept on deck to escape the heat and coal-dust laden atmosphere below, braving being lashed by intense rain in the early morning.

Two weeks of breakdowns, so frequent that some said they were the result of deliberate action; botched exercises and fraught, frantic signals from the flag berating officers and ordering summary punishments. Luckily, the *Yaroslavich* managed to avoid the ignominy of being ordered out of line to take station to starboard of the flagship. This would have been the ultimate shame.

In a way that reflected the fact that nobody, from the fleet commander to Enkvist, who had charge of the cruiser squadron, seemed to know what to do with the old, outmoded cruiser. She couldn't take her place in the line of battle or keep up with the modern cruisers. She was an anomaly, almost making her own arrangements and just generally pottering along with the rest of the Imperial Russian Navy's 2nd Pacific Squadron.

Tension had been high as the fleet nosed its way into the estuary of the Gabon and towards the small, sleepy French colonial capital of Libreville nestled there. The ships followed steam pinnaces that marked out a safe passage and berths in the crystal clear, inviting water. The order to drop anchor had been given outside territorial waters and every eye observed the launch that slid across the placid water towards them from the distant French colonial capital. Those with glasses or telescopes could see the boat bore the fresh fruit and a crate of Champagne for the flagship.

Although no one but Rozhestvensky would be able to sample these gifts, a palpable sense of relaxation came across the officers and men. There would be a friendly reception here, it seemed. Without a telegraph station, there was no way for the colonial authorities to have anything more than the vaguest sense of what was occurring in the wider world.

The hated colliers were still a few days away, and shore leave was granted. Captain Gorchakov had, apparently, reluctantly agreed with Juneau that there was little opportunity for Baxter and Tommy to abscond. The colony was surrounded by jungle rife with cannibals, so rumour had it. Libreville also received little in the way of foreign visitors — indeed, the Russian ships' arrival was probably the most dramatic thing that had ever happened here and the only other vessels in the harbour were fishing boats and a single somewhat dilapidated French coastal freighter. There would therefore be limited chances to escape by sea.

"It hasn't changed much," Baxter commented to Tommy as one of the cruiser's launches crawled across the placid water. The bluejackets at the oars drove the boat forward with power but little co-ordination or smoothness. This was despite the cox'ns best efforts and exhortations, as Ekaterina and a gaggle of officers were in the stern. Ekaterina was resplendent in a light, white summer dress and the officers were bedecked in their smart dress uniforms (and no doubt suffering as a result). As Lieutenant Yefimov, looking sour as always, was in the party Baxter had taken himself to the bows with the excited lad.

"'Ave you bin here before, sir?" Tommy asked unnecessarily.

"Years ago. I was fifteen, so not much older than you," Baxter said. "My father's ship called here on the way to Cape Town. The Land of the Lotus Eaters, he called it."

"Never had lotus," Tommy said, slightly wistfully.

"Me neither, lad. I think it's just an expression."

"It is a reference to Greek mythology, Mr Baxter," Ekaterina said from the stern. Baxter coloured slightly, both at being overheard and at having his lack of a classical education highlighted. He could see Yefimov and some of the other officers who understood English smirking. "It means … it is a place to forget yourself and your woes. But also, the things that make you strive."

"Doesn't sound so bad," Baxter muttered.

"I wouldn't want to forget anything," Tommy blurted. "I've never been somewhere forrin."

"And you will remember this adventure your whole life, Tomas'ka." Ekaterina's voice was indulgent.

"Just stay away from the lotuses," Baxter muttered, making Tommy laugh. "You'll be fine."

A few minutes later, the boat crunched up onto pristine white sand. Baxter jumped over the side with the bluejackets, letting the blood-warm water rise up his legs, and helped pull the launch far enough up so that the lady and officers could disembark without soiling their finery. He'd known exactly how hot it would be here and had commissioned a light linen suit in preparation. It was dry within a few minutes as he wandered up the beach with the rest of the party.

Looking back at the gentle lapping waters of the bay, he saw the beach was already lined with boats. Although there was a small pier, it seemed most crews thought it would be quicker and easier to land here and go straight up into the quiet little town of whitewashed buildings. Merchants were already lining the beachfront to greet the visitors, just as a swarm of what he would call 'bumboats' was beginning to surround the ships.

They reached the breakwater, the soft sand above the tideline making the going slightly harder. As they reached the hard-packed road that ran along the beachfront, Ekaterina gestured to Tommy. "Come along with me now, Tomas'ka," she said quietly, with something approaching an apologetic look at Baxter, just as Yefimov stepped into his path.

The sour Russian officer gave him a rare smile, devoid of any pleasantness. "Enjoy Libreville, Mr Baxter," he said in his poor French. "I hope the meaning of the name is not too ironic for you."

Baxter opened his mouth, colouring slightly as he realised he had been ambushed. There had been a plan forming in his head, to see if there was a British consulate here and take shelter, or even just find a bolthole and hope the business of the squadron wouldn't allow the Russians to tarry long enough to find a couple of errant British citizens.

He couldn't countenance abandoning Tommy, though, and someone on the *Yaroslavich* obviously well understood that. He didn't think it was Juneau, but he could quite believe it was Ekaterina. She knew that keeping the two of them separate guaranteed Baxter's continual compliance. And, he was certain now, she was so much more than the first officer's wife who'd come along for an adventure.

He gritted his teeth briefly, feeling a flash of the old desire to knock Yefimov's block off. He forced a smile and a courteous nod over the smaller man's head to Ekaterina. "Make sure he doesn't get into too much trouble," he said, thinking he sounded affable enough.

Yefimov obviously didn't like being ignored. "*Botsman* Kobach will accompany you," he said, his voice acidic. "To help carry any purchases you make."

Baxter looked blankly at him for a second, until he realised he was referring to the sailor who was still his ever-present shadow. He realised he'd never heard anyone refer to Vasily by his rank and family name — hadn't even known that his rank was bo'sun. That made him a relatively senior non-commissioned officer.

The big man emerged from the press of sailors waiting eagerly to be dismissed to their pleasures. He was smiling agreeably, obviously not overly worried about having to spend his time trailing around after their 'guest'. Baxter had, after all, saved Vasily's life and he seemed to feel he owed Baxter a debt. Baxter had come to value the stolid presence, even though he had no doubt that if push came to shove Vasily would do his duty.

"Well, Vasily, what does a Russian sailor do on liberty?" Baxter said loudly in English. When the bo'sun just stared blankly at him — Vasily was still maintaining the pretence of not understanding even a word of English — he laughed and clapped the man on the shoulder. "Much the same as British sailors do, I shouldn't wonder."

It was the first time in weeks Baxter had set foot on dry land, and he realised with surprise that there was no relief here. He was essentially a prisoner of the Russian fleet, but at least he was at sea. On land, though — that was where things could get more complicated than he liked.

The town was already crawling with sailors. The enlisted men were, in equal parts, excited and bewildered to be somewhere this exotic. Most of them were from farming villages deep within the interior of Russia and had been no further than the Baltic or, at best, some other European port. There was little definition between the town of low stone buildings and wooden huts and the jungle. The sailors marvelled at the trees that loomed overhead, the undreamed-of colours of the enormous flowers; the shapes and sounds of the monkeys that swung about overhead; the great turtles that basked on the beach between the boats.

Contrary to his expectations, Vasily was content to explore the town rather than make for one of the small number of drinking establishments — which mostly just appeared to be open-fronted shacks. Baxter had always relished this part of his seaborne upbringing. He'd had the chance to visit places and experience things most people couldn't even dream of, including Libreville. He was content to wander with his minder, taking in the sights and sounds and smells.

"They tenderise the meat by submerging it in bogs, you know," he told Vasily as the two of them stopped for lunch and a glass of cheap, sour red wine from one of the shacks. "It's monkey."

The Russian glanced with some dismay at his spit of grilled meat, then his eyes narrowed and he looked back up quickly, as though only just realising that Baxter had spoken to him in Russian. A slow smile split the granite block of his face. "Is very good," he replied, in heavily accented English.

It felt like a moment of ... not change, as such as a recognition of some bond of trust.

"Tell me, Vasily," Baxter went on, speaking slowly and carefully, and not just because he had stuck to Russian. "What do you make of our second lieutenant?"

Vasily puffed out his chest slightly. "His Honour is a fine man and a good officer," he said, sounding almost like he was reciting something by rote. "He learned from your English Navy, after all."

That was interesting. Relations between Britain and Russia had not always been as frosty as they currently were, and it hadn't been uncommon for Russian officers to spend time with the Royal Navy. The squadron commander had done exactly this as a captain. Baxter decided against picking the point any further. Vasily was still a non-commissioned officer under Yefimov and he neither wanted to put a strain on their growing friendship or force the man into an indiscretion about a more senior officer.

The wine was also starting to sit sourly in his guts. It was hot, even in the shade of the big tropical trees, and humid. "Well, shall we continue our wanderings? Though I'm not sure how much more of Libreville there is to see."

He was glad of Vasily's company, and not just for the companionship. He wasn't too worried about the cruiser's crew, as they'd accepted him, and the locals would pay him little heed unless he was stupid enough to wander into the jungle — never far away in the small town. Other Russian sailors were another consideration, though. While they may have heard of the British captives, it was likely that was all they knew of him. What they would know was that British ships had hounded them as far as Africa, and the officers had made no secret of the fact they were taking on coal in miserable circumstances because British pressure prevented them from docking to refuel. Tommy was safe enough, particularly with

Ekaterina. If one of the bluejackets did want to start trouble with a British person, they'd pick on him.

He unconsciously cracked the knuckles of his right hand. They'd be welcome to try. He could look after himself, but with the equally big Vasily there as well it was unlikely that there'd be trouble.

A streak of Scottish lad went past with a whoop, chasing the biggest moth he'd ever seen. "Careful, Tommy," he called out, then surreptitiously cast around to see where the rest of the officer's party had got to. This could be his chance. He knew he had limited options to get away from the colony, but getting away from his captors would be a first step. He could work out the rest from there...

"He's a lively boy," Ekaterina commented, appearing right next to him in that startling way she had. She had a knowing smile that suggested she knew exactly what he'd been thinking.

Baxter was getting used to her doing that, though, and didn't startle. "He'll make a good sailor one day," he said. He didn't offer any honorific, and she didn't seem to mind. This was not a place for formality, walking along an unpaved street, low whitewashed buildings on either side.

"A shame you had to get him involved in your attempt to kill my husband."

"Your husband?" It took Baxter a moment to put two and two together — he was accused of attempting to assassinate a particular friend of the Tsar, and also of killing her husband, and it took him longer than it should to realise they were one and the same. That, more than anything else of late, astonished him. Juneau was not someone who gave the impression of being that highly connected.

Her smile was wider than normal, lighting up her whole face. There was real affection in her voice when she spoke of him.

"Yes. He does not like to make much of it." The smile died. "Though you did not answer my question."

He reached for the anger he expected, found it wasn't there. Her deep emerald eyes, so green they were almost black, quelled any thought of the familiar rage. He shrugged. "I did not realise I had been asked a question. But I wish it would occur to someone, *anyone*, that even a perfidious British agent would not risk a child's life in that sort of jaunt."

The smile returned, and her hand rested on his arm very briefly. "If it is any consolation, I believe you when you say you were not trying to attack us." A pause, and she caught her lower lip between her teeth as she thought. Her voice was careful when she spoke again. "Though I am not convinced that you are not somehow connected to the British Intelligence. You have been keeping secrets, after all."

"Beg pardon, Mrs Juneau?"

She looked down at Tommy as he trotted up. "Tomas'ka," she said with a fond smile, and reached into her small handbag to retrieve some small coins. "Run along into the market ahead and buy a mango. Do not be cheated."

Tommy bobbed his head. He seemed as taken with the countess as everyone else aboard, and her naming of him and tone suggested she had a genuine affection for the boy. "Yes, miss," he said, and darted off, weaving through the mixed crowd of sailors and locals.

"Tommy's a canny lad from Edinburgh, miss. He'll know if someone is cheating him."

"You are a cynic, Mr Baxter."

"I'm a sailor, ma'am. We're a practical species."

"Are you, though, Mr Baxter? Are you truly a sailor?" she went on when he just blinked in confusion at her.

The question was asked lightly, but he got the feeling his answers here would carry great weight. "Why yes, ma'am. My father was a Merchant Navy captain and I've been on and around ships since I was ten."

"My husband tells me you were in the Royal Navy."

He felt a tightening in his guts. "For a short spell, yes," he said, perhaps more sharply then he'd intended. If she minded, it didn't show. He forced himself to calm. "For the last little while I've been working ships on the coastal trade — this is the furthest I've been for a year or more."

There was a slight smile, but her eyes were impassive. He was struck by the fact that he didn't really know her; not only that, but no one else aboard truly did. Except maybe her husband. "And this journeying around the world, this is how you learned our language?"

"Well, ma'am, I wouldn't say I spoke Russian. Understand bits of it, maybe."

The smile was still there, but the eyes were sharper. "You sounded very fluent when you were giving orders, when those German *bashi-bazouks* almost sank us."

That took the wind out of his sails. He hadn't even noticed switching language in the heat of the crisis. The venom with which she spoke of the German collier also surprised him, although her crew hadn't really been at fault.

That light touch on his forearm. "Do not worry — I don't think anyone else realised, and your secret is safe with me. Unless it turns out that you are the agent of a foreign and hostile power."

That was too close for comfort. It had been a while since Baxter had thought much about Arbuthnott and tried to unravel what he was about. Life at sea, the intermittent grind of coaling, had driven most such thoughts from his mind. He remained convinced, though, that he was a pawn in some form of illegal enterprise. "I was not aware that a countess would generally have an opinion on such matters," he said, deflecting her queries.

A frown creased her brow. "Do English noblewomen not consider such matters as their husbands' safety?" she asked, with a slight edge to her voice. "Or do English women in general not have opinions?"

"I must confess my experience of the ladies of England is limited — I've spent most of my life at sea. Scottish women, who I grew up with — they are a different matter."

"Well, let me assure you. Where my husband's safety is concerned, I pay close attention."

He was struck again by the thought that she was not just some romantic noblewoman on an adventure, but thought better of mentioning it. She was someone who would only share her secrets when she was good and ready, and he'd never been much for getting into a lady's good graces. He took what he thought was the wisest course and changed the subject. "So, where is your gaggle of officers, Countess?"

"Gaggle, Mr Baxter? I think you mean a group of the Tsar's finest officers." She sniffed haughtily. "Some are making plans to join the hunt for some cannibals who committed the sin of eating two Frenchmen recently. Others have decided to go and harass some poor old man who is the king here. Neither activity appealed to me."

Sometimes, he reflected, she was exactly how he imagined an aristocrat to be. At other times, such as this moment, she seemed far more ... human.

They were coming up on the little market she had despatched Tommy to, Vasily maintaining a respectful distance behind. The crowd was so noisy — not so much rowdy as cheerfully busy — that Baxter didn't really hear the first gunshot. The first he knew of being under fire was a sudden stinging in his arm, followed by searing pain.

He looked down, saw a red stain spreading through his jacket. Looked up at Ekaterina, her eyes wide with shock but not fear. Another round slapped past him, drove splinters from a nearby tree at about chest height.

Adrenalin came with the realisation and time seemed to speed back up. People were shouting in fear and anger, a stampede of panicking feet. Baxter didn't think, just grabbed Ekaterina and lifted her bodily, putting himself between her and the square where the shots had come from.

She was shouting something in Russian as he put a tree between them and the dense patch of undergrowth the shots had come from. She sounded angry, not scared, and had her little automatic in her hand. She couldn't fire as he had her in a bear hug even after they were safe. He heard Vasily thunder past, roaring imprecations as he crashed into the forest in pursuit of the gunman.

It was complete chaos on the street behind them. Libreville was a peaceful enough town, and shots being fired within it were unheard of. Ekaterina was busy with her pistol, working the action to chamber a round as soon as he put her down. "I do not suppose you are armed, Mr Baxter?"

"I have never been fond of firearms, Countess," he said drily. He knew his arm would start hurting properly soon, but it was oddly numb right now — although he could still make use of it. "And I suspect our attempted murderer has already fled with the crowds."

There certainly had been no further shots, and no sign of pursuit. There had been Europeans, including Russian sailors and officers, in the market and he could hear shouting in a range of languages. A moment later, Yefimov's stentorian voice roared out, demanding attendance and obedience. As much as he had come to loathe the man, Baxter relaxed slightly as the Russian officer established some semblance of order. A moment later Vasily re-emerged from the undergrowth, shaking his head at Baxter's inquisitive look.

"Well, as much as I appreciate your concern for my safety," Ekaterina said smartly, "you did prevent me from taking action to defend us. And I can assure you, I am more than capable of defending myself."

Baxter gave her a sour look. "Well, in future I shall make no effort to assist. Did you even see who was shooting at us?"

"At you, Mr Baxter, at you. And no, I did not."

"Well, there we are then."

With a churlish glare she stalked away, tucking her pistol back into a pocket in her light summer dress. He hadn't even noticed she was carrying the weapon, the dress had been cut cleverly enough. Not the sort of thing you would expect a Russian aristocrat to be wearing.

He followed her out into the light. Juneau had arrived, no doubt drawn by the sound of shooting and the sudden panic that followed, and was now holding his wife tightly. The sight sent a stab of something ... odd through Baxter. He couldn't quite put a finger on it. Envy, perhaps?

But that was foolery. She had just admonished him for protecting her, as well as jumping to the conclusion that he was the target anyway. She was also, of course, married to a man he had come to regard as a friend. No, foolishness indeed to think of her as anything other than a conundrum that he may not even want to solve.

"Oh, and I apologise for getting blood on your dress," he called after her. She stopped, turned towards him with what could almost have been a contrite expression. At that moment Tommy emerged from the crowd and Baxter felt a surge of relief when he saw the lad was safe. Obviously a bit shaken, Tommy dashed straight into Ekaterina's open arms. She looked up as she hugged the boy, her eyes meeting Baxter's.

They had that much in common, it seemed — Tommy Dunbar's continued well-being.

The crew of the *Yaroslavich* took the events in the market hard. Depending on who you asked, it was either an attempt to murder the countess or someone being stupid enough to risk her life while attempting to rid them of the troublesome British captive. The clever money was on Baxter being the target of an incompetent assassin — after all, who could wish Ekaterina Juneau harm?

Baxter's slight wound and the subsequent blood on Ekaterina's dress had been the worst of it for either of them. The bullet had scored a channel through the meat of his upper arm, barely requiring stitches from Andropov, the ship's surgeon. "The occasional scar is part and parcel of a seaman's life," the mild-mannered man had observed as he carefully and neatly stitched it up. "Far less worrying than the blow to the head you took in the North Sea."

Baxter's view, as he inspected the scene with Juneau and a representative of the French colonial police, was that the shots had not been aimed at him.

"You are quite sure?" Lieutenant Cassell asked. He was a small, middle-aged man with watery eyes behind round spectacles. Baxter was certain he would be quite wan if he did not have the misfortune (as he would no doubt see it) of being stationed somewhere sunny. They were speaking French, as the language all three had in common.

"Of course I'm not sure, Monsieur. Have you ever been shot at?"

A nervous tick next to the eye. "I have always been fortunate or clever enough to avoid such occurrences."

Well, you're probably in the wrong line of work then. "Well, if you had, you would know that recollections after the fact are always a little … hazy. However, observe." Baxter brandished his wounded arm. "The countess was stood on this side of me, and while the second round was at chest height on me, I believe the countess — while a tall woman — only comes to that height. The assassin was just a poor shot."

"But who would have cause to shoot at my wife?" Juneau said unhappily, wringing his hands. "Surely, though it pains me to say it, you were the more likely target, Mr Baxter?"

Cassell was poking carefully at the trunk of the sadly abused tree with a pair of tweezers. Tutting when he found he could not quite reach, he drew a box across and, standing on it, peered myopically into the bullet hole before delving into it.

"There are Marxists aboard the squadron, Mr Juneau," Baxter said quietly. He'd contemplated switching to Russian so as not give too much away to Cassell. However, he was keeping his own command of that language to himself on the off chance Ekaterina had not already told her husband. "Perhaps this was a politically motivated assassination attempt?"

Juneau did not look happy at that, but half nodded. "I really must persuade her to go ashore at the next safe harbour and take a ship back to Russia," he said. "Even if she was not the target, it has brought home to me that a warship is not a place for a woman. Even one as capable as my wife."

"Well, some good has come of this unfortunate incident, then," Baxter said. His tone, surlier than he'd intended, drew a quizzical gaze from Juneau.

"I am sorry that this happened, Mr Baxter. It is perhaps because of the behaviour of your government…"

Baxter forced a smile, more of a grimace. "Or the Imperial Russian Navy has just decided that I should be shot at as often as possible."

"Ah ha!" Cassell declared triumphantly. The bullet had buried itself thoroughly in the wood, but with a yank he managed to extract it. He threatened to topple off his box, and both Juneau and Baxter put hands up to catch him. The little Frenchman held the round up for them all to squint at. It was heavily deformed, but it was clear that it was a large bullet.

"Perhaps even a point four five-five, as used by your Army, sir," Cassell said, looking over the rim of his glasses at Baxter. "Certainly not smaller than a point four-four."

Baxter shrugged, pressing down on the anger that threatened to bubble over again. "I am no authority on such matters. Anything less than four inches is outside my experience."

Juneau laughed, followed by a confused-looking Cassell, more out of politeness than anything else. The police officer's half-hearted chuckle died away. "Well, I am something of a … hobbyist when it comes to bullets, so I shall give this my utmost attention."

Juneau's smile didn't falter, but there was something forced about his voice. "Well, this shall be a diverting mystery for you, but alas I imagine we will have weighed anchor by the time you deduce anything conclusive."

Cassell drew himself up to his full self-important five foot and some. "I assure you, Mr Juneau, that if I do determine anything of import I shall find a way of telegramming you. It is very likely, after all, that our culprit was a resident of Libreville and not a sailor on your fleet." He tilted his head in a semi-formal bow. "Well, I must be about my duties. Good day, gentlemen."

"We are fortunate," Juneau sighed. "We have found a police officer who is diligent and not just in a hurry to see us and our troubles gone to sea." He shook himself. "Come, we must aboard. It is almost time for the feast of coal."

Baxter scowled. "I almost wish I had achieved something a bit more than a light wounding to save me from that."

"If that had happened in this climate, my friend, you would succumb to an infection far worse than the black fever."

Baxter was certain they had crossed the Equator not long before the squadron dropped its anchors at Libreville. He knew this from his previous visit, through navigation had never been his strong suit. The Russian crews, though, marked the event in the time-honoured way the day after they had weighed and continued their slow journey south.

"It is fascinating, is it not?" he commented to Juneau as they watched the festivities unfold. 'Neptune' had come aboard not long after nine in the morning and mounted his gun carriage, his arrival saluted by the ship's band that now accompanied the slow procession towards the prow, where a giant canvas tub had been set up. The ancient sea god — in fact Vasily — was stalking the ship, preceded by capering devils and barbers with giant razors, half-dressed warriors and Russian peasants, gathering up those who had not crossed the line and herding them forward. It was, in this case, most of the crew. Much hilarity ensued as the neophytes were hunted down.

"What is, Mr Baxter?"

"Having had the opportunity to observe naval and other customs from many different nations, I have noted many differences. Some minor, merely in how a rank or title is styled. For instance, in the Royal Navy you would be a lieutenant-commander not a captain of the second rank. Others are significant. And yet, across all seafaring nations, this pageant is observed with a religious fervour. It may differ in its details, but the intent and the spirit are the same."

"One might even say pagan fervour," Juneau mused. "If the ship's chaplain may not be in earshot."

"I believe he is hiding from a considerably older deity."

"Sensible man."

Baxter turned to face the Russian officer, a slow smile spreading. "You have not seen this done before, have you?" he said, keeping his voice as mild as he could manage.

Juneau shook his head. "Indeed. I have never been so far from home."

"And I understand that officers are not considered exempt from marking this important occasion," Baxter went on. Looking down, he caught the eyes of a hunting party of devils, whose job it was to bring sacrificial victims before the ancient god of the sea. The procession was passing just below them at that moment. He tilted his head very slightly at the first officer, and one of them nodded his understanding.

"I understand that even the flagship's captain has not avoided it. I cannot imagine our own noble captain would subject himself to such an indignity." Juneau turned, a suddenly alarmed expression on his face. "You would not, Mr Baxter!"

"I, of course, most certainly would not. However…" Baxter nodded to the hands who were making a ham-fisted attempt to creep up a companionway and surprise the first officer.

Juneau threw his hands up in mock indignation. "Very well, I must submit myself, it seems!" he declared as he allowed himself to be led away. Baxter noted, as he went, that the normally elegant officer was wearing an older and slightly threadbare uniform.

Two of Neptune's followers grinned at him, a mixture of fear and slyness on their faces. He was the biggest man on the ship, with the exception of Vasily, and no one really knew yet what his status was. Prisoner? Guest? To be included in the ship's customs or not?

Baxter smiled, held his hands out to his sides. "The line, I have crossed many times," he said in deliberately broken Russian. They smiled, ducking their heads before heading off in search of other prey. One of them at least looked more than relieved. "Though Tomas'ka?" he called after them in English. He shook his head when one of them looked back. "He has not."

From somewhere further back there came a muffled cry of trust betrayed and the sound of bare feet slapping on the deck. He heard Ekaterina laughing and tilted himself over the rail to see her leaning back to laugh as the lad made a beeline for cover. She glanced across at him, and her smile didn't go, but changed somewhat. He looked away quickly, confused and unsure of what to make of … any of it, really.

CHAPTER 9

"How goes the day, Master Dunbar?" Baxter asked.

They were far south, now, not far from the Cape, and the temperature at least had dropped off somewhat. The preceding days had dragged past as they crawled further south. Africa, vast beyond comprehension, appeared only as a drab, dun mass forever to port. The baking heat had made everyone lethargic and the tedium had made them tetchy. Only the soporific heat kept tempers from flaring to violence, though Vice-Admiral Rozhestvensky had also let it be known that any ill-discipline would be met with abandonment in an open boat. This had quelled an incipient mutiny by civilian stokers who had been brought on to the biggest ships and ensured that any further trouble was kept well out of sight.

Tommy had become more subdued the further from home they got. His ritual ducking and shaving — and a fine down had started to appear on his chin — had been a high point for him, as in a way it had made him more a part of the shipboard community than Baxter was.

Ekaterina had done what she could to keep the lad's spirits up, though she had passed the word that perhaps Mr Baxter would speak to the boy. After the attempted assassination at Libreville, most of her interactions with Baxter had been at that distance. She communicated with him through intermediaries and passing pleasantries at the dinner table, though he sometimes fancied he caught her watching him. Her gaze was usually assessing and calculating, but he occasionally caught himself hoping there might be something more to it.

"It was all right. I was showed some knot tying."

Baxter noted the boy's glum tone. "And how are you holding up?" he asked quietly. They were in the stern of the ship and there were others nearby, though most gave the prisoners a modicum of space.

Tommy looked up at him, eyes brimming, and Baxter knew exactly what was going through the boy's mind. "It's all right to be scared, Tommy," he said. "You're a long way from home and getting further every day."

A look of indignation replaced the tears that had threatened to fall. "I ain't scared, Mr Baxter! I'm just worried about my ma. She'll be sick with worry about me."

Baxter didn't say that Mrs Dunbar would almost certainly be grieving for her dead son. He cursed himself for getting the boy involved in this. For not standing his ground, for being too hungover to insist that Tommy went home. For being so desperate that he'd taken the job in the first place.

"Do you know where we are, lad?" he said at last, rather than expressing any of that.

"Coast of Africa?" Tommy said sullenly. "Where we've been for months."

That, of course, was a slight exaggeration. "Not far above the Cape," Baxter said. "Which, for centuries, has been a special place for sailors like you and me, Tommy. It's where we'll start heading more east than south. Just imagine that, Tommy — the fabulous Orient!"

That didn't cheer the boy greatly — if anything, mentioning going even further from home made him look more glum. Baxter leant in close, craning his neck and putting a slightly awkward hand on the boy's shoulder. He'd never been any good with children. "And it's a British colony," he said as quietly as he could. He squeezed the shoulder, perhaps a little harder than he should, to warn Tommy not to make a fuss of that.

For once, Tommy seemed to get the hint. "Why're we going this way, anyway? Thought the whole point of the Suez Canal was to cut the journey short?"

Baxter looked down, surprised despite himself, and blew out a breath. "Well, that's a good question and one for the admiral. Some say it's because he's worried the Canal would be too shallow for his big ships, but that's tosh. If I had to guess, I'd say he's scared the Japanese will attack him in the Canal. Which is also rubbish, just as it's nonsense they tried to attack him in the North Sea. But he's an odd fish, Rozhestvensky, and has some strange ideas."

He realised he was perhaps being indiscreet, and when he looked round he realised Ekaterina was on the superstructure overlooking the stern. Watching him with those cool, assessing eyes.

He turned his face back to the sea. The *Yaroslavich* was stationed towards the forward edge of the 2nd Pacific Squadron's rough formation, giving him a magnificent view of the other warships. Even with a clutch of the big old battleships and the destroyers, not to mention the support ships, dispatched through the Canal, it was a magnificent assembly — in terms of numbers, anyway, though he had to admit the Russians had some fine vessels. The setting sun gilded the ships under their canopy of smoke, doing much to disguise the coal dust and the many flaws his experienced eye had picked out.

Looking out to the south and east, the gathering darkness was already deeper than it should have been, presaging a dirty night. It wouldn't be the first time their progress had been hindered by foul weather. Coaling at the German colony of

Angra Pequena, a bit further to the north, had been a miserable business, the worst yet, due to the powerful gale that had come up, at one point driving one of the colliers onto the *Suvorov*'s main guns. They'd resorted to coaling using the ships' own boats until the wind had died down.

Baxter had been half considering an escape attempt there, to the small British colonies on the islands just outside the bay. The weather had put a crimp on that plan, and intelligence brought by the German governor — know universally as 'the Major' — had further hampered him.

He shook his head now, remembering his frustration. "Torpedo schooners," he muttered derisively.

"Wha's that, Mr B?" Tommy asked.

"That idiot German put the idea in Rozhestvensky's head that we're converting sailing schooners into torpedo boats for the Japanese, at Durban on the other side of the Cape of Good Hope. The most preposterous thing I've heard on this ridiculous voyage, as it'd never work." Baxter didn't add that the unsubstantiated rumours had put the Russians on edge, making it harder for him to attempt an escape.

As they drew closer to the southern tip of Africa and the eventual turn north, past Durban, that agitated state only became more acute. If the weather didn't put pay to the plan he'd hinted to Tommy, to make a break for Cape Town or at least somewhere on dry British land, the paranoia settling over the fleet would.

Luckily, for him at least, the British Empire was one on which the sun never set.

Ekaterina glided up next to him, glanced down at the boy. "Tomas'ka," she said with a fond smile. "Run along so Pavel can dress you for dinner."

Tommy bobbed his head. "Yes, miss," he said, and darted off, weaving between the sailors. With a start Baxter realised the exchange had been in Russian, on both sides.

"I think we're in for some foul weather, Countess," Baxter said awkwardly. "I wouldn't necessarily bank on a formal dinner this evening."

"You British, letting your standards slip so easily."

He bristled slightly. "At sea, the weather dictates the standards," he said, voice abrupt to the point of rudeness.

She laughed off his ill temper. "I apologise, Mr Baxter, I have been perhaps … churlish?" Her command of English was perfect, and only the occasional pause like that and the slightest accent gave away that it was not her native language. "Tell me, have you thought further on our unfortunate encounter in Libreville?"

He had. It had gnawed at him during the long, dark hot nights as he lay awake in his cabin or, more frequently, slung a hammock somewhere on deck. He could not shake the feeling that the attempt somehow connected with Arbuthnott and whatever he was scheming. But how had the man got someone there so fast, or even known that Rozhestvensky would be insane enough to go all the way round Africa?

No, far more likely that it was a disaffected sailor or jealous officer. That *had* to be it.

"I have given it some thought, Countess, though with so little information it is hard to see what further we can deduce."

"Well, hopefully that charming French policeman will have some luck with the bullet and fulfils his promise to telegram the squadron."

That was interesting — it seemed Juneau shared everything with his wife rather than seeking to shield her from some things. "And what of you, if I may ask? Perhaps, when we have reached a more developed port, you could await further word while the fleet sails onwards."

Fire flashed in her eyes. "Where my husband goes, Mr Baxter, I go. And how would I catch up with the ship if word did reach me?"

He acknowledged the point, and the implicit rebuke, with a slight nod. She changed course again, throwing his footing off.

"And what do you make of the reports of what awaits us at Durban?" It was asked innocently enough, but there was just that slight edge of cunning in her gaze. She'd obviously overheard some of what he'd been saying to Tommy, so she already knew what he thought. Which meant she was trying to trip him up, trap him somehow. "Does Durban have the facilities to carry out this work?"

Very clever. She was after some information, even the smallest titbit, from his RN days. Any sort of way in, he realised, and wondered again who she *really* was.

"Well, ma'am, it's been a long time since I was in Durban," he said carefully. "So I couldn't say one way or the other." He bowed slightly. "I should go and dress for dinner as well. Good day to you, Countess."

"I shall see you at dinner, Mr Baxter."

Baxter very much doubted that anyone would be dining formally by the time the gale broke. He dined alone in his cabin, a thick sandwich of cold beef and coal dust, perfectly comfortable as the cruiser rose up the side of a wave, lurched over the crest and then almost fell into the following trough; the waves following in an endless progression before eventually destroying themselves on the cape. He could feel the engines thumping as they pushed the ship away from that ironbound shore. Even here he could hear the wind and rain howling about the upper decks — being on the open bridge or anywhere else on deck right now would be beyond miserable, particularly for those new to the sea.

Gorchakov, if he was any kind of seaman, would be on that exposed bridge, overseeing the safety of his ship; but Baxter guessed that duty had fallen to Juneau. He'd already heard people running past his cabin on the way to the heads — most of the junior officers would not be used to weather this dirty.

He was just starting to doze off on his cot when someone started hammering madly on the door. "All right, all right," he grumbled as he pulled himself up and yanked it open. Pavel, Juneau's servant, stood trembling and wild eyed before him. If anything, the man looked even pastier than usual and most certainly should not have been on any errands. He had to grasp the door frame as the cruiser lurched and rolled.

"What is it, man?" Baxter demanded after a long moment, remembering to switch into French, the language he had in common with Pavel. The one he would admit to having in common.

"It is Master Tomas. This great storm has deeply upset him and he has fled into the rest of the ship. Countess Ekaterina, she has gone after him but I am worried — so deeply worried — as it has been so long and all the officers are either on the bridge or prostrated by this gale that will be the end of us all…"

"Calm yourself, Pavel," Baxter growled, then clapped him reassuringly on the shoulder. "This is little more than a hard blow. They're neither of them fool enough to go on deck, so they'll be somewhere below." He could see this did not satisfy Pavel. He pulled on his jacket. "Go back to your quarters and do not stir yourself again until this has blown over — I'll look for Tommy and the countess, make sure they're safe."

Moving through the ship under these conditions was more of a controlled reel than a walk. Even with his knees bent and feet spread it wasn't easy getting about. Baxter enjoyed a good blow as much as any experienced sailor, though. "Just glad I don't have to be on deck," he muttered. Within the armoured shell of the high-sided cruiser the fury of the storm was muted. Those high sides, though, meant she rolled dreadfully. "Now, where would I go if I was a frightened bairn?"

The answer, of course, was into the lower decks. Either amongst the crew, or right into the lower compartments where the motion of the ship and the sound of the gale would both be muted.

Below decks, the old cruiser was cramped and dingy, and right now smelt of fear and vomit. Baxter moved quietly amongst the miserable crew, mostly going un-noticed and unremarked. He guessed Tommy wouldn't go to the lowermost mid-ships decks, towards the great steam boilers and engines that were the beating heart of the ship. The magazines and other compartments devoted to the *Yaroslavich*'s warlike purpose would be off limits. Instead he dived down in the honeycomb of storerooms that filled any space that was not otherwise occupied. Everywhere he turned, there were the cursed sacks of coal, even alongside what fresh food was left and wedged in amongst the hated casks of salt beef and sacks of biscuit; fare that would not have been completely alien to Nelson's sailors.

Light glimmered through the open hatch of one such compartment. He was about to blunder through, calling out cheerfully for Tommy, but the low Russian voices he could hear gave him pause. He was too far away to make out much, but something in the tone and the occasional word he picked up, plus the oddity of sailors being down here at this time, stopped him.

The compartment, he saw as he sidled up to the hatch coaming, was one of the larger food stores, lined with shelves and stacks of barrels. Three or four figures were crouched at the far end, around a lit storm lantern. He slipped through the hatch, keeping low. He knew a sensible man would walk away. There were things that went on amongst the lower decks that the wardroom — to which he tentatively belonged — didn't need to know about as long as they were not prejudicial to discipline or the ship's safety. There was something about this gathering, though, that struck him as conspiratorial.

As he drew closer, he started to make out what they were talking about. Class, wealth, privilege. Capital — a notion of which he only had the vaguest notion. Could this be the revolutionary cell that had been dispensing pamphlets? And, if so, could this be turned to his advantage? He inched closer, crouching down and moving silently behind a bulwark of coal sacks, trying to make out who the conspirators were. The uncertain, flickering light of the storm lantern cast their faces into alternating stark relief and deep shadow. He wasn't sure he'd recognise any of them, even if he did by chance know them.

"So we are agreed," one of them, a younger man, was saying in a hoarse whisper when Baxter got close enough to hear. Dark hair, intense eyes that glinted out of the shadowed sockets. "Now is the time to strike, to create the necessary conditions for our comrades at home to rise up."

A rat-faced sailor nodded earnestly, speaking rapidly in a dialect Baxter was less familiar with and couldn't make out. Rat-face seemed to be the actual leader of the cell, from the way he was clearly giving out orders. Baxter crouched lower as those watery eyes swept the shadows, but no alarm was raised.

He hunkered down as far as he could — no mean feat for a man of his size. The meeting seemed to be concluding, and he remained motionless as they left the compartment. He was plunged into darkness as the youngest man was last out with the lantern, and cursed under his breath — he didn't relish the thought of fumbling his way out of here in the pitch darkness, not with the deck still rolling under him.

He started to move, having given the conspirators about enough time to move on. Someone else in the storeroom obviously had the same notion, muttering and giving him just enough warning to duck and close his eyes as light flared. It wasn't the warm glow of a match, but a harsh electric glare.

He was astonished to see, when he opened his eyes a moment later, Ekaterina crouched on the far side of the compartment, holding a large box that appeared to have an electric lightbulb mounted in the front that cast a pool of light wherever she pointed it. Baxter was so startled to see her, he let out a grunt of surprise. She whirled and he caught a flash of steel that told him she was carrying her automatic. She tucked it away quickly when she saw it was him and moved quickly to switch on the light to provide better illumination.

"Ah ... Mr Baxter." She sounded surprised to see him — which was perhaps natural — but also confused, and that rang oddly with him.

"Countess." He'd never worked out the proper honorific, and didn't much care for such fripperies anyway. Mrs Juneau would just have sounded odd, though. He shifted his feet awkwardly. This was well outside his experience of normal society. "Ahhh ... Pavel was concerned for you and young Tommy and asked me to have a look round for you."

Her expression of confusion deepened but only briefly before her brow cleared. "Ah yes, Tomas'ka. I have yet to find him, though I imagine I will return to my cabin to discover he has returned quite safely and is being fussed over by poor Pavel."

There was something odd going on here, of that Baxter was sure. For one, why was she carrying a pistol while searching the ship? Under normal circumstances, she was in no danger from the crew, of that he had no doubt. She was very much the ship's darling, in fact, and more to the point if any harm befell her Juneau would tear the vessel apart to find and punish the culprit. The fact she had come armed suggested she knew there would be some chance of danger.

"I was just searching in here when those ... individuals came in. Sensing they were up to no good, I hid from them for my own safety."

"Umm ... yes. I had much the same experience, having been drawn in here by the light." Baxter knew he wasn't much for eloquence, but his capacity to string words together in a sentence seemed on the verge of deserting him.

She looked doubtfully at him — while she was tall for a woman, she still had to crane her neck to look up at him when she stepped closer. Her implication was clear. "And what did you make of their conversation?" she asked quietly, her voice in deadly earnest.

He opened his mouth, but closed it again when her warning look told him that she would not brook any claim of ignorance — she wasn't buying his lie that he didn't speak Russian. "It seems to me that mutiny is fomenting aboard," he said. "We had best warn your husband."

"It would seem that way, yes. I must ask you not to speak of this further, though, for your own safety. And that of Tommy. I shall speak to Juneau."

"May I escort you back to your cabin?" he asked, forcing a note of gallantry into his voice.

"You may not," she said sharply, then softened it with a smile that made his knees go slightly weak. She laid a hand on his upper arm, only briefly, and he fought down an urge to take her hand in his. "We would not want people to talk if we were seen leaving a storeroom together."

He was about to ask what they could possibly be talking about when the ship gave a great lurch. They were deep enough in the ship that the roll imparted by the storm, though stomach-turning on the higher decks, had been almost normal until that moment. Ekaterina lost her footing and he reached out to steady her. She caught a shelf upright and braced her legs apart, giving him a cool look as the lurch became more of a roll that seemed to go on forever as the cruiser slid down the reverse of an enormous raise.

Baxter realised he was holding his breath, waiting for the roll to continue all the way into a breech, the ship turning over — which would be fatal for everyone aboard in these conditions, but especially for those as deep below decks as they were. Ekaterina's cool dismissiveness had turned to alarm, the first time he'd seen her in any way discomfited. Then he blew out the breath convulsively as the cruiser righted herself and began a slightly less extreme climb up the next wave.

Before he knew what was happening, she was against him. He could feel her deep, shuddering breaths, the length of her against him as she threw her arms around his neck. For a panicked moment he thought she was just seeking comfort after they'd come so close to danger, then she was pulling his head down to kiss him with a fiery hunger.

He almost froze, then. It had been a long time since he'd kissed a woman, and never one quite like this. Then he found himself responding unconsciously, arms going around her waist to pull her even closer, lift her against him, and they lost themselves in that moment.

She broke away eventually and he found himself almost gasping for breath. She rested her cheek against his chest, hands flat against his shoulders, and he knew it had passed; whatever it was. She wasn't pushing him away, as such, but there was a distance opening between them. He relaxed his grip.

She turned to look up at him, something … unreadable in her expression. She brushed her lips against his, one last time. "It cannot be," she whispered. "I love my husband."

He nodded, jerkily, despite himself. The mention of Juneau, who he had come to think of as a friend — perhaps his only friend in the world, let alone aboard this ship — cooled his ardour. A sudden sense of shame filled him. "Of course."

She laid a warm hand against his cheek, her expression still opaque to him as her eyes met his. She turned without another word and left the storeroom without looking back.

Baxter turned over the night of the storm often in his mind in the following days. The blow had been a bad one, but not the worst he'd ever experienced, and the Russian ships seemed to have weathered it without too much trouble. The longer they spent at sea, of course, the better both officers and crew handled their ships — even when all they mostly did was plod along with the coast of Africa off their port beam. They still didn't perform well in the occasional exercise that

Rozhestvensky ordered.

Baxter found himself, though, increasingly distracted by what else had happened on the night of the storm. He couldn't shake the memory of Ekaterina, her body in his arms, her lips against his. With it came a rush of unaccustomed feelings. Shame was amongst them, but not the chief one. Desire, yes. He could not help a feeling of envy for Juneau, that such a remarkable woman should be his; that even if she wasn't, that an accident of birth should have entitled the Russian to so much when Baxter's own parentage and class meant he could never aspire to anything of that life.

Not unless things changed, and changed radically.

He forced his mind away from those dark thoughts, focusing instead on things that made sense to him — the sea, and the ships that sailed upon it. He couldn't help but smile as he watched Enkvist's lean cruisers charge around further out to sea. From somewhere up ahead, out of his sight as he was taking his ease on the quarter gallery, he could hear the occasional peremptory signal gun from the flagship. The sharp reports were getting more and more frequent as the evolutions broke down into chaos. They were obviously attempting a torpedo drill, and he wished he had a set of glasses to observe the operation more closely.

Juneau, coming off watch, emerged on the little balcony next to him, causing Baxter to start guiltily. The Russian officer didn't seem to notice anything amiss. He looked tired and drawn, cradling an uncharacteristically early glass of brandy. But then, running an old ship on a very long journey under an absolute tartar of a captain would make anyone look tired.

"Torpedoes," Juneau sniffed. "An ungentlemanly weapon, even if they are the only true ship killers. I cannot see them ever replacing the big guns. It would be a sad day if they did."

Baxter had often wondered if a lot of officers in Britain's Navy were, perhaps, overly concerned with gentlemanly conduct and not with winning; it seemed this was not unique to the RN. "I understand the Japanese have already made good use of them," he said carefully.

"And thus we train both to use them and to defend against the enemy torpedo boats. Our new searchlights will sweep the waters constantly once we are closer to Japan."

"Some say that lighting your ships up like Christmas trees will just make you easier targets for night-time torpedo runs." Baxter marvelled at his own restraint in not pointing out the debacle in the North Sea again.

Juneau seemed to acknowledge that with a vague smile. "I gather your new First Naval Lord is a proponent."

Baxter smiled. Being overly concerned with gentlemanly conduct instead of crushing your enemy was a charge that could not be laid at JackyFisher's door. "He is, and more generally in favour of reform." He tried to keep bitterness from his voice, not at the man himself but at the service in general. Fisher had been a breath of fresh air through the Navy's training practises and attitudes, but too late to benefit Baxter. "I served with him, briefly. Met him once."

"Fisher?"

No, the bloody Tsar. Baxter bit back the sour retort, realising it was just to do with his mood and not his friend. "Yes, when he had the North America station, one of my first postings after I was commissioned." Perhaps, though, it was as much to do with Juneau as it was his own mood. Or rather, the woman to whom the Russian Count was married. It was an uncomfortable sensation for him.

"And may I ask — do you feel his reputation is deserved?"

"Depends to what reputation you refer," Baxter said mildly. That had been a happier time in his life. "Brash, aggressive, quite a showman. Utterly ruthless if you cross him or even if you're just in his way. But a hard worker, brilliant, open to new ideas no matter who is bringing them forward. All this and more."

"I met him also, taking the water in Marienbad along with certain of my family. I just wish he was more of a friend to Russia."

The mention of Marienbad, where the great and the … good of Europe went to take the restorative waters, threatened a divide between the two men. It was not somewhere the likes of Baxter would ever find himself.

"Well, if all men on Earth were more of a friend to each other we would all be out of a job," Baxter said with a grin, bludgeoning his threatening foul mood.

"Perhaps that would not be a bad thing."

Yefimov emerged onto the after gallery, a smug smile on his face and a particularly venomous look in his eyes when he looked at Baxter. He bore a folded piece of paper that he held out to Juneau without really looking at him.

A delighted smile spread over Juneau's face. "It seems our friend in Gabon came through after all!" he declared.

"How the devil did he get a message out?" Baxter asked sourly.

"Details are limited, but I believe he took ship to the nearest colony that has a telegram station, sent a message to St Petersburg, who then sent it to us. Is the modern age not magnificent?"

"And what does our French chum have to say?" Baxter wasn't sure why his mood had turned so dark suddenly —

perhaps because of Yefimov's expression, or merely his presence.

Juneau's face fell. "It is the lieutenant's considered opinion that the bullet that almost struck you was of point-four-five-five-inch calibre. Most likely fired from a Webley or similar British revolver, as yours are the only people who use that particular cartridge."

"Well, that puts an interesting face on things," Baxter said, fighting to sound casual and only partially succeeding. "Though I don't imagine it's impossible that Africa might be awash with them. More than a few must have fallen into Boer hands, during the recent unpleasantness, for one thing."

Juneau squinted at him, his expression bemused. "Indeed. It does seem … coincidental, though, does it not?"

Baxter shrugged, discomfited. "Perhaps, but I have seen stranger coincidences at sea."

CHAPTER 10

Passandava Bay, Madagascar, January 1905

"At least we have one friend in the world," Juneau commented, mopping his brow with an already-soiled kerchief.

The *Yaroslavich* barely rocked at her moorings in the beautiful bay, the gentle swell hardly noticeable.

"Do not confuse this for friendship," Baxter said, his dark tone surprising even himself, and for a moment he wondered if he was talking about the nations or their own relationship. "France may seem to view your expedition with some favour. I suspect this is more to do with putting mud in the eye of my own government than any real friendship with you."

"Ah yes. That ancient blood rivalry. This I understand — to a Russian, the holding of grudges is a way of life." Juneau sighed. "I fear we all have a new, common enemy."

Baxter nodded. The French Republic seemed to revel in its status as Britain's arch-enemy, but many — Admiral Fisher included — looked with more concerns at the rise of the young, vigorous German Empire's Navy.

He looked out across the now-oily water. The bay, until recently, had been more or less pristine, but the local authorities had outdone themselves to prepare it as a berth for the 2nd Pacific Squadron, even if they could not provide the docks and shore facilities the squadron desperately needed. The village of Nosy Be was growing into a full-blown town, springing up along the white sands of the beach and into the cleared jungle beyond, and a slight pall of smog lay over everything as the Russian ships kept their boilers at harbour pressure. Where once there would only have been the cry of exotic animals, now there was the sound of industry as the battered Russian ships were prepared for what would be the longest and most difficult stage of the journey — across the Pacific.

The squadron had separated into detachments not long after rounding the Cape and the gale that had hit them, the *Yaroslavich* remaining attached to the battleships as she could not keep up with the faster, more modern cruisers.

There, of course, had been no sign of 'torpedo schooners' as the slow squadron rumbled through the established fishing grounds off Durban. Opinions were divided as to why this was the case, with most of the Russian officers ascribing it to Rozhestvensky's well publicised threat to destroy any vessel that came within torpedo range of his battleships. Wise heads — Juneau amongst them — suspected that the suicide boats never existed.

The authorities in Madagascar were well prepared, forewarned by the arrival of the older ships, despite this being the largest assembly of ships they would ever have seen. After some days off Ile Sainte Marie, the main force had been piloted into Passandava Bay on the north-west coast of the island, to be greeted with some degree of relief and joy by the elements that had come through the Suez Canal. That had been a week and two days ago, and the reunited squadron had settled into harbour life with remarkable speed.

"The Second Pacific Squadron is together again," Juneau commented with some satisfaction. Sweat dripped from his brow as the two men gazed out at the pleasantly calm bay and the green-cloaked mountains that rose beyond the sheltered water. "And reinforcements are on their way. We will need all our strength in the coming months, I fear."

Baxter cocked an eyebrow at the lower inflection of that last statement. Catching the expression, Juneau shrugged. "Word is spreading round the fleet," he said quietly. "The major at Angra Pequena had news for Rozhestvensky, and of course nothing stays secret for long on a warship."

Baxter was astonished that Juneau was telling him all of this, but kept his peace and let the man speak.

"The Japanese Army has taken a key hill overlooking Port Arthur, bringing the remnants of the First Pacific Squadron, not to mention the heart of our fortifications, into range of their heavy guns." Baxter didn't want to imagine what that must have been like — even if no army dragged guns as big as those on battleships to war, the remaining Russian ships would have been fish in the barrel for the Japanese artillery and would have perished swiftly if they had not escaped. And escape would have been a desperate charge into the waiting ships of Togo's fleet. A sigh heaved from deep within the Russian officer. "I fear, increasingly, that we are on a fool's errand."

"I imagine you will go on, though?"

"Oh, I am sure Rozhestvensky has every intention of continuing. He will not understand the import of this news, as it does not pertain to the Navy, and he has his orders."

"He must know our chances of survival, of victory, are minimal."

Baxter paused, realising he had just referred to 'our victory'. Juneau did him the courtesy of not pointing that out beyond a slight tweak of an eyebrow. "Oh, I suspect he has always known this," Juneau went on resignedly. "But he also understands orders, and that His Imperial Majesty is set upon this course. He would not let another man go in his place, nor does he think anyone else would be up to the task."

Baxter nodded. He was getting used to Juneau's odd insights into the Russian court's inner working. "Plus, we've come this far," he said, rather than commenting on that, straightening and stretching his back until something popped. "I had been pretty keen to return to the sea, but months aboard..."

"While the admiral has indicated that we will be moving on swiftly, it would not surprise me if our stay here will be ... protracted. As much as there is a need to hurry, our vessels are all in a sorry state — the bottoms must be cleaned, the boilers maintained, and only our most obtuse officers argue we are ready for combat," Juneau went on. "Rozhestvensky has ordered a curfew and forbidden the officers and men from staying ashore. The order does not, of course, apply to my wife. She has taken lodgings in the, well, town. As the prohibition does not apply to you either, you would be welcome to stay with her. And Tomas'ka, of course."

Baxter opened his mouth to refuse, and realised how churlish that would seem. "Are you not worried that I will attempt escape?"

"My dear Baxter, where would you go? No, it is settled. I will have Vasily bring your things ashore."

They settled into something approaching domestic bliss on the island, in a pleasant and obviously very new bungalow in the colonial style, higher up on the hillside where they could get more of a breeze. Juneau may only have been the first officer of a clapped-out old cruiser not far from the scrapyard, but he also wasn't adverse to using his court influence when it came to it. While the house may have been sparse in its construction and smelled of freshly hewn wood and sap, it was in a fine location. Ekaterina had already settled in with Tommy Dunbar when Baxter arrived, Vasily in tow with his meagre belongings.

It was late afternoon, and Baxter was sweltering despite the light suit he wore. Heat had never bothered him much, but it was humid to the point where the air almost felt like a wet rag in the face. At least up on the hillside it was cooler, and Pavel greeted him with a cold gin and tonic.

"Good lord, I didn't realise how much I'd missed this until this moment," Baxter declared after taking a long pull from the frosted glass, the ice clinking against the side.

"And the tonic will keep away the various miasmas of this place," Ekaterina said from the door onto the veranda, before sweeping in to greet him. Tommy was in tow, but seemed almost shy of him.

"That's why we drink it, ma'am, though I was afflicted with enough tropical diseases as a young'un that my system seems to fight them off." Baxter smiled down at Tommy. "Master Dunbar, good to see you."

Tommy bobbed his head but didn't meet Baxter's gaze. It was indeed good to see the lad, who'd been keeping his distance of late. He realised for the first time that he'd never actually heard where the lad had got to on the night of the storm — what had passed between himself and Ekaterina had driven such thoughts from his mind.

He looked back at Ekaterina sharply, an ungallant thought in his mind, but as always he found himself completely disarmed. She smiled slightly. "Come, let me show you the rest of our humble house."

To many, it would indeed have been humble. To Baxter, after months at sea and before that the cheapest lodgings he could find, it was almost luxurious, and certainly clean. As befitting a man of his rank, Juneau's staff did not stop at Pavel. It turned out that he'd also brought the chef who had served the officers on the *Yaroslavich* — "I engaged him personally,"

Ekaterina told him as they breezed past the kitchen, "And of course the captain has little interest in epicurean delights" — and engaged some local people to keep the house. Baxter's room faced onto the bay, comparatively cool and airy and (he admitted to himself privately) mercifully as far from the master bedroom as it could be.

"Well, I will let you settle in before dinner." She gave him an arch look over her shoulder as she left. "We dress for dinner here, Mr Baxter." There was no sting to her words, and he couldn't help but grin as he flipped open his case.

"Have I done something to offend you, young Tommy?" he said quietly, without turning round. There was a disgusted noise from behind the mosquito netting around the window and the boy emerged into view.

"Miss Ekaterina made me promise…" Tommy said, voice miserable.

"To keep away from me?" Baxter asked, nonplussed.

"Naw, not to tell ye…" Tommy's Edinburgh accent was coming through, sure sign that he was upset.

"Hang this up for me, would you?" Baxter said, keeping his voice level. He handed the lad his other, more formal suit and nodded to the wardrobe in the corner of the room. To think that a few weeks ago this area had been untamed jungle. "And tell me what it is you're not supposed to tell me."

Tommy seemed relieved to have this demand made of him. Baxter would never understand the mindset of children — though Tommy was near enough a young man, almost the age he'd been when he'd joined the Royal Navy.

"She told me to hide, during the storm. From everyone. Hid me away in a cupboard, she did!"

132

"We call them lockers aboard, lad," Baxter said, absently. Breaking the flow of words coming out of the youth to give himself time to think. "But go on."

"She didna say why, just hid me away. Didn't even tell Pavel. Let me out when she got back — she seemed awf'ly upset about something."

Baxter finished unpacking his handful of shirts, neatly laying them side by side on the low net bed. "I see." He absently wandered across to Tommy, ruffled his hair — earning himself a disgusted look. "But if you make a promise to anyone — especially a woman — you should keep it. A man is only as good as his word, lad."

Tommy looked like he couldn't decide to be angry or upset and had settled on somewhere between the two. "So I shouldn't have told ye, aye?"

"No, but I'm glad you did." Baxter closed the case and put it into a corner before he went on. "I thought we were in dangerous waters before, Master Dunbar," he said quietly. "But there is far more going on here than I'd imagined. You must not tell anyone I know what happened, especially the countess."

The thought of lying to her, even by proxy, left a sour taste in Baxter's mouth. But it was becoming increasingly clear that she was up to something, more than just being an adventurous young noblewoman. That something was in danger of drawing both him and Tommy into it.

"And I should keep this promise?" Tommy asked.

Baxter stared out of the window. The squadron spread across the bay, a truly breath-taking assembly of warships. "Yes, yes you should," he said quietly.

"Is this domestic bliss, I wonder?" Ekaterina asked as they made their way through one of the markets that had sprung up in Nosy Be. It was busy with locals and sailors, haggling and bartering for trinkets, fresh fruit and exotic pets. A party of swaggering bluejackets Baxter recognised from the *Yaroslavich* were attempting to haggle over the price of bread with a sharp-looking Arab who obviously had their number.

They weren't so far from areas where other, more basic human interactions were going on — Baxter could hear obviously bawdy singing from an establishment that catered to the enlisted men. Something about Courlander women — he couldn't quite make the lyrics out, but while the details were different the theme would be the same as that of many of the songs he'd heard in the Royal Navy. The rowdiness was why, ostensibly, Vasily Ivanovitch followed in their wake — the big Russian sailor had become a *de facto* part of the odd little household over the last few weeks, despite Juneau's protestations that he didn't think Baxter would attempt an escape.

Baxter caught an arch look from Ekaterina. "Hmm? Oh, I wouldn't know about that, ma'am. I've been at sea most of my life, and before then my mother raised me more or less herself while my father was at sea." He realised how self-pitying that might sound to someone who didn't know him, and sought to shift attention. Esme, one of the local woman engaged by the household, followed on behind with the shopping basket, Vasily hovering protectively beside her. Neither would be any use. "What say you, Master Dunbar?"

Baxter glanced across at the lad, who was ambling along with a grin on his face and his hands — protruding from too-short sleeves — were shoved in his pockets. His arms and legs were tanned, and only a sennit hat saved his face from being as tanned as any sailor. His grin spread further. "Just like the market by the Custom House. Bit warmer though."

"Well, there you have it."

Ekaterina laughed, low and full-throated, and linked her arm through Baxter's, causing the hair on the back of his neck to stand up. He could feel her flank against his arm, the warmth of her, and he wanted nothing more than to scoop her up and...

Well, best not to think about such things.

They had settled into a kind of odd almost-friendship since the night of the storm and what had passed — both what they had seen and what had happened between them. Neither of them spoken of it and — he felt, at least — that they had become increasingly comfortable in each other's company over the past weeks trapped in this tropical bay. Rozhestvensky's plan to plough ahead had come to nothing, just as Juneau had predicted, stymied by interference from St Petersburg.

"You must stop calling me 'ma'am'," she said suddenly, with an almost-convincing impression of both his baritone voice and manner. She looked sideways at him. "My friends call me Ekaterina. Or just Katya."

"As you wish," he said. He caught her enquiring look, shrugged slightly uncomfortably. "Baxter. My friends, such as they are, just call me Baxter."

"Well, Baxter, I have to say that does not surprise me," she said, taking any possible sting out of her words with a smile.

They walked on in companionable silence, aside from stopping and haggling with a storekeeper over the price of mangoes — everything was going up in price as the storekeepers realised how much they could make from the Russian sailors. Ekaterina ruthlessly drove the man down from exorbitantly expensive to merely very expensive, and walked on with a nod to Esme — *pay the man*, the expressive gesture said — and a contented smile. Baxter knew full well that as soon as they were out of earshot, the maid would finalise the transaction and extract a much fairer price from the storekeeper, knowing as she did the true value of the fruit.

There was no need to explain this to Ekaterina, though. She was happy believing the price had been right.

In truth there was no need for them to do this at all. Most of the fleet's aristocracy engaged in far more diverting pursuits such as gambling and hunting. He suspected, though, that Ekaterina actively enjoyed these simple, household pursuits — probably as close as she had ever come to chores.

"After Gabon, I'm surprised you want to be out and about like this," Baxter said after a while, remembering the last time he had escorted her around a market.

She glanced sharply at him, then smiled. "While you are a magnet for trouble, Baxter, I think we are probably quite safe here. The French are our allies, and this community exists only because we are here."

He didn't know why he was suddenly uncomfortable. Why he'd even spoken. Perhaps just the familiarity of the scene, even though Gabon was a thousand and more miles away across a vast landmass. He forced himself to relax, tried to smile. "Well, whether I attracted the trouble depends very much on who you think the target was."

She acknowledged the point with a gracious smile. They were interrupted as a noisy crowd of drunk bluejackets spilled across their path. She wrinkled her nose with distaste as one or two of them, recognising her nature if not her person, made clumsy bows before staggering after their fellows. "Are all sailors like this?" she asked.

He shrugged uncomfortably. "More or less," he said slowly. "You take a man far away from his home, further than he'd ever dreamed of going — whether he has chosen the life or no — and subject him to hard conditions and military discipline. He's going to kick up Bob's a-dying when he's ashore. Of this we can be certain."

"Not the officers, of course."

"No — they find more refined ways to let off steam."

The occasional crackle of distant rifle fire from the hills above the township was a fine illustration of how the gentry wrought their own chaos. Baxter didn't add that more than a few of them would be frequenting the more expensive bawdy houses that had appeared.

"This seems far worse than at previous ports of call, nonetheless," she said, a real note of concern in her voice.

He'd noticed this as well, but hadn't want to voice his suspicions. "The news from the front won't have helped," he said eventually. It was well known in the fleet, at this point, that the garrison they had been sailing to relieve had fallen, the ships of the 1st Pacific Squadron sunk. "And no one knows why we aren't either turning around or cracking on. That, the heat and the shock of the unfamiliar will breed ill-discipline." He didn't want to speak of what would come from that. Mutiny was an ugly word.

"That, or something more political," she said, her voice dark. Baxter's mind flashed back to the coven of revolutionaries they had both overheard, but who had so far remained at large as far as he was able to tell. "Rumours abound of risings in the home country."

That was a reminder of just how isolated they were, stranded at what felt like the edge of the world. A tropical idyll that was rapidly becoming a prison. News filtered through by telegram, although the nearest telegram station was seventy-five miles away and the relay to St. Petersburg uncertain, or from visiting ships. The occasional supply ship from Russia brought mail and news along with such necessaries as heavy winter coats but not sufficient 12-inch shells for the battleships to exercise their main batteries. No one knew exactly what was happening, although the rumours spoke of massacres in response to massive strikes and unrest.

He shook his head. "Ill-discipline, and acts of defiance, yes. But this heat, particularly if you're not used to it, will sap the will of even the most committed revolutionary for any sort of sustained action."

"Perhaps you are right, though they are no doubt among us."

It was the closest they'd come to talking about the cabal they'd uncovered, and he wondered again exactly what she was up to. What game was she playing, and how did he fit into it? He'd guessed, perhaps always known, that she wasn't quite what she appeared to be. He knew how he wanted to fit in to her life, but she'd made it clear that this wasn't on the cards.

"Zinovy Petrovich does his best," she said after a moment, referring to the vice-admiral. "Though even he struggles."

That Baxter couldn't deny. Having met the squadron commander and seen him at work, he had little time for him as a man. He knew ships and the sea, though, and certainly had the force of will to drive this — to Baxter's mind doomed — expedition onwards.

The conversation — muttered quietly between themselves while Vasily, Tommy and Esme talked happily amongst themselves — was cut short by a commotion ahead, the sounds of shouted indignation and then something approaching panic. He and Ekaterina exchanged glances, neither of them needing to say anything — the irony was not lost on either of them.

The crowds were thick enough that they couldn't see what was going on. Ekaterina bit her lip and he noticed her hand drift towards the closure of the bag she carried. "It's probably nothing."

"Well, nonetheless. Vasily, Tommy, stay with the countess and Esme."

Baxter strode towards the sounds of confusion, knowing he was being unnecessarily dramatic but not able to stop himself. People were starting to run around him, mostly away from the noise, but he had the bulk to shoulder through what threatened to become a stampede. A few Russian sailors were moving towards the sound of trouble, and he was glad he'd left Vasily to look after the others.

A rickety stall toppled just ahead of him, scattering people and goods and setting the stallholder to a furious tirade of French. He dashed forward as he realised the sailor who had fallen into the stall was holding a bloody hand over his guts.

The man was half-propped against the rough wooden planking and started to slide down, leaving a red smear across the brightly-coloured local fabric that was on sale. Baxter caught him as he fell, one arm under the man's shoulder. The front of his uniform was stained dark and his face was pale — he must have come some distance despite the wound.

"Help here!" he roared, then remembered to shout in Russian and French. He pulled off his jacket and wadded it, knowing how futile that would be but that he had to try. He pulled the man's hands away from the wound to have a quick look, seeing a deep and long gash, then got the fabric against the bloody mess and pressed the man's hands on it.

"Who did this to you?" he asked quietly in Russian. He'd seen few wounds for someone in his profession, but enough to know it didn't look good.

"Countess…" the man whispered.

Baxter realised he knew the fellow, albeit only in passing — one of the *Yaroslavich*'s foredeck hands. He'd been one of Neptune's helpers at the line-crossing ceremony. "What's that? The countess…?" For a moment he genuinely thought that the sailor was accusing Ekaterina of stabbing him.

"Must … tell … Countess…"

"Tell me what?" Ekaterina asked, appearing from the rapidly dispersing crowd, Vasily and Tommy in tow. Baxter looked up and around instinctively, realising the man could very well have been pursued. He caught a flash of someone vaguely familiar disappearing behind a low, ramshackle warehouse, but Ekaterina laid a hand on his arm to still him as he tried to rise and pursue.

"This evening, Countess…" the dying sailor murmured. "It starts … at the curfew."

He didn't die immediately after that, his voice breaking down into a quiet and increasingly nonsensical ramble.

Ekaterina had one go at getting more out of him. "What happens? What *exactly*?" She didn't seem shocked or horrified, didn't baulk at holding the man's bloodied hand and stroking his brow.

The man didn't say anything more of sense, and by the time a drunk ship's doctor was prised out of a nearby bar, he had died.

Ekaterina felt for his pulse and then gently closed his eyes. "Rest well, Georgy Alexeivich," she whispered, then looked up at the three men crouched or kneeling around her with fierce eyes. "Tommy, run down to the dock and get a boat to the ship immediately." She pressed a coin into his hand. "Tell my husband I need to see him at once. *At once*, those exact words. In English."

Baxter was about to object to the boy being sent by himself, but held his peace. Tommy was proving to be able to look after himself. The lad shot off without demure.

"Vasya, stay with the body until we can send someone for him," Ekaterina went on. The big petty officer bobbed his head in silent assent, clearly ready to keep the solemn vigil without complaint. The countess looked at where he knelt in the growing pool of Georgy's blood. "It seems you and I are in need of a change of clothes, Mr Baxter."

CHAPTER 11

It was close to the 6pm curfew, when all sailors and officers were expected to be back aboard their ships, by the time Juneau arrived, red faced and sweating, at the house. Tommy was in tow, and not long after Vasily reappeared.

Ekaterina had been silent since they'd left the market, a look of stony resolve on her face that brooked no attempt at questioning or conversation on his part. Esme, pale and shaken, was sent home. Pavel hovered, horrified by the fact both his mistress and Baxter were more or less covered in blood that was already sticky and ripe. Luckily, it wasn't far from the scene of the murder to the house and they hadn't attracted too much attention.

"Should we not, at least, have waited for the local authorities?" Baxter asked, gently. The rapid tropical sunset was casting bars of light across the front room of the house, bathing them both in a warm glow. He felt physically clean after a tepid bath and fresh clothes, but he still fancied he could smell the coppery tang of blood on his hands. He sipped a gin and tonic that Pavel insisted on topping up frequently. Baxter didn't object, not least because it gave the nervous servant something to do.

Ekaterina looked like she was about to spit. "What local authorities? This is a Russian matter and will be dealt with by Russians."

"And by me," Baxter said with a flat certainty that surprised himself as much as her. She smiled briefly, a genuine expression that seemed to light up her face. He hesitated before speaking further. "You believe you know who did this?"

The smile went. "Who do you think?" she asked, her voice hard, just as the front door opened and Juneau flew in.

"It is soon? Tonight?" Juneau asked immediately, but Ekaterina made a shushing gesture with a significant glance at Baxter.

Baxter rose, setting down his glass. "I think it's fair to say that I'm in this, whatever it is. And I can't help feeling you're going to need all the help you can get." He stared at them each in turn, but his gaze lingered on Ekaterina, as she seemed to be the one in charge. At least when it came to these matters. Juneau gave an expressive shrug, and the countess nodded as she came to a decision.

"There is clearly a group of revolutionaries on board the *Yaroslavich*," she said. "You have seen this much yourself."

"There are dissidents throughout the fleet, in fact," Juneau went on.

"Hence the higher than average levels of mechanical problems," Baxter said, voice dry.

Juneau gave another one of his shrugs, acknowledging that but also the state of their engineering. "The cell aboard our own ship, it embarrasses me to admit, are more organised and ambitious than the others. They have seen the somewhat poor state of discipline in the squadron, as we languish here, and they are going to seize their moment."

"What they *think* is their moment," Ekaterina said, her voice grim. She had seated herself at the table in one corner of the room and, in the dying light, was carefully disassembling and cleaning her Colt automatic pistol.

"What could they possibly hope to gain?" Baxter asked. "Beyond being on the wrong side of a firing squad?"

"We have pieced some of it together, from the planning session you stumbled upon and some other opportunities, as well as informants among the crew," Ekaterina replied. Baxter was slightly transfixed by the way she was popping the vicious little bullets from the pistol's clip and then reloading them. She handled the weapon with a certain degree of surety. "We know they think they will start a fire here, serve as an example for the other ships. How they plan to do it, though…"

"Killing a friend of the Tsar would be a step along the way," Baxter brooded, staring out of the window before turning back to them. "But why the devil haven't you brought this to the attention of Gorchakov or the admiral's staff?"

"It is no secret that the squadron's command is in disarray, and we are left to our own devices to deal with problems. Gorchakov refuses to believe that anything like this could occur on his most blessed ship — God would not allow such things. We are on a holy crusade, after all."

"Useless bloody idiot!" Baxter exploded. "Maintaining discipline is his first duty!"

Ekaterina made a calm gesture. "When you have quite finished, Mr Baxter," she said coldly. "We do not know who aboard we can trust — there may only be a few conspirators, but I am not confident that we have identified all of them and it would be disastrous if we take even one into our confidence. Who you see here and some few others are all we can rely on. Husband, did you manage to acquire arms without being noticed?"

Juneau managed to look slightly shamefaced, Baxter guessed in part because he was going to disappoint his wife. "Alas, my dear — I believe the conspirators to be on high alert and watching all officers' movements. Luckily Tomas'ka managed to give the appearance of being on a domestic errand when he came aboard, which did not panic anyone. I have my service revolver and there are my sporting guns still in the cabinet in our cabin — though I fear they have not been fired for some time."

"We and the weapons we have will have to be sufficient," Ekaterina said decisively, slotting the clip into the grip of her pistol and tucking it away in her handbag. "Mr Baxter, as you are with us — do you favour a pistol or long gun?"

Juneau broke in. "Mr Baxter doesn't have much time for a gun in less than four-inch calibre," he said.

Baxter grinned as he was reminded of his words, thousands of miles and thirty degrees in temperature ago. "I'm better up close," he admitted.

Ekaterina looked at them as though they were quite mad. Or rather, that they were dangerous amateurs and she was the professional, which was a bizarre notion. "Well, let us be aboard and see what we can do," she said with a sigh.

They returned to the cruiser as quietly as they could, using a hired local boat to transport them across the increasingly oily and detritus-filled water of the bay; an occasional rotting animal carcass floated past, jettisoned from *Esperance* supply ship after her refrigerators broke down. All around them they could hear the evidence of how lax discipline had become. Singing could be heard from many of the ships, different songs perhaps but rendered interchangeable by the obvious drunkenness of the singers. No sentries challenged the boat as a pair of surly locals dipped their oars into the water and drove them forward, the rowlocks creaking.

The *Yaroslavich*, at least, had a semblance of order. Juneau had threatened, encouraged or cajoled his subordinates into standing proper harbour watches in addition to the exercises Rozhestvensky demanded. Gorchakov had not been seen for days, retiring to his cabin or the ship's chapel, and Baxter had yet to decide whether this was a help or a hindrance. A proper guard was being kept, or at least the semblance of one. This night, of course, an alert sentry would be a problem. Even if he wasn't in cahoots with the mutineers, he could accidentally alert them to the return of Juneau.

They'd discussed it in low, hushed tones as the boat pulled to the outer anchorage where the cruiser lay. Ekaterina, it was agreed, was right. Both they and their opponents were few in number — at least they would not be facing the entire crew or even a significant faction of it, as officers had over the centuries of seafaring when mutinies occurred. It also meant they could not risk rousing the crew — while most would be obedient, it would alert their quarry and they could not trust every man implicitly. Instead, they would effectively be carrying forward a 'cutting out' expedition on their own ship.

Baxter realised, as the boat slid towards the stern, that his hands shook slightly and his stomach churned acid. Boarding actions were things one talked about when training, but it had been years since the Royal Navy or any other had carried one out in anger. Particularly when unarmed, he admitted to himself wryly. He knew this was utter insanity, that he was risking life and limb to help people who held him captive and had dragged him and Tommy to the far side of the world. But at the same time, Juneau and Ekaterina at least were his friends.

And, he realised with a sudden fierce grin, how could be pass up the opportunity to do something like this?

The two oarsmen grinned back at him. Juneau had convinced them that they were only sneaking aboard to play a practical joke on a brother officer, and had mistaken his expression for humour at the coming japes.

Baxter turned back into the bows as the bulk of the cruiser filled the sky in front of them. She was lit up — there was no reason not to be in a friendly harbour — but it was dark at the waterline as the skiff slid up to the stern, the oars out of the water so it came alongside with only the sound of the oily water running along the sides.

His grin faded as he readied himself, poised to make the jump. Juneau had tried to dissuade him, arguing this should be his own duty as the first officer, but he had insisted. He told himself it was because the choice was logical, not that he was trying to impress Ekaterina.

At Juneau's hissed command, the boatmen fended their fragile wooden vessel off with their oars, one scraping along the barnacle-encrusted hull. The noise was almost shattering in the dim silence that had enveloped them, but it was too late now. Baxter reached up, but as he suspected the quarter gallery was higher than even he could reach. He crouched as the boat came broadside on to the cruiser, launched himself up to catch the smooth oak railing. One hand slipped and for a moment he thought he was about to disappear into the murky water. Someone behind him gasped in alarm. Then his plimsolls found purchase and he vaulted lightly onto the deck, crouching in the dimness. He turned and stuck his hand out, receiving a line thrown up from below.

He looped it over the rail and had barely finished knotting it before Juneau was with him, revolver in hand. They'd agreed that Vasily would hand Ekaterina up, but as Baxter glanced back he realised she was shimmying up the rope to join them.

"Remember, quiet as we can," she said as she arrived. "My husband, do not discharge that."

Juneau switched his grip on his Nagant revolver with a tight smile, holding the weapon by the barrel. "It will make an excellent club."

"You're all quite mad," Baxter said, realising as he did that he was probably madder than any of them. "Let's be about this."

They went as a group through the silent, dark wardroom. It seemed oddly empty and devoid of life now the officers and their menagerie of dogs were mostly ashore. Beyond it were the officer's quarters on either side of a narrow corridor. Baxter cracked the door very slightly and peered out, but drew back sharply when he realised there was someone at the door to Juneau's quarters.

He held a finger to his lips, raised his other hand and pointed. He didn't wait to see if they had understood his half-seen signs. He opened the door just far enough and twisted out. His ma, rest her, had often commented how light he was on his feet for such a big lad and he made best use of that now as he covered the distance between himself and the interloper in a few long strides.

He grabbed a handful of collar, hauled the man away from the first officer's quarters and lifted him against the opposite wall, putting his hand across his mouth.

Yefimov glared at him, a mix of fear and anger in his eyes. Juneau was with them a split-second later, whispering quickly in French as Baxter put the older man down. "Sorry, old chap," he whispered, causing Yefimov's eyes to narrow in anger.

Baxter caught an odd flash in the lieutenant's eyes, then Yefimov seemed to come to a decision and clicked his heels together, bowing towards Juneau and rattling off French too fast for Baxter to follow.

Juneau replied, then turned with a small smile to Baxter and translated for his benefit. "It seems we are not completely alone — Lieutenant Yefimov had realised that things were amiss and that the revolutionaries have already seized control of the armoury. He'd come here as he knew I have some fowling pieces and wanted to arm himself."

Something didn't quite ring true about that, but Baxter put it out of his mind — now was the time for decisive action, not rumination, if the revolutionaries had already seized the ship's small arms.

Juneau quickly unlocked his cabin door and ushered them all into the cramped space. Yefimov's eyes widened in surprise when he saw Ekaterina with them, but he made no comment. Nothing about this situation was within the bounds of normality, so a pistol-wielding noblewoman wasn't going to throw him off his pace too far.

"So, if the revolutionaries are armed, our task is even harder," Juneau said, switching to French.

"Let us call them what they are," Yefimov spat. "Mutineers."

"The technicalities can wait," Ekaterina said, her voice imperious. "We must prevent them distributing arms to any of the crew who might be foolish enough to rise with them."

"Who amongst the officers are aboard?" Juneau asked his deputy, his voice patient.

It wasn't a good picture. The doctor was aboard, seeing to his duties, and the quartermaster as well, inspecting the stores. A handful of the other juniors. The officers with permission to be ashore were expected back imminently, as part of the mad rush to return to berths before the curfew and the lowering of the flags at day's end.

"I'll see to the armoury," Baxter said, glancing at Vasily who nodded heavily. The ship didn't carry a lot in the way of small arms — gone were the days of close-action necessitating sailors to fire on their opposite numbers, let alone boarding. It seemed they had other plans than to try to rouse the entire crew, though. "Best that those who are already armed should make their way to the main magazine."

Neither Juneau nor Ekaterina could muster an objection, but neither looked happy. Juneau unlocked a long, low chest in one corner and produced a rather fine looking hunting rifle, the furniture in a well-polished dark oak and the brass fitting gleaming. He handed that and a box of heavy bullets to Yefimov, then produced an equally finely-made double-barrelled shotgun and cartridges that went to Vasily. The big petty officer looked delighted to be given the use of such a weapon, breaking it open and loading it without any need for instruction.

"Perhaps I should attempt to rouse some of the other officers and such crewmen as are in a fit state," Yefimov offered.

Juneau thought about that for a moment, his lips pursed. "Very well — see who is aboard and awake. Quick as you can, though, as we shall not wait." He looked between all of them, his expression stern. "We know what we need to do. Move fast, and for God's sake take care of yourselves." His gaze lingered on his wife, then he nodded sharply and they filed silently out of the cabin.

The armoury wasn't far from officer's country clustered in the stern. If it was anything like those on RN ships, it would be little more than a locker with racks of rifles, pistols and possibly even some cutlasses.

Baxter stole silently down a companionway, Vasily as light on his feet not far behind with the shotgun broken over his arm. He could hear voices ahead, not many — but hard for him to say exactly. He wanted to get as close as he could before any noise, for instance the firing of a fowling piece, could alert them or their compatriots. But he also needed to succeed and do it quickly so they could get to the magazine and help the others.

A soft noise from an adjoining compartment startled him. He whipped round, but rather than an ambush or a lookout he saw Tommy's face grinning from the open hatchway.

He darted in, pushing the boy back. As far as he or anyone else knew, the young Scotsman was supposed to be ashore, in the care of Pavel. Juneau had brought him back from the ship and they'd all but locked him in his room. "What the de'il do you mean, sneaking back aboard?" Baxter whispered, his expression making up for the lack of volume.

Tommy barely quailed. "Thought I could help," the lad protested in an equally low voice. "Pavel was saying how worried he was, how few you were. I've already scouted down there, there're only three of the buggers."

"Language," Baxter said almost automatically, then ruffled the boy's hair. "Well, that's one more than us — even with the best will in the world you won't match up to a full-grown sailor, not for a few years yet. But they don't know we're coming." He looked down. "I mean it this time, lad — stay here."

Ignoring the look of disappointment on Tommy's face he went back out and gestured Vasily forward. They went down a companionway onto the lower deck, the steps creaking slightly under their feet. The mutineers were so confident that they were undetected they hadn't even posted a look out, but a particularly loose tread caused a cessation of the chatter. "What was that?" one of them whispered.

A moment later, a slightly tentative voice called out. "Hey, shipmate?" in an innocent tone that tried to suggest they had nothing to do with the armoury hatch standing open.

"It's just me, Vasily Ivanovitch," the big Russian at his shoulder said cheerfully, without missing a beat. He winked at Baxter as he looked back, surprise on his face.

"Vasya who has been guarding the British spy?"

"The same, though I have been relieved of that duty and glad to be away from the officers."

They were almost at the door, and Baxter could feel his palms sweating. Almost there…

A head emerged from the hatchway, an uncertain smile on its face. Baxter lunged forward, grabbing a handful of shirt, and with a great heave hurled the man across the narrow gangway. The mutineer hit with a sickening *thump* but Baxter didn't have time to check on his first victim. He went through the hatch, low and fast, and his shoulder connected with the upper chest of the one behind, sending him sprawling through a pyramid of stacked rifles. Vasily was through like a shot, wielding the expensive shotgun like a club to drop the third revolutionary in the room.

Baxter rose, breathing hard, and kicked the man he'd collided with in the midriff, causing him to double up with an agonised gasp. He wouldn't be calling for help any time soon. He was astonished that they'd actually succeeded at that.

"Is he deid?" Tommy asked querulously from outside. Baxter rolled his eyes but didn't snap at the boy as he went back out and crouched by the man he'd thrown into the bulkhead. Reaching out, he felt for a pulse. It was there, albeit thready, but from the dent in his skull and the way his eyes were rolled up showing only whites he'd be surprised if the fellow lasted the night. "No, he's still with us." He didn't add anything else, for instance that even if the wretch recovered he'd be shot as a mutineer. "Is there any chance in hell you'll do like you're told and stay out of trouble?"

Tommy shook his head firmly. Baxter shrugged. If the mutineers succeeded in damaging the ship or even blowing it up, the lad would be as much at risk as everyone else.

Vasily emerged, having tied the other two up with the sort of quick efficiency only an experienced sailor could manage. He handed a heavy Nagant revolver to Baxter, who took it without demure this time. They'd got away with it at the armoury, but he knew turning down a weapon had been pure bravado. The big Russian had a few of the awkward rifles slung over his shoulder, no doubt in case they met any more loyal bluejackets, and carried a sack that clinked with the sound of gunmetal. He handed it to Tommy, then shook his head firmly as he looked pointedly at the hand holding it.

Baxter grinned mirthlessly. "Well, on we go then."

The magazines were deep below the waterline, where they were well protected. Hoists allowed them to serve the batteries above, once the ready lockers had been expended. That was something Baxter knew was inevitable, given the Russian penchant for enthusiastic but inaccurate fire.

They found a couple of nervous looking bluejackets and a midshipman Baxter didn't recognise guarding the first of the magazines. They had a belaying pin and the middy's dirk between them, and gratefully received the firearms once Baxter had reassured himself that they were indeed loyal and had been left there by Juneau.

It felt surreal, creeping through the darkened and slightly ill-smelling decks of the ship he had come to know and think of almost as his own. He could hear snoring on either side, and somewhere singing. At least the ever-present, cloying stench of the coal, the feel and taste of it on everything, had abated as they burned the stocks down.

That peace, the lives contained within this steel shell, could be shattered in an instant if they failed, if they couldn't stop the revolutionaries carrying out their insane plan.

"Can't let myself think about that now," Baxter muttered. Vasily, knowing this part of the ship far better than he could, put a hand on his shoulder to stop him. They were approaching the central magazine, where the bulk of shells and propellant for all the artillery was stored before being portioned out to compartments that served the individual weapons and batteries. They found Ekaterina at the top of a companionway that led down to one of the two hatches. She was crouched in a most unladylike manner, staring intently down the companionway with her pistol levelled. She turned at their approach — their clanking did make stealth slightly harder — and smiled slightly.

"Juneau and a few others approach from the far side," she whispered. "There are four in the magazine, preparing fuses, and we will take them by surprise."

Baxter sucked in a breath. If they gave the revolutionaries no chance of escape, he suspected they would choose suicide, and an explosive suicide at that. Nothing awaited them but the firing squad anyway. It was too late to do anything about it now. "Do we think this is all of them?" he asked, keeping his voice low and clutching the unfamiliar pistol.

She glanced at him and he fought to relax his grip. "Try not to miss if you have to fire that," was all she said in response, then rose smoothly and started creeping down the steps.

"Stay here," Baxter said to Tommy before he followed her. "I mean it this time."

It was beyond madness, really. If he'd had any sense, he'd have waited at the house until the inevitable disaster occurred, then seen about getting himself and the lad out of Madagascar.

The very thought of abandoning *her*, though, made him feel sick to his stomach. And he'd never been one for running from a fight.

The revolutionaries here were on guard, at least. Baxter could see the shadow of one passing to and fro across the open hatchway, occasionally coming close enough to peer out. Perhaps they were worried that their comrades were late getting back.

He wanted to nudge Ekaterina, who was leading them, out of the way so he could dive in first. Something about her cool poise and confidence held him back, right up until the point that the first shot was fired.

None of them had time to think. The guard on this side stuck his head out of the door, seeing them rather than the expected comrades. He opened his mouth to shout at the same time as he raised his revolver. Baxter was already launching forwards, but the time for subtlety and quiet was gone. Ekaterina's pistol cracked, surprisingly loud, and he tasted powder smoke. The Bolshevik cried out and span away, pulling the trigger as he fell. The bullet went past him close enough that he felt the hot wind on his face, and the noise and the tang of the smoke triggered something visceral.

Baxter exploded into the magazine, casting about with a cold, furious clarity. The circular compartment was lined with racks bearing gleaming shells, chests of bagged propellant and cases of belts for the machine guns. If any of them was hit by a stray round, it could be disastrous.

Juneau was already at the opposite hatch, wrestling with a revolutionary who was trying to stab him with a clasp knife. Baxter started forward to help, then realised there were two more, one of them vaguely known to him, who were quickly slicing open powder bags.

Juneau would have to wait. Not wanting to risk his poor aim, Baxter instead threw the heavy revolver. It smacked into the nearest, not hard enough to put him over but enough to distract him from preparing his own weapon to fire into the open powder.

It seemed they had chosen death before capture. Couldn't have that.

The one he'd hit with the gun went down fast, a solid blow to a long rodent-like jaw that Baxter knew he'd be feeling the next day. His mate was faster, and though he'd dropped his rifle he had a knife and from the way he sent it darting towards Baxter's guts he knew how to use it.

Baxter caught the knife hand with a downward-sweeping forearm block, jabbed for the man's face. Hissed as blood was drawn as the knifeman turned his blade and danced out of the way of the blow. He kicked low, for the shins, grunted in triumph as the man staggered.

There was a feral, cornered look in the sailor's eyes as he cast around, knowing he was doomed but wanting a final act of defiance. He launched his knife at Baxter and dove for the discarded rifle. Baxter landed hard on him, ignoring the knife. He felt the other man's ribs crack, butted him hard on the bridge of the nose as he tried to squirm round. Got his hands around his throat and, vision going red, squeezed until he felt something pop and his victim go limp.

He rose, breathing hard, not knowing or caring if he'd killed the mutineer. His shoulder stung where the flying blade had caught him and blood dripped hot down his fingers. He didn't care much about that either.

There was an odd silence in the compartment that suggested things had either gone well or were about to go much worse. Turning slowly, trying to master his rage, he saw the former was the case. Juneau had his man down and was holding him at pistol-point. Ekaterina and Vasily were both there, and the little bugger Tommy had somehow found his way in.

Good job he had, too. The knife, having slashed Baxter, had knocked an oil lantern some utter buffoon had brought in off its perch. Tommy lay across the open case of powder bags it had fallen towards, pale and shaking, with the lantern held away from his chest in both hands.

"Ah ya blighter," Tommy yelped suddenly, as the heat of the lantern finally got through the adrenalin. Vasily had it out of his hands in a jiff and Ekaterina was gathering him into a tight hug. Her eyes, meeting Baxter's over the lad's tousled hair, held a mix of fascination and horror.

CHAPTER 12

"You are lucky no tendons were severed," Dr Andropov told Baxter as he peered at the wound in his arm by flickering gas light. "This would be easier in my sickbay."

"The sickbay on a ship neither Mr Baxter nor I have been near for days, good doctor?" Ekaterina said serenely.

Watery blue eyes regarded her from behind round spectacles. "Indeed, my lady," Andropov said evenly.

"And if I had been aboard, I'd have been bloody lucky not to have been blown up, let alone not lose the use of a hand," Baxter grunted, trying not to wince as the doctor bent over the upwards cut in his forearm with needle and thread in hand.

The wound in his shoulder was slight — the blade had merely caught him on the way to its true target of the lamp. The slash in his arm had been deliberate and deeper. Oddly enough, despite years at sea on both warships and merchantmen, he'd never been seriously injured, but he had picked up his fair share of this type of knock.

"As I was, indeed," Andropov said gently. "There." He dabbed the wound with surgical spirits without warning, causing Baxter to flinch slightly, and commenced bandaging it.

Baxter looked across the room at Ekaterina, who was cradling a neat whisky in her hands and staring broodingly at the medical tableau. They had been spirited, along with Tommy, from the ship as soon as the magazine was secure. It was better for everyone if the official story — and it would come out at the courts martial — did not involve any of them. Juneau and Vasily had remained aboard.

"How are your other patients, Doctor?" Ekaterina asked guardedly.

"Those who are likely to live will do so, until the firing squads," Andropov said. There was no trace of bitterness in his voice; like many doctors Baxter had met in the course of his life at sea he had a fatalistic streak. "But I should attend to them."

He rose, washed his hands in the basin provided and rolled down the sleeves of his linen shirt. He was in mufti, preparing as he had been for a night ashore, and he looked every inch a colonial doctor as he gathered up his straw hat and bid them all good night.

"How do you feel, Baxter?" Ekaterina asked after a moment.

He bit back on the urge to sound off with fake bravado. "In truth, lucky to be alive," he said. His whole body ached, aside from those bits that were actively painful, but despite that he felt his heartbeat quicken again as their eyes met. "Such events do tend to put things in perspective…"

She rose before he could say anything else, particularly anything potentially embarrassing. "There is truth in that, Mr Baxter," she said quietly, not meeting his eyes.

He sat back, slightly deflated. "And you, ma'am?" he said, letting an unfortunate level of formality creep back into his voice. "You shot a man this evening, and that is no small thing."

"You killed one with your bare hands," she shot back, then stopped with a look that suggested she didn't know why she was angry. "I apologise, Mr Baxter. I am tired — I shall look in on Tommy and retire, I think."

"I imagine we all need rest," he said, keeping his voice as mild as possible.

"You were very brave," she said quietly from the doorway.

"I have a thick skin, Mrs Juneau," he said, looking into the shadowed corner of the room.

"I wasn't talking about the stitches, Mr Baxter."

"Neither was I. Good night, ma'am."

"Good night, Mr Baxter."

Baxter was unable to sleep, tossing and turning under a thin sheet despite the fatigue. Although he'd tried his best, he'd come within a hand's breadth of killing both him and Tommy, again, and that gnawed at him. Charging headlong into the fight like that was exactly the sort of blockheaded behaviour that hadn't helped his cause in the RN.

The door creaking open at some point — the heavy night was still pitch dark — brought him bolt upright. For a moment he thought it was Tommy, looking for someone to talk to, but Andropov had given him a sleeping draught and Pavel was watching over him.

Ekaterina was a dimly-seen form through the mosquito netting; then she lifted a flap and slipped inside. She wore a robe belted loosely over a light nightdress. Her eyes widened slightly when she saw he was bare chested, and he hurriedly pulled himself up and the sweat-soaked sheet up to his shoulders.

"This is … quite improper…" Baxter mumbled.

There was no preamble "I didn't want to leave things like that," she said, in her pristine broken English. "Between us."

"There was nothing between us," he said, trying and failing to meet her steady gaze.

She sat on the edge of the bed, and shifted closer to him. "I should very much like there to be." Her voice was quiet, but it wasn't a shy whisper.

"Your husband…"

She reached out, very gently touched his cheek and turned his face, leaning forward until they were almost nose-to-nose. Her robe had fallen open and her nightdress was very thin indeed. "Is a good, kind, and honourable man who I love very much, and he loves me. In his way." Her other hand stole up his leg, bunched the sheet and started pulling it down. "Not in this way. I am, how do you say…?"

A sudden jump of intuition. "A false flag?"

She laughed at the terminology, her whole face lighting up, and he laughed with her. Then she was sliding into his arms, the sheet and her nightwear seeming to disappear of their own volition, and they smothered each other's laughter before they could give the game away.

She was gone the next morning, which was sensible. If it wasn't for the scent of her on the pillow and sheet, he would almost have thought he'd dreamed the whole thing.

They hadn't talked much after, falling asleep side-by-side, so he had no idea what her intentions were. But then, he'd never known what she was after. All he could really do was carry on as normal and see what happened next. That had become his life, in these last few months.

Baxter felt tired and shivery as he pulled himself out of bed and to the wash basin. It had been filled at some point in the early morning, and he guessed that Ekaterina had already been back in her room by that point. He didn't normally sleep that heavily.

"Just an after-effect of the action," he mumbled to himself, and shoved his head into the deep basin of tepid water. He could smell coffee and frying bacon, but his stomach churned at the thought of food.

His shoulder and arm were both stiff and sore, and looking in the mirror he could see a bit of blood through the bandage around his shoulder. They'd been careful last night, gentle, so he didn't think the wounds had been reopened then. He resolved as he dressed to see the doctor.

He found the denizens of the house in the dining room. Ekaterina looked up at his came in with only the politest of welcoming smiles, but there was a slight gleam in her eye.

"Good morning, Mr Baxter," she said as he bent to scratch Maxim behind the ears and then ruffled Tommy's hair, which got him only the vaguest of reproaches from the lad. The big dog was obviously not enjoying the heat and barely opened his eyes. "Did you sleep well?"

"Like the dead, ma'am," he said, fighting to keep a straight face.

Pavel appeared silently, no hint of disapproval or even awareness in his quiet efficiency as he served Baxter his breakfast.

Tommy was picking at his food, eyes downcast and face pale. Baxter regarded him for a few minutes. "You did well last night," he said, his voice level. "In future, you don't get left behind."

Ekaterina's eyes flashed a warning, but Baxter just gave her a slight smile and nodded. He didn't intend to say more, but Tommy needed to hear that. The lad nodded, looked up briefly when Baxter rested a hand on his shoulder.

Young Master Dunbar had already seen more than many men twice his age, including death and danger at very close hand. Baxter had only been a little older when he went to sea, though, and those who chose a maritime life had to become accustomed to such rough and tumble.

"You do not appear hungry, Baxter," Ekaterina said, a note of concern in her voice.

He realised he was only turning his fork over in his hand and poking at the mountain of bacon, fried bread and eggs in front of him. He reached for something humorous to say about appetites, but his brain was slow and before anything came to hand Juneau exploded into the room.

Baxter winced at his cheerful greeting, the noise going right through his head. He mumbled a response, guilt shooting through him despite what Ekaterina had said last night. He had bedded another officer's wife before — one of the many ways, he was coming to realise, he hadn't helped his own case in the RN — but never the wife of a friend.

That friend seemed oblivious to his mood, chattering away cheerfully as he filled a plate. "Well, I have to say that was something of a relief," Juneau said after a few minutes of hearty eating. "Knowing those *ublyudki* were aboard and planning something was wearing on me."

"Language, my husband," Ekaterina said mildly, with a fond smile.

"I imagine not dying was also a relief," Baxter muttered sourly. That was another source of guilt — Juneau had looked to be in dire straits in the magazine but Baxter had prioritised stopping the revolutionaries from blowing the whole thing sky high. It seemed he should have had more faith. "You really should have let the bluejackets go first."

Juneau's mood wasn't punctured by the sour words, he merely shrugged diffidently. "This happened on my watch and I therefore had to deal with it myself," he said simply.

"Not that any of us were there to witness this," Ekaterina said acidly, glaring at Baxter before turning a dutiful smile on her husband. "And have the prisoners been talking?"

"Oh, full confessions are being made," Juneau said.

Baxter shook his head, trying to clear it. Their voices were coming from a great distance away as they talked about the testimony. His arm throbbed painfully and he felt oddly cold, though his shirt was already clinging to his back.

"Though one of them did embellish it somewhat," Juneau was saying as Baxter managed to fight down the nausea and dizziness. Tommy watched him with a concerned expression but Ekaterina was absorbed by what her husband was saying. "Making some wild claims that one of the officers was in contact with British Intelligence, who were rendering aid."

"That would be beyond the pale, even for perfidious Albion," Ekaterina said flatly, then looked up as Baxter pushed his chair back with a loud scrape. He put his head in his hands, feeling the clamminess on his brow. "No offense, Baxter," she said quickly, but he wasn't really listening. His vision was swimming, but there was something important he needed to tell them. If only he could remember…

"I don't think the British government would stoop to such levels," he said, his voice a hoarse whisper. "But those within the intelligence services already have."

Stunned silence greeted that pronouncement. At a whispered command Tommy dashed from the room. Baxter watched his feet trot to the door, the view at an odd angle, and realised that somehow he was on the floor. It was comfortable enough, so he decided to stay put.

The next week or so was a blur of sweat and half-remembered dreams. Of the distant crack of firing squad rifles drifting up from the bay, a jagged interjection into dreams of leering slender daemons feeding him poison (or, as Baxter realised later, Dr Andropov feeding him quinine pills). An ever-changing cast of the daemon's acolytes filtered through the dreams as well, alternating concern for his well-being with trying to drown him in warm water.

"Dr Andropov tells me you came close to death on Wednesday," Ekaterina told him one morning as he lay still, weak and exhausted, under a fresh sheet and in fresh cotton pyjamas. She had pushed the window open and for once a cool sea breeze blew through the room. "He was concerned the infection in your arm would turn gangrenous."

He stirred weakly, trying to see the offending appendage. He could feel it, but he'd known men who'd lost limbs but swore they could still feel a phantom of the appendage. She smiled gently, eased him back and held a glass of water to his lips. "Don't worry, everything is still where it should be. He said the fever would break on Saturday if the rot didn't set in."

"What day is it?" he asked after taking a sip. He wanted more, but she eased the cup away.

"Friday."

"I was always an overachiever." It was a rough quip, but the best he could manage given he felt utterly drained.

She actually smirked. "At least you don't finish everything early."

He blinked, utterly astonished at the innuendo. "Mrs Juneau, I am horrified that you would subject a man in my weakened condition to such bawdy wit."

Her laugh was clear and bright and he sensed the relief that lay behind it. "I really don't know what you mean, Mr Baxter," she said primly, and offered him more water. "Gently, gently. Not too much at once." She sat back, folding her hands in her lap and looking down at him, her smile fading. "You gave us much cause for concern, Baxter," she said softly. "And I am glad you have pulled through."

He lay still, basking in her presence but waiting for the 'but'.

"It pains me to press a man in your weakened condition, but I must know … what you said, just before you collapsed…"

He couldn't tell if she was truly pained, but he could also guess that questioning him in this state was deliberate and felt a flare of old familiar anger.

He stared at her through aching eyes, struck again by how unfathomable she was. But he was tired, and ached from head to toe, and the hot rage had died as quickly as it had come. He owed Arbuthnott and whomever was behind the rogue agent nothing.

So he told her everything.

Nothing more was said of it during his convalescence, though he saw her most days. Tommy was a constant presence, ready to run and fetch anything he needed, and Andropov was a regular visitor.

"You probably should not be out and about, Mr Baxter," the doctor said reprovingly as he arrived to find his patient on the veranda, sipping a long glass of iced mango juice.

"I've never been one to lie around in bed, Doctor, unless I'm truly hungover." Baxter tipped his broad-brimmed straw hat back to regard the cadaverous medical man. "Your ministrations have put me well on the way to mending."

"It is nothing — in cases like this the strength of the patient is the best indicator." Andropov sighed as he took a chair opposite him. "Unless other outside forces intervene," he went on, voice sad.

"Did they shoot the injured men as well?"

Andropov made a wide gesture with his long-fingered, expressive hand. "The Graf argued for clemency, at least until nature ran its course, and as you know Admiral Rozhestvensky has previously refused to sign any death warrants here, but

Gorchakov was insistent on the sentences being carried out. They had to tie poor Alexei Dmitryich into a stretcher and tie that to a post. At least he knew nothing of what was happening."

The speed with which the trials and executions had been carried out astonished Baxter. Even in the RN, with its emphasis on firm discipline, it would have been weeks if not months before a proper court martial could have been carried out; and even for a crime as severe as mutiny the punishment was not always so swiftly enacted.

He knew he'd killed one of them outright, in the heat of the fight, and more or less killed Alexei Dmitryich who's head he'd smashed. Men who had wanted him and everyone else dead. There was nothing he could do about that, and he refused to feel too bad about it. "I haven't heard any more firing squads over the last few days," he said, rather than follow that train of thought further.

Andropov sighed again. "Word has reached the squadron of events in the Motherland. Disturbances, some have said revolutions, and brutal reprisals by the Tsar's army and secret police. That and the conditions here trigger a wave of unrest on the ships. Our lord and master feels, though, that he cannot find a worse punishment than leading these men into certain battle and probable death."

"Too damn hot for them to have achieved much, anyway," Baxter said darkly, mopping his brow. In truth the warmth had been a godsend for him once the fever had broken. "Hard to work up revolutionary fervour when the air feels like a wet blanket."

"If they had succeeded aboard our own ship…"

"That's quite enough, Doctor." Ekaterina's flat, hard voice chopped across the conversation as she stepped out onto the veranda. "As you said yourself, Mr Baxter is still convalescing and it would be well not to trouble him with such matters."

"Of course, your Serenity," Andropov said urbanely, but not before Baxter caught the slightest flash of fear in his eyes.

Ekaterina settled into the other wicker chair and topped up Baxter's glass. "Let us talk of pleasanter things," she said, her voice lighter. "I am joining my husband and the other officers on something of an expedition into the interior, and wondered if you yet feel up to it, Mr Baxter?"

CHAPTER 13

When Baxter finally returned to the cruiser — over Dr Andropov's objections — he found it much changed. Some semblance of military order had returned, the men and officers moving with a bit more purpose. The many exotic pets that had been bought over the last few weeks had been thrown overboard, mercifully close enough to shore to escape, and there was barely a hint of bloodstains on the planking of the quarterdeck where the revolutionaries had been shot. The Russian navy, he was told, laid out tarpaulins first.

It felt good to have a moving deck under his feet again, the sea breeze in his face as the *Yaroslavich* shouldered aside light seas.

"It's the admiral, you see," Juneau said as he joined him by the rail. "The threat of a complete breakdown of discipline brought the man out of his cabin and taking command again."

"Is that what you call it?" Baxter muttered, then shook away the last of the sourness. "The mutiny, I mean — a breakdown of discipline?"

Juneau's smile was disarming. "What else could it be described as, my dear Baxter?"

This was the first time he'd really spoken with Juneau since the night of the 'breakdown of discipline'. He hadn't been deliberately avoiding him, but Juneau had been kept busy with the aftermath. Despite what Ekaterina had said about her marriage, Baxter couldn't quite shake the sense of guilt over having bedded her.

"Fair point," he grunted. "I wasn't here so couldn't say, of course."

The cruiser was steaming in line astern with the faster, newer cruisers of Enkvist's squadron. She was the last ship in the line, trailing slightly, and Baxter looked hungrily along the sleek, grey shapes of the modern warships as they commenced a slight turn to starboard. He had a superb view along the length of the line, and his heart ached with the knowledge that he'd never command a ship like that. The *Yaroslavich* was dumpy and old by comparison, and noticeably the only ship still carrying a vestigial sailing rig.

"When I see a line like this, I wonder how we can ever be beaten," Juneau said wistfully.

"The Japanese line will be just as impressive." Baxter bit back on saying anything more. "Though you have all done an incredible job coming this far. Rozhestvensky seems to be the man for the job."

"Whether he is Togo's equal in battle remains to be seen," Juneau finished the thought for him, though quietly enough that the other officers clustered on the upper deck couldn't overhear. He gave Baxter a brittle smile. "Well, we're about to commence firing practice, and my place is on the bridge."

The whole 2nd Pacific Squadron was on exercise, though the cruisers were some way distant to the big beasts of the line squadrons. No one wanted a repeat of the near-disaster in the North Sea. Steam pinnaces had finished laying out a series of targets — empty salt meat barrels lashed together with flags on them, in time-honoured tradition — and were now hurriedly clearing the area.

Baxter turned, with mild curiosity, to watch the crew of the nearest 4.7-inch gun; he leaned against the railing as much for support as to show a lack of concern. One of the many ways the cruiser showed her age, dating as she did from another era of naval architecture, was in the arrangement of her armament.

Her main guns were 6-inch, single barbette mounts two to a side, fore and aft. The secondary armament of the twelve 4.7s were mounted primarily along the sides, firing through piercings in the manner of the old wooden warships rather than in fully traversable mounts. The gun captain was watching the lieutenant in charge of the starboard battery, who in turn had his eyes on the bridge. Baxter felt a stir of familiar excitement as Juneau called down orders from the bridge wing and the loading proceeded.

The bluejackets were … slapdash, it was fair to say. Not through any fault of their own, but for lack of proper training. He'd seen them at work in the North Sea, though it had been harder to see what was going on in the darkness, and he thought they had improved since then at least. Juneau at least took his duties seriously.

The order came down to fire on their selected target, and Baxter twisted back round just as the great guns spoke, first the two six-inchers and then, in a ragged broadside, the lighter guns. He watched the fall of shot, a scattering of water spouts mostly around the float aside from one errant shot that landed closer to a different target. The other ships unleashed their own broadsides a moment later, a heavy crash of guns even at that distance, and he watched their own fall of shot with increasing dismay.

"I really need to get off this ship, Tommy and Ekaterina as well."

No sooner had he muttered that when something clanged heavily behind, to the sound of much hilarity. One of the loaders had fumbled a shell, and it was rolling across the deck. Men shrieked and leapt away, either thinking this was amusing or worried that the shell would detonate. Baxter reacted without thought, jumping down to the gundeck — managing

not to fall flat on his face as his knees threatened to buckle —
and got his foot on the shell. "Not like that, you *bashi-bazouks*!"
he snarled. "Take this seriously, would you?"

They stopped, staring at him with their mouths open. He
may have been a pale shadow of himself after the fever, but his
rage was towering and, he realised, he'd roared at them in
passable Russian.

Well, he was in it now. He may as well wade forward. He
bent, scooped the shell up and shoved it into a loader's arms.
"Like this — like you're holding a baby," he went on, lowering
his voice and trying to inject some humour into it. "Don't be
shy, it won't explode until the pointy end hits an enemy ship.
Now, did you remember to open the bloody breech?"

The gun captain nodded uncertainly.

"Well, that's a start."

He took them through the correct methodology for loading
quickly and safely, then had to reach out and stop the gun
captain leaping forward to pull the firing lanyard. This, he
suspected, was their favourite part — most sailors loved a
good bang. "Remember, firing fast is good. Firing accurately is
better. Firing fast *and* hitting your target is what we're aiming
for." He stripped off his linen jacket. "Let's do this properly,
shall we?"

The rest of the afternoon was spent in honest toil, until
Baxter's hands shook slightly with fatigue and his vision swam;
sweat stuck grime and powder residue to his skin. Pretty soon
he was instructing the neighbouring gun, the diffident
lieutenant — Koenig, he thought — who was supposed to be
in charge taking instruction with his men. At one point he
caught Juneau watching him from the bridge, but no word
came down for him to butt out. The cruiser line came about to
fire the port weapons, by which time at least one of their

compatriots managed a near enough miss or two that their target floats were looking in a shabby way. The *Yaroslavich*'s target still floated unsullied and defiant.

While the ship was manoeuvring and their colleagues on the other side were having their go, Baxter took the crews through a few dry firing runs, then gathered them around him.

"Remember, fast and accurate if you can — but accurate if you can't." The ship was starting to turn again — the flag had ordered that no vessel was to return to port without having first hit her target — and the orders were coming down for the starboard battery to prepare. "Now let's show those bastards how it's done, eh?"

He took command of one of the guns. He knew he shouldn't, that it could be seen as an insult to the Russian gun captain, but it had been years since he'd laid artillery and he sorely missed it. "You fire when I give the signal, though," he told the burly, shaven-headed man, who gave him a smile that was mostly metal.

He peered through the crude gunsight, which gave a little magnification, and used hand signals and grunted commands to get the rest of the crew to lay the weapon on target.

He held his breath, held his fire. Waited. The six-inches spat flame and smoke and noise, briefly obscuring his vision, but he knew they wouldn't hit. The rest of the 4.7s fired, similarly wide. Then he raised his hand and chopped it down sharply. The gun to his left fired, the shell sending splinters hurtling through the flag on the target. Cheers went up as it started to topple, then Baxter's own gun went off with a crash, hurtling back on its springs next to him and deafening him with the report. A second later and one of the big casks that made up the raft exploded under a direct hit; he staggered back from the gun with a triumphant grin as the gunners pounded him on the back and Juneau raised his cap in salute.

It was a small victory, but a victory nonetheless. And exactly what this crew needed.

Some of the cruisers were still firing on their targets when the *Yaroslavich* and the other ships that had achieved 'victory' turned back to the bay, sailing away from the rapidly setting sun. With their own guns housed, it was easy to hear the heavy thunder of the big battleships' batteries, long tongues of flame licking out in the gathering darkness. Baxter shuddered to think how much ammunition was being used, particularly as the expected resupply of 12-inch armour-piercing shells had so far not arrived.

Dinner that evening in the wardroom was a raucous, cheerful and informal affair.

"Gorchakov, of course, is not happy," Juneau told Baxter quietly. "I had to pretend I couldn't hear his orders to have you dragged away and prevented from interfering. Even after we started hitting he remained unconvinced you had anything to do with it."

On a personal level, Baxter was gratified that Juneau had backed him like that. Professionally, he was horrified that command aboard the cruiser had broken down to that point and that he was the cause of it.

"I have some influence, you know," Juneau said cheerfully, and slightly drunkenly. "I could arrange for you to be offered a commission. There are many honourable precedents — even John Paul Jones, you know…"

Baxter looked at him in surprise. Everyone, by now, knew that he was a former RN officer, but only Ekaterina knew under what circumstances — that had been part of his confession. Juneau gave no hint of having been informed, though, and seemed to be making the offer out of genuine kindness. And self-interest, of course. Baxter couldn't make claims to be the greatest officer ever to have trod a deck, but he'd shown himself to be competent. More than most around the table, for all that they were genial, could claim.

He returned Juneau's earnest stare and realised that he was tempted. He owed Britain and the Royal Navy nothing, and as Juneau said there was a long and proud tradition of former officers serving other navies, often in disgrace. Naval tradition vaunted Lord Cochrane rather than holding him up as a villain.

But Britain and Russia had been enemies in the past and tensions were high enough that they had almost gone to war because of the very actions of this squadron. And, with a few exceptions, he didn't think he'd find going up against his old comrades palatable.

"And if I politely decline, Juneau, will Tommy and I be put ashore here?" It occurred to him that he must now be trusted by them, if he was being offered a rank, respect and station.

"Ah. Officially the orders stand, but I am sure we can find a way to circumvent them without getting into too much trouble. It would be considerably easier to put Tomas'ka at liberty if you wore the Tsar's uniform, of course."

Juneau's gaze was deliberately artless, as he laid a devil's bargain in front of his 'guest'. The only trouble with that offer, of course, was that it would be tantamount to abandoning the boy more than ten thousand miles from home. With the best will in the world, he would get himself into trouble before he got back.

"How about this, Mr Juneau," Baxter said, carefully and formally. "Your wife has, I assume, told you what I told her?"

"The pertinent details, yes."

"My offer is that I will remain aboard." He said this with a slight smile, acknowledging he might actually have no choice in that. "I will continue to train your men in gunnery. As a … consulting gunner, shall we say?"

"And that would not conflict with any sense of duty you might have?"

"I very much doubt it. Think of it as self-preservation — if we do run into any enemy ships while I'm aboard, I don't want to be killed because your lot can't shoot back." Juneau laughed at that, then his expression grew serious as Baxter lowered his voice. "I'll also help you find this British agent you have aboard, if such a thing exists."

"Surely that does offer some moral conflict for you?"

Baxter shook his head firmly. "Not in the slightest. Their plot involved me dying, and I take exception to that. I also do not think they have the best interests of either of our countries at heart."

Juneau took a moment, regarding Baxter thoughtfully, then nodded. "And in return?"

"I imagine we will be passing Singapore, or some other colony. It would not be a great effort to put us ashore."

"I imagine it would also be a good opportunity to put my wife ashore as well." Juneau smiled a thin smile, and there was a sad knowing in it. Baxter was taken slightly aback by the expression. Did he know what had happened between his wife and Baxter, or was it more of an understanding that the Russians were sailing towards almost certain destruction?

The moment passed as one of the officers — Koenig, who Baxter had more or less supplanted earlier that day — rose to offer a toast to the gunnery of the Russian navy, which would surely sweep all before it. Juneau caught Baxter's eyes with a knowing expression, and nodded very slightly.

"Blithering idiots, all of them!"

Baxter looked up at Juneau's angry explosion, surprised to hear his normally mild-mannered friend vent like that. The count threw down the telegram he had been reading. "I have received word from a cousin," he said bitterly. He didn't expand further and Baxter didn't ask — Juneau did not like to reference his family connections. "Apparently, our good Captain Nikolai Klado has finally convinced our illustrious leaders to assemble the scraps we left in the Baltic and dispatch anything that still floats as a third Pacific Squadron."

Baxter put his head back and sighed. He knew he should be angry as well, but he still felt physically drained and exhausted after his illness. Plus, Juneau was angry enough for the both of them. "They are sending those men to their deaths," he said simply. He didn't mention that their own ship — and he realised he had come to think of the *Yaroslavich* as his ship — would have been one of those dregs if it wasn't for her first officer's influence.

"Everyone knows that except, it seems, Klado and our superiors." The Russian sounded more bitter than Baxter had ever heard.

"When do they sail?"

Juneau's laugh was harsh. "They are already on their way. Cousin Alexander only just thought to mention it to me while providing news of my family."

That simple statement hid a depth of meaning. Russia, as far as anyone of them knew, was still gripped by unrest that bordered on bloody revolution — and Juneau's family would be caught right in the middle of it. It was easy not to think of such matters, trapped as they were in this odd sweltering half-life.

"Everyone is well?" Ekaterina asked from the other side of the breakfast table, her voice mild.

Baxter hid a smile. Just the sound of her voice excited him. She glanced at him, sensing his attention, and gave him a slight smile of her own. Juneau had been aboard ship a lot in the last couple of weeks. When Baxter didn't accompany him to provide his experience and expertise, he had spent many happy hours with Ekaterina.

Baxter didn't know what to make of her or this odd arrangement they had found themselves in; he knew he should feel guilty about stolen nights with his friend's wife, even if what Ekaterina had said was true. He was just — happier? — more content, perhaps? — than he had been for a very long time, and he clung to it with every ounce of his returning strength.

Juneau took a deep breath and a hold on his emotions. "All is well, and stability seems to be returning, just as it is here." His eyes were clouded — they all knew that stability in the Motherland would have been achieved more severely than it had been here.

"Rozhestvensky will not be happy," Baxter said thoughtfully, pushing away his plate. Pavel collected it, approval at the amount eaten evident. Maxim looked up from where he sprawled, panting, in the coolest part of the room, and then rested his head with a forlorn expression as he realised there would be no scraps right now.

"He has always been dead set against having a squadron of self-sinkers — he barely tolerates the *Yaroslavich* and others of her age. I have heard he has tried to resign at least once — I fear he will do something rash to try to avoid dear Nebagatov's reinforcements."

Ekaterina's expression had hardened as she thought. "This may offer us an opportunity," she said, and Baxter marvelled again at how completely she could shift. At one moment a refined lady of leisure, talking of family matters; the next a hard-headed woman determined, it seemed, to protect that family by any means necessary. Including putting herself into harm's way, pistol blazing.

Juneau cocked his head. He often deferred to his wife in these matters, and not just because she obviously knew more than a mere naval officer could. Baxter looked between the two of them. He knew Ekaterina, intimately, and yet in many ways she remained a mystery to him. He realised at that point that it might be vital for him to know more — for his own safety. To understand how that switch could happen and where this most unladylike expertise seemed to come from.

"How so?" Juneau asked when Ekaterina sank back in her chair, expression thoughtful.

"The admiral, it seems to me, will put to sea shortly," she said at last. "The Tsar has given him no option but to press on and try to secure a victory before he can be further hampered. Our friend aboard will almost certainly want to report any new movements to his superiors, and there are only so many ways that can be achieved."

"Only two, in fact!" Juneau said with a smile. "The local post office, or the telegraph office in Diego-Suarez."

"Indeed." Ekaterina's responding smile was predatory. "The latter being expensive, and difficult to get permission to use. The post office is therefore more likely. Luckily, I happen to have struck up a ... friendship with the postmaster's wife."

Baxter tried not to stare at her, his previous feelings evaporating in a chill of apprehension. When she spoke like this, he realised, she sounded not unlike Arbuthnott. She went on in that cold, bloodless manner. "Her husband, it seems, can be absentminded about his keys, so has developed a shocking habit of leaving a spare set with his wife. She, ah, shall we say prefers the company of ladies and has been starved of it, certainly within the class she thinks of herself. I just need some sort of excuse to get her to give me access to the post box before it is dispatched."

Baxter realised Juneau was as uncomfortable as he was with that proposition, and at the apparent lack of concern on Ekaterina's part. Then Baxter smiled. "The wife, she is French?"

Ekaterina nodded, with narrowed eyes. Baxter smiled, without much humour, aware of the reason why the idea had come to him.

"Well, the French do love a scandal. Tell her you're concerned one of the *Yaroslavich*'s officers is carrying on an affair with your … sister, shall we say?" It occurred to him that he had no idea what family she had, beyond her husband. There were certainly no children. "If the fleet is about to leave, our friend will no doubt want to communicate this to his paramour…"

Juneau frowned at Baxter, as though surprised that he should come up with something so underhanded, then shrugged. "It has merit," the Russian officer said, with a glance at Ekaterina.

"It could work." She pulled at her lower lip, an uncharacteristic gesture. "I should like more surety."

"I could watch the post office as well," Tommy piped up from the doorway. He'd finished breakfast some time ago — he ate ever greater amounts and faster — and they'd all thought he'd been off about his day. He was light on his feet, that one.

"One of these days, young Tommy," Baxter said with exaggerated patience, "your habit of turning up at just the right moment will get you into trouble…"

"Will get me into trouble, I ken." The boy slid onto a chair. "Who're we watching for?"

Ekaterina's eyes sparkled with amusement, her serious expression disappearing. "Well, Baxter, your country starts training its young men for war when they're barely older."

"To prepare them for when we're at war," Baxter growled. He realised he would have to accept that Tommy would get himself involved, no matter what he said, so it was better to know what he was up to. "But then, I suppose we *are* at war."

Ekaterina's eyes were a deep shade of green as she regarded him and for once he had an inkling of what she was thinking. Then she nodded. "Very well — let us make plans swiftly. We do not know how long we will tarry here."

CHAPTER 14

They had even less time than they'd expected. Vice-Admiral Rozhestvensky was indeed determined to be away before the obsolete and unsuitable ships of the 3rd Pacific Squadron could catch up to him, and he threw his newly recovered energy into making that happen.

The squadron had lingered almost two months trapped in Nosy Be – Nossibeisk, as the Russians had come to call it. It seemed Rozhestvensky, had had enough of his Tsar and his commanders prevaricating and changing his orders and the 2nd Pacific Squadron was thrown into preparations for departure. Boats hurried here and there between the ships. A number of deputations from the Hamburg-Amerika company were seen going aboard the flag, Rozhestvensky no doubt negotiating for continued fuelling.

Juneau's time was spent in preparing his ship — and it was clear to all that it was *his* ship now, not Gorchakov's — to sail. Which meant Baxter, Ekaterina and Tommy had the task of hunting the snake in their midst.

"Tommy doesn't cease to amaze me," Baxter said quietly as he escorted Ekaterina to the post office. They walked arm in arm, Ekaterina just close enough to his side to be decent.

"I don't know why, Baxter. He has many of your qualities." He actually found himself blushing at the unexpected compliment, and a small smile danced around her lips. "He has, however, not yet picked up any of your flaws."

The smile took away any possible sting from the words. The object of their discussion was nowhere to be seen, but they knew he was about as he'd summoned them.

182

Unbeknownst to any of them, Tommy had somehow developed something of a gang during the weeks of forced inactivity. It was composed primarily of local children, with some less well-to-do colonial offspring, and they had been watching the post office, noting the comings and goings of Russian officers. Tommy was well enough known by the *Yaroslavich*'s officers that he had to keep a low profile, but he'd been able to confirm two (Yefimov and Koenig) going in to send letters or packages, with another two that had been seen by Tommy's followers and tentatively identified. The office had been busy, to the point that it had run out of stamps at least once in the squadron's stay – there was no way to guarantee if any of them were, in fact, British agents.

"In all seriousness, Baxter, you are a leader of men — though you may not realise it. And Tommy has already learned a lot from you." She patted his arm. "Now, it is probably best that I go and see Madame Larousse by myself. We have a delicate matter to discuss. Why don't you peruse some stalls? I don't imagine I will be long."

Ekaterina was a while with the postmaster's wife; taking enough time in fact that Baxter was starting to feel more than a bit suspicious just hanging around the streets near the post office. It was one of a handful of brick-built buildings in the settlement that had leapt up around the harbour, up on the hill overlooking Passandava Bay.

It was quite a view from up there, overlooking the spread of warships – those familiar from the long weeks of the journey, others either of the formation that had come via the Suex Canal and had had a much easier journey of it, as well as a clutch of cruisers despatched from the Baltic after the bulk of the squadron was well on its way. He was so lost in the view that he didn't notice Ekaterina until she had taken his arm. She smiled up at him, slightly quizzically. "Sorry," he mumbled.

"You were deep in thought."

"Just enjoying the view," he said cheerfully, deliberately shaking off the dark mood that had threatened to overwhelm him at the thought of all these ships and men sailing towards destruction.

She had a certain glow of excitement about her, slightly flushed cheeks and a gleam in her eyes. "Any luck?"

"Well, it took some tears and a lot of persuasion, but Elaine — Madame Larousse to you, Mr Baxter — was persuaded to part with the keys so I could check the accumulated post for letters to my, ah, sister. Immodest or not. Mr Koenig is a dutiful son who sent a fulsome letter to his parents, in case he should not see them again. Lieutenant Yefimov merely sent a letter to his tailor with new measurements."

"Why the devil would someone send a message to their tailor from here, and it's not like the man has grown at all!"

"Indeed. Particularly when his tailor is, apparently, in Durban."

"Yefimov?" Juneau asked, astonishment clear in his eyes. "He has no love of the British."

"He *appears* to have no love, husband," Ekaterina corrected him. As usual, they were speaking English when they discussed such matters — their command of the language was better than Baxter's command of Russian, and they were less likely to be overheard by someone who could follow the conversation.

"He certainly has no love for you," Baxter pointed out.

Juneau looked slightly hurt by that. Though by no means a man who curried favour and affection from his subordinates, the Russian officer was also one who wanted to get along with everyone. "I had never…"

"Think about it, man," Baxter interrupted, voice harsher than he'd meant. "He's at least a decade older than you, and to give him his due, he's a perfectly competent officer. And there he is, an ageing lieutenant, and you're his superior. And while you're certainly a better officer and seaman, the reason you got that post and he didn't is because of an accident of birth."

Baxter realised he had risen, and the Juneaus were both eyeing him with some trepidation. He realised his blood was up, because suddenly he had seen himself in Yefimov, or at least what he could have ended up as. Perhaps being cashiered from the navy had saved him after all.

He forced himself to breathe out and sit back down. "He may not love the British, Juneau, and he may still love Russia — but like many he is perhaps unhappy with the current state of things."

"Are you sure you're not a revolutionary, Baxter?" Ekaterina said, her teasing tone breaking the tension that his fury had created.

He smiled. "I could very well have been, were I born in Russia."

She gave him a fleeting smile. "Accidents of birth."

There was a gentle knock at the door, and Pavel entered at Juneau's invitation. "The last of the chests is ready to go aboard, Graf," he said in his soft voice. He must have heard the raised voices, but gave no sign of it — ever the consummate servant. If anything, that made Baxter's rage boil again.

"Thank you, Pavel," Juneau said gently. "We will repair aboard immediately."

The steward withdrew as quiet as he had entered.

"We must make arrangements to put Pavel ashore before we reach dangerous waters," Juneau commented as an aside, then shook his head sadly and turned his attention back to the matter at hand. "We, of course, do not have any evidence that Yefimov has behaved in an ill way — not even the Guard Department would arrest a man on so little."

Baxter caught the slight edge of Juneau's tone and also the answering scowl from his wife. "Guard Department?" he asked.

Ekaterina looked slightly pained as Juneau opened his mouth, and he made a placating gesture. "Merely a branch of our police force," he said, his voice very careful. "Specifically charged with countering revolutionary activity and protecting the Royal family."

Baxter felt his lip trying to curl in disgust but managed to stop it. He hadn't had much contact with Britain's intelligence services, until Arbuthnott, but he didn't have much time for what Juneau had just described — a form of secret police. But, he reminded himself, it was a form of police charged in part with keeping Juneau and his family safe — he couldn't fault them for that.

"But you are right, husband — we cannot be sure it *is* him, let alone have charges brought against him," Ekaterina said as though the brief interruption had not happened. "We must observe him, and see if he is the guilty party."

"Indeed. There is, after all, little he will be able to do once we are back at sea — the admiral plans to sail into the deep ocean."

Baxter found himself yearning for that. As much as he had enjoyed the privacy being ashore had afforded him and Ekaterina, he could feel the pull of the sea, the simplicity of that life. The desire to wash away the grime and complication of life on land.

Juneau sighed, and nodded. He didn't look happy, but as usual he seemed content to take his wife's lead in these matters. Which, once again, made Baxter wonder who she actually was. "Well, we should go aboard. There is still much to be done and I suspect the admiral will give orders to weigh anchor sooner rather than later."

"You remember that storm, after the Cape?" Baxter said. He had to raise his voice over the wind that whipped around the quarter gallery, and foaming green water covered his boots as the *Yaroslavich* wallowed her way over another wave.

For as far as the eye could see, there was nothing but a procession of itinerant green-blue mountains that battered into the Russian ships. The squadron, only just reunited at Madagascar, was getting increasingly spread out as the storm descended on them. Baxter caught sight of one of the big battleships — he couldn't tell which — as she went through another wave. A plucky destroyer bobbed in her wake. The smaller ships' coal bunkers would never have sustained them across the Indian Ocean, and they were instead being towed. Baxter didn't envy the crews of the tiny vessels, hurled around as they would be by the coming weather; towing them wouldn't be much fun either, even for the big beasts. They were rearing so far out of the water as they crested waves that the red-painted undersides of the hulls could be seen, freshly scraped of clinging weed.

"How could I forget!" Juneau replied with a grin, bracing his feet apart with his foul weather gear flapping about him. "Why do you ask? I can assure you, I recognise that there is a storm brewing."

Baxter nodded to the darkening sky to the east with a grin. "That isn't a storm — that's a typhoon. It's going to get worse — a lot worse."

"You sound like you relish the prospect."

"What sailor doesn't enjoy a good blow?" Baxter asked, then shrugged. "Out here, my friend, there is only the sea. If you forget that, let yourself worry about other things, you will die. If you focus, trust yourself and your crew, you will live. I find it … liberating."

Juneau was silent, as though he realised quite how much it had taken Baxter to wring those words from himself. Then they both had to cling on to the rail as the cruiser started to crest the largest wave yet. "Well, I think that's my signal to join the captain on the bridge."

Baxter sniffed, looking again at the sky as the first drops of rain hit his face. "You'd best find me some oilskins as well. Get the feeling you're going to need me, and everyone else, before this breaks."

It was as bad as he'd feared, and worse. The typhoon tore down on them like the wrath of an ancient god, hammering into the Russian vessels as it tore up the ocean to ever-more towering heights. Most of the other ships were soon lost in the murk of lashing rain, occasionally glimpsed as terrifyingly fragile children's toys toiling up the sides of mountainous waves and then disappearing over the top.

Baxter had sailed these waters before, learning his trade under his father's tutelage on a sailing brig running up the east coast of Africa from Cape Town. He'd seen some foul weather then, but nothing to compare to this. As he reeled along the upper deck, clutching the lifelines strung fore and aft, he found himself grinning into the face of the storm. Rain stung his skin and the wind pulled at him, opening gaps in his oilskins so he was soon soaked to the skin. Footing on the planking was treacherous and the ship lurched sickeningly as she successfully crested a wave and everyone aboard lived for another few moments.

He pulled himself up the companionway, past the armoured wheelhouse and onto the open bridge. Juneau was braced against the fore railing, next to the speaking tubes that connected him with the wheelhouse and engine room — the two most vital parts of the ship in these seas. The first officer looked haggard and drawn — he'd barely left his post in the hours the typhoon had battered them, whereas Baxter and others had been able to get below to dry off and find something to eat. Even on a modern warship, the galley fires had to be out but Pavel and Lieutenant Koenig had between them contrived a makeshift galley in the blazing heat of the engine room. The repast provided wasn't anything to write home about, but it was hot and most importantly it came with an endless supply of tea. Baxter had never rated the Russian penchant for tarry teas, but he knew now that he'd never be able to live without it.

Of Captain Gorchakov, there had been no sign. Rumour had it he was laid out in his cabin, dead drunk or sick as a dog. Or both.

Baxter clapped Juneau on the shoulder, as much to let him know he was there as to indicate companionship. The Russian mustered a smile, leant close to shout in his ear. "How much longer must we endure this, do you think?"

Baxter shrugged. "No idea!" he roared back cheerfully. "Never seen it this bad!" He was fishing around in the pockets of the slightly too-small oilskins. They were Vasily's, so more or less broad enough for him but too short. With a grunt of triumph he managed to pulled out a thick sandwich, wrapped

189

in oilcloth, and a flask of tea. "The countess had Pavel whip this up. I added a dash of vodka to the tea."

Juneau's smile brightened briefly, then they both leaned forward and grabbed the polished rail. A wall of grey-green water towered above them, rearing up as though it would smash the ship like so much inconsequential flotsam, dashing away the lives held within. The cruiser's bows rose, up and up and up, until it felt like she was almost vertical, that she would tip over backwards, and Baxter had to admit to a thrill of fear, his stomach rising, then there was nothing but foam and green water threatening to engulf them as the ship teetered and then started to slide down the other side.

They breathed for another few moments.

"It's pure, basic seamanship," Juneau shouted, almost as though he was trying to reassure himself. "As long as the engines keep beating and we keep our bows to the oncoming waves, we *will* ride this out!"

"That's the spirit!" Baxter shouted back. He was about to ask where he was needed, but an apparition appeared on the bridge — as though summoned by Juneau's confident words.

It was Yefimov, his face pale with a terror Baxter hadn't thought to see there. He didn't have his foul weather gear on and his uniform clung to his gaunt frame. He looked frantic as he clawed his way along a lifeline. Juneau went to meet him, moving away from Baxter, and his panicking deputy shouted something, his words whipped away by the wind. Baxter knew it could be nothing good, from the man's expression and the way Juneau's mouth dropped open.

Juneau waved Lieutenant Koenig over, shouted in his ear and then gestured for Yefimov and Baxter to follow him. They left the young officer in temporary command and retreated to the brief shelter of the wheelhouse that lay below the bridge.

Vasily Ivanovitch was there, to lend his massive strength to the quartermaster at the wheel. It was an enclosed, armoured space, but even with the shutters up the noise of the wind was barely diminished. "Speak," Juneau almost spat at his subordinate.

"But this is best not overheard…"

"The enlisted men do not speak French," Juneau said coldly, glossing over what Yefimov actually meant. The older man swallowed, tugged at his beard in a nervous gesture.

"I regret to report, Graf, that it has come to my attention that … we … did not catch all of the revolutionaries aboard." That last bit came out in a rush. "And I believe one or more of them has sabotaged the engines."

Baxter stared hard at Yefimov, trying to gauge him.

"I'm sure a common stoker would not know how to sabotage the engines that badly," Juneau said dismissively, then broke off as he saw their informant's expression.

"I am … given to understand that he is an engineer's mate," Yefimov went on, sounding sick. "The problem with educating the peasants, Graf…" This was said with a wan smile that Baxter wanted to wipe off his face with the back of his hand. He wanted to grab the weaselly officer by the front of his shirt and shake the truth out of him. Even in these desperate circumstances, Yefimov was trying to preserve the fiction that he had just stumbled onto this information.

Juneau's eyes widened as he understood the implications. "If we lose power now, we're all dead! Our mutineers are committing suicide!"

Yefimov nodded unhappily. "It seems this is their intention, as they believe themselves to be dead men anyway." There was a flash of anger in his eyes. "They intend to take some aristocrats with them." He swallowed hard, obviously aware that he had perhaps said too much. He clearly wasn't committed to the cause — not to the point of dying, anyway — but he certainly harboured resentment against the established order. Baxter could almost sympathise, if he wasn't such an obvious idiot who had thrown in with Arbuthnott and whomever backed him.

"Well, we must of course stop them," Juneau declared.

"I fear the sabotage has already been undertaken," Yefimov said, his quiet voice miserable. "I did not find out about it until…"

Baxter loomed over him, struggling to control his temper and to hold back from smashing the man against the side of the wheelhouse until either his bones or the metal structure gave. "What have they done?" he snarled, his own voice quiet but filled with menace.

"I do not understand such matters," Yefimov snapped with a touch of his previous hostility.

"And that's the problem with the officer classes in most navies," Baxter rumbled. He gathered a double fistful of Yefimov's sodden uniform jacket, not hurriedly, and then lifted him from the deck with no apparent effort. From the corner of his eye he saw Vasily stir and then subside at Juneau's gesture. "Tell me what you know, you little prick."

Yefimov's brief defiance crumbled. "I believe they have sabotaged the oiling system for the shaft…"

Baxter didn't need to hear more. He dropped Yefimov so suddenly the man collapsed in a wet pile on the deck, spun to Juneau. Engineering wasn't his province but he knew enough to understand how dangerous that was. Juneau clearly knew less, but the look on Baxter's face spurred him to action. He dashed to the wheelhouse's speaking tube and shouted a series of terse questions down it.

A strained silence settled over the cramped space. Baxter positioned himself between the hatch and the traitorous officer in case he had some idea about bolting. Juneau stared fixedly at the speaking tubes, as though willing the chief engineer to respond that everything was fine.

He didn't even want to think what it must be like in the engine room right now, deep below the waterline. Even there they would be feeling the pitch and heave of the ship, and while they were insulated from the wind and the rain the noise and heat would be horrendous as the massive steam engines laboured away at full power.

Juneau lunged his head forward to listen to the engine room's report, barked a response. Baxter couldn't hear what was being said but Juneau's expression told him everything. "It seems Yefimov's intelligence is accurate," Juneau said, managing to muster a certain amount of sarcasm despite the situation becoming even more desperate. "On inspection, the drive shafts are overheating — they are minutes away from having fused entirely, it seems."

"What are we to do?" Yefimov almost wailed from the deck. His jaw snapped shut at Baxter's glance.

"I have ordered revolutions reduced, but that will only give us a little more time. It is impossible to know how much more."

Juneau chewed his lip. Baxter could well understand his conundrum. A ship not making at least some headway and able to keep her bows into the waves was dead. In this storm, there would be no rescue even if anyone survived.

The ship lurched, and Baxter stepped up to throw his strength into the wheel along with Vasily and the two quartermasters. The four of them strained against the natural tendency to turn away from the rising water, and managed to keep her bow on. At least here, with the shutters up, they didn't have to look at what Mother Nature was throwing at them — they just had to follow the orders shouted down from the open bridge.

Juneau was snapping orders for more men to be sent to the wheelhouse. As Baxter had just discovered, it was enormously taxing work. With no end to the storm in sight and conditions on the ship worsening the helmsmen would need to work in shifts. That would only help, though, if they were under power…

"You still have masts, old chap," he heard himself saying, and was surprised at how nonchalant and calm he felt. "I assume they have sails."

Juneau blinked at him. The *Yaroslavich* was, indeed, one of that peculiar breed of ships — a steam ship with an auxiliary sailing rig, albeit not the full hamper she'd been built with thirty years ago.

Understanding came into Juneau's eyes, and trepidation. They both knew the crews had barely trained on the masts and yards, let alone gone through any kind of arduous drill until working them became second nature.

They didn't have any other choice though.

"I will need your help," Juneau said simply.

"You'll have it. I have no desire to die on this bloody ship."

CHAPTER 15

It was verging on complete chaos on deck as the officers, such as could be dragged from their cabins, tried to martial the crew that had been unwillingly driven topside. Men ran back and forth, driven by petty officers — some of whom at least were old enough to have done this before. Baxter threw in where he could, but he rapidly discovered a significant problem with his command of Russian.

"Up the ratlines!" he bellowed to a parcel of sailors who were milling about uncertainly. "The sails, you dolts!" He knew his rage stemmed from frustration at himself. He gestured at the masts, but the men were so overcome by the heave and pitch of the ship, the incredible noise of the wind and rain, that they merely stared at him blankly if they met his gaze at all. Juneau was on deck with him, leaving Koenig in charge on the bridge, but was having little more success.

"The trick is just to get a scrap of sail up," he roared in Juneau's ear. "Anything more and it'll carry away and we're fucked!"

"The trick is to get it up quickly — the chief engineer tells me the shafts are on the verge of seizing entirely and we will have to stop revolutions in about a minute!"

It was rapidly becoming clear that this wasn't going to be a quick operation. The bluejackets didn't understand how much depended on them getting this done and were baulking at clambering up the ratlines, despite the threat of violence from burly petty officers. The handful of, for the most part, junior officers who were on deck weren't much better.

"Even if we save the ship, men are going to die," Baxter muttered darkly. And saving the ship was looking increasingly unlikely.

He turned, stared aft. The situation around the mizzen and after masts were no better than the foremast. Turned for'ard again in time to see a man get smashed off the ratlines into one of the light guns and fall limply; those coming after him shying away from their duty. The next wave was building beneath them, the peak rearing above. It was, of course, the biggest yet.

"Right. Not having this." Baxter grabbed Juneau's shoulder. "Send everyone to the foremast! We'll get something there and that might get us over!"

Without waiting for an acknowledgement, he strode forwards. He wanted nothing more than to grab onto a lifeline, but he knew he had to show complete confidence, total competence, now.

There was no point trying to shout orders or encouragement to the men who huddled miserably in any shelter they could find. He couldn't blame them for their unwillingness to go aloft and try to carry out unfamiliar tasks in the worst conditions imaginable. They didn't know that the steady, thumping heartbeat of the engines he could just feel through his boots was about to stop, or that when it stopped they were all dead men if they couldn't manage this task.

Without hesitation, he grabbed onto the ratlines and swung himself out. Water raced past under his back as the cruiser heeled and he didn't let himself think about that, or what a misplaced hand or foot would lead to. He climbed doggedly, the wind dragging at his oilskins and trying to snatch him away from the flimsy safety of the ropes. He didn't look down, didn't give any indication he was interested if anyone was following him. Hand over hand, one foot at a time, knowing they were running out of time but that if he hurried he would fall and drown. His muscles burned and limbs shook from the cold — it appeared that he hadn't fully recovered his strength after the fever. He couldn't pause, though.

"Tommy better not bloody show up," he growled, and found himself throwing his head back to laugh his defiance at the racing clouds and rain.

Up and up, until he came to the crosstrees. He allowed himself a moment to pause and breathe, try to recover his strength. He allowed himself to look down for the first time, and picked out Juneau back at his station on the bridge. Even at that distance, he could read his friend's expression.

The engines had been shut down.

But below him, strung out along the rope ladders that led to the crosstrees, a line of bluejackets struggled up towards him. He would only admit it to himself later, but an extraordinary sense of relief shot through him when he saw those resolute faces turned up towards him. Vasily was there at the front, and Lieutenant Koenig just behind him. Relief, and a towering pride.

He looped an arm around a rope and pushed them past him out onto the yard, doing what he could to send the lighter men out to the extremes. He yelled simple instructions into the face of each as they reached him. Koenig needed no encouragement, gamely clambering past him. Now they just had to hope that the rarely-used or inspected ropes and the canvas that had spent most of its life furled had not rotted through...

The ship had lost way entirely as Baxter fumbled his way out onto the yard last of all. The mountain of water was right on them and, without the great brass screws turning to drive them forward, her bow had started to fall off. So little time...

He didn't think about it, just shoved his feet securely into the loops of rope that hung below the thick wood. Here, close to the mast, was bad enough — the lighter men further out were being tossed about and subject to wild gyrations as the mast swung with the ship's roll. He knew that shaking and now frozen hands wouldn't be able to undo lashings that had been tied for years. Instead, he fished out the clasp knife Vasily had given him. He almost dropped it as, with numb fingers, he struggled to open the folding blade. Those nearest to him caught the idea and started pulling their own knives — even in this modern age, a working blade was still vital equipment for anyone at sea. He gave it a moment to allow the idea to spread all the way along the mast — there was no shouting of orders in this wind — and brought the keen edge down on his lashings. The steel sliced straight through with a minimum of sawing and wet canvas battered against his legs as the sail let go.

Ideally they would have released at the same time, allowing the sail to belly out and draw, but co-ordination had been impossible and the canvas sagged and flapped, threatening to flog itself to pieces against the mast. The wind that pounded them was strong enough that they couldn't carry anything more than a storm reef, but that hadn't been heeded by everyone. There followed a scramble to even things out, the sailors somehow interpreting his wild hand gestures.

We're too late, he thought. The cruiser was heeled right over and there was only the Indian Ocean beneath his boots. There was nothing he could do as one of the bluejackets slipped and fell, his scream torn away by the wind. No time to worry about that now. All he could do was hang on to the yard. At least if the ship did broach to, the impact would probably kill him outright...

But the sail was drawing now, the fall of canvas evened out, and even the scrap they had loosed was enough to put a little bit of headway on the cruiser. He caught a glimpse of Juneau yelling into his speaking tube and the cruiser turned, turned, turned, slowly at first and then with increasing speed. She staggered as she reached the crest of the wave at an oblique angle, hung there, teetering.

And then a great cheer went up as, almost peacefully, she started to slide down the far side.

That sail, hurriedly handled and having been furled on the yard for so long, gave not long after the cruiser had survived the enormous wave. More sails were being shaken loose on the other masts, though, reefed almost to the point of being tablecloths but providing just enough draw to keep the cruiser ploughing onwards. They lost four in the end, the abused canvas splitting in the wind, but they couldn't bend any replacements from the paltry sailmakers' store, and they had to make do with the others. The crew worked itself to the point of exhaustion, and beyond, in the following hours. Juneau had to be carried below having passed out at his station. Despite not being an officer, Baxter stood a watch until he couldn't stand anymore — Juneau, returning to the bridge, had had to order Vasily to manhandle him below.

Once the sails were rigged, and the hands were in the discipline of handling them, Baxter had no doubt they would survive. Crisis, it seemed, was an excellent way of bringing a crew together. At some point, after Juneau ordered him below, he slept. He didn't know for how long — night and day had become moot concepts in the endless twilight of the typhoon — but he awoke to a gentler motion. He lay in his cot for a while, the clothes he'd fallen into bed in stiff with dried-in salt, and contemplated not emerging for another few hours. Some residual sense of duty, though, made him drag his stiff limbs up onto deck.

He emerged, bleary-eyed and blinking, into watery sunlight and broken clouds scudding overhead. The sea was unhappy, short and choppy with white caps, but gone were the gargantuan waves of the last few hours. He could just make out a few other ships in the distance, their plumes of smoke being whipped away by the still-stiff breeze. The *Yaroslavich* was still under sail, the reefs shaken out, and the sight of those great arcs of canvas stiff in the breeze stirred something deep within him.

"Ah, Mr Baxter," Ekaterina said. "Awake at last, I see."

He turned slowly and regarded her with a bemused look and a slightly raised eyebrow. There was a twinkle of amusement in her eyes and a small smile played about her lips. He wanted nothing more than to put his arms around her, crush her against him, feel her strong frame move. Really wouldn't be the done thing, though.

"Indeed, Countess," he replied, matching her tone. "Did you sleep well? I trust the slight roughness didn't disturb you?"

Her eyes were shadowed with fatigue, he noticed, and there was dried blood on her skirt. He knew she had been at work in the sickbay for much of the storm, helping to tend the inevitable cuts and abrasions, not to mention broken bones and dislocated joints.

"I slept tolerably well, thank you," she said, the smile spreading into an enormous grin. A moment later, they were both almost doubled up with the almost hysterical laughter that came with relief, with the sense that they had dodged death. Again.

They drew a few bemused and indeed concerned looks from the sailors who were moving listlessly around the deck, and that brought back some semblance of calm.

"Did we lose anyone?" he asked once he had recovered his breath. "Aside from the poor sod who fell from the mast?"

Her own expression became serious. "No, God be praised. Many injuries, and the doctor does worry about one or two — but no other dead."

"It seems miracles never cease," he said, leaning his forearms on the oak rail and staring out to sea. There was always an odd quality to the air and the light after a big storm, matching his mixed sense of fatigue and relief. But, now the danger of the typhoon had passed, other pressing matters bubbled up in his mind. "Juneau has told you who warned us about the sabotage?" he asked quietly, having glanced about to make sure that no one he knew spoke English was within earshot.

She nodded. "This, more or less, confirms our suspicions," she replied in the same low tone.

"The question now, is — what can we do about it?"

She shrugged. "Inform the captain and have him arrested," she said in a tone so nonchalant he was taken completely aback.

"Who *are* you?" he blurted. "Truthfully?"

She just gave him one of her enigmatic smiles. "You should, perhaps, change your clothes," was all she said in reply.

He sighed and shrugged, once again resigned to never knowing the truth of her. "As you require," he said, bowing and turning to head below decks.

"And Mr Baxter? Perhaps a bath?"

"Captain Gorchakov," Juneau said, his voice carefully neutral, "will not hear of it, countenance it, or agree to take any action upon it."

The three of them were taking tea in the small receiving room attached to Juneau's cabin. The space should have belonged to a junior officer, but apparently his influence knew no bounds and it had been the simplest task for the ship's carpenter to turn it into a well-appointed sitting room. Baxter did not ask where the officer who should have occupied the cabin was berthed.

It felt odd to him, taking his ease in the Juneaus inner sanctum. The feeling had never struck him when they had shared a villa those long weeks in Madagascar, but while Pavel had tried to make the cabin feel spacious it still felt very … intimate. He hadn't been here since the day he'd first stumbled upon Ekaterina, which felt like a year or more ago.

"He feels that any suggestion of dishonesty, corruption or, indeed, treason about one of his officers can only reflect ill upon the personage making the accusation and that, unless actual evidence can be brought forward, Mr Yefimov should be given the courtesy of being treated with the same respect any other officer is due."

Silence fell. Baxter sipped the tea in his bone china cup, relishing the strong, smoky flavour. "Yefimov wouldn't be a protégé of the captain's, would he?" he asked at last.

Juneau smiled briefly. "He would. Indeed, I have been given to understand he would have been the first officer under him if I had not been appointed."

"And, of course, as we are giving him the respect due any officer, I am sure we are prevented from making a search of his quarters," Ekaterina said, her voice tart.

Juneau dropped into the free chair. "You are quite correct," he said, then tilted his head back. "Though I suspect the cur has learned his lesson and we will have heard the last of his machinations. His, how do you say, cat's paws having shown themselves to be dangerously unreliable, he would be wise to keep his head down."

"I wouldn't be too sure," Baxter said thoughtfully, turning his mind to his own interaction with Arbuthnott. "As the Scottish play would have it, he's waded in blood so deep, it's nearer to go over. Or somesuch."

Both of his companions regarded him with some surprise, though he could not be sure if it was because he knew Shakespeare or because they did not and had no idea what he was talking about. "He'll certainly want to get off this ship as soon as he can," he soldiered on doggedly.

"That much is true. His occasional bluster aside, it is clear he is disillusioned with this mission and does not want to throw his life away — particularly for a service that has ill-treated him."

It was Baxter's turn to be surprised at Juneau's frank assessment. "Everyone aboard should be disillusioned," he said. "We all know Port Arthur is fallen and the First Squadron is no more. The mission is over."

"It has changed only," Ekaterina said sharply. "We will fight through to Vladivostok and strike back from there."

Baxter exchanged a glance with Juneau. It seemed he had not yet told his wife of the intention to put her ashore at Singapore or some other neutral port. It was also a relief to him that she apparently knew little about the realities of naval warfare — he'd become a little worried about the extent of her expertise.

"Well, these are matters for the admirals," Juneau said, slightly uncomfortable. "Let us turn our minds back to the problems at hand. Whether or not our friend sensibly keeps his head down or not, he has been involved in a number of attempts on both mine and my wife's life, not to mention putting my ship at risk. I will not stand for that."

"And there are the remains of the revolutionary cell aboard," said Ekaterina, as though the risk to her own life was of little importance. "Our friend has, ah, not been able to furnish us with their names."

"I'm sure that's because he doesn't know them, not because they will be able to identify him as their controller," Baxter said sourly.

"Indeed," Juneau said, taking a swallow of tea and then peering into the depths of his cup. "I feel something stronger may be required," he said, reaching for the decanter himself rather than ringing for Pavel.

"I thought you'd never ask," Baxter said.

"It will be difficult to interrogate the engine room staff without causing a great deal of ill will, of course," Juneau said out of nowhere, once they had drinks in hand. "Particularly while repairs to the engine are on-going."

The cruiser was still under sail, and even in the light airs that had followed the typhoon she was more or less keeping pace with the rest of the squadron as it coalesced out of the great emptiness of the Indian Ocean. A number of the ships had been damaged and they clustered around the overworked *Kamchatka* and the other repair ships.

Juneau had ordered a reduction of revolutions to zero not a moment too soon — while no permanent damage had been done, repairs to the overheated shafts were required, and the damage to the oiling system had to be made good.

"With any luck the wind will have come out of their sails," Baxter said.

"Which is not to say that they shouldn't be rooted out and shot," Ekaterina said, her voice taking on a flat, hard edge that chilled him.

"Yes, well. Yefimov, however, is perhaps more of a threat in the long term." Baxter looked between Juneau and Ekaterina — husband and wife, one his friend and one, perhaps, his lover. It was hard to say. A smile spread over his face. "What do you say to a bit of a *ruse de guerre?*"

The days stretched out, feeling as long as the horizon was far, as the battered Russian ships made their slow way across the Indian Ocean. The typhoon had claimed lives but, miraculously, no ships. In the aftermath of its fury the seas were relatively placid. Out of sight of land and with barely a scrap of cloud in the sky, the crews basked in the warmth and relative peace when they weren't called upon for the feast of coal or other more mundane tasks.

Men fished from the *Yaroslavich*'s side when they were able to take their leisure, or watched the albatrosses that turned overhead, the only other living things moving above the water. On the surface, at least, everything was calm. Peaceful, even, a far cry from their warlike purpose. Huge sharks drifted in the squadron's wake, setting upon anything that was thrown overboard.

Baxter could feel a tension on board, though. Rumour of the attempted sabotage had spread through the ship, not quite as fast as wildfire but just as dangerous. While some may have been sympathetic to the revolutionaries before, that had changed with the attempt to send them all to the bottom and now the bluejackets regarded each other — and particularly the engine room crew — with some suspicion.

It was reflected, to an extent, in the wardroom. They'd managed to keep their suspicions of Yefimov under wraps, but the other officers had picked up that the tension between Juneau and his immediate subordinate was coming to a head. Sadly, they had split along lines of loyalty, with most of the cadre of older officers aligning with Yefimov and, by extension, the captain, while the younger officers supported Juneau.

"It seems word had got out that I attempted to have our friend removed," Juneau commented. "And that has turned some, including Dr Andropov, against me even if they were not aligned with him to begin with. It's not the, how do you say, 'done thing'?"

"And, of course, the reason for you taking that extreme step is not known."

"No — Captain Gorchakov would not hear of it, just as he would not hear of any actual investigation."

"He can't admit he's backed a wrong 'un. We're going to have to prove it."

"Indeed. If only we could come up with a suitable gambit," Juneau said, his voice tired and frustrated.

Somewhere over the horizon and creeping closer every day was the British colony of Singapore, and not far beyond that waited Japan and her navy. Port Arthur, Russia's hope for a year-round blue-water port and the squadron's goal, now lay in enemy hands, and safe haven lay much further north, at Vladivostok.

All that was the future, though, and seemed almost inconsequential. All it did was set a time limit on the task at hand, to bring down Yefimov and his revolutionary collaborators before they could do more harm.

"In the way of things, the sailors will know or at least suspect who the saboteurs are," Baxter said after further reflection, not lifting his eyes from the wake that ran, straight as an arrow, behind them. "It's entirely possible they will take matters into their own hands."

Juneau shrugged uncomfortably. "It is not unheard of, and while it may rid us of one problem, the effect on discipline and morale would be … undesirable. And that's assuming they even deal with the right people."

"Oh, indeed." Baxter swallowed the last of his pre-dinner drink. "Shall we go in?"

The wardroom was full that evening as the cruiser made her slow way north and east. It was a bubble of light and sound and jollity in the gathering darkness. It felt divorced, insulated, from the concerns of the ship and the wider formation, just as the squadron was isolated from the upheavals back home. They drank cheerfully and copiously, ate well, and celebrated the fact they had survived everything the storm-tossed ocean had thrown at them and would soon come to grips with the enemy.

"Assuming we get that far, of course," Koenig declared cheerily. The young man was flushed with drink and high spirits, perhaps a little too much of both.

"Whatever do you mean, Mr Koenig?" Ekaterina asked from where she held court at one end of the long mahogany table.

Koenig blinked at her as though trying to clear his vision. "Why, the rumours are everywhere in the fleet. The British, it is said, will sail out from Singapore and Hong Kong and bring us to battle. At the very least they will, once again, support Japanese torpedo boats from those ports."

Yefimov raised his gaze from his plate. He had barely spoken all evening, to the point of insolence with Juneau, and ate mechanically.

"Poppycock," Baxter snapped before he could stop himself. "There were no torpedo boats in the North Sea, nor did the suicide schooners appear off the coast of Africa."

"And even if they did," Juneau said, "we have more than enough force to defend ourselves successfully."

Baxter was slightly taken aback by his friend's sudden enthusiasm for fighting the Royal Navy. He was also puzzled by his own reaction to the statement — he owed his old service little and certainly no loyalty, but he could not let that lie; felt a flicker of choler. "Even with the bulk of the fleet in home waters," he said, slowly and carefully, trying to inject a note of friendly rivalry into his voice, "what is left out here is, I'm sure, more than a match for this ... collection of ships."

Uproar greeted that pronouncement, some of it angry, some taking it in good part. Yefimov was staring at him, an odd look of calculation in his eyes.

"Well, it is moot of course," Ekaterina said, her voice carrying easily through the hubbub. "We are painted ships on a painted sea, and none know where we are. We will be past Singapore and Hong Kong before any ambush can be organised, I am quite sure."

"Well, this is true enough," Baxter commented gruffly, and raised his glass to her. "Indeed, I am sure we will slip past the Japanese islands just as easily." He was careful, despite his irritation, not to hint at the plan he and Juneau agreed that some of them at least would be going ashore before they reached the Sea of Japan.

"This is not what we want though!" Koenig protested hotly. "We must bring all to battle!"

A slightly embarrassed pause followed the outburst. "I think Mr Koenig has had slightly too much wine," Juneau said after a moment. Baxter suddenly got the feeling a game was being played here, from the way the first officer's voice teetered between disapproval and humorous indulgence.

The moment passed, Koenig apologised profusely to much laughter, and the dinner progressed as the ship sailed on into the night. Baxter felt his humour improving as the wine and vodka flowed, though he could not shake the feeling Yefimov was watching, carefully. He might even say balefully.

"Well, I think that went rather well," Juneau said genially as the door to his cabin swung shut.

"It was a pleasant enough dinner," Baxter said, trying to keep any sourness out of his voice. That was made harder by the fact that both count and countess were trying to suppress enormous grins and failing. "What are you two playing at?" he snapped.

His anger broke the dam of their self-control and they both broke down in laughter, Ekaterina falling into a chair and Juneau doubling up and clutching his midriff. "I am indeed sorry, my friend," Juneau said as he regained his breath. He took off his spectacles to wipe his eyes. "Our little piece of theatre there would not have worked if you were in on it."

"No offense, Baxter," Ekaterina said. "You have many virtues, but we both felt acting is not one of them."

He felt himself flush, but their humour was infectious and he felt the tide of anger subside. "Can I assume some devious plan has been set in motion to trap our friend?"

Ekaterina's eyes sparkled, but there was a hard edge to the humour. "You can, Baxter. You can indeed."

CHAPTER 16

"He hasn't fallen for it," Ekaterina fretted.

Baxter glanced at her, surprised to hear a note of frustration and concern in her voice. Of all of them, she seemed to be the most unflappable. "He will," he said, unsure if he was as confident as he sounded or just wanted to be. "This is too good and opportunity for him to complete his mission. Even if he had given up hope on it, this will rouse him from that."

She chewed her lower lip briefly. "He may choose to, what is it you say, keep his head down?"

He was beginning to notice that when she was agitated or concerned, her English broke down very slightly. He wanted to put his arms around her, hold her, reassure her. But even putting a hand on her shoulder, while they stood on the stern gallery, would not have been appropriate. Instead he shrugged. "Sometimes plans don't work, no matter how careful you are. If he is intent on survival at this point, on avoiding notice, he will make no further sabotage attempts — and that, in itself, is no bad thing."

"We need him to tell us who the remaining mutineers are!" she snapped, voice rising a bit too far.

"And we will find another way to identify them if we have to," he said, making a slightly placating gesture with his hand.

"Given what Yefimov has done to you, personally, I find myself surprised by your pragmatism."

He shrugged, slightly uncomfortably. "Well, I'm used to people who have crossed me not getting their just desserts — they don't always deserve 'em either. And it's like I said before — we sailors are a pragmatic bunch. Sometimes things don't go the way you may want them to. Instead of railing against it, you just have to change your course."

She took a deep breath, hands locked around the gleaming polished wood of the railing. Her fingers were long, but not delicate — he knew from personal experience how strong her grip was. "You are right, of course," she said in a small voice, and the look she gave him spoke volumes. Of her understanding, that she was of a class and station that could never fully appreciate the notion of *not* being able to exact retribution for slight or injustice if they chose.

The gulf between them had rarely felt as wide as it did at that moment.

He broke the spell with a grin. "Of course, I'm sure Vasily and I, if we cornered the man, could get him singing."

She smiled, but it was one tinged with the memory of what he'd done the night of the mutiny. The way he'd killed a man with his bare hands. "Thank you for the offer, Baxter, but I fear our friend must be caught red-handed."

He bowed, his expression grave. "Of course, your Serenity," he said with mock-seriousness, and her smile widened as he used the correct form of address for a Russian Countess.

There was a shout from the masthead, dimly heard over the churn of the screws only a few yards below their feet. The excitement was clear, though.

Land had been sighted.

They left the Malay peninsula, a dull, low, sullen landmass, in their wake two days later. The only settlement of size was, of course, Singapore, and that was British. There could be no safe haven for the squadron there, not even an opportunity to hove-to beyond territorial waters to take on coal.

There had certainly been no sallies of naval vessels, British or Japanese, or any suicide attacks by torpedo boats based there. The squadron had barely seemed to be noticed as it chugged slowly past, towing its cape of coal smoke with it. It was as though they had been forgotten about by the world at large; that disappearing into the vast stretch of empty seas had been tantamount to falling from the face of the world.

"Hong Kong, then," Baxter said quietly to Juneau. They had convened in his cabin, just the two of them.

"Both to deal with our friend, and for you all to go ashore," Juneau said, his voice glum.

Baxter shared the feeling that they were an odd little family, had been since Madagascar, and Hong Kong would be where they would part ways. "Singapore would have been my preference," he said gruffly. "But I could not, in good conscience, leave a job half finished."

He knew that was a lie — he'd left plenty of things unfinished in his twenty and some years on the face of the Earth. His career in the RN, for one, and everything he had drifted between since. Yes, there had been external forces at work — but he realised there were times he could have stood his ground but had chosen to walk away.

It was a startling realisation, brought about by an acknowledgement that he had come this far not because it was something to be doing. Not just because of how he had come to feel about Ekaterina, his friendship with Juneau and some of the other Russians. It was time he saw something through, and putting a stop to Yefimov's skulduggery had become that thing. And through thwarting Yefimov, putting one in Arbuthnott's eye.

"Well, the point of decision will be soon, I feel," Juneau said, his voice only slightly less morose. "Our friend will have to make his move, if he wants to take advantage of this intelligence. Beyond that — well, then we are on course for the Sea of Japan and anything else he does is moot."

There was a gentle tap at the hatch to the cabin, and the two men exchanged glances. Some shared instinct told them that their quarry knew the same thing.

Tommy's faced appeared around the hatch at Baxter's summons, an excited grin on his face. "'E's on the move, yer 'onours, and her ladyship thinks 'e's making an attempt to contact the shadow."

The look of shared understanding became shared purpose and they rose. For some days now, a merchantman flying a Swedish flag had been following a parallel course to the squadron's, closer inshore. Just keeping the Russian ships in sight, while remaining close enough to friendly ports to escape interference.

It could have been a perfectly innocent ship, a merchantman going about honest business. There was just something about her, though, about the way she was behaving, that made them all think that she was up to something. She didn't even look Swedish.

Baxter reached into the locker next to his cot and pulled out the service revolver Juneau had entrusted him with. He knew exactly how much of a gesture of good faith that had been.

He offered it grip-first to the Russian. "You're better with this than I am."

Juneau took it without demure — he'd seen what the bigger man could do with his fists. "Well then, let's see what he's about, shall we?"

"It astonishes me," Baxter commented as they moved through the decks, following Tommy's eager lead, "that the countess has such an instinct for such things. Even I find myself following her instructions with little question."

"She is an astonishing woman," Juneau said with a slight, knowing smile.

Baxter had a sudden flash of insight. "It's very … unusual for the security police to employ women," he said casually.

"Only the one woman, as far as I know," Juneau said. "It helps, of course, that she is an aristocrat, though I doubt not being of high birth would ever had held her back." He stopped and turned to Baxter with a wan smile, laying a hand on his arm. "I have said too much. I would be obliged if you did not mention that to anyone."

Baxter grinned. "Least of all your wife."

Tommy turned to glare at them. "Would you two hod your chattering?" he snapped, taking both of them aback. "We're almost there." The lad gave them another hard look, and then led them round a turn to where Ekaterina was waiting, standing almost casually by one of the hatches from the superstructure onto the upper deck.

"He is in climbing up to the rear watch post," she said, keeping her voice low but not indulging in melodramatic whispering. "I believe he has an electric torch."

It was one of two options they'd considered. He would either try to steal a boat and make for a friendly shore; or the merchantman was in fact a shadow and he would attempt to signal her. Using one of the lamps mounted on the bridge wings would have been too obvious. "We must move immediately. Come, Tommy."

Baxter regarded her with new eyes, now that her husband had confirmed what she was. He had to admit, he would have found the whole notion absurd if it wasn't for her obvious capability and almost unconsciously commanding attitude.

She disappeared back the way they'd come, Tommy in tow. They didn't need to discuss a plan — unlike the mad dash to the ship to head off the mutiny, they'd had time to consider this and had guessed correctly what Yefimov's approach would be. Baxter and Juneau headed up on deck.

Baxter squinted up into the darkness. He'd spent a lot of time up those masts during the typhoon, and while he didn't normally mind heights, he didn't feel enamoured with the idea of going up again so soon. It had to be done, though, and done quickly. He could see a faint shimmer, light against the hazy dimness of the night, that must be Yefimov finally dragging himself onto the platform two thirds of the way up the mast.

He didn't even ask Juneau who should go up, just started scrambling up the lines. He went fast, hand over hand, driving up with his legs. He had to be fast, but he had to be quiet as well. Yefimov had some complicated information to communicate – much of it false – but it wouldn't take him all night.

He could hear the fellow muttering to himself as he finally managed to get himself settled. It was quiet enough up here, tens of feet over the deck and with barely any breeze, that he could hear the sound of a notebook being thumbed through.

Baxter paused below the platform, in a bit of a quandary. He knew he had the advantage of size and speed, and the fact he was comfortable working at this height. Yefimov had been conspicuously absent during the mad scramble up the masts in the storm. The traitorous bastard might have a pistol, though, and be prepared to use it. Baxter would be very vulnerable as he came up through the hatch in the underside of the platform.

He smiled grimly. There was a reason seasoned sailors in the RN had disparaged that easy route as 'the lubber's hole'. Moving fast so he didn't have time to second-guess himself, and relying only on his arms, briefly he swung himself out from the rope ladder and swarmed up through the rigging, Went out, using the ship's slight roll to give himself momentum, and swung up over the watch post's wooden bulwark. Almost missed a handhold right at the end, but didn't let himself think about that as he landed lightly on the platform, next to the unconscious body of the lookout.

He needn't have bothered risking his neck like that. Yefimov was facing in the opposite direction, back towards the land, and was muttering to himself as he glared down into the bulb of the torch he was holding. Baxter caught something about the device's parentage as he crept forward, covering the scant feet between the two of them. Yefimov hit the thing on the side, then swore copiously as it flickered into life, beaming straight into his eyes and almost dropped the thing.

Baxter could have laughed at the utter farcical incompetence of the whole situation.

"You've really not thought this through, have you?" he said softly, when he was standing right behind Yefimov.

Yefimov, already dazzled, jumped in surprise, spun round to blink up at Baxter. "What is the meaning of this?" he blustered. Men like Yefimov were always able to switch that on, no matter the situation. "How dare you interfere in my duties!"

He knew the gig was up, though, and was just going through the motions. Baxter glanced over the side of the platform, made out Juneau. The first officer was starting his own climb up, unwilling or unable to leave this to Baxter.

"It's done," he called down, pitching his voice to carry but not loud enough to wake people.

Baxter escorted the surly Yefimov back to the deck. It was a dangerous stretch, or would have been if the fight hadn't gone out of the man. Juneau, waiting at the base of the mast, pulled himself up to his full height and linked his hands behind his back as Yefimov launched into an explanation that rapidly trailed off when he got no response. Baxter handed Juneau the confiscated notebook, which he flicked through with a studied casualness.

"I see you have more instructions for your tailor in London," he said coldly.

Yefimov, realising just how much they knew, looked like he was about to weep.

"These are ridiculous measurements," Juneau went on. "Though they look eerily like a longitude and latitude, and a likely time of arrival. Which would be embarrassing, taking delivery of a garment that would be large even on Mr Baxter here," Juneau went on. He stalked forward, eyeing his subordinate. "But you must have known this plan was likely to fail, that as soon as you started flashing messages, as soon as you resorted to violence, that your perfidy would be discovered. Not even you are arrogant enough to think any of us would be fooled for long."

"He was planning to flee the ship," Baxter said. "We're not far from a number of friendly harbours. Friendly to the likes of him, anyway." Yefimov stared daggers at him, opened his mouth to speak. He was almost an afterthought in the conversation, though. "I imagine he was signalling the freighter to arrange a pick-up."

"He wouldn't be able to steal one of the larger boats easily,' Juneau replied. "Even a small one would need a few hands to get over the side and then sail to land."

"The revolutionary cell, what's left of 'em," Baxter said with cold certainty, and was pleased to see the traitor throw his hands up in disgusted surrender. Really, it was astonishing that he had lasted this long. "They've probably already got a boat ready to be launched — he wouldn't want to stay aboard much longer anyway."

Juneau's eyes lit up at the thought of capturing the last of the vipers who had threatened him, those close to him and his ship. "Go — gather up Vasily and those others we trust and make a search of the vessel. As quietly as you can!"

"And this wretch?"

"Mr Yefimov and I will go and see Captain Gorchakov," Juneau said firmly, his tone and demeanour reassuring Baxter he had the situation under control. "It is past time we put a stop to this nonsense."

The deck of a ship during the night could be an eerily quiet place. Just the gentle lap of the waves against the hull, the hiss of water passing under the bowsprit and gurgling down the sides. If the ship was under power there would be the deep thump of the engines that burned night and day, felt rather than heard, but instead the *Yaroslavich* sailed north and east with no sound beyond the creak of the auxiliary sailing rig. It would be days before the engine was ready for use again.

High above them, light spilled from the wheelhouse and glowed from the open bridge, but all was shadow as Baxter led Vasily, Koenig and two other trusted hands towards where one of the smaller ship's boats was stowed. They had already checked two of the other likely vessels, working on the assumption there would only be a handful of men and they would want something they could launch quickly and quietly. They would aim to make their escape unnoticed, and if they couldn't do that they would want to get away fast.

He held his hand up as he heard whispering voices ahead. Three dimly seen shapes, little more than shadows, crouched in the shelter of the smooth, white-painted curve of the boat.

They were speaking guttural peasant Russian, so quietly he couldn't make out much. He didn't need to understand them, though, to pick up the tension and worry; and understood enough to pick up — after a few minutes — that they were indeed waiting on Yefimov and were concerned that he was overdue.

Baxter didn't need to hear any more, satisfied that these were the remaining revolutionaries. There was no other reason for them to be hiding in a position to steal a boat — and someone had certainly put the boat into a state for it to be launched. All that was required was for them to swing it out over the side and lower away. He'd only waited as long as he had as he felt it only fair that he made sure before visiting violence upon them.

Once he had that certainty, however, he didn't give them a chance to ready themselves; there was no demand for surrender.

He led his party forward in a rush, Vasily at his heels. Koenig and the other two, all of whom were slightly perplexed and slow having being turfed from their beds, were hesitant but followed on.

They saw Baxter just before he reached them. The first man rose to his feet, hands coming up in fists, and went down as Baxter's right jab connected with his chin. Vasily, not to be outdone, grabbed the second in a massive bearhug, lifting him cleanly off his feet and trapping his hands by his sides.

The third man backed away, hands up pleadingly, as Baxter closed on him, the three sailors on his heels. He glanced once over his shoulder as Baxter reached for him, then without a word threw himself backwards over the railing, disappearing in the dark water with barely a sound.

Koenig rushed to the rail, opening his mouth to shout "man overboard". Baxter put a hand on his shoulder to still him.

"Let him go — we would just shoot him anyway." It came out in a voice that sounded tired and flat even to his ears. He felt exhausted for no particular reason. He suspected that it wasn't the after-effects of the fever, or not that alone. They'd been living on a knife-edge of suspense and adrenalin since Ekaterina and Juneau had put their plan into operation, and now that it appeared to be concluded — to have succeeded, in fact — the tension drained out of him.

Koenig looked back at him, surprised, acknowledgement of his point but a sense of duty to a fellow sailor warring on his face. Nobody liked to leave a man behind in the water, but his fate was already sealed. The young officer looked unhappy, but nodded.

And with that, the menace of revolution on the cruiser appeared to have ended.

Gorchakov's voice was raised in anger as Baxter approached the captain's cabin, though it sounded reedy and petulant rather than the full-throated roar he had been subject to all those months ago, when he had first come aboard against his will. It was hard to make out the words, but from the way Juneau's voice was raised in protest he guessed the interview was not going entirely as planned.

The sentry outside the captain's cabin raised a hand and shook his head at Baxter's enquiring glance. No words were needed — no admittance would be given. Baxter didn't want to bring down Gorchakov's wrath on the sentry by trying to challenge the situation. Instead, he retired a few steps and waited. He didn't have to wait long. The click of shoes on the decking, a long but brisk stride, announced the approach of Ekaterina. She glanced at him, one eyebrow raised, and he nodded. Mission accomplished. She gave him a smile and swept past. He glanced down and saw she was carrying a revolver in one hand, held by the barrel to make it clear she was not about to offend anyone with it. It was a type of weapon he was familiar with — a .455 Webley.

She merely glanced at the sentry as she approached, and his hand dropped back to his side. He may have been a sailor under Gorchakov's command, but everyone knew she was a countess and was, more to the point, not someone who took 'no' for an answer. He knocked on the hatch and opened it at Gorchakov's bark, stepping back smartly. She paused just over the hatch coaming and beckoned Baxter.

He wasn't sure if he wanted to go in there, but she beckoned again with a more impatient gesture. He sighed and straightened, stepping through after her. Gorchakov was breathing hard, his face flushed, and that didn't fill him with confidence. Yefimov's slightly smug expression confirmed his suspicions. "And what is he doing here?" Gorchakov ground out, his French as always flat and uninflected.

"He is a witness to what has transpired, Captain," Ekaterina said coolly. In comparison, her command of the language was better even than her English.

Gorchakov turned hot, angry eyes on her. Baxter realised he hadn't seen the man at less than a distance for months, and now that he thought about it, it had been weeks since he'd seen him at all. He looked pale, shaky, and somehow diminished.

But then, he is diminished. Baxter didn't know much about the man, but he was clearly no seaman, no more than he was a capable captain. He had gradually relinquished command to Juneau, since well before the storm that had nearly done for them all.

"As are you, no doubt?" Gorchakov said, his voice so far beyond polite it bordered on churlish.

"I am, yes, and I am also one of his intended victims," Ekaterina replied, gesturing sharply to the prisoner. She gave no hint of having been offended by his tone. She carefully laid the pistol on his desk. "This is the weapon, I believe, that was discharged at me in Gabon. You will see, if you break it, that two rounds have been fired."

Yefimov had paled when he saw the weapon. Gorchakov merely glanced at it dismissively. "I have never known a man," he said, his voice shaking with growing anger, "so determined to prove his point and undermine a subordinate, that he would go to such lengths and draw so many people into his madness!"

They all stared at Gorchakov, surprised despite themselves. Even Ekaterina, normally so poised, seemed taken aback by Gorchakov's determination to bend and twist the facts until they suited him. "Sir…" Juneau began.

"Enough!" Gorchakov bellowed. His rage seemed to lend him strength again, if only for a little while. "This will end! Mr Yefimov, you may go about your duties with my apologies. Captain of the second rank Juneau, you may consider yourself warned — if this occurs again, I will break you. I shall consider any necessary disciplinary measures. As to your so-called witness here — confine him to his quarters, where he belongs."

Baxter couldn't help the look of utter contempt that crossed his face. "You may be interested to know," he said, in slow and deliberately insolent Russian, "that I have captured the remaining revolutionaries. They await your pleasure in irons — all but the one who chose self-murder." He had the satisfaction, at least, of seeing Yefimov's mask crumble, before Gorchakov's temper properly snapped.

CHAPTER 17

"Of all the absurd, blind, obstinate idiocies visited upon us and this squadron!" Juneau stormed, pacing the length of his cabin — not a great many strides, even for a short man like him. "This has to be the most iniquitous!"

"I might even be tempted to suggest the Gorchakov is in on it as well," Ekaterina said, her voice dark.

Baxter watched them both, surprised they couldn't see what was going on. But then, they were both used to being on the right side of this sort of situation. "It's nothing like that," he said mildly. "As you've said yourself, Juneau, Yefimov is his favourite. Would have been his first officer if you hadn't been foisted upon him."

Juneau accepted that with a gracious wave that also invited him to keep speaking.

"I'm quite prepared to believe that Gorchakov has accepted everything you both said to him, and just doesn't want to admit to having favoured a man in the pay of British Intelligence. Or he has just come down on the side of his man, rather than the man imposed upon him. Either way, you have become an embarrassment to him."

Ekaterina cocked her head and gave him a shrewd look.

Juneau looked unhappy, but nodded. "Justice, it seems, is quite a mutable thing."

"For your kind," Baxter said, his voice harsher than he'd meant it to be, "yes."

Somewhere above, a drummer began beating; the summons for off-duty crew to come and witness punishment. Juneau put on his dress uniform cap, his unhappy expression deepening.

Once again Gorchakov had abdicated responsibilities to him, and he would have to oversee the execution of the remaining — or what they hoped were the remaining — mutineers. They had been convicted at a summary court martial the day before and would soon be marched onto the cruiser's foredeck.

"And meanwhile, Yefimov goes about his business, appointed a *de facto* aide to the captain," Juneau said bitterly, then strode from the cabin without another word.

Ekaterina and Baxter remained seated. What was about to transpire on deck was not for the eyes of civilians, and on the off chance that Gorchakov actually appeared for the proceedings Baxter remained below. Juneau had studiously ignored his orders to have Baxter confined to quarters again, knowing he would get away with it as Gorchakov so rarely left his cabin.

From above, they could hear Juneau reading the charges and sentence, as the regulations required, then the rattle of rifles being prepared and the sharp bark of orders. An odd silence, not peaceful in any way, settled over the ship. It wasn't a complete silence, because a ship was never completely silent, but quiet enough that they could hear someone sobbing. He could only guess it was one of the men about to die.

Juneau's voice, almost gentle, cut through the sobbing. The rifles cracked, not quite as one, and two heavy thuds told Baxter the deed was done. He cocked his head as he heard an officer call for a *coup de grâce*, and a moment later a pistol popped, discharged at close range into the head of a mortally wounded prisoner to put him out of his suffering.

Not a duty Baxter would have relished.

"They deserved it," Ekaterina said quietly. He couldn't tell if her voice was filled with certainty or whether she was trying to convince herself.

"You'll get no argument from me," he said shortly, rising and crossing to a porthole. The crew sounded muted as they dispersed from their solemn duty of witnessing the executions — the Marxists may have come close to killing them all, but few men enjoyed the spectacle of a former crewmate's body being torn by heavy bullets fired at close range. It would be worse, of course, for the firing squad. No doubt Juneau had already ordered an extra tot of vodka for the men who'd had that unpleasant task.

The ships of the reunited squadron sprawled off to port, once again lost to the sight of the world and their own high command. The enormous armada was hoved to and taking on coal, and judging from how high the colliers sat in the water it was the last of their immediate supply. The *Yaroslavich*, under sail as she had been for some days, was at least spared this.

"Always in such a rush," he murmured. Normally that would have suited him — indeed, he had been aching to be at sea after the weeks of enforced inactivity in the last idyllic bay they had rested him. He just felt … drained. As though he needed time to rest and gather his strength again. "I'm surprised Rozhestvensky is in such a hurry to meet with Togo."

"I am told the admiral is less concerned with finding the enemy, and that we are to run the Japanese gauntlet for Vladivostok after all," she said drily. "The problem is we are being pursued — by ships of our own navy no less."

For Baxter, it summed up the madness of the whole expedition. Rumour had it that Rozhestvensky had stopped communicating with his superiors and certainly refused to let them know where he was. The Admiralty had ignored everything he said to them and had fallen in with Captain Klado's idea to try to swamp the enemy with enough ships that they would not be able to deal with them all, even when those ships had no business being out of coastal waters or were so old and decrepit they were liable to sink with no provocation.

"He runs from his own countrymen like the French ran from Nelson," Baxter grunted.

"Let us hope we do not succumb to the same fate," Ekaterina said by his side — close by his side. He was acutely conscious of her presence, the warmth of her body so close to his. "Alas, your and my husband's plan for us all to go ashore in Hong Kong will be foiled by Yefimov still being at large."

"Well, there's nothing to stop us from…" Baxter started saying, before his brain caught up with his mouth.

"As soon as he manages to get ashore, he will make for the nearest telegraph office and communicate with his handlers, and at that point they will know … what I am, and that you have been helping us. We cannot risk going ashore, even here. Ironically, this is probably the safest place for us now."

"Their reach cannot be that far. The nearest land is French Cochin, after all, and there's no love for Britain there."

"We cannot know that — attempts on our lives have been made in a French colony before." She smiled at him, raised a hand as though to lay it on his cheek and then dropped it suddenly, gaze lowering. "And thank you for confirming what you had cooked up with Cristov."

He knew then that he would never out-think her or out-manoeuvre her. "Your husband is now safe from the revolutionaries," he pointed out. "Your work is done — if you went ashore here…"

"The quickest way back to Russia and relative safety is to remain aboard — we are bound for Vladivostok after all. We are bound together, all of us, and will see this through to the end. I do not think you ever intended to leave the ship, in truth, though you may not have realised that yet. I just worry that, as we have failed to stop Yefimov, he will manage to put in motion some sort of display off Hong Kong that will drag our two countries into war. That we put that idea into his head."

Baxter pursed his lips. "I doubt he will try that, knowing as he does now that it was a trap. He will keep his head down and try to pretend this was all a bad dream. Even if he does, there wouldn't be enough time for Arbuthnott to organise something surreptitious in the China Station. The bastard isn't all-powerful, after all, and as you say — we are in a bit of a rush."

The most frenetic activity, he realised as he squinted out of the porthole, was an increasingly fraught exchange of signals between a number of ships — the flash of signal lamps and jerky hoists of flags, to his eye, certainly looked fraught.

"I feel, my lady," he said, "that something is afoot."

"It is ... inconceivable!"

Juneau's face was almost purple with apoplectic rage. He paced the length of the wardroom and threw himself down in one of the armchairs. Maxim rose from his place in front of the fire and laid his head on his master's knee, staring at him with huge eyes.

The wardroom had remained a place of odd tensions and forced formality, full awareness of what had transpired between the two most senior officers now commonplace. That meant most of the officers avoided the comfortable lounge unless they absolutely had to. Formal dinners were cold and joyless affairs that were finished as quickly as possible.

Machinations in the rest of the force, however, were at the root of Juneau's increasingly dyspeptic mood this day. "They have won every competition, devoured every feast of coal faster than anyone, and carried the efficiency pendant every day from the very Baltic!" he stormed.

Baxter poured a generous brandy for his friend, and an even more generous one for himself. "Who has done what, exactly?" he asked drily.

"That pompous ass Bukhvostoff has doomed us all!" Juneau snapped, then raised his brandy balloon in a slightly shaky hand and took a draw. It seemed to calm him. "Do you know what he said, at the formal dinner before the squadron left? 'There will be no victory, but we will know how to die'."

Baxter racked his brain for the name while Juneau declaimed. "Captain of the *Oryol*?"

"*Alexander III*," Juneau corrected him. "An equally vital ship, but not one that should have been put in the charge of that … that … *nincompoop*."

Baxter struggled to restrain a grin at the use of the English idiom.

"You may smile, my friend, but this man has succeeded where every machination of Britain, Japan and Mother Nature herself have failed. Contrary to the initial plan, we will not be able to strike while the iron is hot, but must now wait to resupply — as his ship is out of coal."

Baxter blinked in surprise. As Juneau had said, *Alexander III* had consistently feasted faster than the other ships, always being first to signal she had completed coaling. "They lied?"

"Oh, they were not dishonest — merely lazy and incompetent. The officers made a rough assessment based on what they thought had come aboard, rather than precise measures. It only came to light because of the need for exact endurance for the run to Vladivostok. She will not make it, and as a quarter of the main battle line she is too critical to leave behind."

Baxter dropped into a chair across the cold fireplace from his friend. "So any attempt to break through cannot be made without resupply. Do we know what the admiral's intentions are?"

"I do not know that he even knows what his intentions are, and I am told he barely shares his council with Konstantin or his other staff officers anymore. The cruisers and sundry small vessels will be the last to know. Mark my words, though — this will have taken the fire out of him.

"Shore leave has finally been granted," Juneau said heavily some days later. "Yefimov is ordered ashore in the first boat to, ah, conduct important business for the captain. At the telegraph office."

The squadron rode at anchor in Cam Ranh Bay, in French Cochin. The warm water was clear and blue and a beach of white and yellow sand rose to forest in the distance. On the surface, it was a peaceful scene entirely at odds with their martial purpose. On closer inspection, though, it was clear that this had once been a powerful fortification of the French Empire. Collapsed barrack blocks, mouldering ramparts and rusty ironwork were slowly being overwhelmed by the jungle. All that remained of the colonial presence was a desperate little town of once-whitewashed buildings, hanging on despite no longer having a purpose.

Baxter felt his mouth quirk at the irony of that. "It is madness, but a depressingly familiar one," he sighed. "Every navy seems to be subject to this nepotism. However, I'm told we will only remain here long enough to coal, so I see little danger of him being able to get up to too much mischief."

"Gorchakov seems to be becoming increasingly irrational — every attempt to take action against our friend, he sees an attack upon his own authority. Which, if I am truthful, I fatally undermined weeks ago." Juneau's voice was tinged with the slightest hint of regret. Not that he had undermined Gorchakov in particular, Baxter suspected, but rather at the notion of having undermined his captain — no matter how incompetent he was.

"Well, we're where we are — we'll have to do what we can."

"Ekaterina will go ashore as well, and try to keep an eye on him." Juneau shook his head at Baxter's hopeful expression. "You are expressly forbidden from going ashore, I am afraid. And no, this is not an order I can quietly ignore. The captain was most specific."

"Well, I had best occupy my time as best I can," Baxter said, trying not to sound churlish as he poured himself another drink.

"If you had not noticed, morale aboard this ship is as low as the rest of the fleet," Juneau said, his voice tinged with coldness. "The flag is … completely passive. No orders have been given, not even for drills. We must find a way to keep the men active and distracted. I fear the consequences if we do not, even in this damnable heat."

Baxter carefully put his glass down. "You're right, of course," he said, by way of a tacit apology. "Well, we may not have orders to drill, but that doesn't mean we're not allowed to."

"Colliers are also expected daily," Juneau said, his voice weary. "And with the engines repaired we will be expected to raise steam again. That at least will provide some distraction."

"The joy." Baxter picked up his discarded glass and stared down into the amber liquid, before drinking it off.

Confusion and uncertainty. They weighed on the squadron. With no clear instructions or even an indication of what Admiral Rozhestvensky's intentions were, speculation was rife when men had the energy for it.

Baxter, despite the soggy weight of the air, felt tension ramping up inside him as he watched the ship's boats pulling for the tiny town, crammed with sailors and officers relieved to be away from the cramped and filthy confines of their ship.

It wasn't that he particularly wanted to be ashore, though being able to stretch his legs would help. It was the fact that Yefimov was in the stern of one of those boats and Ekaterina, accompanied by Vasily and Tommy, in another.

Baxter leaned on the rail, forearms crossed on the polished mahogany and straw hat pulled low over his eyes against the glare of the rising sun, and stared hard after the boats. Ekaterina did not look back, but Yefimov turned on his bench to stare back at the ship. Even at that range, Baxter felt their glares lock. Yefimov looked triumphant — an expression he had worn since the fateful interview with Gorchakov and Juneau — and raised a hand in contemptuous salute to Juneau.

"Bastard," Baxter muttered under his breath, straightening and wrapping his hands around the rail, squeezing and twisting it in lieu of Yefimov's throat.

A discreet cough at his shoulder drew a baleful look that caused poor Koenig to quail. "I believe we were going to be drilling the crews in accurate gun-laying?" the diffident young officer asked in his flawless but careful French.

Baxter forced himself to master his anger. "We are indeed, Mr Koenig. I see you have drawn the short straw and will not be going ashore."

"I had the option," Koenig said, almost piously. "But I feel we have much work to do and little time before we must put these skills into action."

Baxter nodded. "Good lad."

They had even less time in Cam Ranh Bay — as perfect a natural harbour for desperately needed maintenance as anyone could ask for — than anyone had anticipated. A French cruiser, flying the flag of the station commander Admiral de Jonquières, had visited not long after their arrival. That evening the sleek vessel slipped into the harbour again, having exchanged courtesies and identification with the destroyer pickets. The fast, dangerous vessels were the only ships in the squadron that remained active, burning precious coal as they patrolled relentlessly in case the Japanese should try a sneak attack. Or, as some Russian officers maintained, *another* sneak attack.

It didn't take long after the French admiral's boat had put off from the *Suvorov* for signals to start flying, ordering preparations be made for the squadron to put to sea the following day.

By that point, of course, the rumours were already flying. Rozhestvensky was known to have agreed, finally, to wait for the arrival of the 3rd Pacific Squadron — or rather, to follow the Admiralty's orders to wait.

"I heard Togo is prowling the coast with his full force," Koenig said excitedly over dinner.

"We are close to Japan now," Dr Andropov said, his voice more measured. "But as far as I understand things, being a mere medical man rather than a fighting officer, it is still … a bit far? More likely pressure has been brought to bear on the French to evict us — we have already outstayed our welcome by some margin."

"I heard the Japanese were already at the outskirts of Vladivostok!" a particularly young and impressionable lieutenant exclaimed. "We are sailing to their rescue now!"

That led to a round of tolerably good-natured abuse that left the young man red-faced but otherwise unharmed. Only Juneau did not engage in the ribbing — he sat massaging his forehead at his end of the table, paying rather more attention to his wine than to the food. It was the best fare they'd had for some time, fresh supplies having being brought aboard that morning.

"The French are our allies!" the young man protested weakly. "They would not evict us…"

"The French are profiting handsomely from you," Baxter corrected him, not ungently. "Where do you think that steak came from?" he went on as the boy gave a puzzled look. "Still, various governments will be pressuring them to enforce the rules of neutrality."

"Where is Mr Yefimov?" Juneau asked suddenly, raising his head from his hand. His voice was harsh and strained.

An uncomfortable silence fell over the assemblage. The second officer had been a brooding, silent presence for so long that his absence had barely been noted. "I … I believe he has retired to his cabin. I understand he ate something ashore that disagreed with him." The last part of Koenig's sentence came out in a rush as Juneau's eyebrows knitted together.

"Well — he should have reported it to me!" Juneau snapped. He looked as though he was going to say more, but bit it off. Disciplinary matters were best not aired over the dining table.

After that, the dinner lapsed into by-now familiar morose silence and broke up not long after. Andropov retired to see to his malaria cases in the sickbay and the officers of the watch left to take up their stations. Soon it was just Baxter and

Juneau. Feeling sweaty and a bit shaky, Baxter called for Pavel — who doubled up as the senior wardroom steward — and sent him off to raid their dwindling supply of gin and tonic.

"I notice the countess did not join us," he said mildly, once the welcome cool drinks had been delivered.

"What of it?" Juneau flared, furious gaze turned on Baxter.

Baxter felt a stir of his own temper, but tamped it down. "I merely worried that she too had been laid low while ashore," he said. He found himself worried Juneau knew about the … affair was the wrong word. Entanglement, perhaps.

Juneau sagged back in his chair and took up the gin. "I find myself liking this peculiarly British drink more and more," he said in a different, milder tone. The glass he raised was half-toast, half-apology for his temper. "Katya was entirely, how do you say, fagged out? And has retired."

"Inactivity can be tiring, just as it wears on the morale."

Juneau gave him an odd look. "Oh, I doubt she has been inactive at all."

CHAPTER 18

They did not realise that Yefimov was missing until they were already at sea. Moving almost forty warships of all sizes through the narrow mouth of the harbour had been a time-consuming and, at times, hair-raising experience, even though the cruiser squadrons had been the first out to secure the surrounding sea.

The ships formed a great arc, almost five miles long, beyond the mouth of the bay. The *Yaroslavich* was standing well out, on station to repel any attack. The crew was on high alert, British cruisers having being sighted observing the fleet's departure from beyond the edge of French territorial waters. The French Admiral steamed with them, escorting them towards that territorial limit — not as a watchman but a polite host seeing his guests on their way.

"The flagship has signalled for all commanders," Juneau said. He had invited Baxter to join him on the wide, open bridge — it was his domain now, and Gorchakov was a rare sight indeed on it. "And of course Gorchakov wanted his aide."

"Who was nowhere to be found?" Baxter asked.

"Who was, indeed, complete and glaring in his absence." Juneau's voice was dark as he raised glasses to sweep the seascape again. "It appears he deserted in Cam Ranh — he was last seen heading for the telegraph office. Beyond that, there has been no other sighting."

"Could he be hiding there?"

Juneau pursed his lips and then shook his head. "No, the town is too small. And even if he had laid low there, he will already be on his way somewhere larger. Somewhere that will allow him to disappear."

"He will be weeks if he goes overland or even by river," Baxter said confidently. "By the time he has got anywhere to do anything, assuming he survives the journey, we will be safely north. Away from this damnable heat," he added as an afterthought, mopping his brow.

"You sound like you speak with experience."

"Of travel inland in these parts? Not direct experience, no — I've spoken with old hands who've done the coastal trade here. I much prefer blue water sailing."

"That's as may be, of course, but we think he did stop at the telegraph station first. Unfortunately my wife hadn't had time to ... cultivate contacts, as she had done at Nossibeisk. We do not know what he told his masters."

Baxter felt his heart sink. It was entirely possible, then, that the Juneaus' plan had backfired and backfired badly. As Ekaterina had said, he would now be stuck aboard this ship until they were safely in Russian waters; that was the least of their issues now assuming Yefimov was aiming to cause more mischief rather than just fleeing for his life.

He quirked a smile. He'd never, in his worst nightmares, imagined considering Russian waters as being safe. Then he shrugged. "Well, our course has been set for us, then."

"Indeed. The damnable thing is the admiral promised his French counterpart that he would not interfere with anything shipping even if we feel like it might be bound for Japan — so we cannot even stop and search any ships he might be taking, if he was to try to get to Hong Kong by sea."

"He won't," Baxter said. "Yefimov is, in essence, a cautious man." He hesitated to say cowardly. "And he cannot know that we have orders not to molest shipping. No, he will go by river. And hopefully the river will claim him."

Juneau raised an eyebrow at the vehemence in Baxter's voice.

"I think I'm allowed to think ill of the fellow, don't you?"

"That is … reasonable." Juneau raised his glass in salute.

Ever onwards, ever northwards — that's what Vice-Admiral Rozhestvensky told his assembled commanders that day. Gorchakov, without Yefimov to confide in, grudgingly told his officers at a conference in his cabin. Baxter heard all of this second hand from Juneau after the event. It seemed that, for most of the officers and crew, he was more or less one of them; but for Gorchakov he was still a prisoner and, at best, an inconvenience.

"It's clear, though, that Juneau now runs the ship and the captain has little or no real influence," Ekaterina told Baxter over breakfast. They were dining in the adjunct to Juneau's cabin. With Yefimov gone, the wardroom was returning to some semblance of normality — or at least a pastiche of it — and there were a few off-duty officers breaking their own fasts before the day became too hot to contemplate food. That meant that it was no longer a suitable space for any sort of private conversation.

Baxter looked across the rim of his coffee cup as she spoke, struck again by what a remarkable woman she was. And she was striking. Not beautiful, but her strong-boned face and cool eyes that almost matched her raven hair would turn plenty of heads. More important than her looks, though, was her cool, clear mind. Her way of looking right through people and getting exactly what she wanted from them.

And, he had to admit wryly, she'd done exactly that with him. He knew it, but knowing it did not break her hold over him. He'd certainly never imagined sitting down to breakfast with a countess — at his lowest point, broke and broken down in Edinburgh, he might even had punched a man who'd predicted this. Least of all a noblewoman he'd bedded, although those long hot nights on Madagascar seemed like a half-remembered dream now.

He realised she was watching him, obviously expecting some kind of comment. "Well, she could do worse for a commanding officer," he said after taking a swallow of still-scalding coffee. "Juneau's a damn fine officer. I'd be happy to sail into action under his command."

"And you may have an opportunity to test that theory," she said with a slight smile.

He suppressed a frown, knowing she was right but not wanting to admit it.

The subject of their discussion burst in at that point, stripping off his uniform jacket with a grateful sigh as he came off watch. Juneau glanced between then, an odd expression playing briefly over his face. Baxter wondered if he'd expected to find a slightly less domestic scene.

"We are moving, husband?" Ekaterina enquired.

"We are, but not far," he replied, nodding a greeting to Baxter and securing a cup of coffee. "Ever northwards and ever onwards, it seems, means merely the next bay north while we wait for the Third Squadron. It sometimes seems to me that we will be trapped on this infernal journey for the rest of eternity, like some punishment meted out by Baba Yaga."

"Finishing the journey could mean a battle," Baxter pointed out. "Not everyone is in such a rush to face that."

Juneau grinned at him. "Many men who wear a uniform crave it, though. And I for one would prefer that to this interminable heat."

Baxter thought back to what little action he had seen during this brief stint in the Royal Navy, and even the experience of being under fire from this very ship. He wasn't entirely certain he'd ever craved action, though the thought of it did not fill him with trepidation. Before he could put any of that into words, though, there was a gentle rap on the door. Pavel, serving them this morning and leaving the wardroom to the lesser stewards, glided silently to it and exchanged a handful of words with the visitor before returning with a slip of paper.

Juneau glanced at it, no doubt expecting a message about some minor happening, then straightened and reread it carefully. He shot a glance at Baxter. "It seems you were wrong, my friend. A report has reached us from Cam Ranh — Yefimov was seen boarding a fishing vessel late yesterday, which immediately put off and headed north."

Silence greeted that pronouncement, but it was not prolonged. Ekaterina put down her tea with a decisive gesture. "I have a sudden desire," she said, without a hint of irony and with a great deal of asperity, "to go on a pleasure cruise."

"I dunnae ken why you're all in such a rush," Tommy commented as they watched one of the cruiser's steam pinnaces being prepared. "Sure oor friend has already made his report by cable."

Baxter glanced down at the lad, surprised. Perhaps it was the time he was spending with Ekaterina, but he seemed to be developing an astute understanding of his own. "True. We haven't been able to confirm whether or not he did send anything from the telegraph office. It's difficult, not to mention expensive, to send details by cable, though. He might have given them some warning of our position, may even have blown Ekaterina's cover, but the real information will be in his head."

"So we're going after him? What chance in hell do we have?"

Baxter pursed his lips. It was a difficult question. Yefimov had a head start, but less than he might imagine. Baxter and Juneau had poured over charts while Ekaterina oversaw preparations for her 'jaunt up the coast'. They knew when the fishing boat he'd hired had left, knew the currents and the prevailing wind, what the weather had been doing. The hired crew knew the waters better than them, admittedly, but not necessarily much beyond Cam Ranh.

Against that, though, was the challenge of picking out the right fishing boat and managing to close with it. Many boats plied these waters, small and large, and they only had the vaguest description of what they were looking for. Not to mention the possibility of foul weather and the ever-present pirates who still plagued these waters.

He shrugged. "We have to try."

"Well, ah'm coming with ye."

Baxter glanced down at Tommy — even in the last couple of months he'd grown enough that there was less 'down' in the look. "And if I say no and try to prevent it, I imagine you will find a way on board."

The lad's grin was broad and self-confident. "You are learning," he said, dropping easily into Russian.

Baxter laughed and tousled his hair, causing Tommy to duck in annoyance. "Well, you'd best get your kit," he said, knowing the lad was right. He was just going to keep finding ways to get himself into trouble, so he may as well do it under Baxter's watchful eye.

He turned his suspicious gaze to the preparations being made as Tommy hurried off. The cruiser carried two steam pinnaces — a larger complement than many ships her size — and one had already been swayed out and sat in the lee of the ship as supplies were passed down. Vasily and the three other bluejackets who would crew the boat were already aboard, and the big petty officer was busy checking over the 3-pounder Hotchkiss gun mounted in the bow.

"I'm trusting my wife to you, Baxter," Juneau said, appearing at his side in that way he had.

Baxter glanced at his friend, his captor. The man he had cuckolded. He wondered again how much Juneau knew. Whether he even cared. "She'll be looking after us as much as we her."

Juneau shook his head doubtfully. "On land, perhaps, or in political manoeuvrings. But out there, on the water, she will be in your hands…"

A number of options flashed through Baxter's mind, all of them shades of bravado. Instead he nodded. "Well, if there's one thing I know, Second Captain Juneau, it's handling boats."

If the journey thus far — those bits that had not involved storm or intrigue, at least — had been oddly peaceful, their 'cruise' up the coast of Cochin towards Hong Kong was idyllic. They were freed at last of the machinations on the cruiser and the pressure of being surrounded by so many men. The one thing they were not free of was coal, and they still found themselves stepping around sacks of the foul stuff, stored in every available space — even the small boiler had a voracious appetite and they were steaming much further than the little vessel was designed for. The coast, always on their port side, varied only minimally between Mangrove swamps, muddy estuaries and the rolling greenery of coastal jungle.

The pinnace was, of course, a much smaller vessel and much of her interior space was taken up with the tiny engine and boiler rooms, along with the sundry stores they required. It was still a 50-footer, though, and steamed with a small crew. Tommy, Vasily and the three other bluejackets bunked in the largest space, and after the crowded confines of the *Yaroslavich*'s mess decks it must have seemed blissful, particularly as they stood watches by twos, one at the wheel and the other in the engine room, tending the small furnace that drove them on at a decent clip.

The ship's carpenter had hurriedly turned the second, slightly smaller compartment in front of the wheelhouse into two tiny cabins and an even smaller galley-like wardroom. Ekaterina, of course, enjoyed the comforts of the slightly larger space, while Baxter's resembled a cupboard with a bunk in it. He barely fit below decks anyway, particularly given how close it was, and was content to spend most of his time at the wheel or otherwise on deck, keeping an eye out.

The coastal waters were busy with small fishing vessels, most clinging close in shore but others venturing into deeper water. There was a lively trade as well, most of it still reliant on the wind, and Ekaterina delighted in sitting with Baxter on deck as he identified the wonderful variety of local vessels on the first full day of the voyage.

"That 'un, with a lateen rig — the big triangular sail," he told her almost absently. "She's an Arab, and has come a bloody long way. Pardon my French."

"That was not French, Mr Baxter, but was English of a most vulgar kind," she said primly — the small smile playing about her lips gave the lie to any attempt at sternness, though. He could feel her gaze on him as he swept the horizon again. "Will we stay close to shore for the whole journey?"

"I'll follow the coast of Cochin round for a while yet," he said, commencing another sweep. Ekaterina had closely questioned the men who had made the initial report, sailors from the *Yaroslavich* who had thought it odd to see one of their officers going aboard, and had further refined their description of the boat. "If we don't pick him up then, we'll steer more or less nor-east around Hainan and on to Hong Kong."

"And how long will this take?"

"To go all the way? It's seven hundred-odd miles, so if we maintain this speed then five days or so. We've got plenty of supplies though."

She sighed almost theatrically and sat back along the bench that ran around the forward part of the pinnace. "I don't know if I'll be able to cope with the tedium," she said with a reasonable imitation of an upper class English accent and a slightly arch look in his direction.

He smiled, feeling a stir of excitement that he tamped down. The pinnace may have been large for a ship's boat, but they were still cheek by jowl with the crew. "My dear Countess, I thought this pleasure cruise was your idea?"

"Don't be so obtuse, Baxter," she shot back. "Well, I imagine we will catch up with them sooner than that anyway."

He looked up, judging the handful of clouds in the otherwise deep blue bowl of the sky. "They've got a favourable wind, and the fishing boats in these parts are fairly quick in the water. However, he's not got much of a head start and the boats are not designed for long voyages. I shouldn't wander if they put in at a harbour to resupply or indeed stay in a safe anchorage during the nights. My main worry, then, is that we will overshoot. Assuming, of course, that he doesn't change vessels."

"I doubt he has the funds for that," Ekaterina said firmly. "I searched his quarters again and found a reasonable amount of currency that he'd abandoned. I think he panicked and bolted once he was ashore, rather than planning this. You think we have a chance of intercepting him?"

He thought about that for a few moments before answering. He didn't want to say he had a feeling, that his gut said they would. He could feel it, though, in his bones. A certainty that they were reaching a conclusion with Yefimov. That his prey was close, and would be in his hands soon enough. He couldn't explain it, so didn't try, merely nodded. "I'd say we've got a good chance. Not today, though."

She rose, ran a hand very lightly down his arm. "In that case," she said, in a low husky voice, "leave Tommy to keep a watch and come below."

He swallowed hard after she'd gone, then raised his voice in the direction of the crew cabin. "Master Dunbar, a job for you!"

CHAPTER 19

They sailed on in that way for what felt like a peaceful age, maintaining a steady fifteen knots during the day with the little engine chugging away and their own little cape of smoke following them. They anchored in shallow water at night — navigating busy coastal waters in the dark was never a great idea, and their quarry was unlikely to push on through the dark.

Baxter and Ekaterina always said good night to each other, carefully and publicly, before the rest of the crew retired to the foredeck or cabin. At some point, there would be a rustle of cloth and Ekaterina, half-seen and glorious in the dimness, would slip into his bunk beside him. They didn't always make love, but just the closeness in the cloying darkness was enough for him.

"What of the sailors, though?" he whispered one night, after they subsided next to each other. Her body moulded against him, their skin tacked together with sweat. Her complete lack of even a light nightdress would have scandalised any society lady. He felt her raise her head and sensed rather than saw her raised eyebrow. "I mean, won't they talk?"

She shrugged, breasts rising against his ribs. "They are peasants — the doings of their betters is none of their concern."

It was said without any sort of condescension or rancour, just a plain statement of facts; a rare glimpse into a world he'd only ever encountered at a distance before. He wondered where he fitted into her scheme, her view of the world. Almost as though she sensed his thoughts, she turned closer against him and raised a hand to run her fingers languidly down the side of his face. He felt the softness of her hair against his cheek, and rapidly lost his train of thought.

Early the next day, Baxter shaped their course further to the east, and tried hard to ignore the insolent grins of the men under his command. His and Ekaterina's business may have been none of their concern, but that didn't mean they didn't know what was going on. He pushed those thoughts aside. The seas were running smooth and long, but he was aware they were only in a small vessel and wanted to remain within an easy steam of the coast in case it did turn on them. His gut told him Yefimov's vessel would do the same thing.

"He won't think he's being chased," he explained to Tommy in the small deck wheelhouse as he adjusted their heading. "And he knows the squadron won't move for days, possibly more than a week."

"And he's a man who values his own skin," the lad commented thoughtfully. "He'll want to make sure the journey's as safe as possible."

Baxter smiled. Tommy was sharp, no doubt about it. The months aboard the Russian ship had taken the soft, pallid edges off him, and he was fitter and healthier. The oddest change was that he had more or less lost his Leith accent, and his English now had a trace of Russian about it.

It didn't make him feel less guilty about accidentally dragging Tommy along for this mad ride, but there was nothing he could do about that now — and the lad had proved himself invaluable. He just had to work out a way to get him home to his ma when all this was over.

"So we'll just saunter along, going a little bit faster than a sailing boat can go even with these favourable winds, and keep a sharp eye out. Won't we lad?"

Tommy grinned and hefted the enormous pair of field glasses the Russians had entrusted him with. They looked ridiculously out of proportion, but he didn't seem to have any problems holding them up to scan the horizon for their quarry.

"Well, best jump up to the bows then," Baxter said, then nodded to Vasily to take the wheel. "I think I'll join you."

The land was now little more than a shadow to the west and north — and at some point it would become apparent a little north of east as well, as they raised Hainan. Beyond that, of course, was Hong Kong. British bastion in the Orient since the Opium Wars and home of the China Station.

"We're not far, are we?" Ekaterina asked. She lounged along one of the benches in the stern of the boat, having turned what had been spartan accommodation into luxury with the addition of cushions and blankets. She had a book open in her lap, and seeing her looking so relaxed almost fooled him into believing that this *was* a pleasure cruiser. Her eyes were hard and assessing, puncturing any nascent delusion.

"From Hong Kong? Another two days, all things being equal."

"Not much time to catch our quarry." Her tone made it clear that she knew he was considering other things. He realised, perhaps for the first time consciously, just how conflicted he was. A sensible man would just keep going into Hong Kong, get himself and Tommy to safety. Not to mention ensure Ekaterina didn't steam headlong into the middle of a war. He was confident he could overpower even Vasily, and they wouldn't even know what was happening until they were steaming into the harbour — it would be a simple matter to surrender to the first Royal Navy ship he saw.

But... He looked into those level green eyes, and knew she would never forgive him for that. And he wouldn't forgive himself. He shook those thoughts off. "We'll have him before Hong Kong. Tomorrow, I'd warrant." He raised his voice and switched into Russian. "But only if our lookouts do their damned jobs!"

Tommy flashed a grin over his shoulder, elbowed the other lookout in the ribs to encourage him to keep a sharper lookout. Baxter picked up a spare set of field glasses and went forward to join them, followed by Ekaterina's full throated laughter.

Baxter wasn't far wrong with his assessment. They spotted what could very well be their quarry in late morning on the following day, with the low rolling hills of Hainan on their port quarter and Hong Kong barely more than a day's sail away if the sweet cool wind maintained its direction.

She was a pretty enough barky, for a working vessel, sliding through the water with the wind just where she wanted it to make the best speed. Baxter held her in the view of his field glasses, riding the pinnace's roll unconsciously in order to keep the view steady.

"You've got sharp eyes, lad," he said to Tommy, who had summoned him into the bows. The view was hazy and the fishing boat was some distance off, but she certainly matched the description.

"Alexei and I spotted her at the same time," the boy said in Russian, causing the burly young sailor who shared the watch to bob his head in pleasure.

"An extra tot of vodka, then," Baxter said, then saw Tommy's smile. "Not for you, lad — when you're a bit older."

"Ah'm keepin' track," the boy said grumpily. "You think it's oor friend, though?"

"I think it could be." Baxter turned. "Vasily, increase revolutions to full. Let's get a closer look."

The increased thumping of the engines brought Ekaterina on deck as the pinnace surged forward, water burbling as it sluiced down its side. Her hair was down and the wind whipped it around her face. She grinned as their game little vessel surged over a wave, her footing as sure as any experienced sailor's, and he felt his heart surge at the sight of her.

"We have him?" she called forward.

"We might have him," Baxter replied as she made her way forward until they didn't need to raise their voices. "The local fishing boats are remarkably swift with the wind a bit abaft. I think we've got the legs on her, but not by much."

"And if it isn't him, will we have wasted time?"

"We're more or less following the course we're on, but we'll be burning extra coal." He felt a bone-deep certainty that he had taken the right course of action. "It's worth the risk though."

She nodded, took the glasses from him without asking and put them to her own eyes. "Yes. Yes, I think you are right."

Baxter felt the excitement build in the little crew as the day wore on and the certainty rose in them that they were, in fact, closing on their quarry. A succession of watchmen in the bows reported the view becoming clearer and sharper as they closed, slowly but surely; with clarity came certainty that it was their Vietnamese fishing vessel.

"What happens when we close with her?" Vasily asked, startling Baxter with his deep rumbling voice. The big Russian petty officer rarely spoke except to give orders to subordinates, and almost never asked a question. It wasn't that he was stupid — far from it — or lacked initiative; he had a petty officer's inherent confidence in his own abilities, and if an officer's orders didn't make sense he usually just found a way to work them round until they did.

"Well, we'll see how they react," Baxter said after a moment's thought. "Could be they'll hand him over without fuss — after all, they were paid to sail him to Hong Kong, not fight a boatload of angry Russians. Could be we'll have to take him by force."

A slow smile crept over Vasily's face. He didn't appear to be a man who courted danger, but he also wasn't someone who shied away from it. "Shall I clear away the gun?" he asked after a pause. That explained his expression — like many bluejackets, he did enjoy the noise and activity of gunnery.

Baxter pursed his lips. He didn't anticipate needing it, but it would give the men something to do during what would likely be a long sea chase. And it was better to be safe than sorry. He nodded. "Do it quietly, though, Vasily, and no great displays. We don't want to tip our hand if we haven't been recognised."

It did seem that the fishermen hadn't noticed them, let alone taken particular note. Steam vessels weren't uncommon in this area, even if sail was still the prevalent form of locomotion. He could see one or two other vessels in the distance, on the Hong Kong trade no doubt, but the pinnace and the fishing vessel were by far the closest to each other.

That lasted for an hour as they closed gradually with the target vessel. After Vasily had cleared the gun and arranged the little three-pound shells ready for use, there was little for those not directly involved with the operation of the boat to do. That meant they all crowded into the bow, watching tensely as the range crawled down.

"This is what it must have been like in the wars against France," Baxter said. He was taking a turn at the wheel, Ekaterina once again sitting in the stern. Her book was nowhere in evidence, though, and he suspected her pistol was in her pocket.

"And against Russia, depending on the year," she said mildly. "But how so?"

"The crew watching a chase avidly, waiting to find out if she was legal prize. Working out what their share of the money would be."

Ekaterina snorted. "You sailors — a mercenary lot."

He shrugged. "It's a hard life, even more so then. You take what compensations you can find. All these poor buggers will get is a bit of extra vodka, of course."

"And you, Mr Baxter? What compensation do you look for?"

It was asked in a completely innocent voice, but there was a wicked glint in her eye when she said it. He couldn't help but smile back. "A roof over my head, even if it does pitch about, and food every day is good enough," he said. "Though the current company is … delightful."

Tommy's call from for'ard forestalled further conversation. "She's seen us!" A moment later. "She's shaking out more sail."

"Vasily, take the wheel!" Baxter ordered, cheerful conversation and all thoughts of compensation banished. He scrambled forward once the big man had the wheel again. The fishing boat was indeed forging ahead — she hadn't had much more in the way of canvas to spread on the single mast, but what little there had been had given her a couple of knots. She was quite clearly fleeing now, but he could not yet say why — whether they thought the pinnace was the oddest pirate vessel ever to ply these waters, or whether Yefimov was indeed aboard and had demanded it.

That question was answered a second later. He'd not long put glasses to his eyes that a Westerner emerged from the little deckhouse of the low vessel. He focused quickly, and they were close enough that he could more or less recognise Yefimov. The Russian was shading his eyes as he stared back at the pinnace, before turning to shout something at the crew.

A feral smile split Baxter's face. "There's our man!" he called out. "Tommy, jump down to the engine room and tell the engineer I want every extra knot he can manage!"

"The engine room, aye," Tommy muttered, though Baxter couldn't tell if he was being sarcastic or just acknowledging orders. It was a grand title for the adjoining cubby holes that housed the engine and boiler, after all.

Now that their quarry was confirmed, the tension aboard ratcheted up. The harassed engineer's mate who had charge of their propulsion managed to squeeze a few more knots out of the engine, but with dire warnings of both fuel consumption and the long term viability of the machinery. It took him a little while to do so, which allowed the fishing boat to open her lead slightly before they started clawing back distance.

"He must have paid them well," Baxter commented, watching the opposing sailors' efforts.

"Or he's threatening them — his service pistol was not in his cabin," Ekaterina countered. "Tommy and I searched it carefully. Can we catch them before nightfall?"

Baxter chewed his lower lip. Glanced at the little Russian ensign they had broken out on the flagstaff to gauge windspeed and direction. Glanced over the side at the rushing green water of the South China Sea. "If this wind holds or freshens and maintains direction, probably not. And they could very well lose us in the darkness."

"And, now he knows he is being hunted, he will want to — crack on, is it? — until he reaches the safety of Hong Kong."

"Indeed." He was watching the fishing boat carefully, and realised Yefimov was starting back at him through a set of glasses. "Vasily, how far would you say we are? One, two miles?"

The big Russian petty officer squinted, then shrugged. "Maybe a little more than two."

"I think we shall try the range of the Hotchkiss in a little while."

"Gunfire?" Ekaterina asked. "Is that wise?"

Baxter turned a slow circle, sweeping the sea all around. There was still other shipping around, including a smudge of smoke on the horizon that could have been a bigger steamship. "Probably not, but it is just a small gun. I doubt it will attract too much attention. We'll try a warning shot or two once the range has closed. And Vasily? Issue the rifles, if you please."

Yefimov was not evading him this time.

They commenced firing a half hour later. It was still long for the little popgun and Baxter had it on its highest elevation. The goal, of course, was not to hit the boat but to drop shells into the water close enough that they would take the hint.

The Hotchkiss went off with a crash as he pulled the firing lanyard and everyone held their breath and watched for the fall of shot as the pinnace shot out of the little cloud of smoke. The waterspout as it landed was pitiful compared even with the *Yaroslavich*'s secondary armament, but its effect on the chase was almost comical. Baxter did feel a bit guilty about putting the fishermen — probably honest, hardworking folk who had been offered an undreamed of amount to do a simple job — in harm's way. They were now trapped in a nightmare of someone actually firing on them, and there was obvious consternation on deck even though the shooting had been remarkably poor.

"Well, let's not stand about, eh?" Baxter said to the scratch gun crew he had assembled. There wasn't the same need for rapid fire as there would be in a full on battle, but he knew that first round probably wouldn't do the trick.

"They're starting to bring the sails down!" someone cried out with delight.

"He's brandishing a weapon!" Tommy reported almost at the same instance. "He's not giving up that easily."

There was a brief confusion on the fishing boat, some men trying to bring the sails down in a panic and others, equally disconcerted, obeying Yefimov's orders at gunpoint. The end result was that, though the chase didn't stop, she lost a lot of headway and allowed the pinnace to close faster.

"Right, let's see if we can land this a little closer," Baxter said, squinting along the barrel. The gun didn't even have a proper gunsight and he was having to do everything by eye and guesswork. He dropped the elevation slightly and waited until the pinnace's bow had started to drop down a wave. "Stand clear!"

This time, the shell landed close enough that the wind carried the waterspout over the stern. Yefimov whipped round, actually brandishing the pistol at them. Baxter grinned fiercely around the circle of crew.

"Baxter…" Ekaterina said.

"One second if you please, Countess," he said gruffly. This was his element, his role in life. While he had long since accepted her as a superior in most ways, he was not to be interrupted in his execution of this duty.

The third shell he laid a lot more carefully. Although the second shot had landed close, Yefimov still seemed to have control of the crew. He crouched over the gun, staring along its length, as the swell caused his target to bob in and out of sight. There was no science to this, barely any skill — intuition told him when to step back and fire again.

The Hotchkiss gun fired a variety of three-pound shells. They hadn't thought to stow solid practice rounds when preparing for the expedition, so had been hurling standard steel, black-powder-filled shells with a delayed fuse.

The shot, as even Baxter had to admit, was spectacularly lucky. They'd come close enough to fire on a flatter trajectory and the round went low over the fishing vessel and clean through her mainsail before bursting on the surface of the water. The explosion did no harm but it did drench the entire boat with spray. Even at that range, though, they heard the canvas tear as the sail split down the middle. The sudden loss of thrust threatened to turn the boat over, even with the crew — obviously experienced — managing to get the remnants down and the vessel under control.

Yefimov threw his hands up in disgust and then, with a baleful look towards the closing pinnace, threw his revolver overboard.

They were closing fast with their target now. Ekaterina's stern, slightly alarmed voice cut through the start of the cheering. "Marcus!"

Baxter turned, her use of his given name finally getting his attention, and followed the direction she had aimed her glasses. Taking up his own pair, he was startled to see the low, lean shape of a cruiser closing at speed, the White Ensign of the Royal Navy snapping from her flagstaff.

CHAPTER 20

"Russian pinnace, what is your business?"

Baxter listened to the voice shouting slowly in English from below decks. Yefimov sat opposite him, pale and wide eyed, as Baxter kept the muzzle of a revolver pointed at his belly. The traitor glanced over his shoulder, obviously trying to get a look out of the porthole; trying to see if he could do anything to effect his salvation.

"I may be a terrible shot, old chap," Baxter said urbanely, "but even I won't miss at this range. I'm told being gutshot is … not pleasant."

Yefimov subsided, glaring at him.

"Russian pinnace, I repeat, what is your business?"

Despite the speaking trumpet distorting the voice, Baxter had the vague and unpleasant feeling that he knew the owner.

"We were out for a cruise," Ekaterina called back in frosty English. She had been keeping out of sight behind the deckhouse, stepping into view as the cruiser came up alongside — the sudden appearance of a woman, and an attractive one at that, calculated to discomfit the RN officer speaking. "We happened upon a deserter from our ship. He is now in custody."

The voice became considerably more affable. The light coming in through the small porthole was occluded by the much bigger ship coming alongside, her engines idling. The pinnace rocked in the wash and Yefimov's eyes darted for the hatchway. Baxter twitched the muzzle of the gun and he subsided.

"Fortuitous for you, my lady," the fellow shouted, and Baxter was now certain he knew the voice. "Though we heard you firing on those poor chaps."

The Vietnamese fishing vessel was already underway with all possible sail set, beating away into the wind to turn round and make for home. Baxter couldn't blame them. They'd still done well out of the incident — Ekaterina had insisted that Yefimov pay them what was promised, and she had compensated them generously for the destroyed sail. The whole thing had been a miserable experience for them, though.

"I trust none of them were hurt?" the speaker went on, and Baxter felt a cold rage settle over him as he finally recognised the voice. No, not settle — resurface from where he had buried it. *Bradshaw.*

"They were paid for the damages," Ekaterina called back, her voice still cold despite Bradshaw's obvious attempts at being charming. The dapper young officer Baxter had known had always thought of himself as being a lady's man, and had some success to validate that opinion. Baxter suspected that their clash over a young lady in Portsmouth was what had brought Bradshaw into the coterie that had plotted against him aboard the *Doyle*; it wasn't surprising he would try flirting on the high seas.

But what ship was he assigned to, now, and in what role? He had patronage, certainly, but probably not enough to have seen him elevated to command rank — not even the sort of small, old ships one generally found on the further-flung stations.

There was silence from the British warship which now lay barely more than twenty yards from them. Baxter stared at Yefimov, wondering if after all this the blighter was going to get away with it. He toyed with the idea of shooting him right then and there. While he wouldn't be the first man Baxter had killed, he would be the first one he'd killed in cold blood — and while he was many things, he wasn't a murderer.

"I'm afraid, my lady, that I need to come aboard and ensure that everything is as it should be," Bradshaw shouted across a moment later. In the background, Baxter could hear orders being called out to lower away one of the ship's boats.

He saw hope spring in Yefimov's eyes at this new development. If Yefimov could convince Bradshaw that he was in the employ of British Naval Intelligence, things could get extremely uncomfortable. The bastard might actually get away with it, and continue to cause trouble for them.

"You shall do no such thing!" Ekaterina replied. "This is a ship of the Imperial Russian Navy and as such is sovereign territory — you shall not step aboard without an invitation."

"Well — I suggest you invite me on board when I get there." Even through the speaking trumpet, there was an air of menace in Bradshaw's voice now. There was no doubt that the British ship outgunned them, as surely as they would outgun the little boat he would be pulled across in.

Baxter rose quickly and smoothly, and Yefimov didn't even see the right hook that laid him out cold. Baxter didn't have time to mess around with tying and gagging the man. He knew how quickly a Royal Navy crew would get a boat away, and how keen Bradshaw was to get invited aboard by Ekaterina.

He didn't hurry as he made his way on deck and towards the Hotchkiss gun. Vasily caught his eye and raised a ponderous eyebrow. Baxter casually gestured to the weapon, which the petty officer had just finished housing after the brief 'action', and Vasily nodded his understanding. The two of them converged on it.

Baxter glanced towards the British ship without appearing to give her too much attention. He recognised her at once as an

Apollo-class protected cruiser, old but still powerful — probably more than a match for the *Yaroslavich* herself. He knew there were a few assigned to the China Station, though at least she wasn't flying an admiral's pennant.

That should make the bluff slightly easier.

Bradshaw's skiff was already halfway between the two vessels, close enough that Baxter could tell immediately that the arrogant little shit hadn't changed. He sat erect and proud in his hot weather uniform, an expectant expression on his face. Perhaps a little plumper around the middle and in his face.

The haughty expression dissolved into something like confusion when he appeared to recognise what Baxter and Vasily were doing. The weapon was still pointed forward, over the pinnace's stem, and it was very clear that they were — calmly, without any hint of hurry or panic — loading it. At Vasily's direction some of the Russian bluejackets were also preparing the long, cumbersome rifles brought on deck in case Yefimov had decided to make a fight of it.

"I say, ah…" Bradshaw was close enough that he didn't need to shout, and his consternation caused Ekaterina to turn to see what was going on behind her. Her eyes widened when she saw the martial preparations. Baxter met her eyes and winked.

She turned back, any hint of surprise gone from her face and nothing but cold superiority showing. "As I said, this is a Russian warship. You are not invited nor permitted to come aboard."

Bradshaw didn't like that, not one bit. Baxter recalled that he didn't like it when someone stood up to him — particularly not a woman. He nodded to Vasily, and between them they trained the long gun on the boat. He knew he should keep his head down — there was a reasonable chance Bradshaw wouldn't even remember him, but he shouldn't really be taking that risk.

He stepped up to the railing, leaning on it and staring hard at the officer.

Bradshaw had ordered a halt to the boat's progress but seemed determined to blister it out. "How dare you aim a weapon at me!" he snapped, face reddening. Baxter could tell he was becoming flustered as a slight Highlands accent crept into his voice. "Not only is it deeply discourteous, you must know that you are significantly outgunned!"

It was true. The cruiser — HMS *Iphigenia*, Baxter was fairly sure — was not cleared for action but there was no way they could escape her broadside guns, let alone the turret-mounted six-inch guns, if it came to a shooting match.

"However, do you really want to risk war between our nations?" Ekaterina asked, her tone more reasonable. She'd cottoned on to the bluff. "Even if we were all to die here, word would still get out. And you are civilised people — if you sink us, there will be survivors in the water and you will not leave them there. You should also know that I am connected to the Imperial family."

That really took the wind out of Bradshaw's sails, but he gave no indication of ordering a withdrawal to the ship.

Baxter spoke up, making no attempt at sounding Russian. "And whatever happens, sir, you should know — if it does come to shooting, you will almost certainly be hit first."

Bradshaw's mouth dropped open at the obvious threat. Baxter couldn't quite tell, at that distance, if the little prick recognised him. He couldn't see the faces of the British sailors crewing the boat, but he could tell from the set of their shoulders that they were deeply unhappy about the whole thing.

"Well . , I, ah, must confer with the captain," Bradshaw stammered, then snapped orders that turned the boat and sent it skimming back across the water.

"I don't believe he gave us any instructions to remain stationary, did he?" Baxter asked Ekaterina. She shook her head with a smile. "Tommy, jump down to the engine room and get us full steam ahead. Vasily, a course directly away from the cruiser as soon as we have headway."

"They could still open fire on us."

Baxter shrugged. "We're sunk either way unless they decide the doings of mad Russians are not worth the bother. My money's on them coming to that exact conclusion. Sinking us would be worth less than the shells they'd fire."

"You knew that officer." Ekaterina's voice was certain, delivering a statement not asking a question.

Baxter nodded briefly, and his hard expression obviously startled Ekaterina. "Bradshaw. He was senior to me on my first posting, but only just. He's done well for himself."

"Bad blood?" she asked softly.

"I'll tell you about it sometime," he said, knowing he never would. It was a painful episode and one he could live without revisiting. "The important thing, though, is that he's a coward. He'll run back to *Iphigenia* and report that everything is in order."

Ekaterina was obviously a fine enough judge of character that she didn't press the point and they lapsed into a comfortable silence, both of them watching the British ship as the pinnace gathered way. Vasily followed his orders exactly and soon they were steaming directly away from their potential killer. It would be hours before they would clear the effective range of *Iphigenia*'s main battery, of course, but the further away they got the better chance of surviving if the British ship did open fire.

She gave no sign of clearing for action or even turning some of her secondary guns on the pinnace, however.

"There — she's getting under way," Ekaterina said after ten minutes of tense silence.

"And turning for Hong Kong." He flashed her a smile. "Mad Russians — not worth the bother."

Her own smile lit up her face. She wasn't a woman much given to idiot grins, which made the rare expression even more startling. "Well, this has been quite an adventure, but I feel we should cut the cruise short and return to the *Yaroslavich*, yes?"

He inclined his head. "I shall plot a course for Cochin immediately, my lady."

They found the squadron at sea just off Van Phong Bay, slightly further north than Cam Ranh, from where they had been evicted.

They had taken their time heading back south and west — to conserve fuel and protect the over-strained machinery, Baxter told himself, nothing more — and arrived a little after Easter. They'd celebrated the feast day as best they could, putting in to a small Vietnamese village to buy stringy beef at an exorbitant price. "It is a very important festival in Russia," Ekaterina explained with an unconcerned shrug. "Surely it is so in Britain as well?"

It was Baxter's turn to shrug. "I've never taken much note of such things," he said gruffly. "Don't recall the Navy making much of a hullaballoo about it though."

Ekaterina's expression conveyed exactly what she thought of such heathens, but later she and the crew had done their best to show Baxter and Tommy how the resurrection should be celebrated, dining around the mess table in the front cabin with an odd mix of boiled beef and local vegetables. They'd drained the last of the small keg of vodka that had been put aboard, and the more adventurous had tried the local rice wine they'd re-provisioned with. Even Yefimov had been invited — though a traitor and deserter, he was still Russian.

His presence and the rudimentary feast could not detract from the high spirits aboard. They had succeeded in doing something many would have thought next to impossible. They'd found the proverbial needle in a haystack, and chased away a meddling British cruiser, and they were not far from a return to the safety and stability of their own ship.

They knew the squadron was at sea when, two days later, they saw the enormous cloud of black coal smoke that hung over the assemblage. They had been part of it for so long, seeing it from below, that Baxter hadn't really appreciated just how dense and, well, enormous it was. It was like the Russians' very own storm cloud following the squadron around.

"Well, if the Japanese need to find us they won't have to look hard," he muttered to Tommy. "Vasily…"

"Towards the devil's cloud, yes," the big petty officer said cheerfully. Vasily seemed far more outgoing in these situations — he was, of course, away from any officers and enlisted men were often more at their ease in those circumstances.

Baxter felt a palpable sense of excitement from the bluejackets as the pinnace bobbed its way across the waves towards the ships, expecting to find the *Yaroslavich* at her normal station on the edge of the formation. They were on the move! The bows were pointed north, and the course set for Vladivostok. Baxter scrutinised the formation to see if the much-prophesised and dreaded 3rd Pacific Squadron had joined, but there seemed to be the usual number of ships.

Perhaps Rozhestvensky had finally made good on his threat to continue without waiting?

As with many things on this journey, though, the activity was not what it appeared to be. Not long after they first sighted the ships, it became clear they were jostling into position to sail into Van Phong Bay.

"It was my understanding that we were *en route* there before our pleasure cruise began?" Ekaterina commented. "To coal and await the third squadron."

Baxter smiled at her use of the phrase 'pleasure cruise'. It had been very far from that, but as it turned out there had been compensations. He lowered his field glasses. "Indeed. I have the *Yaroslavich* in sight, so we will know what's what soon enough. Vasily, fire a blank to get their attention, if you please."

"Are you sure that's wise?" Tommy asked. "They're reet jumpy, remember?"

"I know Tomas'ka is speaking a form of English, but sometimes…"

Baxter's smile became a grin. "The lad has a point — we don't want them to think they're about to come under attack. We'll send up a flare when we're a bit closer."

Under his obvious pleasure at seeing the pinnace returned, Juneau appeared worn and haggard. "Well, I see you have been successful," he said completely unnecessarily. They were standing outside Yefimov's cabin, where the disgraced officer was now under arrest. "And I am glad to see you all safely returned." This with a particular smile at his wife, but which encompassed Baxter at the periphery.

"What the devil is going on with the squadron?" Baxter asked. He could not help a note of annoyance — just like the bluejackets, the prospect of finally being on the move, of charging north into danger and resolution, had got his blood up. "We've been away more than a week, and yet it seems only just to be arriving at Van Phong."

"Oh, we have been here for a few days. Long enough for there to be a mutiny on the *Oryol*, in fact. Then de Jonquières returned and ordered us to move on again — in accordance with the strict rules of neutrality. It seems Rozhestvensky is no longer trying to pretend he cares, though — as soon as the French admiral had sailed away we turned around and returned."

"And for how long does he intend to keep this up?"

"As before," Juneau said, slightly shortly. "Until the third squadron arrives or we run so low on coal we have no other option but to go on."

Baxter sighed, rubbed his brow. "My apologies, Juneau. It's been a trying trip, in many ways."

The Russian's blue eyes were light as he glanced between his wife and Baxter. "I'm sure it was relaxing in other ways. But you should both go and rest. Mr Yefimov and I must have words."

"Be careful, my husband," Ekaterina said. "Yefimov seems subdued, but now that he is close to his protector…"

"Oh, the captain will be no help to him now — or to anyone else," Juneau said bleakly, without explaining further.

"Then he may become desperate."

Juneau gave her a tight smile and patted the grip of the Nagant revolver he wore holstered on his hip. "I have taken precautions, my love. Now, go and get cleaned up and rest, both you. That's an order."

Baxter and Ekaterina both nodded and turned up the passageway as Juneau went in to see their prisoner. Neither of them spoke and they did not touch, but they walked close together. He was certain now that Juneau was aware of their liaison, and either didn't mind or actively approved. There was no way they could talk about it now, and he knew there was no point thinking about the future at this juncture. Well, not the future before the voyage to Vladivostok.

"Well, my lady..." Baxter began as they reached the door to her cabin. A single gunshot, a sharp *pop*, prevented further dialogue. He spun, but Ekaterina was even faster, running back down the way they had come. It was only a few short steps and her automatic had appeared in her hand as she burst through the door and came up short with a gasp.

A thousand things flew through Baxter's mind as he followed her in. He was ashamed that one of them was the thought that Yefimov had overpowered and killed Juneau, which would free Ekaterina...

The smell of cordite hit his nostrils, overlaying the copper tang of blood. Juneau was over by the porthole, unlatching it. The sunlight streaming through illuminated the cloud of acrid powder smoke that swirled and danced as it started to disperse. Baxter felt an overwhelming sense of relief that his friend was still alive.

The same could not be said for Yefimov. He slumped in the chair he'd been tied to, head back, and the porthole Juneau was opening was splattered with blood and chunks of brain. Baxter walked round, swallowing gorge. The hole in Yefimov's brow, just above his left eye, was deceptively small — the Nagant fired a powerful round and it had made a mess of the back of the traitor's head. Blood and pulped brain matter dripped from the ragged, fist-sized hole there and pooled on the decking. Baxter noted that one of Yefimov's hands was free, scored bloody — no doubt as he pulled it free from his bonds.

"He came for me, you see," Juneau said in a slightly distracted voice. He sounded calm — too calm, in fact. Baxter stepped around the expanding pool of blood to his side. He was shaking, very slightly. "He managed to work his hand free. I'd shot him before I'd even thought about it."

Baxter reached out and gently took the still-smoking revolver from Juneau's hand; he gave it up without resistance. The barrel was warm to the touch and Baxter worked the ejection lever to remove the remaining live rounds before placing it on a side table and pocketing the bullets.

Baxter glanced across at Ekaterina. Her eyes were wide, the merest hint of a tear at the corner of her eye. He knew she had been thinking the same thing, as they rushed here, and the thought of her husband being dead had obviously terrified her. He felt an agonising stab of jealousy and fought it down. "Sounds like he didn't give you a choice, my friend," he said. He could hear the sound of feet beyond the door, moved quickly to block it before people could come barging in.

"Everything is under control," he told Lieutenant Koenig, the leader of the pack running here. "Second Captain Juneau is in shock. He and the countess will go to his cabin. Please ask Dr Andropov to attend him, and alert Pavel that he will need a drink. A stiff one."

"I heard a gunshot, will the doctor not be needed…" Koenig began, and quailed at Baxter's scowl.

"Mr Yefimov is beyond any medical assistance," he said bluntly. "Detail a party to collect his body and prepare it for burial. And someone to clean this mess up."

"You're a good man to have around in a crisis," Ekaterina said as she took her husband's arm. She was still pale, but had composed herself. "You keep your head."

Baxter shrugged. "I'm a sailor, ma'am, who's survived more than a few years at sea."

She smiled, slightly sadly, and patted his arm as she escorted a shaking Juneau from the cabin.

"He's sleeping," Ekaterina said later, as she and Baxter relaxed over a pot of tea in the Juneaus' receiving cabin. "So try to keep your voice down."

Baxter cocked his head and looked at her inquisitively. The shock and worry of before had been replaced by something else. Almost as though she was angry with her husband.

"It wasn't his fault, you know. We should have had Yefimov watched at all times, or at least tied him better."

She shot him a slightly scathing, but also vaguely amused look. "Well, Juneau will be pleased he fooled at least one person."

That took Baxter aback. He opened his mouth, closed it again and thought. "You think…"

"I suspect. It's more or less how I would have set it up."

Occasionally, she said things that left him chilled to the bone. No — not what she said, but the way she said it. Clinically, almost casually.

"Well, he's no longer a threat to us…"

"Oh, don't be so naïve!" She slumped back in her chair, took up her beverage. "Yes, he was a threat, but one under control."

"You sound angry that he's dead?"

"Because I wanted to question him, get intelligence on who his backers are and what they're planning."

"Well, I think we already know that," he said gruffly, starting to feel his anger stir. He knew her response to hearing the shot, and relief at seeing Juneau alive, was making him behave in an utterly irrational and churlish manner.

"We know what you have told us," she said, her voice slightly caustic, then relented and waved a hand in apology. "And while I have no doubt you are telling the truth, as far as you understand it, I would like to have more … corroboration?"

Of course he was telling her the truth, because he knew he was hers, now. He was beginning to realise, though, that she would never be his. Not truly. That stung him, right down to his core, but it was something he knew he would learn to live with. Just as he'd learned to live with other disappointments.

She was staring levelly at him, almost as though she could look through his skull and read whatever was going through his mind. Given he'd always been something of an open book and she was unusually perceptive, it was likely she was doing exactly that. "Well, at least he isn't a danger to us anymore," he reiterated, by way of attempting a distraction.

"And that is why, I think, Cristov did it — Yefimov was a threat to the two people he cares about most in the world." Baxter raised his eyebrows in surprise. "Oh, my husband has taken quite a shine to you," she said, her eyes now dancing with amusement. "It might have been one of the things that has kept you alive."

"There's more than one?"

"I'm told you have your uses." A wicked smile was playing over Ekaterina's mouth now, then her expression became stormy again. "I am given to understand that Gorchakov's health has deteriorated to the point that he has been confined to his bed by Dr Andropov. I fear this may break our good captain entirely, and depending on who replaces him things could change around here. Significantly."

"Has this been reported to the admiral's staff?"

"Not as yet, no."

He shrugged. "Well, I'm sure there's still a good chance the good captain will recover his health and wits and reassume command. I'm sure there's no need to inform the staff until such time as we are *absolutely* certain he will not make a recovery. Which probably won't be until we're thoroughly at sea and with no easy option for him to be replaced. Sadly."

She looked at him quizzically, and then grinned. "You are truly a practical species, you sailors."

"I couldn't possibly know what you mean."

She nodded. "I will speak to Dr Andropov. This will put a large burden on Juneau, you know."

"He's already carrying it, and he's got some good officers to support him."

"And a good friend."

Baxter rose rather than responding to that, wondering just how true that really was. He wasn't sure hoping someone was dead to free his wife fit the definition of a 'good friend'. "So, what next?"

"We bury Yefimov, as a good Christian should be, but with little ceremony as he was a traitor. And then, I'm told — ever onwards, ever northwards."

She couldn't hide the scorn in her voice.

CHAPTER 21

The Straits of Tsushima. Morning, 27th May 1905

"Damn this fog."

Baxter glanced across the open bridge at Lieutenant Koenig's exclamation. The young officer was an indistinct shape in the heavy fog that blanketed what was now the Imperial Russian Navy's Pacific Fleet, since the 3rd Squadron had finally joined up.

"This fog, if it holds, could be the only thing that gets us through to Vladivostok," he pointed out, moving across to join Koenig in staring east, towards Japan. Trying to make anything out was hopeless, of course. They were steaming more or less blind. Somewhere to starboard the rest of the fleet was the occasional fleetingly-seen glimpse, when the fog banks broke, or more commonly a dark shape the lookouts were just about aware of.

"True," Koenig admittedly ruefully. Like a lot of the younger officers, he appeared to remain devoted to the idea of forcing a decisive engagement at this point. While Baxter agreed it *would* be a deciding match, he was less sure that it would go the way some of the Russians still believed it would. "It does mean we don't even know if Togo and his ships are even at sea."

They had limited intelligence on what the Japanese movements were. With Port Arthur taken and the independent cruiser squadron at Vladivostok contained, they knew Togo would have taken the opportunity to return to port to resupply and refit. Their own hold ups, particularly the interminable weeks at Van Phong while they waited for the reinforcements, had been a gift to their enemy.

Baxter sniffed the damp air. "If he isn't at sea, he'll be ready to put to sea quickly. We're not far from a number of ports."

"It begs the question of why the admiral chose to come this way," Koenig muttered, looking vaguely abashed at having the temerity to question the fleet's commander.

"He doesn't have any choice — the ships are worn and in need of maintenance, even without having to worry about coal," Baxter said, his voice gentle. He couldn't blame Koenig for his tension, which was shared by most aboard. "This is the most direct route to Vladivostok."

It was also, of course, the most dangerous. The straits between Korea and Japan were relatively narrow and easy to cover, and the Japanese owned both shores. Rozhestvensky had timed his arrival well, approaching at night in the hopes of slipping through, and the fog had been a bonus.

Baxter had allowed himself to start hoping that they might actually pull this off. It wouldn't be a victory, but they would have survived as a formation and, with time to refit and resupply, could become an effective fighting force.

Juneau arrived on the bridge. There were bags under his eyes, which remained slightly haunted by what he'd done. None of them had spoken of what had transpired with 'their friend', and didn't even speak his name. Baxter was still unsure whether Juneau had, in fact, murdered the traitor, or whether it had been a shooting in self-defence.

"I gather congratulations are in order, First Captain," he greeted his friend.

Juneau gave him a wan smile that was still genuine. "Thank you. It was confirmed this morning. Gorchakov will be transferred to one of the hospital ships today, and a shore hospital at the earliest convenience."

"Your first command?"

"Of any real substance, yes." Juneau took his glasses off and wiped them with a silk handkerchief. "I hope it does not last merely a day."

Juneau straightened, and adjusted the hang of his double-breasted, black overcoat. It hadn't seen the light of day for quite some time, and hung loosely about him. "Well, gentlemen, at least we are out of that interminable heat! This weather suits my Russian soul better."

There was a murmur of agreement and some laughter that helped break the tension.

"Hello, who's that?" Koenig said almost to himself, the mild interjection sending ice water down Baxter's back. "Oh, it's just the *Orel*."

A break in the fog had revealed the hospital ship, trailing a bit behind the fleet. In accordance with international custom and law, she was fully illuminated, the red crosses on her white-painted superstructure serving to make it clear that she was not a legitimate target. It was the decent thing to do, but the glow of her lights in the fog risked drawing enemy attention.

"Who's that she's signalling, though?" someone else asked. Any number of people were now staring at the ship — any break in the monotony of the fogbound early morning.

Orel was signalling to port, more or less across *Yaroslavich*'s stern. Juneau led a small procession to the other wing of the bridge to scour the sea scape for the mysterious communicant.

"*Orel*'s signalling as though that's a ship in the fleet, but she looks like a merchantman," Juneau said, confusion apparent in his voice.

Baxter had the distant vessel in his field glasses now, studied her carefully. "She's a merchantman," he said slowly. "But she's an armed one."

"Is it the *Ural?*" Juneau asked, referring to the armed merchant cruiser assigned to close escort of the fleet auxiliaries.

Baxter felt a gnawing sense of doubt and growing dread. "She's off station if she is. Could have got lost in the fog, I suppose." That wouldn't be unusual. "Or one of the ships sent out to create a diversion, trying to rejoin."

Rozhestvensky had trimmed the fleet down somewhat during the final approach, sending most of the transports away and detaching the less useful warships to try to distract the Japanese. Juneau and Baxter hadn't even raised the possibility of Ekaterina or Tommy departing on those vessels. They were still in a war zone and subject to attack, true, but it was more a common understanding that the four of them were going on together.

The hospital ship was taking the opportunity of a break in the weather to signal the other ships in her vicinity with her lamp. It all seemed terribly … routine, though.

"There goes our armed merchantman, turning back into the fog bank."

"I don't think that was any of our compatriots," Baxter said, that sense of dread growing with every passing moment. "She's definitely a warship, though."

"Japanese?" Koenig asked, and Baxter had to stifle an urge to throttle the young man. He was growing to be a competent officer, but he could still be remarkably obtuse.

Juncau didn't bother responding. "Mr Koenig, signal the flag — possible sighting of enemy warship. Add our position and the time of first sighting."

Baxter was certain it wasn't a 'possible' sighting. No other navy would be foolish enough to operate in these contested waters. The newly minted captain had to be cautious in his reports, of course.

"Are we going to quarters, Graf?"

Juneau thought about it for a few moments, but not too long. He had come into his own, now that he was formally in charge, and there was a new decisiveness to him. "No — she'll shadow us but stay out of range." Juneau stepped back to the railing beside Baxter and lowered his voice as he switched from French to English. "Well, I think we can assume she was Japanese, and therefore Togo will soon be aware of our position."

"Technology marches on." A few years ago, this would have been less of a problem as the picket ship would have to race to within visual range of either a relay point or Togo's flagship to signal a position that could very well be out of date. Now, with wireless telegraph, Togo would put to sea once he knew the enemy was in the area and be kept up to date by the shadowing vessels.

"Well, that's it then."

Juneau nodded, his own expression bleak. Baxter felt a frustration right in the pit of his stomach — they had made it this far and were barely a hundred nautical miles from their destination. It would be hard for them to avoid a battle now, and unless Togo was more incompetent than his record suggested it would not be a Russian victory. From the look on Juneau's face, he was thinking the same thing.

"No need to alarm the other officers or the crew," Juneau said after a moment.

Time enough for that later. Baxter sought about for something to change the subject. "How is the countess?" he said eventually.

"Still laid low by sea sickness," Juneau said unhappily. "She has managed a journey close to sixteen thousand nautical miles with few issues, and is struck down now — I can only assume there is something particular to the motion of the Sea of Japan that does not agree with her."

"If we're about to engage the enemy, it would be as well if she and Tommy were below decks."

"Oh, agreed."

"Where do you want me?"

"Wherever you feel you can do most good — you have been training the secondary batteries, and this close to the Japanese Home Islands we may actually encounter torpedo boats."

It was a tacit acknowledgement that Baxter had slotted into the chain of command, though without any specific duties. He didn't and would never wear a Russian uniform, but the ship's purser had outfitted him in something that looked a bit like one without any of the insignia or braid.

"Aye, Captain."

Juneau's smile had more warmth in it this time. "I will certainly get used to hearing that." His expression became more serious. "However, there is something you must do for me. Concerning my wife, and Tomas'ka. And Pavel."

"And Maxim."

Juneau took his glasses off and peered myopically at the lenses, already misted over again. "I should really have lodged him ashore in Cam Ranh. I should have put all of you ashore. But, yes, Maxim as well."

The fog cleared to a patchy mist over the course of the morning, and from the *Yaroslavich*'s position to port of the labouring fleet auxiliaries they had a perfect view of the Japanese cruisers as they steamed up past the Russian lines on a parallel course.

"I make it eleven," Juneau said without lowering his old-fashioned, finely-wrought telescope. "They appear content to steam just out of our maximum range."

"They're just making sure we don't go anywhere." Baxter found himself oddly calm now that the die was cast and action seemed inevitable. The mix of excitement and apprehension on the bridge was palpable in the slightly rushed, too loud conversations going on. "This isn't the main force, and some of those ships are bloody ancient — think the lead cruisers are that bizarre French design with the single massive main gun. Though I've no idea what in God's name that monstrosity is."

He lowered his glasses and pointed with the blade of his hand towards an odd, dumpy ship with twin big guns — probably twelve-inchers — in barbettes rather than turrets, one on each side.

Juneau smiled, obviously pleased to have more knowledge of at least some naval matters. "That's the *Chinyen* — the Japanese took her from the Chinese a decade ago." He patted the railing in front of him. "She's not as ... venerable as this girl, but nor is she new."

"What an odd battle this will be — some of the most modern ships afloat, and any number of relics of the last century. I shouldn't be surprised to see *Victory* herself come sailing into the fight."

"Having the Third Division here is bad enough." Juneau gestured to the four battleships that comprised a full third of their line of battle. "They shouldn't even be at sea, let alone out of coastal waters, and while they do mount ten-inch guns they'll still be out-ranged by the Japanese."

"Flagship is hoisting a signal, Graf," Koenig reported, and they turned all eyes forward. To an untrained eye or on paper, the Imperial Russian Pacific Fleet was grand enough, eleven battleships and nine cruisers along with a clutch of destroyers, armed merchantmen and dispatch boats. As Juneau had said, though, some of those battleships should have been scrapped years ago and were holding the fleet's speed to less than ten knots when speed was the only thing that might have saved them.

They could just about make out of the hoist on Rozhestvensky's flagship, offset as they were from the main line of battle. They dutifully waited for the signals to be passed down the line until their own ineffectual commanding admiral, Oskar Enkvist on the *Oleg*, repeated it.

Clear for action.

"Today is the anniversary of the Tsar and Tsarina's coronation," Juneau said, almost wistfully, then nodded decisively to Koenig. With Yefimov dead and Gorchakov strapped to his cot, raving and delusional (or so it was said), the young man was now Juneau's deputy. "Mr Koenig, you may clear for action."

"I'll see to the secondary guns," Baxter said.

Juneau stopped him as he turned, stuck out his hand. "Good luck."

Baxter shook the proffered hand firmly. "To us all."

Clearing for action had been a rush of activity and excitement. Non-essential items and personnel were struck down into the hold and ammunition for the cruiser's armament was brought up to the ready lockers. The tompions, stoppers put into the gun muzzles to keep the barrels clean and dry, were pulled out. In the sickbay, Andropov and his two attendants laid out the gleaming instruments of their grisly trade. They weren't at quarters so the crews didn't assemble at their stations for combat, but in all other respects the ship was prepared for what was to come.

For a while at least, what was to come seemed to be the fleet continuing on its steady way. Rozhestvensky seemed to be ignoring the shadowing Japanese cruisers. There was little point chasing the fleet enemy ships, though. Short of some contrivance or cunning device they would not be able to bring the enemy to action. All the cruisers had to do was turn away until they were ready to offer battle. That would happen when their own battle line appeared.

Occasionally, a gun thumped, making everyone jump as the tension increased. The smattering of shots seemed to be skirmishing or accidental discharges, though, and did not presage the general cannonade.

Vasily had appeared silently by Baxter's side as the preparations began. He had long since stopped being his guard, but somehow had never returned to his own usual duties.

Baxter noticed preparations for some sort of ceremony on the foredeck. "What the devil's going on there?" he asked.

"A mass will be celebrated. For the coronation."

"Damned odd time to be having a church service," Baxter grumbled.

Vasily shrugged, in that silently expressive way the Russian peasant had. It was a shrug that said it wasn't his place to question such matters, but perhaps the eve of a fight wasn't such a bad time to invoke a deity's help. "You will not attend?"

"Never been much of a church-going man, Vasily, but you go ahead."

Preparations for the service were stalled, however, by the sound of gunfire to the east. Everyone stopped in their tracks. Some stared upwards as they listened intently, others scanned to starboard. It wasn't the encompassing thunder of a general action, though, but the sporadic crack of lighter guns. "A skirmish — probably our own lighter vessels driving off destroyers," Baxter decided, then shooed the gun crews towards the foredeck as an announcement was made for all hands to muster for church. "Go, pray!"

He remained with the port battery, staring out towards the tail end of the Japanese cruiser line which was now keeping pace with the Russian ships. They were still miles away, and mostly all he could see was the dark smudge of their coal smoke. Juneau was still up on the bridge, over on the port wing and looking in the same direction as the sonorous tones of the Russian Orthodox priest got the service underway.

He heard a light footstep behind him, didn't need to turn to see who it was. "Master Dunbar, you should be tending to the countess."

"Ah wanted to see what was going on."

Baxter lowered his glasses and turned. "I can't blame you for that, but I need you to listen to me now. It's going to get very, very dangerous on deck, particularly if we end up in the thick of it. Heavy shells are going to go straight through our sides and men are going to die. So you can stay on deck for now — I imagine her ladyship will want updates — but as soon as the fighting starts I want you below decks." He saw the lad's rebellious expression starting to take shape. "You need to look after the countess — it'll be the most important job you can do." That got through to him. "I want you to promise me, now — your word as a man that you'll stay by her side."

Tommy nodded jerkily, eyes like saucers. For the most part this had been a jolly jape for him. Baxter needed him to understand, though, that what was coming was no grand adventure.

"All right — off with you and tell Ekaterina what's occurring."

Baxter turned back to his watch-keeping. He was sweeping the sea when a small smoke cloud caught his eye; lean grey shapes beneath it on a closing course. "Destroyers on the port quarter!" he bellowed. "Closing fast!"

Juneau waved an acknowledgement, and a second later a bugle sounded from the bridge.

Action stations!

The three Japanese destroyers came on with great dash, slim rakish little vessels that stirred Baxter's blood to see. "They're probably probing," he said, to no one in particular and mostly to himself. "They won't try a full torpedo run in broad daylight." The Russian lines would be a tempting target for a spread of torpedoes, but the fast light ships would be chewed up long before they got into range.

The *Yaroslavich* was deployed about a mile to the west of the main cruiser formation that brought up the rear of the fleet, there to warn of and spoil such an attack. Baxter wasn't overly familiar with the Russian signalling system — he wasn't trusted enough for *that* information — but he guessed the flags that had run smoothly aloft said something like 'destroyers sighted' and 'am engaging the enemy'. Sure enough, the fore port six-inch gun spoke with a terrible roar, the long barrel crashing back into the barbette as it spat a long tongue of flame and smoke towards the Japanese ships. A moment later the aft port gun fired and he watched for the fall of shot.

Twin splashes rose ahead of the lead destroyer. "Short, but on the right line," Baxter muttered. From the barbette pits he could hear the cadenced shouting of the gun crews reloading. The destroyers were already well within the range of the six-inchers — something for which the lookouts would have to be chastised for — and it wouldn't be long until they were in range of the secondary batteries. The quick-firing 4.7-inch guns were designed for exactly this sort of close-in work, and he could tell their crews were chafing to open fire.

"Mr Baxter!" Koenig shouted down from the bridge. His next words were mostly swallowed by the crash of the main guns firing again, but he caught 'at will' and knew what he was being ordered to do.

He looked along the line of gun crews, their expectant faces turned to him. There were two guns next to each other, more or less amidships, and one fore and aft on the other side of the main gun barbettes. He stepped back until they could all see him. "Ready and lay your weapons! You may commence independent fire when Number Two gun fires!"

He stepped forward again. There was no point trying to co-ordinate broadsides against such small, fast-moving targets and he'd trained each gun crew to work independently. He crouched over the gunsight of the number two weapon. It was a simple enough sight, crude even, and his target bobbed up and down in the small magnified view. He had to think of it in that way, just a target, not a ship not so dissimilar to some he'd served on, crewed by people who may look different to him but were cut from the same cloth.

He stepped back and pulled the firing lanyard. The gun cracked, not as loud as the six-inch but still deafening, and a second later the rest of the battery fired. A moment later both the big guns fired at the same time and the lead destroyer disappeared in a cluster of waterspouts and spray — remarkably good shooting. A cheer went up from at least one of the bluejackets, dying as soon as the Japanese ship came flying out of the cloud, still intact but — seen through glasses at least — some damage obvious around the prow.

At that point the destroyers' three-inch popguns opened up, the ships firing in turn as they veered away from the Russian line. They were at extreme range and primarily intended for killing torpedo boats. Only one shell came close enough for its spout to splash against the side of the cruiser, and then the destroyers were speeding out of range, chased by continued but ineffective Russian fire.

"Cease fire! Cease fire!" Baxter bellowed once it was clear the enemy ships were out of accurate range. He had no doubt that the Russian crews, with the bit between their teeth, would continue to expend ammunition uselessly. "Sponge and house your guns!"

The six-inchers gave the impudent little ships one more round each and desisted.

He looked along the line of gun crews. "Bloody good shooting, all of you! Certainly a step up from the North Sea!"

Grins answered his joke but he struggled to match them. The *Yaroslavich* had fired her first rounds of the battle, but he knew a long day lay ahead.

There was no warning when the battle commenced properly. The men had their lunch, with an extra tot of vodka in celebration of the auspicious day, and if it wasn't for the silent and sullen presence of the enemy forces and the fact the ship was cleared for action, it could almost have been a normal day of steaming. Ever onwards, ever northwards. Conversation in the wardroom was desultory and Juneau, who normally drove the socialisation, was still on the bridge. Just after noon, the squadron turned onto its final heading, towards Vladivostok.

Baxter went to see Ekaterina in her cabin a little bit after that. She looked pale but defiant, sitting in a chair by the porthole so she could peer out. She smiled over her shoulder as Pavel let him in. "Mr Baxter, how delightful of you to visit," she said, and he was shocked at how gaunt she had become since he'd last seen her. The seasickness must be taking a terrible toll on her.

"My lady. Do I find you well?"

She waved a hand languidly. "It seems I improve in the afternoons, and the firing of the guns earlier certainly stirred the blood. I take it we are not yet engaged fully?"

"We seem to have manoeuvring and skirmishing. I shall ask the captain to come down and tell you more."

She reached out a hand to take one of his, pressing her lips to his knuckles. "That is kind of you, but I wouldn't disturb him now." She looked up at him, eyes large in her face. "I imagine he has asked you to look to my safety while this is all going on?"

He smiled. "Of course."

She scowled. "I don't need looking after," she snapped, letting go of his hand then relenting. "I would ask you to do the same for me, and look after Juneau. The bridge is a terribly exposed place."

He crouched next to her so he could look her in the eyes without her having to crane her head back. "I'll do you a deal, Katya," he said, voice deadly serious. "If I know you're safe — as safe as you can be in the middle of a battle — I can focus entirely on keeping your husband out of harm's way. As much as I can, in the middle of a battle. Tommy'll stay with you."

She glared at him, then sank back in her chair. "Very well," she said almost petulantly, then sighed. "You are excellent for looking after people, Baxter, but you do not have anyone to — what is the expression? — watch your back."

"There's Vasily. And I've managed to make it to the ripe old age of twenty-six mostly by myself."

She blinked at him in surprise. "You are barely halfway to thirty?"

"A lot of the men aboard are younger," he said with a shrug. He'd never even wondered how old she was, though she looked barely older than himself. He rose. "I should return to my station," he said gently. "Promise me you'll go below. And keep Tommy with you — I don't want him wondering around in a battle."

She nodded without speaking, taking his hand again. She used it to draw him down until she could put her arms around his neck and kiss him. It was a long, deep and not particularly chaste kiss. "Keep safe," she whispered, and he found himself unable to speak in turn. He nodded, and hurried from the cabin.

He went from there to the deck and up onto the bridge to try to get an idea of the enemy's disposition. Tommy, normally forbidden from the bridge, took the opportunity to trail after him. As they watched, the lead Russian division — made up of the modern *Borodino* battleships — commenced a turn in line.

"What the devil is he playing at?" Baxter wondered aloud. The second ship of the leading division seemed to be turning in the wrong direction, being subjected to a barrage of signals from the flagship. Baxter could imagine the admiral hurling yet another pair of field glasses into the sea, a habit much commented on during exercises.

"I think he's trying to form line abreast," Juneau commented, lowering his telescope. "But Bukhvostov in *Alexander III* has stymied him. There — he has cancelled the order."

None of the other divisions had followed, and a few minutes later a break in the persistent mist showed two parallel lines of big ships, led by four battleships. They were flying the rising sun and turning onto a south-westerly course to intercept the Russian fleet.

The Japanese battle line had arrived. It was steaming to cross the Russian T, the classic tactic every naval commander strived for. The Russian battleships were now in two lines, the *Borodinos* coming back onto their original heading and the second division on a parallel course but trailing.

"This is not a formation to fight in," Juneau commented, voice flat.

Baxter caught Tommy's quizzical glance. "The fleet's main firepower is now sailing straight into the Japanese broadsides and only the front ships are able to bring their fore guns to bear, unless Togo turns to parallel them. The two lines will mask each other's fire as well. Things are going to start getting bloody."

As Baxter spoke, the Russian van fired its secondary batteries, ranging the Japanese ships.

"Tommy, lad, time to go below."

CHAPTER 22

"This Togo fellow knows his business," Baxter shouted to Lieutenant Koenig. The *Yaroslavich* was in a lull in her own battle, but the continuous thunder of the big ships battering each other was loud despite being miles away. And Baxter's ears were still ringing from an hour or more of relatively continuous firing.

Koenig was touring the ship during this break, getting damage and casualty reports to pass to Juneau. *If he lives through this*, Baxter thought, *he'd make a fine officer.*

The Russian fleet was already starting to tumble into disarray, despite early on surpassing their previous gunnery efforts. Rozhestvensky's flagship, the *Suvorov* had staggered out of line and didn't seem capable of doing much except receive a pounding whenever the Japanese line went past. She was certainly not issuing any orders from the commander. The *Oslyabya*, an older ship and the flagship of the fleet's second in command Rear-Admiral Folkersam, was also lagging.

"We've lost both flagships," Koenig muttered miserably. "Command now lies with Nebogatov in the third division, and he is hardly inspiring."

"Well, the admiral did issue orders that the ship at the head of the line leads the way to Vladivostok, so he obviously felt the same way." Baxter had to agree — he hadn't really been inspired by many in the fleet above the rank of second captain, but the young officer didn't need to hear that. Instead he clapped Koenig on the shoulder, rocking him on his feet. "Well, at least we're mostly intact, and I'm told we haven't even lost anyone!"

This much was true. Togo's ships seemed to be concentrating on the modern Russian units, utterly ignoring the ships that had been sent along just to draw fire. While the *Yaroslavich* had fired on anything that had come into range, she'd only taken a few rounds in response, only two of which had hit. The enemy appeared to be using high explosive rather than armour-piercing shells, causing damage on the upper works but, mercifully, not penetrating to anywhere vital.

"There goes the *Oslyabya*!" someone groaned nearby.

Baxter snapped his glasses back up. The big old battleship was indeed turning all the way over — she'd been listing heavily for a while and now her funnels had touched the water. Seen at a distance, he could almost be dispassionate about watching the tiny figures of the crew throwing themselves into the water. Her port screw was still turning as it came into view. She was the first total casualty of the fight.

"Three fifty," Koenig said, his voice dead. "Many hours until nightfall."

Too many. Though they still outnumbered the enemy battle line, Togo had already shown himself to be the master of this part of the world's seas.

"Here they come again!" a lookout shouted. Then, more formally. "Enemy cruisers to port!"

That was the pattern for the rest of the day. The Russian lines ploughed on, ever northwards towards Vladivostok. Gun smoke mixed with the drifting banks of fog and made visibility patchy at best. Togo's big ships mostly concentrated on their counterparts, a battle of comparatively epic proportion mercifully at arm's length from the old cruisers labouring along with the auxiliaries. An occasional twelve-inch shell still came their way when the Japanese line had no other targets. They were not left unmolested by the Japanese cruisers and destroyers, however, which passed through the slower Russian formation repeatedly, firing on targets as they bore.

"Where the hell is Enkvist?" Baxter ground out as they watched, impotently, the plucky little seagoing tug *Rus* finally going down a bit after four. Ironically, enemy action hadn't done for her. She'd been accidentally rammed by the big auxiliary cruiser charged with close protection of the support ships, and the *Yaroslavich* couldn't even slow to pick up survivors — the enemy light units would obliterate any stationary target. Of the bigger, modern cruisers that were supposed to be looking after the support ships, there had been little sign since the firing commenced in earnest.

"I'm sure he's doing something vital," Juneau said, his voice tired. It was the first time they had spoken since they'd cleared for action, what felt like an age ago. Baxter had gone up to the bridge to try to get a better view of the action, and had been greeted by Pavel with a cup of smoky sweet tea that had been most restorative.

He couldn't see much more of the rolling battle, but he could see the damage they'd taken. It still wasn't bad, but more than he'd thought — in the thick of the fighting, he'd only noticed when near misses had slapped shell splinters into the sides and one light gun hit that had ricocheted off the hull at an oblique angle, terrifyingly close to the gun he'd been laying at the time.

"We need to think about the night," Baxter said, after they'd stood side by side in silence and contemplated the horror going on around them.

"You think we'll make it that far? Sunset won't be for another three and a half hours."

"I think we might. We're giving as good as we get, or close enough, and the enemy is mostly going after the mainline units. Night-time is when we might be able to lose them, but it's also when the torpedo boats and destroyers will go to work properly."

"We have our orders..."

"Look around you, man!" Baxter's raised voice drew glances from all over the bridge, even though they were speaking English, and he lowered his voice but still spoke urgently. "Command has broken down entirely. The flag is out of action and we've not heard from the admiral. His deputy's gone. I assume Nebogatov is in charge but there have been no signals. Enkvist is obviously evading combat. At some point, you are going to have to consider the survival of this ship."

Juneau closed his eyes, almost as though he were in pain. Baxter didn't envy him the burdens of command, particularly in the midst of a fleet action when the fleet appeared to have no command. "You're right, of course, but we also cannot abandon our charges. Let me think on it."

"At the very least I ... recommend that you confer with the other captains on a course of action."

"Thank you, Mr Baxter. You may return to your station — once you have finished your tea, of course."

As rebukes went, it wasn't a stinging one. Baxter grinned — it was good to belong to a crew again, even one in such dire straits.

They almost didn't make it to nightfall.

The fighting had become monotonous. The noise of the main units slugging it out had become so constant and all-encompassing Baxter could nearly ignore it. The two hours since he and Juneau had spoken had become a grinding hell of repetitive action. The gun crews under his charge firing and reloading while the main guns assaulted their eardrums as enemy ships came in on one heading, then run to the other side to assist the opposite battery as the Japanese passed them by and all the while shells were crashing down around them.

More and more were hitting the *Yaroslavich* as well as falling in the sea on either side, and now it became clear why the enemy was using explosive rather than armour-piercing shells. The blasts were lethal on the upper works, the explosions and fragments tearing into exposed gun crews and setting fires that they were struggling to put out.

Baxter realised the real danger was the fire. Picking himself up from behind the shelter of one of his guns after a shell from an enemy cruiser, fired at extreme range as a parting gift, had burst against the superstructure twenty yards away, he surveyed a scene of devastation. Broken men, or the parts of men, littered the deck. One of the gunners was lying, crying softly, against the gun he'd sheltered behind — the man was so badly burned Baxter couldn't recognise him. There was no time to pause to give him comfort or even shout for a medical orderly, though, as he could see one of the many piles of coals bags had started to smoulder, the heat of the explosion enough to set the jute bag alight.

He surged forward, seizing the first sack of coal. It was already well alight, the fabric threatening to come apart in his hands and spill smoking black lumps across the wooden deck. He ignored the pain as flames played over his skin. Two long strides and a great heave saw a shower of coal go over the side, and he turned to see a number of men staring at him wide eyed with confusion. "The coal! Get it over the side now, you idiots!" he bellowed.

It was almost comical, watching the realisation sink in. He lunged forward to grab the next bag and suddenly a dozen pairs of hands were doing the same thing, getting rid of that pile. Others were taking up the cry, nobody waiting for orders or permission, the Russian peasant sailor's naturally ingrained obedience overcome by the fear of burning to death. Within minutes the decks were clear of the hateful and suddenly dangerous stuff, a rain of it going over both sides. Some men were actually laughing, verging on hysterical, as they laboured to throw the precious fuel over the side.

"We all suffered the black fever," Vasily said, when he saw Baxter looking at two men who were throwing lumps of coal at each other. "And now we vomit our feast back out."

"Would that we had time to sluice the decks and get rid of the dust," Koenig said as he struggled to get a sack over the edge. Vasily strode past him, a sack in each hand, and effortlessly launched them into the sea. The officer, finally getting rid of his own burden, gestured at yet more enemy ships closing to range.

"They'll burn well enough of their own accord," Baxter said. Even at distance, he could see the battleships were having the same problems, and one of them at least seemed to be a raging inferno. Another had gone under, unremarked while they worked. "Stand to your guns!"

Around dusk, a trio of enemy destroyers made a determined attempt on the *Yaroslavich*, charging in through the cruiser's sustained fire and closing until the one-inch Hotchkiss revolving cannon and the machine guns could come into play, hurling a hail of hot lead at the incoming vessels.

"Keep firing!" Baxter yelled. "They're going for a torpedo run!"

The loader of the gun beside him screamed and fell to the deck, clutching at his bleeding face and dropping the shell he was about to ram into the 4.7's hot breech. Baxter stopped it with his foot, scooped it up and rammed it home, only just getting his hands out of the way as another gunner closed the breech. There was no real need to sight now, the destroyers were so close, and the shell burst near the little ship's main gun, tearing the crew apart. Other men stepped forward, almost heedless of the danger, and the returned shot smashed the firing port Baxter was at. He felt heat on his face and was hurled back by the blast. He lay staring at the sky, numb for a moment, but the stinging pain from a dozen little cuts told him he was still alive.

Men, bluejackets, *his* crew, were screaming around him. The Japanese shell had smashed into the bulwark above the firing port but not torn it entirely. The effects had nonetheless been devastating, hot shards of metal slashing into the crew. Two were dead outright and one man seemed to be trying to hold one side of his face onto his head. The loader was saved only because his face had already been torn off by the preceding hit and he'd already fallen. Vasily was by his side, trying to pull him away. Baxter shook him off and scrambled through the blood and spilled viscera to the gun. "Help me here!" he shouted, or thought he did — mostly all he could hear was ringing.

The gun was intact, although the damage to the surrounding hull plating limited its traverse. The crew had almost finished reloading — he caught the breech block as the cruiser heaved and rolled, swinging it closed. Vasily threw his own enormous strength into bringing the weapon to bear once more, the mounting's scream of protest as terrible as the howls of wounded men, and they fired at less than a thousand yards.

Baxter never saw what happened to that shot. The noise had been thunderous and continuous for hours, but the explosion that rocked everyone on their feet was by far the loudest thing he'd ever heard.

"What in…" Jumping up onto the gun mounting to get a better view over the bulwark, Baxter looked instinctively towards the main battle — something like that could only have been a battleship going up. If it had been their own ship, he wouldn't be alive to consider it. Sure enough, even without his glasses — lost at some point during the action — he could make out the enormous column of smoke that marked the passing of one of the big battleships. He could see the bows of something, already mostly sunk bare moments after the explosion. "Good God. Eight hundred men or more." It was unlikely anyone would have survived that.

He turned back to the more immediate problems, and saw the destroyers were sheering off. Lines of white bubbles, three of them, showed where they'd launched their lethal loads at the cruiser.

"*Torpedo!*" he roared. Someone on the bridge at least seemed to be paying attention and the cruiser was already turning away from the incoming paths. "Come on come on come…" he whispered. The first weapon went wide, the second missed the turning bows by a whisker and he braced himself, knowing the third would be a hit…

There was a *clunk* they all felt through the soles of their feet as the torpedo hit somewhere deep below. The expected detonation never happened, though, and it seemed to him that the entire crew blew out a breath of relief. A dud.

"I heard the explosion," Ekaterina said as she cleaned and dressed Baxter's cuts twenty minutes later, He hadn't had time to have the burned skin of his hands and forearms seen to, but luckily they had not been too badly scorched and she gently dabbed salve onto them.

The sickbay had been transformed into a charnel house. Casualties had been pouring in over the last few hours and the normally diffident Andropov and his assistants had been working like the Russian heroes of old to save as many as they could. It couldn't be all of them, though there were fewer dead being carried out for summary burial than there were wounded being brought in.

"I'm told it was the *Borodino*," Baxter said, voice flat with fatigue. "Most likely a magazine explosion. *Suvorov* finally went around the same time, which means we just have one modern battleship left."

"We are going to lose this fight, aren't we? Just as you predicted."

He'd not been surprised to find her and Tommy here, working amongst the wounded, bringing succour and comfort where they could, tending to the least badly injured who just needed stitches or a bandage. He couldn't muster any anger at that — he'd known all along she wouldn't be able to sit still below the waterline, and the sickbay was one of the safer places anyway. Maxim padded along after her, and the big gentle dog's presence seemed to have a calming effect on many of the wounded.

"We've already lost — now it's about getting as many ships to safety." He met her eyes. "I take no satisfaction in being right."

The sickbay was lit only by electric bulbs, making it hard to keep track of the day. Baxter guessed the last rays of a dying sun would be lighting the sea above, filtered to an ominous red by smoke. They were enjoying a respite, having lost the destroyers that had been hounding them in a fog bank. They were certainly not alone on the sea, there being dozens of ships still within twenty miles, but for now they were able to lick their wounds and bury their dead.

"So what do we do now?"

"Well, I'm not the captain. But the captain's a sensible man who listens to advice, so I imagine he's preparing for the night — that's when the torpedo boats will come out to hunt." He nodded to a man who lay quietly on one side of the crowded sickbay, his chest covered with bandages. "What happened to Khetoslav Andreivic?"

Ekaterina sighed. "By the time he got to one sack the coal itself was on fire. He held it against his chest to stop it collapsing. The doctor thinks he will survive, assuming the rest of us do."

"We just need to get through the night with as little damage as possible," Baxter said.

Juneau convened his officers in the wardroom to talk about exactly that not long after darkness had completely fallen. They were close to Japanese harbours, but it would still take the enemy torpedo boats time to reach the area and find targets. Nonetheless, there was a palpable sense of urgency in the compartment.

"It is clear," Juneau began, in a strong voice, "that this battle is lost."

A morbid silence greeted this pronouncement. No one could disagree with the assessment, but it was still shocking to hear it stated so bluntly by the captain.

"We have also had no contact with anyone of flag rank, and no orders. While we may be able to find the auxiliaries tomorrow, my suspicion is that they will scatter under cover of darkness. Those with officers more competent than the *Kamchatka*'s."

A murmur of amusement greeted that. The troublesome *Kamchatka* repair ship had strayed too close to the main battle and had been sunk almost as an afterthought by the Japanese battleships. While the loss of life was mourned, few would weep to see that ship's passing.

"Our goal, therefore, is to get ourselves and any other ships we may fall in with to Vladivostok. We will make steam north east, to take ourselves away from the last reported positions of the Japanese fleet, then attempt to cut west and trust to the weather and luck to avoid anything heavier than us. Our main concern, however, are the enemy light units. While we are not as tempting a target as the bigger ships, we are still a target and if any stumble upon us we can expect to be attacked. This close to enemy ports in both the Home Islands and Korea, I think we can assume a rather larger number than we faced at Dogger Bank."

This with a sardonic bow in Baxter's direction. He rolled his eyes.

"Will we run with searchlights on, in case?" a young officer asked.

Juneau shook his head. "No, no I am in agreement with Nebogatov on this — that will only serve to attract them. We will remain cleared for action but will stand the men down to eat and rest — they have done very well indeed today, better than any captain deserves. As have you all.

"However, the respite will only be short and we must be ready to close up as soon as any enemy vessels are detected. I also intend to bolster the armaments of the pinnaces and set them to patrol as we steam. I would ask for volun…"

Baxter had his hand in the air before he could really think about it, a second before Koenig and three other officers raised theirs. Juneau smiled with genuine pleasure. "Very well. Mr Baxter, you shall have one. Sava shall take the other — I am sorry, Koenig, I need you aboard with me."

Koenig made a valiant attempt not to look too crestfallen, and clapped Saveliy Romanovich on the shoulder.

The assembly broke up not long after that, but Juneau drew Baxter aside. "Are you sure about this?" he asked seriously. "You have done much aboard, but this is perhaps a step too far."

He knew Juneau wasn't asking about going into danger, although this certainly fit that description. By taking command of a vessel, even one as paltry as an armed steam pinnace, against allies of his home country, he was taking a direct and personal stake in the action in a way that running a battery of guns did not imply.

"We're all on this journey, Captain Juneau — right to the end." Baxter nodded to Juneau. "And I haven't forgotten my promise about the others."

CHAPTER 23

They put the pinnaces in the water not long after the conference finished. Miraculously, neither of them had been damaged by the enemy fire despite their prominent position amidships on the upper deck — well, nothing that the carpenter couldn't make right with some plugs. Juneau had ordered two of the one-pounder rotary cannon dismounted and mounted behind the wheelhouse of each of the little vessels, giving them considerably more close-in firepower — which would be vital for this sort of work. An extra machine gun had gone into the bows as well.

"You'll need to be careful firing the rotary gun," the gunnery officer said dourly as he prepared to clamber back up the ladder into the cruiser. Baxter hadn't got to know the man terribly well, but the bloodied bandage around his head, with his battered cap perched above, suggested he'd done his duty. "I won't answer for stability or indeed the hull if you go firing everything continuously."

Baxter nodded and saw him off before summoning his little crew to gather around. Unlike the officers, the bluejackets had been detailed for the job rather than being given the opportunity to volunteer, though he was pleased to see Vasily and most of the sailors who had gone on the 'pleasure cruise' with him and Ekaterina were aboard. He was also relieved and a little surprised to see young Tommy was nowhere in evidence. But then, he was more likely to stow away rather than present himself for duty.

They crowded into the stern of the boat, a circle of grimy tired faces, but ones which had fight left in them.

"If you're looking for a stirring speech about duty and honour and dying for the Motherland, you've come to the wrong shop," Baxter said, to a few answering grins. "My Russian's not that good, it's not my Motherland, and I've got no intention of dying here. So remember — keep your eyes sharp, as we're not just looking for boats but torpedo tracks. Report any you see immediately. Don't fire at anything unless I give the order, and when I do, give 'em hell." He nodded sharply. "Carry on."

The night was chaotic. The sounds of savage close-range combat sounded from all around — some only a few miles away but others almost to the horizon, showing just how scattered the Russian fleet had become. The muzzle flash of guns and darting searchlight beams illuminated the drifting banks of fog like a surreal, low-level thunderstorm.

The first few hours of the cold night were dull for the crew of the *Yaroslavich* and her little tenders. They chugged north and east, moving towards the invisible point on the map Juneau had picked for their attempt to run to safety. Everyone's senses were strained to the limit, looking for a shadow moving the way it shouldn't or for the tell-tale track of bubbles; the sound of steam pistons thumping in the night. They seemed to be cocooned in their own little shroud of darkness, though, more than three miles from the cruiser, and once the fear and tension of being separated from the bigger ship passed it started to feel almost … normal.

Baxter wasn't usually someone to worry, to check and double-check every preparation, but as the night wore on he found himself time and again by the hastily-installed rack of flare guns, ensuring they were properly loaded with the pre-arranged signal colours and that the damp hadn't got to them. They would be vital if any Japanese vessels did attack, but also

301

dangerous to his own fragile little command as he'd be more or less signalling their position when he launched one.

There was nothing to salve that, though — the survival of the cruiser was all that mattered. Once he'd satisfied himself, he would walk a circuit of the twenty-foot-long craft, checking each of the watchmen on duty was awake and staring out into the darkness with them. At a quarter past the hour, he would stare to starboard, waiting for the brief flash of a light that would tell him the cruiser was still where she should be.

The routine and the gentle rocking of the boat began to lull all of them into a sense of security that was not warranted — so that when action came, it was almost unexpected. It was Vasily who spotted the sleek torpedo boats as they coasted by on low revolutions, intent on getting into position to launch without the noise giving them away.

"Enemy vessel," Vasily whispered to Baxter, shaking his shoulder and pointing.

Baxter snapped out of the upright doze he'd fallen into, cursing himself. The Japanese boat was barely a hundred yards away, a shadow sliding across the water, and no doubt there were more beyond it. It was a sleek vessel, something over a hundred feet long but low to the water. Dangerous, designed for speed and manoeuvrability to stay alive rather than carrying any armour, its devastating but temperamental hitting power contained within the prominent torpedo tubes.

It was certainly much bigger than their own vessel and more heavily armed — his job wasn't to try to destroy the torpedo boats, though, just disrupt their attacks and warn the cruiser.

They were running without lights, and Vasily had used his head in not shouting a warning. Baxter nudged the helmsman and whispered a course change to bring them even closer to the barely-seen enemy vessel. He held his breath, judging the speed and distance, knowing he risked either losing their target in the foggy night or being spotted themselves. Instinct told him when the balance point had been reached. "Torpedo boat on the port side, forty yards — open fire!"

Vasily fired the three pounder almost at once, a long stab of fire that was dazzling in the darkness. The rotary cannon opened up a second later, a series of sharp cracks as the experienced gunner cranked the handle at a steady rate, firing off half the magazine. The bluejacket on the machine gun in the bows was considerably less restrained, spraying heavy bullets all over the ocean. The flare that Baxter sent up — *red warning torpedo boats* — was almost an afterthought, casting everything in a ghastly red light.

A moment later the *Yaroslavich* sent up illumination shells from the two six-inchers on his side, an almost festive array of lights that drifted gently over the ocean and picked out the Japanese boats in stark relief. They increased speed as soon as they were lit up; all but the one that had borne the brunt of the pinnace's initial fire. Vasily's shells had pocked its hull around the engine room while the rotary cannon had hit the bridge at least once. Their shells and bullets, which would have been harmless against even a destroyer, had the desired effect on the lightly-armoured target. He could see men running to their own Hotchkiss guns, though, and other weapons being trained round on to them.

"Come about and full steam ahead!" Baxter shouted into the wheelhouse. "Forward gun and machine gun, fire as you bear!"

Now there was a fine judgement to be made. They'd done their job, spotting and foiling the sneak attack. Their role now wasn't too try to fight off the boats but to harass them, right up until the point the cruiser could engage with her secondary batteries — at which point, Baxter didn't want to be anywhere near them.

The machine gunner was firing again, at a rate that would almost certainly eat through their ammunition before the night was over. The enemy was close enough that he could hear them shouting, close enough that he could make out words that meant nothing to him and cries of pain that meant even less.

The torpedo boat seemed still to be under command and under discipline, Japanese sailors dashing to one of the guns mounted in her stern despite the machine-gun fire peppering it.

"Get another round into it!" Baxter roared to Vasily over the burp of the rotary cannon firing. They could barely miss at that range, and after that all he could hear was groans of pain.

One of the other torpedo boats was firing back now, aiming for their muzzle flashes, and he resisted the urge to duck as a shell whistled low overhead — he had to set an example. "Yuri, get fire on that forward enemy gun! Fire at the muzzle flash!"

The Japanese weapon fired again, maybe something a little heavier than their own gun, and the shell landed close enough its waterspout doused the deck and soaked Baxter. One of his crew was screaming in pain, obviously caught by a shell splinter from the near miss. The machine gun was having the desired effect, though, and a second later Vasily managed to land a direct hit with the Hotchkiss, silencing the enemy weapon.

"Cease fire!" he shouted, then again, more loudly. "Save your ammunition, Goddammit!"

He ran into the bows, straining to see into the eerily lit night. The illumination shells made things only a bit lighter and cast everything in an odd, actinic light, but enough for him to track the enemy boats and guess when they would launch. It was instinct, more than anything else, that told him when the moment had come. Some combination of the noise the tubes made and the splash of the weapons going into the water, perhaps, or maybe just his own judgement of when he would have fired. He grabbed a flare gun from the second rack and sent a green flare into the sky.

Torpedoes port!

Another salvo of illumination shells went up, followed swiftly by the gunners reloading and discharging high explosives at the weaving torpedo boats as they attempted to withdraw. Juneau had obviously been alert for the signal and he put the cruiser hard to port, turning into the torpedo tracks, getting the bow across until they were running down the *Yaroslavich*'s starboard side. There was no devastating explosion, so Baxter assumed they'd managed to dodge everything or they'd got lucky again and any warheads that had hit were duds.

"Let them go!" Baxter shouted, as he saw Vasily starting to swing the main gun round to bear on the retreating torpedo boats. As much as he wanted to make sure they couldn't return to harass the cruiser, their main weapons were spent and Baxter had to conserve ammunition. It was, after all, going to be a long night.

Dawn found the cruiser back on a westerly course. The fog that Koenig had been damning the previous morning was blown to tattered shreds scudding across the seascape. A few ships could be seen in the distance, hard to tell who's at the range they were at. Often, they could only tell from the plumes of dirty black smoke that they were not alone on the sea.

Baxter's eyes were grimy from lack of sleep and his almost constant vigil, staring out in the darkness, straining for any hint or glimpse of the sleek, darting torpedo boats or the larger and more dangerous destroyers.

"Do you think they'll come again?" Vasily rumbled by his side. It was the first time the stolid Russian, to his recollection, had asked a direct question.

Baxter rubbed his eyes tiredly. "I doubt it — not the torpedo boats, anyway. It would be suicide, now that we can see them coming. The destroyers, though…" He brought his glasses up, the view wavering more due to fatigue than the choppy motion of the pinnace. He squinted, lowered the glasses from the aching sockets and rubbed his eyes before raising them again.

Something … something in the nearest bank of fog. A light breeze stirred the grey curtain, and he knew he had done what he had consistently chastised his Russian comrades for — underestimated the enemy. Almost fatally.

"Three torpedo boats on the port bow, five hundred yards — Yuri, Vasily, open fire!" Baxter's heart was crashing in his chest, his brain racing. The enemy had got dangerously close to the cruiser by using the fog, skipping in across the rolling grey waves. "Yuri, Vasily, fire at will! Helm, come about and put our bow to the cruiser, full speed ahead."

That would put them on an intercept course, increasing the accuracy of his gunners, but should also let the rotary cannon in the stern bear shortly. It also meant, of course, that he was charging straight into closing fire — almost as soon as he had that thought, the Japanese crews started returning fire.

He dashed back towards the wheelhouse just as the pinnace shuddered to a near miss that drove shell splinters into her hull and, from the screams, into one of his men. The angry chatter of the machine gun cut out suddenly — perhaps the screaming was Yuri — but Vasily maintained a steady fire. Baxter reached for a flare gun and realised the rack was gone, the side of the wheelhouse torn out by the near miss. He spun, tracking the half-seen boats in the dawn twilight. The cruiser would be alert by now, of course, even at two miles they would be able to hear the gunfire, particularly now that the rotary cannon had opened up as well. There was no sign of illumination shells or direct fire from the big ship, though.

He lunged into the wheelhouse, scrabbling for the flare gun that was part of the boat's standard equipment. Seized on the polished wood grip, got his left hand on the brass tube and clicked a lever to break the weapon open. He stared down at the Cyrillic lettering on the base of the flare gun, then spun to the helmsman. "What colour!" he shouted in frantic Russian, knowing he couldn't confuse the cruiser's exhausted crew.

The bluejacket blinked, obviously unused to his commander being able to speak the language. "The colour, man! I can't read this godforsaken lettering!"

"Green, sir," the fellow managed to stammer out, and Baxter only just cleared the little cabin before he fired the flare, knowing it was probably already too late.

It was light enough now that he could make out the big, stolid shape of the cruiser, her funnels belching smoke as she began her turn to avoid the torpedoes that had already launched, and he felt nothing but a cold lump in his guts as the white trails ran straight and true to their target. Vasily and the gunner on the rotary cannon were still blasting away, joined by the gunners on the cruiser. He could hear Yuri yelling at his loader, telling him to find more belts of ammunition for the machine gun, and a moment later a fluent stream of invective told him the Maxim machine gun was spent. Baxter had known that would happen at some point, and had done his best to curtail the trigger-happy gunner. He couldn't bring himself to chastise his people for using up ammunition now, though — it didn't matter anymore.

A cheer went up as a torpedo boat dropped away from the formation, smoke boiling from a ragged tear in its flimsy hull, but his eyes remained locked on the Russian cruiser. Somehow, Juneau had managed to get her bows towards the lethal weapons that rushed towards her, managing to dodge the first two. Baxter started breathing again, almost letting himself believe they had once more avoided calamity. Then an enormous plume of water rose in the cruiser's stern and a moment later the pinnace lifted in the water, the shockwave of the underwater explosion battering the hull and throwing them from their feet. As he pulled himself onto his knees to stare at the ship, he knew her journey was over.

The Japanese seemed content to leave them alone as the lacklustre day finished breaking. The *Yaroslavich* was listing, but not too badly, and she was dead in the water. As Baxter had predicted just before the final assault, it was now too light for the torpedo boats and the big ships were busy elsewhere. He couldn't see them, but he could hear the thump of heavy guns not too far away.

He brought the pinnace alongside the lamed warship at Juneau's signal. There was an odd, stunned silence aboard, as though the detonation had killed or incapacitated everyone. Then Juneau's tired, drawn face appeared at the head of the ladder as he pulled himself up. He didn't look angry or even particularly desperate, but that didn't lighten Baxter's mood. The knowledge that he had failed, that at the last the enemy had managed to sneak past a guard he and the others had maintained all night, gnawed at him.

It must have shown on his face as he pulled himself wearily over the side and stood, clothes still damp from the drenching they'd all taken, staring about desolately. The crew lay or sat listlessly, the fight knocked out of them by that cruel blow at the end of a vicious night. Juneau, though, embraced him and kissed him on each cheek. "Well, my friend. You and the others kept us safe through the night, as you had been ordered. No one could have asked for more."

"What's our status?" Baxter asked gruffly, trying not to let his gratitude for Juneau's consoling words show. That wouldn't do.

Juneau led him to one side and lowered his voice. "We're stopped, and taking on water," he said. "The torpedo holed us not far from the stern and sheered one of the screw shafts cleanly, damaging the other."

Below the waterline. Once that would have been the safest place for anyone in a naval battle, just so long as the ship floated. The torpedo had changed all of that. "Losses?" Baxter asked in a sick voice.

"Many, including Chief Engineer Kurylov. It must have been hell down there, trying to stem the damage and get hatches shut." Juneau laid a hand on Baxter's arm. "Ekaterina and Tommy are safe — they are still helping in the sickbay."

"Well, we've been without the screws before," Baxter said, forcing himself to sound and feel confident. "We can…"

Juneau's glum expression stopped him in his tracks. "We can get a few sails up, but the masts and rigging were badly damaged during the fighting yesterday — shell splinters for the most part."

"Well, we can start splicing and mending now."

"We took on no spares," Juneau said, his voice suddenly anguished. "We didn't think…"

Pavel was making his way across the deck towards them, a tray balanced in one hand with glasses of hot tea steaming on it. Where everything around them was grimy and torn, bloodstains and scorch-marks on the once-pristine decks, the captain's steward was still neat and dapper. Baxter took the tea with a grateful nod and sipped at the scalding liquid. "I am afraid the wardroom, Graf, has been somewhat destroyed and the galley damaged," Pavel reported to his commander in his very formal French. "We are doing what we can."

"The crew must be fed and given tea as well," Juneau said, his voice slightly reproving.

Pavel, always a slightly bent over old man, drew himself up as far as he could. "This is being seen to, your Serenity." His French had become positively frosty.

"I am sorry, dutiful old friend," Juneau said with a wry smile. "I was angry because I had not thought of it myself."

Ekaterina at that moment appeared from the ship's superstructure. Where Pavel had somehow managed to remain neat and tidy, she looked as exhausted and dirty as the rest of them. Dry blood stained the front of the simple smock she wore and her hair was tied back in an old scarf. When their eyes met across the deck, though, Baxter felt his heart skip a beat.

She smiled at him and nodded a greeting. She emerged into the weak sunlight, helping Tommy pull a cart carrying an enormous, dented silver samovar that had once been in the wardroom. Her voice rang out, cool and clear. "Come, my friends," gesturing at the nearest sailors. She was followed by the cooks, including the wardroom cook, bearing platters of cured meat and ship's biscuit. While some men shuffled forward to receive their allotment — and there was no pushing to get to the front or to receive more than their fair share —

others remained collapsed. Ekaterina started filling tin mugs from the samovar and taking them to those too exhausted to move.

Baxter couldn't help but smile. Whatever else happened this day, he knew she had cemented her legend. "She's going to fight, when it comes time to leave," he said.

"She is, but you must not let her." Juneau's voice was hard, and when he glanced down at the smaller man he saw steel in his stare, and something else. Grief, possessiveness. Jealousy? "I have placed many burdens on you, and you have shouldered them without complaint. This is the most important one."

"And what will you do?"

"Oh, I'm not giving up yet. We'll try to get some sort of steerage way on her and plot a course for Vladivostok. We have come this far, and it would seem a shame to give up now. If luck is with us, you will not even have to pry my wife from my loving arms."

There was a glitter in Juneau's eyes that confirmed for Baxter that he knew exactly what had passed between him and Ekaterina. Baxter felt a fresh stab of guilt, ridiculous as it was in this dire situation. It wasn't an emotion he was used to, and he quickly sought to change the subject.

"If luck does not hold, and we come upon the enemy?"

"Oh, I doubt we will be coming upon anything — but if the enemy finds us, I shall discharge a few shells for the sake of honour and then signal my surrender. I am no fool, to die pointlessly for Tsar and the Motherland."

CHAPTER 24

A tense silence hung over the open bridge as the *Yaroslavich* limped towards her final destination. By some miracle, a junior engineering officer had managed to effect enough of a repair to the one intact drive shaft to start the starboard screw turning. Baxter had no idea how, but the man deserved a medal for achieving it. At the same time, he and any other spare hand had been put to work trying to get at least a scrap of sail up on the pole masts. Now a few square yards of patched canvas flapped in the gentle breeze. It was hard to say whether they were adding anything, but Juneau had left them up.

"We have no other option but to sail straight for Vladivostok," Juneau had said after he'd sent his best, strongest men to the helm to keep the cruiser on course as she made a handful of knots towards safety. "And pray that we are either not seen or not considered worth a few shells."

With their own immediate danger past, every available pair of eyes were turned to scanning the sea. Alert not just for possible enemy attacks, but searching even more keenly for a friendly ship. Yesterday's fog had been burned down and blown away to a few drifting banks by the bright sun and stiff breeze, a mixed blessing as it could no longer hide them. They'd been hearing gunnery again for a few minutes, but distantly.

"I have them," Koenig called down from the lookout nest halfway up the midships mast. "A little south-west of our current course."

Every head on the bridge, including those without glasses or a telescope, swivelled in the indicated direction. Even Ekaterina was there, holding a finely made pair of binoculars.

Baxter squinted through his considerably plainer Imperial Russian Navy-issue set. What was left of the the rolling mix of fog and smoke still made it hard to make out what was going on, and then he managed to fix the image of a ship in the magnified view. Clearly a battleship, and even though he'd never seen her before there was something about her construction that told him she'd been built in a British shipyard — as most of the Japanese fleet had been.

"That must be the main Japanese line," Baxter said without lowering the field glasses. A few voices murmured agreement.

As he watched, the ship's main guns fired. She looked like a clever toy at this distance, spitting pyrotechnics for the amusement of children. Up close, though, she would be a thing of terrible power, and being on the receiving end of that fire would be both terrifying and devastating.

The distant sparkle of muzzle flashes at least told them the general direction of their own ships. He looked beyond the line of enemy ships emerging from the fog and could just make out grey shapes that must be the remnants of the Russian battle line — he couldn't get an exact count, but there were certainly a number of battleships there, huddled into a bay on the Korean coast. Not as many as they had started yesterday with. Waterspouts were rising all around them as the Japanese pounded them.

"I'm going up to the crosstrees," Baxter said, turning and almost bumping into a young officer — little more than a teenaged boy — who was standing by the head of the ladder, clutching a note and looking around despondently, trying to decide which senior officer wasn't going to tear his head off for disturbing them.

Baxter stuck his hand out. He had an odd feeling in his guts. "I'll give it to him," he said softly. After a moment's hesitation the boy handed it over — no doubt a breach of regulations, but they were past such considerations now.

Baxter desperately wanted to read what was scrawled there, but it wasn't his place to do so. Instead, he touched Juneau on the shoulder and passed him the slip of paper.

Juneau glanced at it, then looked again more intently. He took his glasses off to pinch the bridge of his nose, and just seemed to deflate. All of the fight went out of him in that moment. "It's over," he said tiredly, then raised his voice until everyone on the bridge could hear him. "From the radio room. Admiral Nebogatov has signalled the surrender of the units under his command."

There was a stunned silence amongst the assembled officers. After a moment, there came a susurration of whispered voices as those ratings who had a smattering of French relayed what had been said to their comrades. The news would spread like wildfire around the ship, as news always did.

"But why are they still firing?" a plaintive voice asked. The code for surrender was not specific to Russia, and was indeed universal.

"It will take a few minutes for a cease fire order to be sent round," Juneau said. Baxter thought he sounded unsure, and his expression confirmed that.

"Well, a good job the Japanese can't shoot worth a damn!" someone else declared, trying to force a brash note into his voice and receiving only cold stares in response.

The firing continued, the steady rumble of a bombardment rather than a petering out to nothing. It was too far away for any of them to see much. "The battle line has come to a complete stop," Koenig called down from his perch. "I think … yes, I think they are hauling up white flags."

"The enemy continues to fire though." Juneau's voice was bitter.

"Because they do not understand the concept of surrender," Ekaterina commented, her voice clear and ringing — defiant even. It was hard to say whether she found that admirable or infuriating. She sounded so confident that none on the bridge disagreed.

"A cruiser is running!" Koenig burst out, his voice rising in excitement. "The *Izumrud*, I think!"

Silence fell again over the assembled officers and crew, though it was one Baxter found hard to read. On one hand, he could feel their desire to cheer at the final show of defiance. On the other, particularly amongst the older officers, there would be disapproval of running after striking the colours, a most dishonourable act. The Japanese fire, which had finally started to abate, picked up again. Baxter, sweeping the sea, finally found the Russian ship, the blue cross of St. Peter flying proudly from her mastheads. Waterspouts were rising all around her as she charged away from the otherwise passive Russian line. Swinging his glasses round, he picked up a pair of Japanese cruisers speeding up and changing course to pursue.

It was a flash of defiance, and only that. The rest of the Russian line was hauling up Japanese flags now, desperately trying to convince the enemy that they had truly surrendered. Baxter lowered his glasses and turned away.

This was a moment on which he would not and should not intrude, or even view. The humiliation of the proud Russian fleet was total, and he knew it would be a blow that would be felt as far away as St. Petersburg. It would not be felt as keenly as it was right now, on the bridge of this isolated Russian cruiser.

He could almost feel the morale crumbling around him. All of their hopes and high claims had come to naught, and not just in defeat but in surrender — although he could not fault Nebogatov for not condemning his men to a senseless death. For a second, the cruiser hung on a knife edge.

Then Juneau's voice rung out across the bridge, pitched loud enough to be heard on the lower decks. He spoke in Russian, the language of the common bluejacket, but his words were for all of them. "So the battle line has surrendered! Well, that was their choice and I cannot judge them for it. But the fleet has not surrendered, do you hear me? Not while this cruiser floats and I draw breath! And we will not be the only ones, for sure — you all saw the *Izumrud* put mud in Togo's eye!"

Baxter felt the faintest flicker of a smile — that was one way of describing what the errant cruiser had done. He also felt a stir of hope, or if not that then defiance. They were still afloat, and under power after a fashion. And it seemed he was not the only one who felt it. Cheering started on the lower decks, where previously listless ratings stood staring up at their captain. It was weak at first, then more and more throats took up the wordless roar of pride and defiance. The officers were shouting, pounding each other on the back as they were all caught up in the moment. Even Ekaterina's voice, rising above the predominantly bass rumble.

Baxter didn't join in. He was too much of a realist to let that ember of hope rise to flame within him, and he knew just how the odds were stacked against them. He raised his glasses to give himself something to do, a reason not to be joining in the cheering. What he saw made him bark a short, bitter laugh — he'd been more right than he could possibly have known.

He turned. Juneau was surrounded by a knot of officers cheering themselves hoarse, the focal point for their re-found enthusiasm. Baxter was a little surprised at his normally diffident friend — while he had never heard a 'death before dishonour' speech, he reckoned Juneau had made a decent job of it.

He caught his friend's eyes, and pointed to the enemy warship closing on them from the east.

"Well, it was nice while it lasted," Juneau said tiredly, leaning against the bridge railing and lowering his head. He took his glasses off and rubbed his bloodshot eyes, the fire and fight of a few minutes ago drained out of him by the appearance of the enemy ship.

Baxter had the closing Japanese vessel in his glasses, studying it carefully. "I think … I make her a merchant cruiser."

Koenig was also observing closely. "I agree with Mr Baxter. Though I think there might be something else, smaller, behind her."

"It could be the Imperial Yacht itself!" Juneau snapped. "As we can barely manoeuvre, I have no option but to strike to her."

Baxter's fists clenched around the wood railing. The enemy ship was coming on in a fine old fashion, white water creaming along her bows as she ploughed through the waves. She was a converted civilian vessel, though, a small merchantman with a pair of light guns — probably four-inchers — in the bow and no doubt more down the sides. She was no doubt intended for scouting and commerce raiding — indeed, it had been a similar ship that had first spotted the fleet a long day ago. Under normal circumstances, her captain should not even have been considering taking on the *Yaroslavich*, old as she was.

"He's insane," Koenig breathed, watching the converted freighter approach from a little off their starboard quarter.

"Or he's realised we're lame and will find a spot he can bombard us from without us being able to retaliate," Baxter ground out. To have come this far, and be so close…

"Like the *Vladimir* and *Pervaz-i-Bahri*," Juneau said, and smiled at Baxter's blank look. "One of our illustrious predecessors who fought the barbarian Turk in the last century, the first time steamships fought each other. *Vladimir* won by using her superior speed to sit on his opponent's stern and rake her."

"Well, we're like to receive the same treatment," Baxter growled. He knew Juneau was right, that they would have to surrender.

"She's in range of our main guns, I believe," Lieutenant Alexeev, the gunnery officer, said. "If we can bring them to bear."

"She'll be in range of her own artillery shortly as well — I'm surprised they've not tried a ranging shot, though."

The words were barely out of Baxter's mouth when a sharp *crack* reached his ears, followed by a second. Looking back, he saw the gun smoke being whipped away from the enemy cruiser's forward guns, just as the shells raised waterspouts fifty yards ahead of the *Yaroslavich*. The Japanese fired again, the shells again landing ahead of her target.

"If we could just bring our bows round a little, I could return with one of the main guns," Alexeev insisted. Juneau hesitated, though Baxter knew it was not indecision but calculation. Given the precariously balanced steering arrangements, if they came off course, they might never get back on it.

"More gunfire will attract other Japanese ships, even if we defeat this one," Koenig pointed out, his calm assessment at odds with his previously fire-breathing attitude.

Another pair of shells landed ahead of them. "Surprisingly poor practice from them," Juneau commented.

Baxter was less convinced. He swung his glasses from the armed merchantman to the spot where yet another pair of shells fell into the sea. The Japanese ship was closing on them quickly and was well within range of her guns. Despite the decreasing range, the rounds were always landing about fifty yards ahead of the cruiser. "No," he said absently. "Remarkably good practice — she's putting rounds across our bows, not missing us."

"Do they want us to surrender?" Juneau wondered. A few minutes ago he had been contemplating just that, but there was a hint of anger in his voice that suggested he would fight if the enemy presumed to demand his surrender.

"They certainly appear to want to talk," Baxter replied, watching as signal flags jerked up the merchant cruiser's masts and then unfurled in the slight cross-breeze.

"If we were to make a sharp turn, we could bring our full broadside to bear!" Alexeev said urgently.

"And would then not to be able to come back on course. Doomed, perhaps forever, to sail the world as some sort of Flying Russian. No — we will see what they want. It would be churlish not to. What do the signals say, Koenig?"

"It … it appears to be gibberish, Graf. It must be coded, signals meant for nearby allies rather than us." Koenig let his glasses drop. "Why don't they just get on with it?" he snapped furiously, tears glittering in his eyes.

Baxter quirked a smile. "It's plain alphabet, Mr Koenig, and not gibberish — English."

"Close enough," Juneau said with a slight smile, demonstrating once again that peculiar upper-class habit of being able to find humour in any situation. "Let's see — yes, they are in fact demanding our surrender."

Baxter felt a trickle of cold sweat down his back. There were any number of reasons why the Japanese would be signalling in English, the most likely being they didn't have any French or Russian speakers, and knew their quarry probably didn't speak Japanese.

But ... some instinct told him something else was going on here. He raised his glasses again and scrutinised the Japanese ship. She was still coming up fast from astern, just far enough off their beam that they could make out her signals but still carefully placed to be outside the firing arc of the guns in the stern barbettes. They were at point-blank range now, and he directed his particular attention to the bridge that sat proud on the ship's tall superstructure.

Ekaterina got there first. "I do not think there are only Japanese sailors on that bridge," she said, her voice hard. "Look to the right of who I think must be the captain."

The ship's commanding officer was easy enough to make out, a silvery haired man standing bolt-upright dead centre of the bridge, returning their own stares. They were still too far away to make out much more detail than that, but Baxter had to concur that at least one of the men on the bridge was European. And there was something about his frame, his posture. "Well — we know the English Navy has observers aboard some ships."

"More signals going up, Graf." Koenig, now he knew what he was reading, was able to make them out this time. "Reveal ... no, release British subjects. Unharmed."

A new, tense silence fell across the knot of officers. Baxter didn't drop his gaze from the closing ship, but he could feel accusatory stares boring into his back. "Arbuthnott," he spat, feeling a sudden hot rage boiling up within him. It must have shown on his face, as everyone stepped back slightly as he turned to face them. He glowered at Juneau. "We should talk privately."

Privately, of course, meant Ekaterina as well. At some point, Baxter had come to the same conclusion as Juneau obviously had — this was far more her world than it was theirs.

"This is the *ublyudok* who first set this up? Who sent you out to attack us?" she asked, not even trying to hide the scepticism in her voice. "You are sure?"

Baxter nodded sharply. They had not retired below decks, which would have ensured them full privacy, but huddled in the corner of the bridge away from the Japanese ship. He was acutely conscious of the fact that he cut a distinctive figure, and it perhaps would not go well with him if he was seen conspiring with Russians. However, none of them wanted to be away from the centre of command for any length of time. "Well, I couldn't make out his face clearly — but I'm pretty sure it's that scrawny bastard."

"Language, Mr Baxter," Juneau said, voice distracted. "But how could he even know you were here?"

"He must have been receiving reports from Yefimov." Juneau flinched at the name — they'd all been careful not to use it since the second officer's unfortunate demise. "And this is a distinctive ship."

Juneau rubbed at his forehead, a sure sign of the pressure he was under. "That could be the cruiser that shadowed the fleet off the Malay peninsula, her true colours revealed at last."

"It does not matter how he has found us, just that he has," Ekaterina, practical as ever, cut in. "What shall we do about this?"

Juneau stared out to sea, thinking. It was oddly peaceful as the *Yaroslavich* chugged towards her destination. For the first time since early the previous morning, there was no significant gunfire to be heard — the enemy cruiser just seemed content to close with them, sure of her eventual triumph without needing to fight. The grand drama of the main fleet's surrender was already done and forgotten, as they faced their own crisis.

"It seems to me," the captain said eventually, "that if we hand Mr Baxter over, then he is as good as dead."

Ekaterina's eyes were cool as she gazed levelly at Baxter. "If we try and fight, we risk many more deaths. Perhaps…"

She didn't finish the sentence, but even so Baxter felt like he'd been kicked in the guts. He'd always known she was ice-cold, ruthless when she had to be, but to be on the receiving end when he'd thought he might have meant something to her…

"She's right," he said, his voice sounding flint-hard to his ears as he struggled to hide any emotion. "No point risking the ship or the crew on my account. Best just to…"

"I will not just hand him over without a fight, after how much…" Juneau broke in hotly.

"If I might finish," she interrupted them both icily. "Perhaps it would be best if Mr Baxter and a few others attempt to make a break for it in one of the pinnaces. If he was to leave now, he might be able to put sufficient distance between the cruiser and himself to go unnoticed as we surrender."

"He would not be doing it alone," Juneau said quietly, his own voice matching hers for firmness. "You will be going with him, my love, as will Tommy and others. We have no way of knowing how the Japanese will treat prisoners. As you said yourself, they do not understand the concept of surrender."

Baxter shook his head. "There is only a slim chance of me getting away in the pinnace," he said flatly. He couldn't escape the suspicion that Ekaterina had been about to suggest handing him over without demure but had realised her husband would not brook it. "It is best, if we are to try this, if I go alone. He won't be interested in Tommy."

"Your Arbuthnott will not be best pleased when he discovers you have fled the ship," Juneau pointed out. "It is perhaps best if the countess is safely away at that point — particularly as she was a target for the initial … operation."

Baxter smiled grimly at the way Juneau had avoided using the word 'attack', though they all now knew that was what had brought him aboard. It seemed like a lifetime ago now. There was a mute appeal in Juneau's eyes, and Baxter realised he had no intention of surrendering — or at least not without a fight. And Baxter had made a promise to him.

"That's a good point," he said, avoiding her gaze. She was a perceptive woman and he was sure she would guess what both men were thinking. "Very well — we'd best be about assembling everyone who will be going. Quick as we can."

"I will not abandon my husband," Ekaterina said, not for the first time, and Baxter doubted it would be the last. "I will…"

Baxter rounded on her. "I don't want to go either!" he snapped. "But…" He struggled for words, as he always did at moments like these, with everything boiling away inside him. "But I have my orders," he said quietly. "As do you."

"I am not to be ordered around by my husband, or by you, or by any man!" she flared.

"The orders come from the captain of this ship," he said softly. "And at sea, that transcends everything else. Even any deity you should chose to name."

She stared at him, eyes bright with furious tears, then turned without another word and stalked away. He hoped to gather whatever essentials she needed, as time was so terribly short.

The pinnaces were in the water, Vasily a reassuring presence in the wheelhouse of the one he was to take charge of. Mr Koenig had been given charge of the second, a steady pair of hands and — according to Juneau — no longer vital as he was planning on surrendering the ship. Men were streaming down the sides into those vessels, along with Juneau's dog Maxim and the other wardroom animals to have survived. There were walking wounded amongst them, but after some discussion with Andropov it had been decided that the seriously injured .were better off remaining aboard. Tommy sat disconsolately in the stern, a pitiful sack of possessions between his feet.

The Japanese cruiser was hidden from his view by the *Yaroslavich*'s superstructure, but she was making her presence and impatience known with the occasional, peremptory gun dropping shells closer and closer to the Russian ship. They were no longer short of time, Baxter knew, but out of it.

He looked around, telling himself his eyes were burning because of fatigue and the waft of smoke from the funnels. The ship had been home to him for seven months, even if that has started with imprisonment aboard, and he found himself loathe to depart her now. More of a home that anywhere he had been for years, and this crew of mad Russians more of a family than he knew he deserved. The bluejackets and officers who remained aboard looked on now, no resentment in their eyes even though some at least must have guessed they were going to fight to cover this escape.

"We are fully loaded," Koenig called up to him.

"Stand by." Baxter turned and found Ekaterina with his eyes. She was speaking with low urgency to her husband, who once again shook his head firmly. She turned away from him suddenly, shot Baxter a furious glare and, without another word to either of them, stepped into the bosun's chair that would lower her into Mr Koenig's pinnace. Juneau had been holding his hand out to her as she moved away, and he stood for a disconsolate second, looking down at the pleading appendage, before shaking himself and walking over to Baxter.

"She is barely a mile away — you had best go," Juneau said quietly. "I will give you as much time as I can."

"By stalling before surrendering?"

"Something like that. But remember, Mr Baxter, anything I do, I do for the honour of the Imperial Russian Navy."

It was a benediction, of sorts, an instruction to Baxter not to carry any burden. He held out his hand. "Well."

Juneau shook it. "God speed, Marcus. Get everyone to safety."

"If luck is on my side," Baxter said. Lady Luck was the sailor's god, cruel and fickle, and he'd long since let go of the notion any other higher power paid heed to him.

There was nothing more to be said, and with a last look around the battered and scorched deck he swung himself over the side and descended into his command.

CHAPTER 25

"Why are we doing this if Mr Juneau is just going to surrender?" Tommy asked as the two little boats chugged away from the *Yaroslavich*.

Baxter hadn't been surprised to find the lad in his boat, even though he'd been sticking like glue to Ekaterina for the last few weeks. He'd been grateful for it during the fighting, as she'd managed to keep him out of harm's way.

"Well, for one we're mostly taking able-bodied and competent seamen to Vladivostok, which will help the ships stationed there. We also don't know how the Japanese will treat their prisoners," Baxter said, trying not to sound evasive. "Particularly the countess — they didn't seem overly keen on even allowing the main fleet to surrender, mind."

"But they specifically asked for us to be handed over," Tommy protested.

Baxter sighed — he'd been hoping that information wouldn't have reached the lad's ears. "True, and that's why we're running for it," he said. "I don't trust the men who want us to be handed over."

"But I'm just a wain, and an … innocent?"

"You're neither of those things anymore, lad, and more than that you're a witness." The gnawing guilt of bringing Tommy along on this mad adventure again bit hard at Baxter when he said that. The boy should not be in this situation, but there was no helping that now. "Once we make it to Vladivostok I'll find a way to get us both home quietly."

He was fairly certain Arbuthnott was operating without official consent or probably knowledge, and he did not therefore risk the censure of the law if he did reappear in the British Isles.

"Wha' makes you think this Arbuthnott won't keep after you?" Tommy said, his nasal and slightly wheedling tone at odds with the sharpness of his questioning. "He's got pull, else he wouldn't even be here."

"There will be British observers on a number of Japanese ships, as we're allies. And he might have pulled some strings to get here, but the fact he's obviously pretty desperate to get us both now suggests he doesn't want this to go any further. And you have a nasty and suspicious mind."

Tommy lapsed into silence, but obviously wasn't happy with any of the responses.

Baxter ducked into the wheelhouse to save himself from further questions. "How is the engine holding out?" he asked Vasily. They'd been pushing the little boat to its limits over the last few days.

"Well enough," the big petty officer replied dourly. "Though Anton will not vouch for it all the way to Vladivostok if we maintain this speed."

"Once we're well enough clear we'll reduce speed and try to nurse her the rest of the way. The important thing is to get far enough away that when the captain hauls down the colours we'll go unnoticed."

"You do not actually think he's planning on surrendering?" Vasily asked, his expression and tone remaining level and stolid.

"Everyone seems to be a bloody mind-reader," Baxter muttered. Everyone but him always seemed to know what others were thinking. But, he admitted to himself, he'd known all along that Juneau wasn't planning on surrendering.

He turned and found Koenig's vessel, keeping station twenty yards to starboard. They'd talked about splitting up as quickly as possible, reducing any chance of detection, but had agreed that remaining within mutual support distance would be more important. Ekaterina was a splash of lighter colours in the stern, no doubt taking a break from her self-appointed duty of caring for the lightly-wounded packed into the flimsy hull.

She must have seen him looking and straightened up. He felt his heart surge at the sight of her, tall and proud in the bobbing boat, her challenging gaze felt even sixty feet away. He knew they weren't out of danger, that despite the *Yaroslavich*'s valour there was little chance the armed merchantman wouldn't run them down, and the thought of her wounding or death filled with him with far more dread than the thought of his own demise.

"Ah, fuck it," he said, then raised his voice. "Mr Koenig, close on me if you please!" he roared across the gulf of water, then turned to Vasily. "Reduce to one quarter."

Behind them, the *Yaroslavich* opened fire.

The two little boats chugged along close enough that their fenders occasionally crunched together. Baxter stood with one foot on the rail, leaning forward to confer with Koenig and Ekaterina. They were far enough away from the battle developing between the two cruisers that he didn't have to raise his voice much.

"Technically, Mr Baxter, I am in command," Koenig said, voice mildly reproving. "And as the senior…"

"Well, consider this an act of mutiny, Mr Koenig," Baxter said. "You also have wounded aboard, not to mention the countess."

The young officer closed his eyes. Baxter knew he wanted nothing more than to return to his ship, as Juneau had without doubt engaged in battle by this point rather than firing a few rounds for the honour of the flag. Glancing back, he could see geysers rising around the Russian ship. Juneau had put his helm over and slowed almost to a crawl, and either the Japanese gunners had been thrown off by that or weren't as well trained as the battleship crews.

"Very well. We will maintain course towards Vladivostok but at a slower…"

"You'll go hell for leather and don't wait for us," Baxter broke in, his voice hard. "Get these people to safety. Oh, and one more thing…"

He turned and grabbed Tommy's collar in one smooth motion, lifting him easily. The boy let out a startled *urk* and didn't even try to fight it, astonished perhaps by Baxter's strength. Before anything more could be said, he hoisted the lad over the intervening water and dumped him in an undignified heap at Ekaterina's feet. They all chose to ignore the stream of invective coming out of him.

The men aboard Koenig's pinnace had obviously gathered some notion of what they intended. There had been no calls for volunteers, and no man had been detailed to change vessel. There was a spontaneous movement, though, men jumping from the pinnace that would be going to safety onto the one that was about to charge into danger. He felt a stir of pride at that, particularly as no men tried to go the other way.

"Hard port, Vasily," Baxter snapped over his shoulder, as he saw walking wounded men trying to join his own command. He turned back to the other vessel. "Good luck to you, all of you!"

The distance was already opening between them. Ekaterina remained silent, but raised a hand as Vasily took the pinnace round in an arc back towards the fight. Baxter raised his cap in salute as Koenig's crew cheered them on their way.

"We're not returning to the ship?" Vasily asked. As Baxter's *de facto* second in command, he seemed a lot more conversational than normal. Which, to be honest, was not saying much.

"No." With the men who had joined them, Baxter had thirty sailors aboard. Returning that many able-bodied sailors would not change the outcome of the battle. He had something altogether riskier in mind. "We'll attack the enemy cruiser directly."

"With what — that popgun on the front? Not many shells left."

"With everything we have, including our fists."

A slow smile spread across the normally impassive bluejacket's face. "That I would like to see, you punching an enemy ship."

"Then get me close enough, Chief Petty Officer."

"As you say, sir."

The *Yaroslavich* was taking hits now, bursts of flame appearing across her upper deck. Baxter knew that his guess about the enemy's artillery was about right, and that if Juneau could get even one of his six-inch guns to bear he could do some real damage.

He had Vasily steer wide of the engaged vessel, to ensure no near misses would hit them, but close enough that they could still use the cruiser's bulk for cover. "And where would you like to punch this enemy cruiser?" Vasily asked drily.

"Let's see what condition she's in. Stand by on the forward guns!"

They came round the *Yaroslavich*'s stern and saw the enemy lying not a mile off, her side flashing as the five light guns mounted without protection along the port side fired. As they watched, one of Russian great guns fired and a six-inch shell smashed a hole in the armed merchantman's stern. That was the problem with using converted merchant ships, Baxter thought grimly — they didn't have armour protection to speak of or any of the other protections a purpose-designed warship had. They were a good stopgap, and he had to admit one of them had proved its worth in finding the Russian ships, but you didn't want to get into a knock-down fight in one.

"Where that shell just hit — that will do nicely!"

Despite that hit, the Japanese were clearly starting to get the advantage. The captain — or one of his 'advisors' — had realised just how damaged the target vessel was, and he was manoeuvring to take advantage of that, trying to get into a blind spot for the main guns.

"I'm going forward," Baxter told Vasily, then scrambled along the narrow gangway. The little vessel was rolling and pitching now as it crashed across the water in its mad headlong dash towards destruction.

"They've seen us," one of the crewmen in the bows said, then spat into the water creaming past the bows.

Baxter could see a number of Japanese sailors pointing towards them, others running towards the stern with rifles. Even a single hit from one of the four-inch guns she mounted would do for them, but Baxter had been counting on the enemy not wanting to divert any of his weak main battery from the cruiser.

The gamble, it seemed, had paid off.

"Ignatyiv, if you would put fire onto those riflemen please — and don't worry about the ammunition this time!"

There were grins all round as the machine gunner, a small but broad and swarthy man, shifted uncomfortably before crouching down behind his weapon. "Right, gentlemen, let's see if we can do something about his main guns."

The *Yaroslavich* was starting to score more hits against the cruiser with her secondary batteries, the crews Baxter had spent most time with. Careful shiphandling was going to put her across the Russian ship's bows, though, where the main guns couldn't hit her and only some of the 4.7s could. From there she could lob shells along the length of the Russian ship, and at that range could barely miss. It would be carnage aboard if that was allowed to happen.

Baxter almost burst into laughter at the ridiculousness of their own course, which chased the relatively fast Japanese ship around the sluggish *Yaroslavich*.

He ducked down behind the pinnace's Hotchkiss gun as one of the bluejackets swung the breach closed with the distinctive clang of steel on steel. At this speed, they weren't much of a gunnery platform, and were closing fast enough that the guns mounted along the freighter's sides would soon be out of reach anyway. Ignatyiv was blazing away at the Japanese riflemen, keeping their heads down to some degree but by no means suppressing them entirely. Bullets started to smack into the water around them, and someone cried out as one hit the railing and drove splinters across the deck.

All of this was secondary in Baxter's attention. Not ignored, just put to one side as he concentrated in the right moment to pull the firing lanyard. He stepped back smartly and pulled it at the same time, the little Hotchkiss gun crashing out flame and smoke as it spat a shell into the superstructure about four feet to the left of the gun he'd been aiming at. Men went down, visible at this close range, but others were already running to replace them. Some of the main guns were being brought to bear on them as the enemy realised they were more than just a distraction.

"Faster, lads!" he shouted to the men bringing up one of the last of their three-pound shells, then flinched as a much larger round hit the sea behind them, close enough that the pinnace rose by the stern. For a moment he thought they might actually go over, then the whirling screw dropped back into the sea.

"Remarkably good practise," he said, forcing a light tone into his voice as he looked round at his crew. "Let's show them how it's done."

It took a moment to recover the shell, dropped as a result of the near miss. This would be his last shot, he knew, and took the time to make it count. They were barely two hundred yards from the auxiliary cruiser and he was staring down the muzzle of one of her guns, at maximum depression, as he pulled the lanyard. He didn't see exactly where the shell hit, but when the burst of smoke cleared the men around started cheering as they saw the enemy gun had been bent right back and torn half off its mounting.

Baxter didn't cheer, because he'd seen the dazed and bloodied gunner staggering to the weapon, obviously too badly injured to realise the weapon was in a worse state than he was. "Don't do it," he whispered, but even the force of his personality could not still the Japanese sailor at that range. The shell burst in the breech, of course, tearing apart the gunner and everyone else within range in a storm of hot steel. The explosion seemed to stun the riflemen firing on the pinnace, buying them a few precious moments to get into the lee of the cruiser.

"Daft fucker," Ignatyiv said, turning away from his machine gun to grin at Baxter. A moment later his face exploded into gore that spattered across the gun crew as a heavy rifle round took him in the back of the head.

That single moment of horror, the cheerful grin dissolving into destruction, threatened to take the fragile momentum out of the men he had led on this dangerous attack. Then they crashed into the side of the Japanese ship, Vasily hitting surprisingly hard and smashing in the pinnace's bow even though he'd started a turn to starboard to bring them alongside rather than ram.

There was nothing else for it.

"Get grapnels up into that hole!" Baxter shouted. He seized one of the coiled lines they'd prepared and whirled it around his head before hurling it up into the jagged metal mouth torn into the ship's side. It clanged and snagged, but didn't take properly and fell into the sea. Faces were starting to appeared above them, followed by rifle barrels.

"You three, get that damn machine gun pointed upwards and keep them off us!" He coiled the line as he rapped out orders. The rope was heavy with water as he spun the grapnel. This time it caught, along with one of the other grapnels. The three men he'd detailed to the heavy Maxim machine gun had managed to lift it out of its mounting and now one of them was crouched with the water-cooling jacket on his shoulder, hands over his ears and a grimace on his face as his mates used the extra elevation to give the rest of them covering fire.

"Come on, your bastards!" Baxter shouted, securing the end of his rope and swinging himself out over the water as the damaged pinnace drifted a bit away from the cruiser's side. The rope sagged alarmingly and for a heart-stopping moment he thought the grapnel was coming loose, then he got Japanese steel under his feet and pulled himself up the side. It wasn't far, but it felt like the longest climb he'd ever had to complete —

even more nerve-wracking than going up the *Yaroslavich*'s masts in the typhoon.

The rent in the ship's hull was as sharp and jagged as it had looked, the metal still hot to the touch. He didn't have time to be careful, but somehow managed to pull himself into the devastated inner compartment without anything more than a few scratches. He straightened up and took stock of his surroundings.

At least one person had died in here, but it was hard to say how many. He saw a leg, standing eerily upright in the middle of the devastation, but no sign of the body it had been attached to scant minutes ago. It reeked of burnt flesh and blood and spilled guts and he knew the sailors couldn't be allowed to linger here. It was easy to cheer the death of an enemy at distance, and do the things that made those deaths happen, but in close action even the bravest or most bloodthirsty man could lose his stomach for it.

His boarding party was coming up the side now. "Secure the hatch," he said brusquely as he pushed them through the carnage, not giving them time to think about what they were walking through.

The hatch had been torn out by the explosion, along with much of the bulkhead, but the bluejackets obediently crouched where it had been, aiming their rifles along the corridor beyond.

"Where's Vasily?" he asked the last man up.

"He has been injured, sir, and remains on the pinnace."

That caught him off guard — the enormous sailor had seemed so utterly indestructible, untouchable, that him being wounded seemed like an ill omen. He couldn't let that stop him now.

"Sir…" someone else said, and he looked round to see the sailor was offering him the polished wooden grip of a revolver.

"Well, not my brightest moment — leading a boarding action without a weapon!" He took the pistol, though he knew he wouldn't do much good with it.

"What now, sir?"

He realised, as they huddled around him in the corridor beyond the charnel room, that he had no particular plan. He hadn't even expected to get this far.

He didn't let that sudden doubt show. He had a decent force, even with Vasily and Ignatyiv out of the fight, and they had spirit. "We take the bridge." Arbuthnott was likely to be on the bridge, and that made it as good a plan as any.

The inside of the ship was much the same as any other he'd been on, with the exception that any script he saw was, of course, in Japanese. Orienting himself from the fact they'd entered by the stern and knowing they wanted to go up and forward, he led his little group of intrepid boarders deeper in.

It didn't take the Japanese long to find them, although they tried to move quietly — greatly aided by the fact the *Yaroslavich* was still peppering the ship with what guns she could bring to bear.

He heard them first, shouted orders and the rattle of rifles being prepared. What he wasn't expecting was a young officer wielding a sword and leading a bayonet charge down the companionway towards them, the enemy sailors letting out a blood-chilling battle cry.

Baxter was so startled he jerked the trigger of his revolver three times without really looking. The Russians fired at the same time, the noise and stench of gunpowder overpowering in the enclosed space, and still three Japanese made it through the fusillade, two of them bayoneting the sailor in front of him as he tried desperately to work his rifle's bolt. He went down screaming and Baxter shot the first man. The hammer dropped into a dud cartridge and he dropped the weapon as he twisted aside from a desperate bayonet thrust. He was acting on instinct now, underpinned by the rage that was always there but had been kept on a tight leash for months.

He let it out now, a great roaring rush of fury, grabbing the polished wooden furniture of the rifle and using it as a lever to slam the hapless enemy sailor into the wall before driving the brass buttplate into his face. He felt bone crunch, definitely more than just the nose, and the man dropped in an untidy heap. The other sailors were bludgeoning the third survivor down, hammering until he was well and truly incapacitated, and probably dead.

Baxter stalked forward, the anger pulsing through him now. The Japanese sailors weren't the focus of it, but they would bear the brunt of it. The sword-wielding officer was bleeding from two small-calibre wounds in his chest but still weakly scrabbling for his sword. Baxter kicked him in the head on the way past. "Stay with me," he ground out and, abandoning all attempts at stealth, headed for the bridge.

They were confronted by two steep flights of metal steps to the bridge of the cruiser, with light plating welded on to the sides as an afterthought when she'd been repurposed. It wasn't unlike the arrangement on the *Yaroslavich*, Baxter thought, as he considered the problem.

The rage had cooled as they'd fought their way here. The Japanese ship didn't seem to have a large crew, or at least no longer had one, and they'd only met scattered parties on the way here. He'd still lost people, though, either killed outright or too seriously injured to keep going. The ship was still taking fire from the Russian cruiser, but so far this seemed to be a single-ship duel.

He didn't fancy the idea of trying to storm the bridge up those ladders but couldn't see any other access point. He certainly couldn't ask any of the sailors to lead the way.

"Well, well, Mr Baxter, this is a pretty pickle, ain't it?"

He stiffened at the horribly familiar tone behind him. He'd become so fixated on the problem, so convinced that they were secure behind, that he hadn't heard the party of Japanese sailors creep up behind them. He had detailed someone to keep watch, little Fridrik, but he was down and a Japanese sailor was pulling a larger knife from his back.

Most of Baxter's attention was on the big European following the sailors into the space below the bridge. His face was as familiar as his voice, although they'd only spent a few hours in each other's company before.

"Billings," he spat, naming the former RN petty officer who had been Arbuthnott's hatchet wielder aboard the yacht where all this had started.

"I'm touched that you remember me," Billings said urbanely. He had a much larger pistol in his hand than the one he'd tried to intimidate Baxter with before. "Now, why don't you tell your lads to lay down their arms, and pass on the cap'n's promise that they'll be well treated if they surrender now."

Baxter licked his lips. Billings had fifteen men with him, more than they could feasibly deal with after their own losses and without the element of surprise being on their side. Fighting now would be suicide for all of them, whereas surrendering would just likely mean death for him.

"That annoying little Jock sprog with you, by any chance?" Billings said, bringing the big Webley pistol up and thumbing the hammer back theatrically.

338

"Tommy? He died," Baxter extemporised desperately.

"Really? Our man aboard…"

"Malaria, long after Yefimov had been shot," Baxter said.

"You 'ear that, sir?" Billings shouted up the ladder.

"I did," Arbuthnott's nasal voice came from above, the first time they'd heard any noise from the bridge. "Well, take care of the situation please, Billings."

Baxter felt his muscles tense. Deal with the situation. Deal with it. Casually ending his life. Billings tutted and Japanese rifles came up to point at the tense and confused Russian bluejackets, none of whom had enough English to follow what was happening.

Baxter opened his mouth to order his men to lay down their arms, and the world exploded in tearing noise.

He dived for cover as soon as bullets started ripping through the space. A lot of his people were already crouched and threw themselves flat. He didn't know where the fire was coming from or which side was firing, but it was loud enough that he had to cover his ears as the large, fast rounds tore Japanese sailors from their feet. One managed to get off a round that smacked into the deck by his head, and then the firing stopped an eternal second or two after it had started.

Baxter leapt to his feet, driving forward at Billings who was down, clutching a wound in his shoulder but not dead. The burly petty officer tried to bring his revolver up and Baxter kicked it from his hand, before he dropped a blow into his head that started somewhere up in the clouds and knocked the man clean out.

"Billings? I say, Billings?" Arbuthnott's querulous voice cut through the stunned silence. The intermittent firing of the main guns of both ships had finally come to an end, as though some uneasy truce had fallen while this peculiar tableau played out.

Baxter held up his hand to keep the sailors quiet and moved to the hatch that the Japanese had come through and from which the machine-gun fire had come. He dropped into a crouch and took a quick peer round, then sighed in relief.

"Nice of you to join us, Vasily," he whispered. The Russian sailor's answering grin was tight with pain and he moved stiffly as he and the other sailor they'd left behind rose and hauled the machine gun up into the compartment. Both men were injured, and he hated to think how hard it must have been for them to haul the heavy Maxim gun up here. Now it was here, though, they could put it to good use — *more* good use, he corrected himself, looking around at the dead and dying Japanese sailors sprawled out around them.

"How many belts do we left have left?" Baxter whispered. Vasily shrugged and held up the half belt remaining — barely enough for a couple of seconds' fire.

"Well, we'll have to make do," Baxter said with a vicious grin, looking up at the deckhead — the virtually unarmoured barrier between them and the bridge above.

The sailor who had previously stood in for the machine gun's tripod flat out refused to repeat the experience, tapping his ear and shaking his head to indicate he'd suffered more than enough of that duty. They didn't have time to argue about it — the longer they left it, the more time the bridge crew would have to prepare for them. In the end, though it had left a bad taste in his mouth, he'd let the Russians quickly stack a few dead bodies for Vasily to prop the Maxim gun on.

"Arbuthnott," Baxter called up the stairs. He didn't know how many men were up there, but guessed more than a few. They were all keeping very still and very quiet. "Arbuthnott,

I'm going to give you this one chance to surrender. It seems reasonable, given you gave me the same chance."

There was a sullen pause. "Ah, Mr Baxter. Can I assume that Billings is dead?"

"No. I don't … deal with situations, was that what you said? I don't shoot unarmed prisoners. Which means, if you surrender now, you get to live."

"And, one assumes, I'll be handed over to the Russians?"

"Of course. You have some crimes to answer for."

Arbuthnott, if anything, sounded even more officious when he spoke next. "Do you have any idea what that would lead to? What a trial, and what I may reveal, would do to relations between our countries?"

"I imagine there might be a war," Baxter said, making himself sound more casual than he felt. "It seems to me that's what you want."

"The situation is entirely more fluid and complicated than someone like you could possibly understand," the intelligence agent said, sounding like every other posh officer Baxter had ever served with. "I can assure you, my goal was never a war with Russia. Or at least, not an extensive one…"

"You wanted a naval panic," Baxter said, the words like lead in his mouth. "Maybe a bit of shooting between the fleets, and then a massively increased spend on ships."

"Ah, you understand after all." Arbuthnott sounded almost paternal. "Now, why don't we stop all this foolishness and…"

Baxter had had enough. He looked over to Vasily, and nodded sharply.

The machine gun's fire lasted a handful of seconds before the greedy weapon had sucked in the last of its ammunition belt, but the sound was still stunning. Wood fragments and dust rained down from the section of ceiling Vasily had fired into, roughly where they guessed the captain's chair would be.

Baxter took the steep ladder two steps at a time, pulling himself up with his hands as much as driving with his feet. He didn't really expect the fire to have done any damage, but that wasn't the point of it. He exploded onto the bridge while the crew were still recovering. He roared, fired the Webley he'd taken from Billings with no expectation of hitting anything, and the Russians responded with their own guttural war cries as they came up both ladders.

He pistol-whipped a Japanese subaltern down, punched a petty officer who came at him with a knife so hard he flew halfway across the bridge. A blood-curdling scream emanated from another young officer as the first bluejacket up the other ladder put a bayonet into his belly, then a shot rang out as one the enemy sailors seemed to remember he was armed. More shots, but he couldn't tell who was shooting at what because all he could see was the tall figure and pale, aquiline features of Arbuthnott.

The rogue intelligence agent was backing up, hands — bloody from where he'd been trying to tend to the dreadfully wounded captain slumped in his chair — held out in front of him in a gesture that was almost placating. Ignoring the bullets that whizzed past him, Baxter stalked forward, barely breaking stride to throw a Japanese sailor through a shell hole in the side of the enclosed bridge.

"Now, Mr Baxter…" Arbuthnott stammered. The sounds of fighting had died down, but Baxter could barely hear the agent over the pounding of his own pulse in his ears. He could only guess that his people had won, as no one was trying to attack him. "Everything I did was for the good of the Service! We need more funding, to stand up…"

"Why ... the fuck ... would I care about the good of the Service?" Baxter asked, his voice dangerously low and calm. He reached out, grabbing a handful of Arbuthnott's linen jacket, and hauled him off his feet with no apparent effort, carrying him towards one of the open wings of the bridge. He didn't have a plan, he'd never really had a plan. All he knew was that there should be some sort of consequence for Arbuthnott, that he had to be made to understand that it was not right, proper or decent for him to play with people's lives in this way.

Before Baxter realised what he was doing, he was dangling the babbling intelligence agent over the side of the bridge wing. There was a dampness in the crotch of Arbuthnott's suit trousers, sharp tang of urine in the air cutting smoke and burnt gunpowder. Baxter brought one first back, but Vasily was there at his side, one hand on his arm.

"This is not good," he said simply, shaking his head firmly. "We do not kill prisoners."

Baxter looked at him, nostrils flared and eyes furious, then slowly brought himself under control. "You're right," he said, and dropped his struggling prisoner.

Anything else that might have been said was lost in a great tearing noise, the sounds of tortured metal sheering and hulls grinding together, the cruiser losing way so suddenly it threw them all from their feet.

.

CHAPTER 26

"You've made your point, Juneau!" Baxter called up from the stern of their appropriated boat. "Honour has been satisfied."

The Russian captain, standing at the top of the boarding ladder as the last of the evacuees descended into the cutter, nodded. "I believe you are right, Baxter," he replied. "And I see you have made yours." He gestured expansively to the prisoner tied up in the bows. Arbuthnott's broken ankle was splinted and they'd acquired morphine from the Japanese cruiser's infirmary. It was mostly to shut him up, rather than out of any real pity on Baxter's part. Billings had been left in the care of Dr Andropov and would remain aboard the *Yaroslavich*.

"That was quite something, my friend," Juneau went on after a moment's pause. "Boarding an enemy vessel with only thirty men, and carrying her."

Baxter shrugged. "You had already chewed her up very well, Captain, we merely finished the job."

The two men grinned at each other, both realising they could get trapped in a vicious circle of attributing the small victory to each other. "You had best get under way," Juneau said, his smile fading. "I do not know how long we will remain unmolested."

The Japanese cruiser was sinking. Having lost steerage when he had torn up the bridge, she had cut directly across the *Yaroslavich*'s bows. Unable to manoeuvre effectively, Juneau had instead increased revolutions and rammed his tormenter, the old-fashioned and armoured bows of his vessel sheering through the flimsy sides of the converted freighter. The remaining crew had taken to some of the ship's boats — luckily, the action had not been furious enough to smash them all to splinters — and Baxter and his people had had to fight to ensure they got two. Their trusty pinnace had slipped below the water by the time they'd finish storming the ship, the damage from the collision proving more extensive than Baxter had realised.

The Russian cruiser was in little better condition. She'd taken a number of hits in her last battle, although the real problem remained the damage to her engines. Having turned off the course they had laboured onto, there was no way Juneau could bring the cruiser back round. His choice now was all stop and drift until they were found or sail directly for Japan.

Juneau had chosen to remain where he was, the cruiser's great beating hearts that had brought them all the way around the world stilled now. As many officers and sailors as possible were being packed into the longboat and cutter Baxter had appropriated from the Japanese cruiser, but some would remain behind in the hope of being encountered by a friendly ship.

"First Japanese flag you see, you surrender, do you hear?" he said. "Honour really has been satisfied."

Juneau didn't look happy, but nodded. "There is nothing else for it," he agreed. "We cannot fight her."

"I will of course make a full report and deliver your logs — I may yet see you in Vladivostok."

"Perhaps. And I doubt this war will last much longer, so even if we are taken we will not long be prisoners." Juneau nodded with considerably more crispness. "Are you sure you can make it? We're still some distance from Vladivostok."

Baxter shrugged. "A paltry distance — Bligh had much further to go and managed it."

"In that case, on your way, Mr Baxter. That's an order."

"I'm not under your command," Baxter replied with a grin, then — bracing his feet apart to keep stable — rose and offered Juneau the smartest salute he had ever managed. Juneau returned it with equal formality, then Baxter turned his face to the oarsmen who looked up expectantly at him. They had a long way to go still, he knew.

"All right, lads," he said, switching into Russian. "Prepare to cast off."

It took them two days to complete the journey that, for most of them, had begun as far away as the Baltic. The men had rowed like heroes, officers included, and there had been enough hands to on each boat that they could switch people out. Baxter was careful to ration the contents of the small water cask Juneau had put aboard, along with some ship's biscuit and salt meat that kept the men sustained. Along with the boats, they had captured some Japanese provisions, but to a man the bluejackets rejected the dried fish and rice. A small jar of pickled vegetables had been declared acceptable, even if some of it had been unidentifiable.

A westerly breeze, warm and gentle, had sprung up in the morning of the second day. At first it had been unfavourable but shifted about mid-morning to a westerly direction, and they'd been able to rig the boats' masts and rest the oarsmen until it came time to navigate into the sheltered harbour or Vladivostok.

Somehow, they had managed to avoid the enemy, and indeed had barely seen any other ships. Baxter had found himself torn between hoping to see Koenig's pinnace along the way, and willing them to make a swift passage. None of them relaxed, though, until the afternoon of the second day when a lookout in the bow called out the words they had been waiting for. "Land! Dead ahead!"

They all strained their eyes and peered ahead. Gradually, low sullen hills started to take shape out of the haze. Baxter consulted the chart Juneau had given him, spreading it across Vasily's broad back. The big petty officer had been grazed by a shell splinter as they had made their final approach to the enemy ship — a lucky escape indeed, not least because it had excused him time at the boards.

Having checked the chart, he went forward, past the single pole mast with its big sail, to stare at the approaching land mass through his binoculars. He had one boot up on the rail, not far from Arbuthnott's head. As always, he had to resist the urge to kick the man and felt the familiar stir of anger course through him as he came close. It wouldn't have been worth the effort, though. As well as his injured ankle, the man had been relentlessly seasick for the entire journey, and Baxter had kept him dosed with morphine to keep him quiet and less of a problem.

The rogue agent was a problem for when they got ashore, and Baxter made himself ignore the recumbent and gently muttering figure as he focused on the approaching land and started to pick out recognisable features. He couldn't quite believe it, particularly as he'd only ever been average at navigation.

"Russky Island, gentlemen," he announced loudly, once he was certain. "And beyond that, Vladivostok!"

A great cheer went up. Baxter let them cheer for a few minutes — for one thing, it would let the following longboat know they were almost home — and then raised his voice. "All right! Let's get this mast down and then stand to the oars. And I want us to come in smartly, do you hear?"

The wind had veered to an extent that they would have to tack endlessly to pass between Russky Island and the mainland if they'd tried to do it under sail. It would be a hard row, but faster than trying to go in under canvas.

Despite their exhaustion, the men set to with a will and it wasn't long before the oars were creaking in the rowlocks, driving the little wooden boats towards safety. It took them the rest of the day to creep round the headland before making a dogleg turn and into the deep, capacious harbour of Vladivostok. It should have been thronged with the ships of the Pacific Fleet, the anchorage crowded with the great steel behemoths. As it was, the meagre independent cruiser squadron that made this their home port formed the bulk of the warships present, sleek and dangerous shapes that had been nowhere to be seen when the Pacific Fleet was being destroyed. Baxter was too tired to worry much about that, now — all he wanted was a hot bath, a steak and enough vodka to knock him out between clean sheets.

Maybe, a traitorous part of his mind though, maybe with Ekaterina next to him. There was nothing to say she would have forgiven him, of course.

As the tired oarsmen pulled slowly towards the nearest pier, they were cheered to see some familiar vessels, including a pair of destroyers and the armoured yacht *Almaz*. They exchanged greetings with the crew of the latter as they pulled slowly towards the pier, the tired sailors lining the yacht's rail to cheer the little boats on as they made their slow way inland.

"What word of any other escapees?" Baxter asked, after he had identified the ship they were from and her probable fate.

"If anyone else made it, they haven't made it here," the captain replied, his voice showing what he thought of the idea of any others breaking through the ring of Japanese steel. "Some may have turned back or made for neutral water."

"And any other boats from the *Yaroslavich*?" Baxter asked anxiously. "A pinnace?"

They were starting to get out of shouting distance and could barely hear each other over the cheers. The shake of the burly captain's head was clear even at that range, and an apologetic shrug. *Not that I have seen*, the gestures said. Baxter stood in the stern to scan the collection of small vessels at the pier, and felt his heart grow cold when he realised he could not see Koenig's pinnace.

A guardboat chugged out to intercept them as they bobbed across the dirty, oily water of the harbour. "What ship?" someone demanded in French, then again in Russian. Despite the fact they had come in past a destroyer picket and under the guns of the shore defences, this was the first time they had been challenged. But then, two tiny boats perhaps did not pose much of a threat. Anyone turning a pair of glasses on them would have seen the crews were in Russian naval uniforms, after all.

Baxter pulled himself up straight in the stern. "*Yaroslavich*, of the Pacific Fleet!" he shouted back, sounding perhaps slightly angrier than was warranted.

The moments of silence that followed that announcement spoke to the surprise aboard the little steam ship that had swung round to parallel their course. Then came a slightly bemused hail. "Welcome to Vladivostok!"

"Lovely to be here," Baxter said quietly in Russian. "After all, we did come all this way to visit this shithole."

A ripple of laughter ran through the tired sailors. In truth, Russia's far eastern port wasn't much to look at, beyond the characteristically Eastern Orthodox domes of the church that

349

loomed above everything, gleaming white in the late afternoon sun. It represented safety, he thought tiredly as he threw a line up to a couple of sailors who had come out to meet them on the pier. He tried not to think about Koenig's pinnace, about Ekaterina and Tommy. It was a big harbour and he may just not have seen the boat.

For the first time in weeks — since Madagascar, in fact — he got dry land under his feet, scrambling up the slippery iron rungs of the ladder built into the pier. The sudden lack of motion under him made him feel slightly nauseous, but that sense was quickly dispelled by the mix of uniformed men and officious-looking civilians marching swiftly towards them. At least two of the men were carrying rifles slung over their shoulders, and one of the men not in uniform looked suspiciously like a police officer.

"Perhaps they've seen we have a prisoner," he muttered as Vasily joined him. "Get him up out of the boat, would you?"

Something about the way the men moved, the way the two with rifles were unslinging them, made him nervous. Made him think that they were, perhaps, here not just for Arbuthnott. He tried to dismiss those thoughts — if the worst had happened and Koenig's boat hadn't made it through, after all, then they would not know anything was amiss. It could just be a greeting party for survivors, and they had come armed in case the crews of the boats were unruly or were deserters.

Baxter squared his shoulders, despite the fatigue that washed through him. Rather than stand and wait for them, he went to meet them — and whatever came next — head on.

EPILOGUE

The waves marched away towards a far horizon, cold and slate grey. A few hundred miles to the south, these waters were the grave of many men Baxter had come to think of as comrades. Some as friends. Many more, hopefully, had survived and were either interned in neutral ports or prisoners of the Japanese.

Here, the sea wasn't so different to the icy expanse of the Baltic or the equally miserable North Sea — home waters for many of those men. A far cry from the turbulent but sweltering climes they had struggled through for much of their 18,000-mile journey to disaster.

"And I've come full circle as well," Baxter muttered, shoving his hands into the pockets of the slightly too-small borrowed greatcoat he wore against the early spring chill. "It's a less sinkable prison, but still a prison."

He glanced across at one of his impassive, plain-clothed guards. *Okhrana* men, he knew. The Tsar's Guard Department. They stared back at him, unmoved and unmoving. Probably didn't even understand a word he was saying. He toyed again with the idea of trying to make a break for it, but they wouldn't let him take these constitutionals on the hill overlooking the Pacific if they weren't confident of forestalling any escape attempt. And, as always, gnawing at the back of his mind was a worry of what had become of Tommy and Ekaterina.

He heard boot heels on paving stones, turned to see Lieutenant Koenig striding purposefully towards him, a diffident smile on his face. "Marcus Baxter," the Russian officer greeted him.

"Mr Koenig," Baxter said, masking how pleased he was to see the young lieutenant. "Still alive, I see."

Baxter was pleased, he realised, not just because Koenig being here meant Ekaterina and her charge were safely landed, but for his own sake. Koenig had shown himself to be a capable officer and a good man; the sort the Imperial Russian Navy would desperately need in the next few years.

Assuming his career wasn't completely derailed by the debacle he'd been caught up in.

"I am, indeed alive. As is everyone else on the pinnace." Koenig looked slightly uncomfortable. "All are safe and well."

Baxter felt a release of pent-up tension at that news. He had been in Vladivostok for almost a week, in the custody of the *Okhrana* along with Arbuthnott, and they had told him absolutely nothing. About anything, but especially what had become of his crewmates.

"Very well done, Mr Koenig," was all he said. "Fine seamanship."

Koenig actually blushed slightly at the praise. "Luck, more than anything, and the fact we had a steam engine. Not quite in the same league as bringing two open boats in."

Baxter shrugged uncomfortably. "Two open boats crewed by good seamen," he said. "Any news of the *Yaroslavich*?"

Koenig's face fell. "None," he said. "Nor of much of the rest of the fleet. Enkvist managed to extricate his cruisers, but has disappeared. Nebogatov gave up without a fight."

"It was a fight he couldn't win," Baxter pointed out, managing to keep his voice calm. "And many men will see their homes again because he chose not to fight it. And Rozhestvensky?"

"As far as anyone can tell, injured and probably a prisoner. He was taken off the *Suvorov* by destroyer, and I have heard reports they were captured."

The discussion of the absolute destruction, in operational terms, of the once-proud fleet was obviously depressing Koenig, and Baxter cast around for something to change the subject. There didn't seem to be a lot else to say.

"The *Grafinya* has asked me…" Koenig blurted, revealing another source of his unhappiness. "She has asked me to tell you that she cannot see you and will not receive you. She has, further, instructed me to deliver this letter."

Koenig held out an envelope. Baxter recognised Ekaterina's elegant copper plate on the front. He took it, feeling the weight of the paper. Turned it over and saw she had formally sealed it with wax. Anything to be doing anything, as a great cold gulf had opened up inside him.

She cannot see you and will not receive you. The dismissal was … impersonal. So very aristocratic.

He held it dumbly, unsure what to make of it all. Not knowing if he wanted to open it, or if it was better to leave such matters in his wake. Make a clean break of things when he left this port. After a moment, in which he was conscious of Koenig's unhappy scrutiny, he tucked it into his coat.

"Tomas'ka," Koenig went on after a moment, "is well, and arrangements are being made to send him home. He sends his best."

Well, that was it then.

"And me?" he asked, not knowing why he was asking Koenig this. He was as unlikely to know as Baxter was.

The lieutenant brightened slightly. "We are to be travelling companions!" he declared. "I am given charge of your custody, with orders to escort you to St. Petersburg."

Koenig made it sound like it would be a jolly jaunt, and at least Baxter would be in the custody of a fellow Naval man, rather than these flint-eyed secret policemen. There was no point protesting that the whole exercise was pointless, that they could put him on a neutral ship right now and never have to think of him again.

"When do we leave?"

"On the next Trans-Siberian express, in three hours."

Baxter barked a laugh. After being in limbo, knowing nothing of what his future held, he was suddenly on the move again. "Well, I have nothing to pack," he said. "So we should have a drink, and toast to an easier journey than our last one."

A NOTE TO THE READER

Dear Reader,

I first became interested in the Russo-Japanese War of 1904/5, and the naval aspects in particular, through reading about the Dogger Bank incident. It's something I'd always heard about, but never knew the full context of. When I delved into it a bit more, I rapidly disappeared down the rabbit hole of the fascinating, epic journey of the 2nd Pacific Squadron. The ill-fated expedition was not the last great military odyssey, but it surely rates as one of the most remarkable. The battle of Tsushima itself was the only fleet engagement where pre-Dreadnoughts formed the majority of the battle lines, and was arguably one of the most immediately decisive naval engagements in history. With the loss of the Pacific Fleet, that had taken on the aura of a crusade for him, Tsar Nicholas II's last gamble had failed and he was forced to the negotiating table with few cards in his hand. The outcome of the war was to shape the next fifty years of international relations in the Pacific.

It is seems odd to me that the wider conflict and Imperial Russian Navy's part in it are not as well-known as they perhaps should be. While only Russia and Japan exchanged ammunition, the other major European powers were involved in one way or the other (and indeed Britain, a staunch ally of Japan at the time, came close to war with Russia over the Dogger Bank incident). While there have been a number of scholarly tomes that were invaluable for research purposes, not much has been written in terms of fiction that I know of. This is my own small contribution to changing this unhappy state of affairs.

How much of the story, then, is fictional and how much is true to the history? Much of the wider story of the voyage and the battle itself I have tried to keep true to the record. In many ways, it was an adventure that wrote itself, a saga filled with eccentric characters, acts of great bravery and humanity and the occasional bout of utter incompetence that required little or no embellishment. The sources I've used do vary in their accounts, and I have written in the gaps between them, occasionally going with interpretations that suit my narrative purposes. I hope I have done justice to the Russian sailors who faced adversity with fortitude and fought with greater courage. In particular, I have endeavoured to avoid the pitfall of making the Russian admiral, Rozhestvensky, the 'Mad Dog' of the British press, when he was a considerably more complex person. He was certainly the man to get his ships all the way from the Baltic to the Sea of Japan, even if he was not perhaps the right man to lead them into battle against Togo.

Baxter, Juneau, Ekaterina, the *Yaroslavich* and everything associated with them are fictional. The ship herself is loosely based on the transitional armoured cruiser *Vladimir Monomakh*, part of the 3rd Pacific Squadron and one of the oldest ships engaged at Tsushima. To the best of my knowledge, the Tsar's secret police — the Guard Department or Okhrana — did not employ women; however history is replete with women who were able to use the influence, wealth, subterfuge or sheer dogged determination to open doors normally closed to their gender. I hope I can be forgiven this minor indulgence. Nor is there any record of any plots or conspiracies to draw Britain into the shooting war through a 'false flag' operation. Naval panics did occur, often an occurrence blown out of all proportion by those who felt the UK's seaborne defences were in need of shoring up.

So why, then, a complicated plot to put a disgruntled ex-RN officer onto Russian ships rather than telling the tale from the point of view of a Russian officer in the squadron? Partly, I wanted someone who was an outside observer to the fascinating and, I think, quite strange society and culture of the Russian Empire and its Navy. Partly because espionage and skulduggery often go hand-in-hand in naval fiction, and this provided a story for my protagonists set against the backdrop of the wider events. And partly because I didn't want a protagonist tied too closely to any one organisation — Marcus Baxter is going to have a long, varied and chequered career around the world…

I am greatly indebted to my good friends Dr Malcolm Kinnear and Paul Hurley, for their insights into Imperial Russian culture and naval architecture respectively, and to Drachinifel for his help with a cover image. As always, the Edinburgh Schismatics writers group has been invaluable with their incisive criticism and boundless encouragement.

It goes without saying that none of this would have been possible without the team at Sapere Books.

Thank you for taking the time to read my debut historical fiction novel — I hope you enjoyed reading it as much as I enjoyed researching and writing it. If you enjoyed it, it would be great if you could drop a review into **Amazon** and **Goodreads** — these can be a great help to authors. You can find me on **Twitter** and **Facebook** for short rambles about my hobbies, other interests and writing:

I'm also developing a blog, mostly about naval history and my great-grandfather's career in the Royal Navy, which can be found here: **timchantauthor.com**

Sapere Books is an exciting new publisher of brilliant fiction and popular history.

To find out more about our latest releases and our monthly bargain books visit our website: **saperebooks.com**

Made in the USA
Columbia, SC
13 June 2022

61702390R00196